DUDLEY PUBLIC LIBRARIES

The loan of this book may be renewed if not required by other
readers, by contacting the library from which it was borrowed.

X

30 NOV 2016

5/8/20

The Greek Mavericks
COLLECTION

July 2019

August 2019

September 2019

October 2019

November 2019

December 2019

Greek Mavericks: For the Greek's Revenge

JENNIE LUCAS

TARA PAMMI

CATHY WILLIAMS

MILLS & BOON

First Published in Great Britain 2019
By Mills & Boon, an imprint of HarperCollins *Publishers*
1 London Bridge Street, London, SE1 9GF

GREEK MAVERICKS: FOR THE GREEK'S REVENGE
© 2019 Harlequin Books S.A.

The Consequence of His Vengeance © Jennie Lucas 2017
Claimed for His Duty © Tara Pammi 2015
Taken by Her Greek Boss © Cathy Williams 2007

ISBN: 978-0-263-276060

1019

THE CONSEQUENCE
OF HIS VENGEANCE

JENNIE LUCAS

To Pippa Roscoe, with best wishes for
a brilliant future. You are going to rock it!!

since he'd broken his arm in mysterious circumstances he wouldn't explain, he'd been home on painkillers, sitting next to her ancient computer with nothing to do.

Could her father have sent Darius a message, pretending to be her?

She glanced at Darius, then decided she didn't care. If her father had interfered, all she could be was grateful, if this was the result.

Her father must have revealed her real reasons for betraying Darius ten years ago. She couldn't imagine he would even be talking to her now otherwise.

But how to know for sure?

Biting her lip, she said awkwardly, "I read about you in the paper this morning. That you sold. Your company, I mean."

"Ah." His jaw set as he turned away. "Right."

His voice was cold. No wonder, Letty thought. She sounded like an idiot. She tried to steady herself. "Congratulations."

"Thank you. It cost ten years of my life."

Ten years. Those two simple words hung between them in silence, like a small raft on an ocean of regret.

Their car entered Manhattan, with all its wealth and savagery. A place she'd avoided since her father's trial and sentencing almost a decade before.

Her heartbeat fluttered in her throat as she looked down at her chapped hands, folded tightly in her lap. "I've thought of you a lot, wondering how you were. Hoping you were well. Hoping you were happy."

Stopping at a red light, Darius abruptly looked at her.

"It was good of you to think of me," he drawled in a low voice, once again with that strange undercurrent. In the cold night of the city, headlights of passing cars moved shadows across the hard lines of his face.

The light changed to green. It was just past ten o'clock,

and the traffic was starting to lessen. Heading north on First Avenue, they passed the United Nations plaza. The buildings had started climbing higher against the sky as they approached Midtown. Turning off Forty-Ninth onto the gracious width of Park Avenue, they approached a newly built glass-and-steel skyscraper on the south side of Central Park.

As he pulled his car into the porte cochere, she was craning her neck back in astonishment. "You live here?"

"I have the top two floors," he said casually, in the way someone might say, *I have tickets to the ballet.*

His door opened, and he handed the keys to a smiling valet who greeted him respectfully by name. Coming around, Darius opened Letty's door. He held out his hand.

She stared at it nervously, then put her hand in his.

He wrapped it tightly in his own. She felt the warmth and roughness of his palm against hers.

He had to know, she thought desperately. He had to. Otherwise, why would he have sought her out? Why wouldn't he still hate her?

He led her through the awe-inspiring lobby, with its minimalist furniture and twenty-foot ceilings.

"Good evening, Mr. Kyrillos," the man at the desk said. "Cold weather we're having. Hope you're staying warm!"

Darius held Letty's hand tightly. She felt like she might catch flame as he drew her across the elegant, cavernous lobby. "I am. Thank you, Perry."

He waved his key fob in front of the elevator's wall panel and pressed the seventieth floor.

His hand gripped hers as the elevator traveled up. She felt the warmth of his body next to hers, just inches away, towering over her. She bit her lip, unable to look at him. She just stared at the electronic numbers displaying the floors as the elevator rose higher and higher. *Sixty-eight, sixty-nine, seventy...*

The bell dinged as the door slid open.

"After you," Darius said.

Glancing at him nervously, she stepped out directly into a dark, high-ceilinged penthouse. He followed her, as the elevator door closed silently behind them.

The rubber soles of her white shoes squeaked against the marble floor as she walked through the foyer beneath the modern crystal chandelier above. She flinched at the noise, embarrassed.

But his handsome face held no expression as he removed his long black overcoat. He didn't turn on any lights. He never looked away from her.

With a gulp, she turned away.

Gripping her purse strap, she walked forward into the shadowy main room. It was two stories high, with sparse, angular furniture in black and gray, and floor-to-ceiling windows twisted around the penthouse in every direction.

Looking from right to left, she could see the dark vista of Central Park, the high-rise buildings to the Hudson River, and the lights of New Jersey beyond it, and to the south, the skyscrapers of Midtown, including the Empire State Building, all the way to the Financial District and the gleaming One World Trade Center.

The sparkling nighttime view provided the only light in the penthouse, aside from a single blue gas fire that flickered in the stark fireplace.

"Incredible," Letty breathed, going up to the windows. Without thinking, she leaned forward, putting her overheated forehead against the cool glass, looking down at Park Avenue far below. The cars and yellow cabs looked tiny, like ants. She felt almost dizzy from being so high off the earth, up in the clouds. It was a little terrifying. "Beautiful."

His reply was husky behind her. "*You* are beautiful, Letitia."

Turning, she looked at him in the soft blue glow of firelight. Then, as she looked more closely…

Her lips parted with an intake of breath.

She'd thought Darius hadn't changed?

He'd changed completely.

At thirty-four, he was no longer a slender youth, but a powerful man. His shoulders had broadened to match his tall height, his body filling out with hard muscle. His dark hair had once been wavy and tousled, like a poet's, but was now cut short, as severe as his chiseled jawline.

Everything about Darius was tightly controlled now, from the cut of his expensive clothes—a black shirt with the top button undone, black trousers, black leather shoes—to his powerful stance. His mouth had once been expressive and tender and kind. Now his lips had a hard twist of arrogance, even cruelty.

He towered over her like a king, in his penthouse with all of New York City at his feet.

At her expression, his jaw tightened. "Letitia…"

"Letty." She managed a smile. "No one calls me Letitia anymore."

"I have never been able to forget you," he continued in a low voice. "Or that summer we were together…"

That summer. A small noise came from the back of her throat as unwanted memories filled her mind. Dancing in the meadow. Kissing the night after her debutante ball. Escaping the prying eyes of servants in Fairholme's enormous garage, steaming up the windows of her father's vintage car collection for weeks on end. She'd been ready to surrender everything.

Darius was the one who'd wanted to wait for marriage to consummate their love.

"Not until you're my wife," he'd whispered as they strained for each other, barely clothed, panting with need in the backseat of a vintage limousine. "Not until you're mine forever."

Forever never came. Their romance had been illicit, forbidden. She was barely eighteen, his boss's daughter; he was six years older, the chauffeur's son.

After a hot summer of innocent passion, her father had been infuriated when he'd discovered their romance. He'd ordered Darius off the estate. For one awful week he and Letty had been apart. Then Darius had called her.

"Let's elope," he'd said. "I'll get a day job to support us. We'll get a studio apartment in the city. Anything as long as we're together."

She'd feared it would hurt his dream of making his fortune, but she couldn't resist. They both knew there was no chance of a real wedding, not when her father would try to stop the marriage. So they'd planned to elope to Niagara Falls.

But on the night his car waited outside the Fairholme gate, Letty never showed up.

She hadn't returned any of his increasingly frantic phone calls. The next day, she'd even convinced her father to fire Eugenios Kyrillos, Darius's father, who'd been their chauffeur for twenty years.

Even then, Darius had refused to accept their breakup. He'd kept calling, until she'd sent him a single cold message.

I was only using you to get another man's attention. He's rich and can give me the life of luxury I deserve. We're engaged now. Did you really think that someone like me would ever live in a studio apartment with someone like you?

That had done the trick.

But it had been a lie. There had been no other man. At the ripe old age of twenty-eight, Letty was still a virgin.

All these years, she'd promised herself that Darius would never know the truth. He could never know how she'd sacrificed herself, so he'd be able to follow his dreams without guilt or fear. Even if it meant he hated her.

But Darius must have finally found out the truth. It was the only explanation for him seeking her out.

"So you know why I betrayed you ten years ago?" she said in a small voice, unable to meet his eyes. "You forgive me?"

"It doesn't matter," he said roughly. "You're here now."

Her heart pounded as she saw the dark hunger in his eyes.

She looked down at the coffee stain on her uniform, the smear of ketchup near the cheerful name tag still on her left breast: LETTY! She whispered, "You can't still…want me?"

"You're wrong." He pulled her handbag off her shoulder. It felt unspeakably erotic. He pulled off her coat, dropping it to the marble floor. "I wanted you then." Cupping her face with both hands, he whispered, "I want you now."

Electricity ran up and down her body. Involuntarily, she licked her lips.

His gaze fell to her mouth.

Tangling his hands in her hair, he pulled out her ponytail, and her long dark hair tumbled down her shoulders. He stroked down her cheek, tilting back her head.

He was so much taller. He towered over her in every way.

She felt crazy butterflies, like she'd gone back in time and was eighteen again. Being with him now, all the anguish and grief and weariness of the last ten years seemed to disappear like a bad dream.

"I've missed you for so long," she choked out. "You're all I've dreamed about…"

He pressed a finger to her lips. At the contact, fire flashed from her mouth and down to her breasts. Sparks crackled between them in the shadowy penthouse, as she breathed in his woodsy, musky scent. Tension coiled low and deep in her belly.

Pulling her body tight against his own, he lowered his mouth to hers.

His kiss was hot and demanding. The stubble on his rough jawline scratched her delicate skin as he gripped her hard against him. She kissed him back with desperate need.

A low growl came from the back of his throat, and he pushed her back against the wall. His hands ran down her body to rip apart the front buttons of her white dress. She gasped as her naked skin was exposed, along with her plain white bra and panties.

"Take this off," he whispered, and he pulled her white dress off her body, dropping it to the floor. Kneeling in front of her, he pulled off her white shoes, one by one. She was nearly naked, standing in front of the floor-to-ceiling windows that revealed the whole city.

Rising to his full height, he kissed her. His mouth plundered hers, searing her to the core. She realized her hands were unbuttoning his black shirt to feel the warmth of his skin, the hard muscles of his body. She stroked his chest, dusted with dark hair, and trembled. He felt like steel wrapped in satin, hard and soft.

She desperately wanted to feel him against her, all of him. She wanted to be lost in him—

As he kissed her, his hands roamed over her shoulders, her hips, her breasts. Her fingers twisted in his hair. She felt dizzy with longing as he pressed her against the wall, kissing her with savage desire, nipping at her lips until they bruised.

He kissed down her throat, reaching beneath the white cotton fabric of her bra to cup her bare breasts. She felt his rough warm hands against her naked skin, and her taut nipples ached, until with a low curse he reached around and unhooked the clasp of her bra.

She heard his intake of breath as it fell to the floor. She now wore only panties, while he was still fully dressed, with his black shirt unbuttoned to reveal his bare chest. As he lowered his head, taking her exposed breasts fully in his hands, her head fell back, hair tumbling down, as she gripped his bare, muscular shoulders.

She gasped as she felt the wet heat of his mouth envelop a taut nipple. Lightning shot down her body as he suckled her in his stark, shadowy penthouse, with its spectacular view of nighttime New York at their feet. She moaned softly.

Abruptly, he pulled away. She opened her eyes, feeling dizzy. Her lips parted to ask a question, but before she could remember it, he lifted her into his arms.

She didn't try to resist as he carried her through the great room into an enormous bedroom in the opposite corner. That, too, had windows on both sides, twenty feet high. She could see all of Midtown, from the Chrysler Building to the Empire State, a forest of skyscrapers between two dark rivers with their bright, moving barges.

Manhattan sparkled coldly in the dark night as Darius spread her across his bed, his expression half shadowed. He undid his cuffs and dropped his shirt to the floor.

For the first time, Letty saw the full strength of his hard-muscled torso and powerful arms. His shoulders were broad, narrowing to tight, hard abs. Removing his belt, he kicked off his shoes. Wearing just low-slung black tailored trousers, he climbed onto the bed.

Lowering his head, he kissed her against the pillows, his lips hard and rough. She felt his desire for her; she felt his heavy weight over her. Darius wanted her... He cared...

Something broke, deep inside her heart.

All this time, Letty had thought their love had ended forever. But nothing had changed, she thought in wonder, tangling her hands in his dark hair. *Nothing.* They were the same two people, still young and in love...

He slowly kissed his way down her body, his hands

stroking her. She quivered, helpless beneath his touch. He dropped kisses here and there as he traversed the softness of her belly to the top edge of her white cotton panties. Drawing up, he looked down at her.

"You're mine, Letty," he whispered. "At last."

Then his heavy, hard body crushed hers deliciously, sensually. Her fingertips moved down the warm skin of his back, feeling his muscle, his spine. He moved his hips against hers, and she felt how huge and hard he was for her. Desire coiled low and deep in her belly.

He slid her white cotton panties down her thighs, down her legs. Like a whisper, they were gone.

Pushing her legs apart, he knelt at the foot of the bed. She held her breath, squeezing her eyes shut in the shadowy bedroom as he kissed the tender hollow of each foot. He moved up her calves, his fingertips caressing her skin as he lifted each knee for a slow kiss in the hollow beneath. She shivered as she felt the warmth of his breath on her thighs.

His hands moved beneath her, cupping her backside. Her thighs melted beneath his breath, hips trembling.

Finally, with agonizing slowness, he lowered his head between her legs.

Moving his hands, he kissed her inner thighs, one then the other. She felt his breath against the most intimate part of her and tried to squirm away, but he held her firmly.

Spreading her wide, he took a long, deep taste. The pleasure was intense. She choked out a gasp.

Holding her hips down against the bed, he forced her to accept the pleasure, working her with his tongue, twirling against her aching nub for long exquisite moments, then lapping her with the full width of his tongue.

She forgot to breathe, held by ruthless pleasure like a butterfly pinned to a wall. Her hips lifted involuntarily off the bed as she soared, and she gripped the white bedspread so she didn't fly up into the sky.

Waves of pleasure crashed against radiating joy. She'd never stopped loving him. And now he'd forgiven her. He wanted her. He loved her, too...

Twisting and gasping beneath his mouth, she exploded with a cry of pure happiness that seemed to last forever.

Instantly lifting his body, he pushed her arms above her head, gripping her wrists against the pillow, and positioned his hips between her legs. As she was still soaring between ecstasy and joy, he ruthlessly impaled her.

She felt him push all the way inside her, the entire enormous length of him going deep, to the heart. Her eyes flew open in shock and pain.

His back straightened at the moment he tore through the barrier that he clearly had not expected. Feeling her flinch, he looked down at her in shock.

"You were—a virgin?" he panted.

She nodded, closing her eyes and twisting her head away so he couldn't see the threatening tears. She didn't want to mar the beauty of their night, but the pain cut deep.

He held himself still inside her.

"You can't be," he said hoarsely. "How, after all these years?"

Letty looked up at him, her throat aching. And she said the only thing she could say. The words that she'd repressed for ten years, but that had never stopped burning inside her.

"Because I love you, Darius," she whispered.

CHAPTER TWO

DARIUS STARED DOWN at her. Letitia Spencer, a virgin?

Impossible. Not in a million years.

But her words shocked him even more.

"What do you mean, *you love me*?" he choked out.

Her dark eyelashes trembled against her pale skin. Then those big, beautiful hazel eyes shone up at him from the shadows of the bed as she whispered, "I never stopped loving you."

Looking down at her beautiful heart-shaped face, Darius was overwhelmed by emotion. Not the good kind, either.

He felt the cold burn of slow-rising rage.

Once, he'd loved Letty Spencer so much he'd thought he'd die without her. She'd been his angel. His goddess. He'd put her on such a pedestal, he'd even insisted they wait to make love. He'd wanted to marry her.

The memory made him writhe with shame.

How far she'd fallen. Today, she'd sent him a message—her first direct communication with him since she'd dumped him so coldly ten years before—offering him her body. For money.

All afternoon, Darius had tried to ignore her message, to laugh it off. He'd gotten over Letty years ago. He wasn't interested in paying a hundred thousand dollars to have her in his bed tonight. He didn't pay for sex. Women fought for his attention now. Supermodels fell into his bed for the price of a phone call.

But the part of him that still couldn't completely forget the past relished the idea of seeing her one last time.

Only this time, she'd be the one begging. He'd be the one to reject her.

As he'd signed the contracts that afternoon to formally sell his company, built on a mobile messaging app with five hundred million users worldwide, to a massive tech conglomerate for the price of twenty billion dollars, he'd barely listened to his lawyers droning on. Holding 90 percent of equity in the company made him the beneficiary of an eighteen-billion-dollar fortune, minus taxes.

But instead of rejoicing in the triumphant payoff of ten years of relentless work, he'd been picturing Letitia, the woman who'd once betrayed him. Imagining her trying to seduce him with an exotic dance of the seven veils. Picturing her wearing nothing but a black negligee. Begging him to take her to bed, so she could perform Olympic-level sexual feats for his pleasure.

After the papers were signed, he practically ran out of the office, away from all the congratulations and celebrations. All he could think about was Letty and her offer.

He'd spent hours trying to talk himself out of it. Then, gritting his teeth, he'd driven to the Brooklyn diner when the message said she'd be getting off work.

He didn't intend to actually sleep with her, he told himself. He'd only wanted to make her feel as small and ashamed as he'd once felt. To see her humiliated. To see her beg to give him pleasure.

Then he'd planned to tell her he no longer found her attractive, and toss the money in her face. He'd watch her take it and slink away in shame. And for the rest of his life he'd know that he'd won.

What did he care about a hundred thousand dollars? It was nothing. It would be worth it to see her abject humiliation. After her savagely calculated betrayal, he craved vengeance far more than sex.

Or so he'd thought.

But so far nothing had gone according to plan. Seeing her outside the diner, he'd been shocked at her appearance.

She didn't look like a gold digger. She looked as if she were trying to be invisible, with no makeup, wearing that ridiculous white diner uniform.

But even then, he'd been drawn to her. She managed to be so damn sexy, so sweetly feminine and warm, that any man would want to help her, to take care of her. *To possess her.*

Bringing her back to the penthouse to enjoy his vengeance, Darius had allowed himself a single kiss.

Big mistake.

As he'd felt the soft curves of her body press against his, all his plans for vengeance were forgotten against the ruthless clamor of his body. For ten years, he'd desired this woman; and now she was half-naked in his arms, willing to surrender everything.

Suddenly, it all came down to two simple facts.

She'd sold herself.

He'd bought her.

So why not take her? Why not enjoy her sensual body as a way to finally excise her memory, once and for all?

She'd lied her way through the evening, pretending it was a romantic date, instead of a commercial transaction. He'd almost been surprised.

Until now.

Naked beneath him, Letty looked up, her eyes luminous in that lovely face he'd never been able to forget.

"Say something," she said anxiously.

Darius set his jaw. After her heartless betrayal, followed by ten years of silence, she'd just told him out of the blue she loved him. What could he say in response? Go to hell?

Letitia Spencer. So beautiful. So treacherous. So poisonous.

But now, at last, he understood her goal. She wasn't just playing for a hundred thousand dollars tonight. No. Tonight was just the sample that was supposed to leave him wanting more.

Because he'd seen her face as she left that diner. She was tired. Tired of working. Tired of being poor. Perhaps her father, newly free from prison, had been the one to suggest how to easily change her life—by becoming Darius's wife.

She must have seen his company's sale trumpeted in the newspaper today and decided it was time she made a play for his billions. He almost couldn't blame her. She'd been holding on to her virginity all these years—why not cash in?

She loved him.

Cold, sardonic anger pulsed through him.

She thought he'd learned nothing all these years. She actually thought, if she told him she loved him, he would still swoon at her feet. That he was still the lovesick idiot of long ago.

If Darius had despised her before, it was nothing compared to how he felt about her now.

And yet, he still desired her. Holding himself motionless inside her hot, tight sheath, he was still so hard, he was close to exploding.

That fact enraged him even more.

He wanted to make her pay. Not just for this last insult, but for everything that had gone before. Suddenly, causing her one night of humiliation wasn't nearly enough.

Darius wanted *vengeance*.

He wanted to raise her up, give her hope, then bring it crashing down as she'd once done. Fantastical plans coursed through his skull. He wanted to marry her, fill her with his child. He wanted to make her love him, then coldly spurn her. He wanted to take everything, and leave her penniless and alone.

That wouldn't be revenge. It would be *justice*.

"Darius?" A shadow of worry had crossed her face as she looked up at him, naked on the bed.

Lowering his head, he kissed her almost tenderly. She trembled in his arms, her plump breasts crushed against his naked chest, her amazing hips spread wide for him. Seeing her stretched out on his bed, with the play of shadows and light on the sexy curves of her tantalizing breasts, stretched the limits of his self-control.

"I'm sorry I hurt you, *agape mou*," he said in a low voice. Lie. His lips brushed the sensitive flesh of her cheek. As lightly as a butterfly setting down, he kissed the two tears that had overflowed her lashes. "But the pain won't last." Another lie. He would make sure it lasted the rest of her life. He smiled grimly. "Just wait."

She looked up at him, the picture of wide-eyed innocence. Then sighed, relaxing in surrender.

The kiss he gave her then was anything but tender. It was demanding, rough, fierce. He had experience, and she did not. He knew how to lure her. How to master her.

Unless—she could be feigning her desire?

No, he thought coldly. He would make sure she did not. That would be one insult he'd not allow her to pay. He would make sure every bit of her pleasure was real.

He stroked her soft body, taking his time, caressing her, until, slowly, she started kissing him back.

She wrapped her arms around his shoulders, pulling his weight back down on her. He shifted his hips, testing her ability to accept him, still rock hard and huge inside her. She whimpered, then exhaled, swaying her hips.

He moved expertly, drawing back slowly, then pushing inside her a second time. She gripped his shoulders, closing her eyes. He suckled a nipple, watching her face carefully. It wasn't until he saw the glow of ecstasy return to her face, and felt her muscles start to tighten around him, that he knew he'd succeeded. Triumph filled him as he began to ride her.

Filling her so deeply, this woman he'd desired for almost a third of his life, he felt light-headed. His body started to shake with pleasure so intense that it was almost like pain. They were so intertwined it was hard to know where one ended and the other began.

Pleasure and pain.

Hatred and desire.

As he thrust into her, sweat covered his body with the effort of keeping control. Her breasts swayed as he thrust inside her, all the way to the hilt. Gasping, she put her hands against the headboard, bracing against the force of his thrust. Her breathing became shallow as her body twisted beneath him with building need.

Her eyes were closed, her head tilted back, as she panted for breath. She moved her hands to his shoulders. He barely noticed her fingernails digging into his skin. He was lost in the sensation of possessing her, filling her, owning her, the glory of her flesh, the sweetness of her skin.

He felt simultaneously lost and found. Every corner of his soul that had ever felt hollow was miraculously filled. His body was pure light.

From a distance, he heard a low ragged shout and realized the sound was coming from his own mouth, releasing emotion he'd kept locked up for a decade. Her voice joined his as she cried out her own joy and grief and pain.

His body spasmed with a final, violent thrust and he poured himself into her, collapsing over her on the bed, their bodies slick with sweat, fused together.

It was much later when he opened his eyes and discovered Letty was sleeping in his arms. He stared down at her in wonder.

He wondered how he'd ever been satisfied by those pallid, skinny supermodels who had filled his bed till now.

Those affairs had been insipid, hollow, dull compared to this fire. Tasting her, feeling her shake, hearing her cry of pleasure had pushed him to the limit.

It's hatred, he realized.

Hatred had made him utterly lose self-control in a way he'd never done before, in a way he'd never imagined possible. As he'd taken possession of her body, after ten years of frustrated desire, he'd slaked his ache in a dark, twisted fantasy of vengeance.

It had been the single best sexual experience of his life.

But as he pulled away from her, he sucked in his breath.

The condom had broken.

He'd worn one, of course. No matter how he might fantasize about revenge, no matter how much he hated her, the last thing he would want was to actually get her pregnant and drag an innocent child into this.

Now he stared down, unable to believe his own eyes. How could the condom have broken?

Had he been too rough, forgetting everything in his need to possess her, to relieve the savage, unrequited desire of ten years?

He'd wanted to brand her forever with the deepest mark of his possession. Had he actually wanted to fill her with his child?

A curse filled his heart.

Unraveling himself from her, he pulled away, rising naked from the bed.

He walked to the window and looked down at the bright skyscrapers of this dark city. His throat was tight as he pressed his hand against the cold glass. Catching his own reflection in the window, he was startled by the cold rage in his eyes.

Disaster. He hadn't done anything like he'd planned. He'd actually slept with Letty. And now…it might be so much worse. His hand tightened against the window. He looked back, and his jaw tightened.

Her fault, he thought. All hers.

"Are you up?" Letty murmured. "Come back to bed."

She was beneath the blankets now, looking sleepy and adorable with her dark hair tumbling over his pillows. She'd covered herself with the comforter. As if he hadn't seen everything, touched everything, tasted everything already.

His body hardened against his will, already desiring her again. He'd just had her, and he already wanted more. He wanted to take her on the bed. Against the wall. Against the window. Again and again. He stared at her in bewildered fury. Truly she was poison.

But did he really imagine after everything that had gone wrong tonight, the gold digger couldn't achieve her ultimate goal—marriage and total command, not just of his fortune, but of his body and soul?

He clawed a hand through his hair.

"Darius, what's wrong?"

He repeated flatly, "You love me?"

"It's true," she whispered.

He took a step toward the bed.

"What is it, Letty?" he said in a low voice. "Did you plan all along to renegotiate the deal? One night isn't enough, is that it? You don't want to be a rental, but a permanent sale?"

She frowned. "What are you talking about?"

Darius's jaw felt so tight it ached. Grabbing gray sweatpants from a sleek built-in drawer, he pulled them up over his naked body. He forced his shoulders to relax, forced himself to face her. When he spoke, his voice was like ice.

"You don't love me. You don't even know what the word means. When I think of how I once adored you, it sickens me. Especially now—now we both know what you really are."

Her forehead creased. "What are you talking about?"

"This night. This whole night. Don't pretend you don't know."

"I don't!"

"Don't play the outraged innocent. You sold your virginity to me for the price of a hundred thousand dollars."

For a moment, his hard words echoed in the shadowy bedroom. The two of them stared at each other in silence.

"What are you talking about?"

"Your email," he said impatiently. "Claiming you needed to pay off some mobster who'd broken your father's arm and threatened to break his whole body if he didn't come up with a hundred thousand dollars within the week." He tilted his head curiously. "Is it true? Or just a convenient excuse?"

Her eyes were wide. "My father's broken arm…" She seemed to shudder as she pulled the blankets up higher against her neck. "I never sent any message."

His lips curved sardonically. "So who did?"

Letty's cheeks were bright red. "I…" Running her hand over her eyes, she said, "So that's why you came for me? You were buying a night in bed?"

"What did you think?"

"I thought…" She faltered. "I thought you'd forgiven me for what I did…"

He snorted. "Ten years ago? You did me a favor. I've been better off without you. Your other fiancé must have realized that fast, since he didn't bother to stick around, either." His jaw set. "What I'll never forgive is what you and your father did to my dad. He died an early death because of you. Lost his job, his life savings. He lost everything, had a heart attack and died." He bared his teeth in a shark-like smile. "Because of you."

"Darius, it's not what you think," she blurted out. "I…"

"Oh, is this the part where you come up with an explanation that makes you look like an innocent saint?" he drawled. "Go on, Letty. Tell me how your betrayal was actually a favor. Explain how you destroyed my family at great personal sacrifice, because you loved me so much." His voice dripped contempt. "Tell me all about your *love*."

She opened her mouth.

Then snapped it closed.

Darius's lip twisted coldly. "That's what I thought."

She blinked fast, her beautiful eyes anguished. She took a deep breath and spoke one small word. "Please..."

But mercy had been burned from his soul. He shrugged. "I thought it would be amusing to see you again. I didn't actually intend to sleep with you, but you were so willing, I finally thought, why not?" He sighed as if bored. "But though I paid for the whole night, I find I've already lost interest." Leaning forward, he confided, "And just as one entrepreneur to another, you sold yourself too cheaply. You could have bartered for a higher price with your virginity. Just a suggestion as you go forward with your new career. What is it called now? Paid mistress? Professional girlfriend?"

"How can you be so cruel?" She shook her head. "When you came to the diner tonight, I saw the same boy I loved..."

"Really?" He tilted his head, quirking a dark eyebrow. "Oh. Right. Since you'd kept your virginity in reserve all these years, you thought if you tossed in a little romance, I'd fall for you like a stone, just like I did back then. 'I love you, Darius. I never stopped loving you,'" he mimicked mockingly.

"Stop!" she cried, covering her ears with her hands. "Please stop!"

Some of her blanket had slipped where she sat on his bed, revealing a curvy breast. He could see the faint pink tip of her nipple, and he could still taste the sweetness of her, still remember how it had felt to be deep inside her.

His breath came hard. Sleeping with her hadn't satiated his desire. To the contrary. He only wanted her more.

The fact she still had such power over him was infuriating.

Turning sharply, he went to his desk. He pulled a cashier's check from a leather binder. Returning to the bed, he tossed it toward her.

"There. I believe this concludes our business."

Letty's lovely face looked dazed as she picked up the cashier's check from the bed. She looked at it.

"If you have another client tonight, don't let me keep you," he drawled.

She briefly closed her eyes and whispered, "You're a monster."

"*I'm* a monster." He barked a low, cruel laugh. "Me?"

Turning away, she rose naked from the bed. He waited, wondering for a split second if she'd toss the check in his face and prove him wrong. If she did…

But she didn't. She just picked up her panties from the floor and walked to the door. He sneered at himself for being naive enough to even imagine the possibility she'd give up her hard-earned money for the sake of honor, or even pride!

She left the bedroom, going out into the great room of the penthouse. He followed, watching as she collected her bra and shoes, then scooped her white dress from the floor. Putting it on after slipping on her panties, she buttoned the dress quickly, leaving gaps where he'd ripped off buttons in his haste to get it off her. She wouldn't meet his eyes.

Darius wanted to force her to look at him. He wanted her humiliated. He wanted her heartbroken. His pride demanded something he couldn't name. *More.*

She stuffed her bra in her handbag and put her bare feet into her shoes and turned to go.

"It's just a shame the condom broke," he said.

She froze. "What?"

"The condom. Of course I was wearing one. But it broke.

So if you wind up pregnant, let me know, won't you?" He gave a hard smile. "We will negotiate a good price."

He was rewarded. She finally turned and looked at him, aghast.

"You'd pay me? For a baby?"

He said coldly, "Why not, when I paid you for the act that created it?" His expression hardened. "I will never marry you, Letty. So your attempt at gold digging ends with that check in your bag. If by some unfortunate chance you become pregnant, selling me our baby would be your only option."

"You're crazy!"

"And you disgust me." He came closer to her, his eyes cold. "I would never allow any child of mine to be raised by you and that criminal you call a father. I would hire a hundred lawyers first," he said softly, "and drive you both into the sea."

For a moment, Letty looked at him, wide-eyed. Then she turned away with a stumble, but not before he saw the sheen of tears in her eyes. She'd become quite the little actress, he thought.

"Please take me home," she whispered.

"Take you home?" Darius gave a sardonic laugh. "You're an employee, not a guest. A temporary employee whose time is now done." His lip curled. "Find your own way home."

CHAPTER THREE

LETTY SHIVERED IN the darkest, coldest hours of the night as she walked to the Lexington Avenue subway station and got on the express train. It was past one in the morning, and she held her bag tightly in the mostly empty compartment, feeling vulnerable and alone.

Arriving at her stop in Brooklyn, she came numbly down the stairs from the elevated station and walked the blocks to her apartment. The streets were dark, the shops all closed. The February—no, it was March now; it was past midnight—wind was icy against her cheeks still raw with tears.

She'd thought it was a miracle when she saw Darius again. She'd thought he'd found out the truth of how she'd sacrificed herself, and he'd come back for her.

Telling him she loved him had felt so right. She'd honestly thought he might tell her the same thing.

How could she have been so wrong?

You disgust me.

She could still hear the contempt in his voice. Wiping her eyes hard, she shivered, trembling as she trudged toward her four-story apartment building.

While many of the nearby buildings were nice, well kept, with flower boxes, hers was an eyesore, with a rickety fire escape clinging to a crumbling brick facade. But the place was cheap, and the landlord had asked no personal questions, which was what she cared about. Plugging in a security code, Letty pushed open the door.

Inside, the temperature felt colder. Two of the foyer's lights were burned out, leaving only a single bare lightbulb to illuminate the mailboxes and the old delivery menus littering the corners of the cracked tile floor.

Even in the middle of the night, noises echoed against the concrete stairwell, a Doppler tangle of tenants yelling, dogs barking, a baby crying. A sour smell came up from beneath the metal stairs as she wearily climbed three flights. She felt wretched, body and soul, torn between her body's sweet ache from their lovemaking and her heart's incandescent grief.

The fourth floor had worn, stained carpet and a bare lightbulb hanging from the ceiling. Going past the doors of her neighbors—some of whom she'd never met even after three years—she reached into her handbag, found her keys and unlocked the dead bolt. The door creaked as she pushed it open.

"Letty! You're back!" Her father looked up eagerly from his easy chair. He'd waited up for her, wrapped in both a robe and a blanket over his flannel pajamas, since the thermostat didn't work properly. Turning off the television, he looked up hopefully. "Well?"

As the door swung shut behind her, Letty stared at him in disbelief. Her handbag dropped to the floor.

"How could you?" she choked out.

"How could I get you and Darius back together so easily?" Her father beamed at her. "All I needed was a good excuse!"

Her voice caught on a sob. "Are you kidding?"

Howard frowned. "Are you and Darius not back together?"

"Of course we're not! How could you send him a message, pretending to be me? Offering me for the night!"

"I was trying to help," he said falteringly. "You've loved him for so long but refused to contact him. Or he you. I thought…"

"What? That if you forced us together, we'd immediately fall back into each other's arms?"

"Well, yes."

As she stared at him, still trembling from the roller coaster of emotion of that night, anger rushed through her.

"You didn't do it for me!" Reaching into her bag, she grabbed the cashier's check and shoved it at him. "You did it for this!"

Her father's hands shook as he grasped the cashier's check. Seeing the amount, his eyes filled with visible relief. "Thank God."

"How could you?" She wanted to shake her father and scream at him for what he'd done. "How could you sell me?"

"*Sell* you?" Her father looked up incredulously. "I didn't sell you!" Struggling to untangle himself from his blanket, he rose from his chair and sat beside her on the sofa. "I figured the two of you would talk and soon realize how you'd been set up. I thought you'd both have a good laugh, and it would be easier for you each to get over your pride. Maybe he'd send money, maybe he wouldn't." His voice cracked. "But either way, you'd be together again. The two of you love each other."

"You did it for love." Letty's eyes narrowed skeptically. "So the fact that you read about Darius's billion-dollar deal this morning had nothing to do with it."

He winced at her sarcasm, then looked down at the floor. His voice trembled a little as he said, "I guess I thought there was no harm in also trying to solve a problem of my own with a…dissatisfied customer."

Glaring at him, Letty opened her mouth to say the cruel words he deserved to hear. Words she'd never be able to take back. Words neither one of them would ever be able to forget. Words that would take her anguish and rage, wrap them up into a tight ball and launch them at her father like a grenade.

Then she looked at him, old and forlorn, sitting beside

her on the sagging sofa. The man she'd once admired and still absolutely loved.

His hair had become white and wispy, barely covering his spotted scalp. His face, once so hearty and handsome, was gaunt with deep wrinkles on his cheeks. He'd shrunk, become thin and bowed. His robe was too big on him now. His near decade in prison had aged him thirty years.

Howard Spencer, a middle-class kid from Oklahoma, had come to New York and built a fortune with only his charm and a good head for numbers. He'd fallen in love with Constance Langford, the only daughter of an old aristocratic family on Long Island. The Langfords had little money left beyond the Fairholme estate, which was in hock up to the eyeballs. But Howard Spencer, delirious with happiness at their marriage, had assured Constance she'd never worry about money again.

He'd kept his promise. While his wife had been alive, he'd been careful and smart and lucky with his investment fund. It was only after his wife's sudden death that he'd become reckless, taking bigger and bigger financial risks, until his once respected hedge fund became a hollowed-out Ponzi scheme, and suddenly eight billion dollars were gone.

The months of Howard's arrest and trial had been awful for Letty, and worrying about him in prison had been even worse. But now, as she looked at the old man he'd somehow become, was the worst of all.

As she looked at his slumped shoulders, his heartbroken eyes—at his broken arm, still hanging uselessly in the cast—she felt her anger evaporate, leaving in its place only grief and despair. Her mouth snapped shut.

Slumping forward, she covered her face with her hands.

The memory of Darius's words floated back to her. *You needed to pay off some mobster who'd broken your father's arm and threatened to break his whole body if he didn't come up with a hundred thousand dollars within the week.*

Chilled, she looked up. "Why didn't you tell me someone broke your arm, Dad? Why did you let me think it was an accident?"

Howard looked down at the floor guiltily. "I didn't want you to worry."

"Worry?" she cried.

His wan cheeks turned pink. "A father's supposed to take care of his daughter, not the other way around."

"So it's true? Some thug broke your arm and threatened you if you didn't pay him back his money?"

"I knew I could handle it." He tried to smile. "And I have. Once I sign over this check, everything will be fine."

"How do you know you won't have more thugs demanding money, once it's known you actually paid someone back?"

Her father looked shocked. "No. Most of the people who invested in my fund were good, civilized people. Not violent!"

Letty ground her teeth. For a man who'd been in a minimum-security federal prison for nine years, he could be surprisingly naive.

"You should have told me."

"Why? What would you have done except worry? Or worse—try to talk to the man yourself and put yourself in danger?" He set his jaw. "Like I said, I didn't know if Darius would actually send the money. But I knew, either way, you would be safe because you'd be with him." He shook his head, trying to smile. "I really thought you and Darius would take one look at each other and be happy again."

Letty sagged back against the sofa cushions. Her father'd really thought he was doing her a favor. That he was reuniting her with a lost love. That he was protecting her, saving her.

She whispered bleakly, "Darius thought I was a gold digger."

Howard looked indignant. "Of course he didn't! Once you told him you hadn't sent the message…"

"He didn't believe me."

"Then…then…he must have believed you were just a good daughter looking out for your father. Darius has so much money now, you can't tell me he'll miss such a small amount. Not after everything you did for *him*!"

"Stop," she choked out. Just remembering how Darius had looked at her when he handed her the cashier's check was enough to make her want to die. But after he'd told her about the threat against her father's life, what choice had she had?

Her father looked bewildered. "Didn't you tell him what happened ten years ago? Why you never ran away with him?"

She flinched as she remembered Darius's acid words. *Go on, Letty. Tell me how your betrayal was actually a favor. Explain how you destroyed my family at great personal sacrifice, because you loved me so much.*

"No," she whispered, "and I never will. Darius doesn't love me. He hates me more than ever."

Howard's wrinkled face looked mournful. "Oh, sweetheart."

"But now I hate him, too." She looked up. "That's the one good thing that happened tonight. *Now I hate him, too.*"

Her father looked anguished. "That was never what I wanted!"

"It's good." Wiping her eyes, she tried to smile. "I've wasted too many years dreaming of him. Missing him. I'm done."

She was.

The Darius Kyrillos she'd loved no longer existed. She saw that now. She'd tried to give him everything, and he'd seduced her with a cold heart. Her love for Darius was burned out of her forever. Her only hope was to try to forget.

But four weeks later, she found out how impossible that would be. She'd never be able to forget Darius Kyrillos now.

She was pregnant with his baby.

She'd taken the pregnancy test, sure it would be negative. When it was positive, she was shocked. But shock soon became a happy daze as Letty imagined a sweet fat baby in her arms, to cuddle and adore.

Then she told her father.

"I'm going to be a grandfather?" Howard was enraptured at the news. "That's wonderful! And when you tell Darius—"

That caused the first chill of fear. Because Letty suddenly recalled this baby wouldn't just be hers, but Darius's.

He hated her.

He'd threatened to take her baby from her.

Letty shook her head violently. "I can never tell him about the baby!"

"Of course you will." Her father patted her on the shoulder. "I know you're angry at him. He must have hurt you very badly. But that's all in the past! A man has a right to know he's going to be a father."

"Why?" She turned to him numbly. "So he can try to take the baby away because he hates me so much?"

"Take the baby?" Her father laughed. "Once Darius finds out you're pregnant, he'll forget his anger and remember how much he loves you. You'll see. The baby will bring you together."

She shook her head. "You're living in a dream world. He told me…"

"What?"

Letty turned away, hearing the echo of that coldly malevolent voice. *I would never allow any child of mine to be raised by you and that criminal you call a father.*

"We need to start saving money," she whispered. "Now."

"Why? Once you're married, money will never be a worry for you again." Howard looked ecstatic. "You and my grandchild will always be cared for."

Letty knew her father couldn't believe Darius wanted to hurt her. But she knew he did.

I would hire a hundred lawyers first and drive you both into the sea.

They had to leave this city as soon as possible.

Under the terms of her father's probation, Howard was required to remain in the state of New York. So they'd go north, move to some little town upstate where no one knew them, where she could find a new job.

There was just one problem. Moving required money. First and last month's rent, a security deposit and transport for Letty, Howard and all their belongings. Money they didn't have. They were barely keeping their heads above water as it was.

Over the next few months, Letty's fears were proved true. No matter how hard she worked, she couldn't save money. Howard was always hungry or needed something urgently. Money disappeared. There were also the added expenses of medical co-payments for Letty's doctor visits, and physical therapy for her father's arm.

There was some good fortune. After Howard had paid off the mobster, no other angry former investors had threatened him, demanding repayment.

But there, their luck ended. Just when Letty was desperate for overtime pay, all the other waitstaff suddenly seemed to want it, too. But warmer summer weather meant fewer customers at the diner craving the fried eggs and chicken fried steak that were the diner's specialties. Her work hours became less, not more.

Each morning when she left for work, her father pretended to look through job listings in the paper, looking shifty-eyed and pale. Pregnancy exhausted her. Each night when she got home from work, almost falling asleep where she stood, she cooked dinner for them both. She'd do the dishes and go to bed. Then the whole day would start again.

Every day, she anxiously counted the savings she kept in her old chipped cookie jar on the kitchen counter. And every day, she looked at the calendar and felt more afraid.

By late August, amid the sticky heat of New York City, Letty was growing frantic. She could no longer hide her baby bump, not even with her father's oversize shirts. Everyone at the diner knew she was pregnant, including her friend and coworker Belle Langtry, who kept teasing her about it.

"Who's the father?" Belle demanded. "Is it Prince Charming? I swear I saw you leave here once with a dark-haired man in a sports car."

No. It wasn't Prince Charming, Letty thought numbly. Her baby's father was no prince, but a selfish, coldhearted beast who wanted to steal her child away.

Finally, as her yearlong lease on the apartment ended, she knew she couldn't wait any longer. She gave two weeks' notice at the diner. She still hadn't saved enough money, but time had run out.

On the first of September, Letty splashed cold water on her face in the darkness before dawn, then looked at her drawn face in the mirror.

Today was the day.

They couldn't rent a truck to move their belongings. No money for that. Instead, they'd just take what would fit in two suitcases on the bus.

They'd have to leave behind all the final memories from Fairholme. From her childhood. From her mother.

The thought made her throat ache.

But Letty was six months pregnant now. Her heart pounded as she put her hand protectively over her baby bump. She knew from the ultrasound at the doctor's office that she was expecting a boy. How had time fled so quickly? In less than three months, by late November, she'd be cuddling her sweet baby in her arms.

Or else she'd be weeping as the baby's coldhearted father took him away from her forever. She still remembered Darius's cold, dark eyes, heard the flat echo of his voice.

If by some unfortunate chance you become pregnant, selling me our baby would be your only option.

She was suddenly terrified she'd waited too long to leave New York.

Going into the tiny kitchen, she tried to keep her voice cheerful as she said, "Dad, I'm going to pick up my last paycheck, then buy bus tickets."

"I still don't understand why Rochester," he said with a scowl.

She sighed. "I told you. My friend Belle knows someone who knows someone who might be able to get me a job there. Everyone says it's nice. I need you to start packing."

"I have other plans today." His voice was peevish.

"Dad, our lease is up in two days. I know it's not fun, but whatever you don't pack, I'm going to have to call the junk dealer to take." Her throat ached. Maybe all their leftover stuff *was* junk, but it was all they had left. Of Fairholme. Of her mother. Her voice tightened. "Look, I know it won't be easy."

Sitting at the peeling Formica table where he was doing the crossword, Howard glared at her with irritation. "You just need to tell that man of yours you're pregnant."

They'd been having this argument for months. She gritted her teeth. "I can't. I told you."

"Poppycock. A man should be given the opportunity to take care of his own child. And you know, Letty," he added gruffly, "I won't always be here to look after you."

Howard—look after her? When was the last time that

had been true, instead of the other way around? She looked at her father, then sighed. "Why don't you believe me?"

"I knew Darius as a boy." Fiddling with his untouched coffee mug, he looked at her seriously. "If you'd just help him see past his anger, he's got a good heart—"

"I'm not gambling on his *good heart*," she said bitterly. "Not after the way he treated me."

Her father looked thoughtful. "I could just call him…"

"No!" Letty shouted. Her eyes blazed. "If you ever go behind my back like that again, I will never talk to you for the rest of my life. Do you understand? *Never.*"

"Okay, okay," he grumbled. "But he's your baby's father. You should just marry him and be happy."

That left her speechless for a minute.

"Just be packed by the time I return," she said finally, and she went out into the gray, rainy September morning. She picked up her last check at the diner—for a pitiful amount, but every dollar would help—and said farewell to her fellow waitress Belle, who'd moved to New York from Texas the previous Christmas.

"Anytime you need anything, you call me, you hear?" Belle hugged her fiercely. "No matter where you are, Rochester or Rome, remember I'm only a phone call away!"

Letty didn't make friends easily, so it was hard to say goodbye to the only real friend she'd made since she'd left Fairholme. The thought of going to yet another new apartment in a new town where she didn't know anyone, in hopes of starting a job that might not even exist, filled her with dread. She tried to smile.

"You too, Belle," she managed. Then, wiping her eyes, she said goodbye to everyone else at the diner and went back out into the rain to deposit her check at the bank and get two one-way bus tickets to Rochester.

When Letty got back home, her hair and clothes were damp with rain. Her father wasn't at the apartment, and his suitcases were empty. All their belongings were still untouched, exactly where she'd left them.

She'd just sort through everything herself, she thought wearily. Once she'd figured out how many boxes they'd have to leave behind, she'd call the junk dealer.

Of the eight billion dollars her father's investment fund had lost, three billion had since been recovered. But the authorities had been careful not to leave him with anything of value. Their possessions had been picked over long ago by the Feds and bankruptcy court.

What was left was all crammed into this tiny apartment. The broken flute her mother had played at Juilliard. The ceramic animals Constance had painted for her daughter as gifts, starting with her first birthday. The leather-bound classic books from her grandfather's collection, water-damaged, so worthless. Except to them. Her great-grandfather's old ship in a bottle. Her grandma Spencer's homemade Christmas ornaments. All would have to be left.

We'll get through it, Letty told herself fiercely. They could still be happy. She'd raise her baby with love, in a snug cottage overlooking a garden of flowers. Her son would have a happy childhood, just as Letty had.

He wouldn't be raised in some stark gray penthouse without a mother, without love…

Letty started digging through the first pile of clutter. She planned to stay up the whole night scrubbing down the apartment, in hopes their landlord might actually give back her security deposit.

Hearing a hard knock at the door, she rose to her feet, overwhelmed with relief. Her father had come back to help. He must have forgotten his key again. Sorting through their possessions would be so much easier with two of them—

Opening the door, she gasped.

Darius stood in her doorway, dressed in a black button-down shirt with well-cut jeans that showed the rugged lines of his powerful body. It was barely noon, but his jaw was dark with five-o'clock shadow.

For a moment, even hating and fearing him as she did, Letty was dazzled by that ruthless masculine beauty.

"Letty," he greeted her coldly. Then his eyes dropped to her baby bump.

With an intake of breath, Letty tried to shut the door in his face.

He blocked her with his powerful shoulder and pushed his way into her apartment.

CHAPTER FOUR

Six months ago Darius had wanted vengeance.

He'd gotten it. He'd ruthlessly taken Letitia Spencer's virginity, then tossed her out into a cold winter's night. He'd seduced her, insulted her. He'd thrown the money in her face, made her feel cheap.

It had been delicious.

But since then, to his dismay, he'd discovered the price of that vengeance.

In Darius's childhood, back on the Greek island where he was born, his grandmother had often told him that vengeance hurt the person who committed it worse than the one who endured it. When the kids at school mocked his illegitimate birth, sneering at his mother's abandonment— *Even your own* mitéra *didn't want you*—his grandmother had told him to ignore them, to take the high road.

He'd tried, but the boys' taunts had only grown worse until he was finally forced to punch them. They'd all been bloodied in the fight, but especially Darius, since it had been one against four.

"So you see I'm right," his grandmother had said gravely, bandaging him afterward. "You were hurt worse."

In Darius's own opinion, that vengeance had been not only justified, but strategic. The boys at school had never taunted him again.

But this time, his grandmother had been proved right. Because Darius's vengeance against Letty had hurt him more than he'd ever imagined.

Instead of quenching the flame, that night together had only built his desire for her into a blazing fire.

He wanted her. Every night for the last six months, he'd

half expected Letty to contact him. Once her prideful anger had faded, surely she would want him back—if not for his body, then obviously for his money.

But she never had. And when he'd remembered the haunted look on her beautiful heart-shaped face the night she'd told him she loved him, the night he'd taken her virginity and tossed her ruthlessly into the dark, he'd had moments when he'd wondered if he might have been wrong.

But how could he be wrong? The evidence spoke for itself.

Still, in the months since their night together, his continual raw desire for her had made him edgy. He'd intended to remain as his company's CEO for a year, guiding his team in the transition after the sale. Instead, he'd gotten into an argument with the head of the conglomerate and left within weeks. Darius could no longer endure working for someone else, but he'd signed a noncompete clause, so couldn't start a new business in the same field.

Bereft of the twenty-hour workdays that had been the entirety of his life for a decade, he hadn't known how to fill his hours. He tried spending some of his fortune. He'd bought a race car, then ten cars, then a race track. He'd bought four planes, all with interiors done in different colors. No. Next he'd tried extreme sports: skydiving, heli-skiing. Yawn.

Worst of all, he'd been surrounded by beautiful women, all keen to get his attention. And he hadn't wanted a single one of them.

He'd been *bored*. Worse. He'd felt frustrated and angry. Because even with the endless freedom of time and money, he couldn't have what he really wanted.

Letty.

Now, seeing her in the flesh, so beautiful—so *pregnant*—he hated himself for ever taking his vengeance. No matter how richly she'd deserved it, look where that thrill of hatred and lust had led.

Pregnant. With his baby.

Even wearing an oversize white T-shirt and baggy jeans, Letty was somehow more sensual, more delectable, than any stick-thin model in a skintight cocktail dress. Letty's pregnancy curves were lush. Her skin glowed. Her breasts had grown enormous. With effort, he forced his gaze down to her belly.

"So it's true," he said in a low voice. "You're pregnant."

She looked frozen. Then she squared her shoulders, tossing her dark ponytail in a futile gesture of bravado. "So?"

"Is the baby mine?"

"Yours?" Her eyes shot sparks of fire, even though she had dark shadows beneath, as if she hadn't been sleeping well. "What makes you think the baby's yours? Maybe I slept with ten men since our night. Maybe I slept with a hundred—"

The thought of her sleeping with other men made Darius sick. "You're lying."

"How do you know?"

"Because your father told me."

The fight went out of her. She went pale. "My...my father?"

"He wanted me to pay for the information, but when I refused, he told me everything. For free."

"Maybe he was lying," she said weakly. She looked as if she might faint.

"Sit down," Darius ordered. "I'll get you a glass of water. Then we'll talk."

She sank into the old pullout sofa, her cheeks pale. It wasn't hard for him to find the kitchen. The apartment was pathetically small—just a postage-stamp-sized living room, surrounded by an even smaller bedroom, bathroom and kitchen.

He looked around him, amazed that the onetime heiress of Fairholme, born into a forty-room mansion, was now living with her father in an apartment the same size as the room her mother had once used to arrange flowers off the solarium.

Old boxes and mementos were packed everywhere. The leftovers of her family's former life—items that obviously weren't valuable enough to be sold, but too precious to be thrown away—were clustered around the old television and piled tightly along the walls. A pillow and folded blanket sat beside the pullout sofa.

Darius walked across the worn carpet to the peeling linoleum of the telephone-booth-sized kitchen. Dust motes floated in the weak gray sunlight. The barred window overlooked an air shaft that faced other apartments, just a few feet away. With the bars across the window, it felt like prison.

It's better than they deserve, he told himself firmly. And it was still nicer than his childhood home in Heraklios. At least this place had electricity, running water. At least this place had a parent.

Darius's own parents had both left him, in different ways, two days after he was born. His unemployed father had discovered his newborn son crying in a basket by his door, left out in the rain by his former lover, a wealthy, spoiled heiress who'd abandoned the child she'd never wanted.

Fired from his job, Eugenios Kyrillos found himself unable to get another. No other rich Greek fathers, it seemed, wanted to risk their daughters' virtue to a chauffeur who didn't know his place. Desperate to find work, he'd departed for America, leaving his baby son to be raised by his grandmother in the desolate house by the sea.

The first time Darius had spoken to his father in person had been at his grandmother's funeral, when he was eleven.

Then his father had taken him from Greece, away from everything and everyone he'd ever known, and brought him to America.

Fairholme had seemed like an exotic palace, where everyone spoke a language he couldn't understand. His father had seemed just as strange, the emotionally distant chauffeur of this grand American king—Howard Spencer.

And look what the Spencers had come to now.

Darius had long ago torn down his grandmother's shack in Heraklios and built a palatial villa. He had a penthouse in Manhattan, a ski chalet in Switzerland, his private race track outside London. His personal fortune was greater than anything Howard Spencer ever dreamed of.

And the Spencers were now living in this tiny, threadbare apartment.

But instead of feeling a sense of triumph, Darius felt strangely unsettled as he walked through her dreary kitchen and poured a glass of water from the tap. Returning to the equally depressing living room, he handed Letty the glass, then looked at the folded blankets and pillow on the floor.

"Who sleeps on the sofa?"

Letty's cheeks turned pink as she looked down at the sagging cushions. "I do."

"You pay all the rent, and your father gets the bedroom?"

"He hasn't been sleeping well. I just want him to be comfortable."

Darius looked at her incredulously. "And you're pregnant."

"What do you care?" she said bitterly. "You're just here to take my baby away."

Well. True. His eyes fell on the empty suitcases. "Where were you planning to go?"

"Anywhere you couldn't find us."

Darius stared down at her grimly. After his conversation with Howard Spencer, he'd had his investigator check up on Letty and found she'd only recently left her job as a waitress. She was still broke. None of the other employees remembered seeing any men around her, except one waitress, Belle, who had described Darius himself.

It seemed that, contrary to all previous assumptions, Letty wasn't a gold digger. Not with other men.

Not even with Darius.

In that, he'd misjudged her. After the way Letty had crushed him so devastatingly ten years ago, informing him that she was leaving him for a richer man, he'd believed Letty was a fortune hunter to the core.

It made sense. His own mother had abandoned him as a two-day-old newborn for the exact same reason. To Calla, Darius had been the embarrassing result of a one-night liaison with her wealthy family's chauffeur. She'd been determined to marry as befitted her station. She'd cared only about money and the social position that went with it.

But Letty wasn't the same. At least not anymore.

Darius abruptly sat down on the sofa beside her. "Why didn't you come to me when you found out you were pregnant? You had to know I would give you everything you needed and more."

"Give? I knew you'd only take!" she said incredulously. "You threatened me!"

He ground his teeth. "We could have come to some arrangement."

"You threatened to buy my baby, and if I tried to refuse, you would take the baby from me and—what were your words?—drive me into the sea?"

Darius didn't like to be reminded of what he'd said six months ago. He'd rationalized his cruelty on the grounds of justice. But now…strictly speaking, he might have sounded a little less than civil, if not outright crazy. Irritated, he glared at her. "Drink your water."

"Why? What did you put into it?" She sniffed the glass.

"Some drug to make me pass out so you can kidnap me to a Park Avenue dungeon?"

He snorted a laugh in spite of himself. "The water came from your tap. Drink it or not. I just thought you looked pale."

She stared at him for a moment, then took a tentative sip.

He looked around the tiny apartment. "Why are you living here?"

"Sadly, the presidential suite at the St. Regis was already booked."

"I mean it, Letty. Why did you stay in New York all these years? You could have just left. Moved west where no one would know you or care about what your father did."

She blinked fast. "I couldn't abandon him. I love him."

The man was a liar and a cheat, so of course Letty loved him. And she'd intended to raise their baby with him in the house, the man Darius blamed for his own father's death. He ground his teeth. "Are you even taking care of yourself? Do you have a doctor?"

"Of course," she said, stung. "How can you ask me that?"

"Because you've been working on your feet all day, until recently. And living in a place like this." He gestured angrily around the threadbare, cluttered apartment. "It never occurred to you I'd want better for our child?"

She glared at him. "*I* wanted better! I wanted my baby's father to be a good man I could trust and love. Instead, I got you, Darius, the worst man on earth!"

"You didn't think so ten years ago."

He immediately wished he could take the words back, because they insinuated that he still cared. Which he didn't.

"Oh, you're actually willing to talk about ten years ago? Fine. Let's talk about it." She briefly closed her eyes. "The reason I never showed up the night we were supposed to elope was because I was protecting you."

His lip curled scornfully. *"Protecting* me."

"Yes." Her expression was cool. "The day we were going to elope, my father told me his investment fund was a fraud. It had stopped making money years before, but he'd continued making payouts to old investors by taking money from new ones. The Feds were already on his tail. I knew what was going to happen." She lifted her luminous gaze. "I couldn't let you get dragged into it. Not with all your big dreams. You'd just started your tech company…" She took a deep breath and whispered, "I couldn't let my father's crime ruin your life, too."

For a moment, Darius's heart twisted as he looked at her beautiful face, her heartbreaking hazel eyes. Then he remembered that he no longer had any heart vulnerable enough to break.

"You're lying. You left me for another man. A rich man who could—how did you express it?—*give you the life of luxury you deserved.*" He snorted. "Though obviously he wasn't much good. He must have dumped you the moment your father was arrested."

"He couldn't dump me." She gave a low laugh. "He never existed."

"What?"

"It was the only way I knew you'd let me go." She lifted her chin and added with deliberate lightness, "I knew your weakness, even then."

"Weakness?" he growled.

"You always said a man could be measured by his money. I knew you wouldn't accept my just breaking up with you without explanation. So I gave you one. I told you I wanted someone richer. I knew you'd believe that."

He stared at her. "It's not true."

"I've always been a terrible liar." She looked sad. "But you still believed it. And immediately stopped calling me."

Darius's cheeks burned as he remembered how he'd felt that day. She was right.

He had loved her beyond reason, had been determined to fight for her at any cost. Until she'd told him she didn't want him because he was poor. He'd believed it instantly. Because money made the man. No money, no man.

His throat felt tight as he looked at her, struggling not to believe she was telling the truth when every fiber of him believed her.

"And my father?" he said hoarsely. "Were you protecting him, too—getting him fired?"

"It's true. I did have him fired. I told Dad I couldn't bear to look at Eugenios because he reminded me of you. I did it because I was afraid my dad might ask him to invest his life savings in the bankrupt investment fund. My dad still believed he could fix everything then. I knew your father would give him his savings. He was loyal to the core."

"Yes, he was," he bit out. His father had always made his employer his top priority, even over his own son.

Darius couldn't remember when his father had ever put his son first, over his job. He hadn't attended Darius's school events, not even his high school graduation. Being eternally at Howard Spencer's beck and call, keeping the ten luxury cars all gleaming and ready, had been Eugenios's total focus in life.

Oh, his father had fed and clothed him and given him a place to live in the two-bedroom apartment over the Fairholme garage that went with his job. But emotionally, they were oceans apart. The two men never talked.

Until that one awful day Darius told his father what he really thought of him...

But that memory was so white-hot with pain, he pushed it from his mind with all the force of a ball thrown from the earth to the moon.

Letty sighed beside him on the sofa. "I was trying to get

your father away from Fairholme before he lost everything. But it was too late. He'd already invested his life savings years before. My dad had accepted it for his fund, even though it was such a small amount," she said in a small voice. "As a favor."

A small amount? His father's life savings! The arrogance of them! Darius's dark eyebrows lowered in fury.

"Howard Spencer is a liar and cheat," he said harshly. "He destroyed people's lives."

"I know," she whispered, looking down. She bit her full, rosy lower lip. "He never meant to."

"He deserves to suffer."

She looked up. "He has suffered. During his arrest and trial, I tried so hard to be strong for him. When he was in prison, I was there every visiting day. I cheered him up. Encouraged him. And all the time, I felt so scared. So alone." She gave him a watery smile. "Sometimes the only thing I had to cling to was you."

"Me?"

"At least I hadn't dragged you down with me," she whispered. "At least you were able to follow your dreams."

Darius stared at her in shock.

Then he narrowed his eyes. She was trying to take credit for his accomplishments. To claim that if not for her sacrifice, he never would have made his fortune. She thought so little of him. Ice chilled his heart.

"And you expect me to be grateful?"

She looked startled. "I—"

"When you found out about your father's crime," he said tightly, "you should have come to me. I was your future husband. Instead, you lied to me. You cut me out of your life. Rather than asking for my help, you apparently believed I was so incompetent and useless, you felt you had to sacrifice yourself to save me."

"No," she gasped, "you've got it all wrong…"

"You never respected me." He forced his voice to remain calm when his shoulders were tight with repressed fury. "Not my intelligence, my judgment or my strength."

"Respected you?" she choked out. "*I loved you.* But I knew what was about to happen. I couldn't let you drown with us. You had nothing—"

"You're right," he said coldly. "I had nothing. No money. No influence. You knew I couldn't pay for lawyers or speak to politicians on your behalf. So you decided I was useless."

"No." She looked pale. "I just meant you had nothing to do with it—"

"You were my fiancée. I had *everything* to do with it. I would have tried to protect you, to comfort you. But you never gave me the chance. Because you believed I would fail."

Her voice sounded strangled. "Darius—"

He held up his hand sharply. "But now I have made my fortune. Everything has changed. And yet you still intended to disappear and keep my child secret from me for the rest of your life." A new, chilling thought occurred to him. "What story did you intend to tell the baby, Letty?"

"I don't know," she whispered.

"What were you going to raise my child to believe? That he or she had no father? That I hadn't wanted him?" An old childhood grief he'd thought long buried suddenly shook the ground beneath his feet, like an earthquake threatening to swallow him whole. "That I'd purposefully abandoned him?"

"I don't know!" Letty cried. "But you said you'd take the baby from me. I had no choice but to run!"

Darius stared at the woman he'd known for most of his life. He'd loved her for such a short, sweet time. He'd hated her far longer.

He himself had been abandoned by everyone who should

have loved him as a child. His whole young life he'd never felt like he really belonged anywhere.

And then there was Letty.

He'd loved her so wildly, so truly, so recklessly. She had finally destroyed what was left of his heart. That had been Darius's final lesson.

He was determined that his child would never learn such a lesson.

Darius's jaw tightened. His child would be surrounded by love from the beginning. His son or daughter would have a solid place in the world and never doubt their worth.

The blindfold of rage and hurt pride lifted from his eyes. He looked at Letty, and suddenly everything became crystal clear. Calm settled over him like rain.

Their child needed both of them.

For the last decade, he'd tried to forget about the Letty he'd once known. About her character. About her kind heart.

He saw now that in Letty's mind, her hurtful lies a decade before hadn't shown disrespect, but love. She really had been trying to protect him. As she still was trying to protect her father.

As she was trying now, in her own misguided way, to protect their child.

Letty hadn't betrayed him. She'd loved him, as recently as February, the night they'd conceived their child. Yes, she'd shown bad judgment ten years ago, lying to him, hiding the truth about her father. She'd continued to show bad judgment today, planning to run away with his child. A chill went down his spine to think of what might have happened if her father hadn't called him today.

But it wasn't entirely her fault. Her love blinded her. It made her weak. And after the cold way he'd treated her, and his threats to take the child, he couldn't blame her for being afraid.

It didn't make her a monster. It wasn't enough of a reason to brutally separate her from their child. Not after he himself had known what it was to have no mother. No father. No real place in the world.

Their baby would have both parents and a secure, settled home.

Darius knew he had to rebuild Letty's trust in him. He had to find a way to strengthen her occasionally faulty judgment with his own. If Darius was wiser, it was because he never allowed love to blind him. He always focused on the bottom line. So what was it here?

The answer was simple.

He had to make Letty his wife.

It was the only way to properly secure their child's future. It would guarantee the stability of two parents and a permanent home.

And also, his body suddenly whispered, marrying Letty would permanently secure her in his bed.

The thought electrified him. That settled it.

"I misjudged you," he said.

Letty glared at him. "Yes!"

"I treated you badly."

"You think?"

"So let me make up for it now." Leaning toward her on the sofa, Darius said, "I want you to marry me, Letty."

Her jaw dropped. "Marry you!"

"I've realized now I blamed everything on you. It wasn't your fault…"

"No."

"It was your father's," he finished grimly. "He's ruined your life. I won't let him ruin our child's."

Her eyes were wide as she put her hands over her large belly. "You're crazy. My father loves the baby, just as he loves me!"

"And what about the next time some thug decides to attack him? What if that man decides to hurt your father's family instead?"

Letty's expression became troubled. Swallowing, she whispered, "That wouldn't happen…"

"No. It won't. Because you and the baby will be miles away from Howard Spencer and safe with me." He rose abruptly to his feet. "You will have to sign a prenuptial agreement…"

"I won't, because I'm not going to marry you."

She wasn't joking or playing coy. She actually sounded serious.

Darius stared down at her in confusion. So many women were dying to marry him, he'd assumed that Letty—jobless, penniless, faced with threats on all sides—would be thrilled at the thought of being his bride. "Of course you want to marry me."

"Marry someone I hate? Who hates me back? No, thanks."

He couldn't believe she was trying to fight him when it was the only practical solution. He gritted his teeth. It was that idea of *love*, once again interfering with all common sense!

"Have you thought this through?" Folding his arms, he regarded her coolly. "I could take you to court. Have you declared an unfit mother, selfishly placing our child at risk."

Letty rose to her feet in turn, matching him toe-to-toe, though he was bigger by a foot in height and at least sixty pounds of muscle. She narrowed her eyes. "You could *try*."

In spite of himself, he almost smiled. Another thing he'd forgotten about her character. She fought harder for others than she ever did for herself.

"You really think you can handle a custody battle? You think there are waves of lawyers out there, willing to support Howard Spencer's daughter pro bono, when all they'd get for their trouble is a lot of bad PR?"

Her cheeks flushed, even as she lifted her chin defiantly. "We'll see, won't we?"

But beneath her bravado, her expression was soft and sad. Her long dark ponytail gleamed in waves down her back, and his eyes strayed to the roundness of her belly and full breasts, voluptuous beyond belief. In this moment, Darius thought she looked like everything desirable in a woman—the perfect image of what any man would dream of in a wife.

He suddenly imagined how she might look in court. Whatever her father's sins, if she did find a good attorney, she could be packaged and sold to the presiding judge as the poor, innocent, poverty-stricken waitress threatened by the cold, power-hungry billionaire. No matter how many legal sharks he hired, Darius wasn't guaranteed to win. There was some small possibility he might lose.

He abruptly changed tack.

"Does our baby deserve to have parents at war? Living in here—" he motioned to the peeling wallpaper, the cracked ceiling "—instead of my penthouse? Does he deserve to grow up in poverty without the protection of his father's name? Without my love?"

Letty looked stricken. "Our baby could still have your love."

"He deserves everything I can provide. Are you really so selfish as to make our child suffer for the sake of your own angry pride?"

He saw emotions struggle on her face. She really was a terrible liar. He knew he was very close to getting what he wanted—her total surrender.

"We could make our marriage work," he murmured. "Our son or daughter would be our priority, always."

"Son," she said unwillingly.

He looked at her sharply.

She took a deep breath, then slowly smiled. "We're having a boy."

"A boy!" The nebulous idea of a baby suddenly solidified in Darius's mind. He could imagine his son smiling, playing soccer, laughing, hugging him. And the fact that she'd revealed that detail proved how close she was to agreeing to his proposal. His resolve solidified. Stepping closer, he said softly, "Marry me, Letty."

Looking uncertain, she bit her lip. "It would be a disaster. Not just for me. For you. Don't you know how much people hate me?"

"Not once you're with me," he said confidently.

"You don't understand how bad it is…"

"I'm sure you're exaggerating." He'd all but won. Now that his unborn child was secure, he was already jumping ahead to the thought of enjoying Letty's surrender in full, imagining her naked and writhing with desire in his arms. He wanted to take her back to the penthouse immediately. Then he remembered. "I am hosting a charity event tonight. The Fall Ball."

She looked impressed in spite of herself. "You're hosting that this year?"

"We can announce our engagement to all of New York."

"It's a mistake!"

"Let me worry about that."

"Okay, but…"

"But what?"

A shadow crossed her face. "But I don't love you anymore."

He felt a strange emotion, deep down inside. He crushed it down before he could identify what it was.

"I do not need your love. I can assure you that you'll never have mine. Love is for children. I just need your compliance." When she still hesitated, he took a deliberate step back. "Or I can walk out that door and go straight to my lawyer."

Letty looked wistful in the gray light from the small window. She sighed sadly. "Have it your way."

"You'll marry me?"

She nodded.

He felt a surge of smug masculine triumph. "Good choice."

Pulling her roughly into his arms, he did what he'd yearned to do for six months and kissed her.

From the moment he felt her lips against his and tasted her sweetness—her mouth, her tongue—he was lost, and at the same time, found. Her lips parted, and as she melted against him, he savored her surrender. His body and long-dead soul roared back to life.

Letty wrenched away. "But first, you'll take me to your charity ball tonight. And see firsthand what it would be like to actually have me as your wife."

"Good—"

"Just remember." She gave him a crooked smile. "You asked for it."

CHAPTER FIVE

LETTY ALMOST DIDN'T leave a note for her father. Her anger at his betrayal was too high. But in the end she didn't want him to worry, so she scribbled a note and left it on the counter.

Out with Darius, and I'm never talking to you again.

Darius had taken one look at her closet and told her he was taking her shopping for the ball. She'd tried to protest, but he'd retorted, "There's no point in announcing our engagement if you turn up at the ball dressed in rags. No one would believe it."

"Fine," she said sulkily. "Waste your money on a ball gown. See if I care."

But she had the sudden disconcerting feeling that her life was no longer her own.

As she climbed into his sports car, her stomach growled with hunger. But she vowed she wasn't going to say a word about it. It was bad enough he was buying her a dress. She wasn't going to ask him for food, like a beggar!

But as Darius climbed into the driver's seat beside her, all her senses went on high alert. Having him so close did strange things to her insides. As he drove through the busy traffic, she glanced at him out of the corner of her eye. His dark hair wasn't even mussed, and his powerful body was relaxed in the leather seat. He looked so much calmer than she felt.

But why wouldn't he be relaxed?

He'd won.

She'd lost.

Simple as that.

Or so Darius thought. Letty clasped her hands together in her lap as she looked out the window. Once he actually saw what life would be like for him with her at his side, he wouldn't be able to get rid of her fast enough. Maybe she and her father could still be on that bus to Rochester tomorrow.

Darius didn't yet see that her family's scandal wasn't something he could master or control. That was why he'd been so angry that she'd protected him ten years ago with her silence. He still somehow thought, if he'd known the truth back then, he could have prevented disaster.

She looked up through the window, seeing flashes of blue sky between the skyscrapers like a strobe light. Darius would get a dose of reality today. He'd discover how toxic the Spencer name was, even now. It had been even worse at the time of her father's arrest and trial, when reporters and angry, tomato-throwing hecklers had camped outside her father's pied-à-terre on Central Park West!

Let Darius get just a glimpse of what he would have been up against if she'd actually followed her heart and married him ten years ago instead of setting him free. He didn't appreciate the way she'd tried to protect him? Fine. Still staring out the window, she wiped her eyes hard. Let him just see.

The rain had stopped. The sky was blue and bright on the first of September. As they drove through Manhattan, puddle-dotted sidewalks were full of gawking tourists, standing still like islands as a current of New Yorkers rushed past them, coming up from the subway, hurrying back to work after lunch.

When their car stopped at a red light, Letty glanced at a fancy chauffeured town car stopped beside them. In the backseat, she saw a man speaking angrily into his phone and staring at a computer tablet, totally wrapped in his own bubble. Rich people lived in a separate world. Letty hadn't fully realized that.

Not until she'd fallen out of it.

After her father's confession that awful night long ago, after she'd tried her best to protect Darius and his father by getting them away from the manor, she'd begged Howard to go to the police and throw himself on their mercy.

He'd loved her, so a few months later he'd done it.

The police and Feds had descended on him like the hardcase criminal they believed him to be. Within six months, he was in prison on a nine-year sentence.

Letty had tried to remain in one of the exclusive small towns on Long Island near Fairholme. But it proved impossible. Too many people recognized her and didn't hesitate to yell or even—more than once—physically take the few dollars in her wallet, saying her father owed them. Manhattan had been even worse, and anyway was way out of her price range. So she'd moved to a working-class neighborhood in Brooklyn where she could be anonymous. No one bothered her. Mostly, people were kind.

But without money or family or friends, Letty had learned the hard way what it meant to struggle and always have too much month at the end of her paycheck.

No one likes self-pity. Help someone else, baby. Letty could almost hear the whisper of her mother's voice, so kind, so warm, so loving. Almost see her mother's eyes glowing with love. *The best way to feel better when you're sad is to help someone who's hurting more.*

Good advice.

Taking a deep breath, Letty turned to Darius in the sports car. "So tell me about your charity, the one benefiting from the Fall Ball tonight."

Driving, he glanced at her out of the corner of his eye. "It provides college scholarships for foster kids."

"Nice," she said, surprised. "But I never pegged you as the society-ball-hosting type."

He shrugged. "I have the time. Might as well use it."

"You could just waste your days dating beautiful women and spending your obscene amounts of money."

He pulled his car to a curb where a valet waited. "That's exactly what I plan to do today."

"You're going on a date?" Then she saw his look and realized he meant her. She blushed. "Oh."

The door opened, and Letty stepped out onto Fifth Avenue, which was lined with exclusive designer shops from famous international brands to quirky boutiques less well-known but every bit as expensive. The last time she'd shopped on this street she'd been a pampered seventeen-year-old looking for a white dress for the graduation ceremony at her private school, Miss Parker's. She hadn't fit into society, even then. She'd been too bookish, too tenderhearted, too socially awkward.

But now Letty was actually scared. She glanced at the people coming out of an exclusive department store, almost expecting one of them to tell her to get lost, that she no longer belonged here.

"Which shop first?" Darius asked, his dark eyes smiling.

"I changed my mind," she muttered. "I don't want to go."

The smile disappeared. "Too late for that."

"Darius…"

Ignoring her protests, he grabbed her hand. Letty tried not to notice the sizzle of electricity from their touching palms as he pulled her into a famous luxury store.

As soon as they passed the doorman into the store's foyer, a salesgirl came up to them, offering a tray of champagne. "Monsieur?"

He took a glass. "Thank you."

Noting Letty's pregnant belly, the salesgirl didn't offer

champagne. "And for madame? Some sparkling water, perhaps, some juice of *pamplemousse*?"

"No, thanks," Letty said, pulling away from Darius. Ducking her head, she pretended to look through the nearest dress racks, sparsely and expensively filled with garments that seemed to be designed for a size zero.

"We require assistance," he said.

"Sir?"

He turned to an elegant white-haired woman, apparently the manager, dressed in an expensive-looking tweed suit. "I need a ball gown for my fiancée."

Fiancée. The word made Letty shiver. But it was true, in a way. She'd agreed to his marriage proposal.

It's not a real engagement, she told herself firmly. She glanced down at her bare left hand. There was no ring. No ring meant it wasn't real. Anyway, the engagement would be over before the end of the night.

"Couture or ready-to-wear, Mr. Kyrillos?" The white-haired woman somehow already knew who he was.

"It's for tonight."

"We can, of course, do any last-minute alterations that madame may require. If you'll please come this way?"

They were led to a private area with a white leather sofa and a three-way mirror, as a succession of salesgirls, under the sharp-eyed direction of the manager, brought in clothes.

"She'll try on everything," Darius said, standing in front of the sofa as his cell phone rang. Lifting it from his pocket, he told Letty, "Come out when you have something to show me."

As salesgirls filled her arms with gowns and gently pushed her toward the changing room, she hesitated. "What do you want to see?"

Looking her body over slowly, Darius gave her a heavy-lidded sensual smile. "Everything."

Beneath his hot gaze, somehow, he made her feel like

a goddess of sex—even at six months pregnant, in her old T-shirt and jeans!

Darius sat down calmly on the white leather sofa, talking into his phone and sipping champagne. She turned away with a sigh to try on gowns for a ball that she was dreading.

Maybe it wouldn't be all bad, she tried to tell herself. She couldn't remember the last time she'd had new clothes. Everything in her closet was either from high school or purchased from the bargain bin at the thrift store. It might be fun to get a dress that was not only pretty, but actually fit.

Then she saw the price tag of the first gown.

Darius looked up expectantly when she came out of the dressing room. His expression changed to a scowl. "Why are you still in your old clothes?"

"The price of these gowns is ridiculous! We can go to the local thrift shop and find a barely used prom dress…"

"Letty."

"I mean it. It's foolish for you to throw money away when you might never see me again after tonight."

"Now you're talking nonsense." He tilted his head, looking her over critically. "Are you not feeling well? Are you hungry? Thirsty? Tired?"

She wasn't going to say a word about being hungry. Wild horses couldn't drag it out of her!

Her stomach growled again.

"Um. I might have missed breakfast."

It wasn't her fault! The baby made her say it!

He looked mad. "You should have told me." He grabbed a glass of sparkling mineral water from a salesgirl. "Here," he said gravely, pushing it into her hand. "Start with that. Breakfast or lunch?"

The cool water tasted delicious, and did make her feel slightly better. "Breakfast?"

Turning to one of the hovering assistants, he ordered, "Have a large breakfast sent down from your café."

"Oh, sir." The salesgirl looked sorrowful. "I'm afraid that's impossible…"

"Of course it's possible for Mr. Kyrillos," the white-haired manager snapped, turning to them with a bright smile. "A pregnant woman must never go hungry. What would madame like?"

"Everything," Darius said. "Send down a tray or two. We'll be here a while. We need a ball gown, but also a great deal more. Shoes, accessories, maternity clothes. Price is no object. We may be here for hours."

"Yes, sir," the woman replied happily, clapping her hands at her assistants, who rushed to obey.

"Darius, you don't need to make a fuss!"

"You're wrong. I can see all too well that I need to be in charge. Because you've always been better at taking care of others than yourself." He drew Letty gently to the white sofa. "Here. Sit down. Take a breath."

"But I left all those dresses in the changing room—"

"They will wait. Relax. You do not have to shop hungry. Breakfast is on its way."

The white leather cushion shifted beneath them, tipping her toward him on the sofa. The edge of her thigh brushed against his. She jumped away with an intake of breath, looking up at him with big eyes.

"I'm not your responsibility."

"You are now." Reaching out, he tucked a long tendril of her dark hair back behind her ear and said softly, "And taking care of you will be my pleasure."

His…pleasure?

A sudden terrifying thought occurred to her.

"Darius," she said haltingly, unable to meet his eyes. "You surely can't think…"

"Think what?"

Taking her courage in her hands, she looked into his dark wicked eyes. However charming he might seem at the moment, she couldn't forget the heartless man he'd revealed himself to be. She couldn't let herself confuse him with the boy she'd once loved. No matter how much Darius's dark eyes, his smile, his kindness might seem the same. *He was nothing like the man she'd loved.*

"You can't think…" She took a deep breath. "That our marriage would be real."

"Of course it will be real. Legal in any court."

"I mean…" She licked her lips, hating him for making her spell it out. "It would just be a marriage of convenience, nothing more. For our baby. We wouldn't… You and I, we would never…"

"You will sleep in my bed, Letty." His dark eyes burned through her. "Naked. Every single night."

His sensual voice swirled around her body like a hot wind, making her toes curl.

She had to resist. She had no intention of sleeping with him again, no matter how seductive he might be. She'd been a virgin till twenty-eight, waiting for love. That love was gone.

"I loved you the night we conceived our baby. Everything has changed. Unlike you, I can't have sex with a cold heart," she said in a low voice. "No love, no sex."

He wrapped her hand in his larger one. She felt his palm against hers, and a shiver ricocheted through Letty's body, deep, to blood and bone. He leaned forward.

"We'll see," he whispered.

CHAPTER SIX

LETTY WAS SAVED when the salesgirls interrupted them with trays of pastries and fruit and juices, followed closely behind by yet more racks of clothes for her to consider.

A proper breakfast tray soon followed with maple bacon pancakes drizzled in maple syrup, hash brown potatoes and hot fried sausages. Thus fortified, Letty spent another hour trying on all the clothes she liked in that luxury store. Then they moved to a designer boutique. Then an exclusive department store.

By the end of the afternoon, Darius had bought her so many bags of clothes, he'd had to call his bodyguard and driver down to Fifth Avenue to carry everything back to the penthouse.

He took her to a world-famous jewelry store where they were ushered to an exclusive, private floor. She tried to protest, for about the thirtieth time. "You really don't need to keep spending more money on me!"

Darius held up a twenty-carat diamond necklace with a critical eye. "You're going to be my wife. Of course you need clothes."

"Those are diamonds."

He grinned. "Hard, sparkling clothes."

She harrumphed. "You're wasting your money."

"So let me waste it. What do you care?" Lifting his eyebrow, he said mildly, "I seem to recall your saying you hate me. So why not make me suffer?"

Why not indeed? Put that way, it didn't sound so unreasonable. "You do have it coming."

Setting the necklace down, he looked at her with a heavily lidded gaze.

"And I intend to take it." Turning back to the jeweler, he nodded toward the diamond necklace. "Starting with that."

But though Darius insisted on buying her an entire wardrobe of fancy clothes, he was never satisfied by any of the ball gowns she tried on. Truth be told, even Letty thought most of them hideous. A hoop skirt on a baby bump? She looked like a cartoon hippo.

In spite of Letty's misgivings, the afternoon flew by in an irresistible whirlwind of small pleasures. Her new wardrobe wasn't comprised of minimalist black and gray clothes as he had originally suggested, currently popular with chic society women, nor were they the plain, sensible, washing-machine-ready clothes she'd worn for the last ten years. No.

Darius had watched her carefully as she'd tried on each outfit, and he seemed to notice the colors that made her face light up with joy. Bright, vivid jewel tones—emerald green, cerulean blue, fuchsia, ruby red—in impractical sensual fabrics like silk.

"We'll take it," he would say immediately.

Letty felt guilty revealing her own pleasure, but she couldn't help herself. For so long, survival had been her only goal. She couldn't remember the last time that her happiness had mattered to anyone, least of all her.

But Darius treated her as if her happiness was actually the main goal.

Because I carry his baby inside me, she told herself, as she changed her clothes yet again in a private dressing room.

But his hot dark gaze had told her it was more than that. He didn't just want custody over their baby.

He wanted to possess Letty, too.

You will sleep in my bed. Naked. Every single night.

She shivered, then tried on yet another formal gown, this one made of a slinky knit fabric in a delicious shade of hot pink, her favorite color.

The dress fell softly over her body. Reaching back, she couldn't quite zip it all the way. She looked at herself in the mirror.

The long stretchy gown fit perfectly over her pregnant body, curving over her full breasts and huge belly. She liked it, but weren't pregnant women supposed to wear tent dresses?

"I want to see," Darius's voice commanded outside the dressing room. She took a deep breath, then came out, her cheeks hot.

"What do you think?" she said timidly.

His expression said everything. He walked slowly around her, looking up and down her body in a way that made her shiver inside.

"That," he said softly, "is the dress."

She bit her lip. "I'm afraid it's too formfitting..."

"It's perfect."

"I couldn't zip it all the way up..."

Drawing close, he wrapped his arms around her. She felt his arms brush against her body as he pulled on the zipper. His eyes never left hers as he towered over her, so close. He made her breathless.

A hint of a smile lifted the edges of his cruel, sensual mouth. He cupped her cheek, then stroked down her throat. "The necklace will be perfect here. Against your skin."

Looking down, she realized how low cut the gown was. Her cheeks went redder. "I shouldn't wear this."

"Why?"

"It's too revealing. Everyone will stare."

"They will stare regardless."

"Because I'm the daughter of a criminal."

"Because you're an incredibly beautiful woman."

At his soft words, Letty's throat suddenly hurt. "You don't realize how much they hate me." Her eyes stung as she pushed away. "When they see me...it'll be like dropping raw meat in a shark tank. And the more they notice me, the more they'll rip me apart." She took a deep breath, tried to smile. "I sound like I'm complaining. I'm not. I can handle it. I'm used to it. But…"

"But what?"

She looked down at the floor.

"Letty?"

She said in a small voice, "I don't want them to say rude things about you at your own party. And they will if I'm your date."

Reaching out, he lifted her chin. "I can take care of myself, *agape mou*," he said in a low voice. "When will you learn that?"

His dark gaze fell to her mouth, and Letty's whole body tightened as, for a moment, she wondered if he was going to kiss her, right there in the luxurious store. For a wild moment, it didn't seem like such a bad idea.

He turned to the nearest salesgirl. "We'll take this dress. Wrap it up. We need shoes to match."

Letty tried on ten pairs before she found stiletto heels that made her gasp at their outrageous beauty.

"Those," Darius said, looking at Letty's face.

"No, I couldn't possibly. They're too impractical. I'll never wear them again!" She looked doubtfully at her feet, wobbling in the high heels. "I'm not even sure I can wear them now."

But even as she protested, she couldn't look away from the beautiful shoes, which were encrusted with glittery pink crystals and had a red sole.

"We'll take them," he told the salesgirl firmly.

Though they pinched Letty's toes and made her wobble ever so slightly, she was filled with joy as she sat down and handed the precious pink crystal stilettos to the salesgirl. She couldn't remember the last time she'd had anything so outrageous, just because of their beauty. And their cost! She was trying not to think about owning shoes worth three months' rent. And when would she ever wear them again? Working as a waitress? Going to the grocery store?

It was wicked, letting him buy her these shoes. Letting him buy her so many things, when after tonight, he'd likely never want to see her again.

She would just leave everything behind, she decided. Most of the clothes could be returned, unworn, with tags. She'd have nothing to feel guilty about when he tossed her out of his life. Nothing!

"Now—" Darius's gaze lingered on her lips, then dropped lower "—lingerie."

Letty made a sound like a squeak. "Forget it!"

"Ah. You intend to wear nothing beneath your gown tonight? I approve."

Her cheeks burned. "Of course I'm going to wear something!"

"Then you need undergarments." He nodded toward three hovering salesgirls. "Get us a selection of lingerie that would suit the gown."

They departed in a rush to obey.

"I hope you don't expect me to try *those* on for you," Letty said sulkily.

"No?" He looked at her lazily. "Maybe later."

Her blush deepened.

Right here, in the exclusive department store, with strangers everywhere, Darius was looking at Letty as if he wanted nothing more than to drag her into a changing room and roughly make love to her. Possibly while she was wearing nothing but those pink crystal stilettos. Not a bad idea...

She blinked, realizing she'd been licking her lips. She put her hand unsteadily to her head. What was happening? Was she losing all her morals over a pair of beautiful shoes and for the body of a dangerously beautiful man?

Except Darius wasn't just beautiful. He was also the only man she'd ever slept with. The only man she'd ever been in love with. She was even now carrying his child deep inside her. He wanted her in his bed. He wanted to marry her. All of those things together were likely to distract any woman.

And with every moment, she felt herself being drawn into his world. Remembering what it was like when money was no object. To be without worry or care.

To be cherished.

It had been a long time since she'd felt that way. She'd been a lonely teenager, far happier spending her time with the estate staff, pets or books instead of other debutantes. At fourteen, she'd fallen hopelessly for Darius, the chauffeur's son, six years older and totally out of her league. Funny now to recall that she'd actually imagined herself to be unhappy then.

She'd discovered soon after what unhappiness really meant, when her beloved mother, the heart of their home, had suddenly fallen ill. She'd wasted away and died within months.

Her father had been gutted. A few years later, he'd gone to prison. Letty had tried to be tough. She'd tried to be strong. She'd hadn't let herself think. Hadn't let herself feel.

But now…

For the first time in years she realized how it felt to be truly looked after. To be cared for. As the salesgirls wrapped up a thousand dollars' worth of silky lingerie, she tried to tell herself it was just an illusion. Exactly like Cinderella. After midnight tonight it would all disappear.

Darius signed the credit card receipt, smiling at her out of the corner of his eye. "Is there anything else you desire?"

Letty looked at him, her heart in her throat. Then she just shook her head.

"It's growing late." He took her hand. "We have one more place to go."

The bodyguard had already left in Darius's sports car filled with bags. As his driver walked ahead, weighed down by yet more bags, toward the waiting town car, Darius never let go of her hand. His dark eyes glowed down at her as the sun slipped down between the skyscrapers, toward a horizon she couldn't see.

Maybe it was the pregnancy hormones, but as they climbed into the back of the elegant car, emotion squeezed her heart as she looked at him. All day, Darius had been beside her, ready to push through any crowds, to make sure that she got—in his opinion—proper attention. When she was thirsty, when she was hungry, when she was tired, he seemed to know even before she did, and like a miracle, whatever she desired would instantly appear.

It was as if she were no longer alone. Someone else was looking out for her. Someone tough and strong. Someone who made her feel safe.

Safe?

She shook herself hard. Darius was dangerous. Selfish. Arrogant and cold.

He frowned at her in the backseat. "Are you crying?"

She wiped her tears. "Nope."

"Letty."

"I'm sorry. I just…" She faltered. "You've been so kind."

"Buying you clothes?" he said incredulously. He gave a low laugh. "Is that all it takes?"

It was more than the clothes, far more, but she couldn't explain. She said miserably, "I shouldn't go with you to the ball tonight."

His mouth turned down grimly. "You're going."

"Don't you understand? It'll only cause you trouble."

"Stop trying to protect me," he said evenly. "I mean it."

"But—"

"It's not your job to protect me. It's my job to protect you now. And our baby. Never again insult me by insinuating

I am incapable of it." At her expression, he said more gently, "Don't you understand, Letty? I will watch over you. I'll make sure no one ever hurts you again. You'll always be taken care of now. You're safe."

She was suddenly shaking as the town car drove down the street. How she wished it were true! How she wished she could believe in him, as she had so long ago.

The car door opened. Looking up in surprise at Darius's driver, who was holding it open, Letty looked back at Darius. He gave her a cheeky grin.

"I'm just dropping you off. This is the best day spa in the city. Collins is bringing your gown and everything else you'll need for the ball tonight. I'll collect you here at eight."

"A day spa? Why?"

"You deserve some pampering. Enjoy yourself." He leaned forward in the car's backseat. She felt his warmth and breathed in his scent as he brushed back her hair and whispered in her ear, "I'll be back for you soon."

As he drew back, her heart beat rapidly, and she felt prickles of sensation and desire course through her body, down her spine and over her skin.

And all he'd done was whisper in her ear!

Oh, this was bad.

Her legs were shaky as she stepped out of the car and was whisked into the gorgeously bright day spa with its tall windows, green plants and kitschy pink furniture. A team of specialists, including massage therapists, beauty therapists, stylists and more, surrounded her, moaning about Letty's cuticles, her tense shoulders, her dry skin…

Hours passed in a flash. Her nails were done and her muscles rubbed and her skin freshened until dewy. Hairstylists and makeup artists came next, and once they were done, it was nearly eight.

Letty put on the new silk bra and panties, the perfectly

fitting pink gown and sparkly stiletto heels. She looked at herself in the mirror.

Her long, freshly shaped dark hair was now glossy and shiny and bouncy from the hairstylist's efforts. Red lipstick made her look glamorous, and her eyes were emphasized with dark liner and even a few false eyelashes for drama. Her full breasts, pushed up by the bra, were laid out like a platter in the knit pink dress, her hips thrust forward by the stilettos, her voluptuous belly the star.

She was dazzled by her own image. She barely recognized herself.

"Wait until Mr. Kyrillos sees you," the proprietress of the spa said with a broad smile. "Our finest creation!" There was a whisper, then a gasp. "He's here!"

Nervously, Letty came down into the foyer. She wondered if he would think she looked silly. She couldn't bear it if her appearance embarrassed him, on top of everything else.

But as Darius came into the foyer, she saw his face. And she knew he approved. Deeply.

"You look incredible," he whispered. "So beautiful."

She gave him a shy smile. "You don't look so bad yourself."

The truth was, she couldn't take her eyes off him. His hard jaw was freshly shaved, and his dark eyes wickedly bright. He looked impossibly handsome, tall and broad-shouldered in his sophisticated black tuxedo, which was obviously tailored. No tuxedo off the rack could have fit his muscled body so perfectly.

Wordlessly, Darius held out his arm.

Wrapping her hand around his hard, thick bicep, she shivered, remembering how six months ago, she'd felt his naked, powerful body over hers. Inside hers. She nearly stumbled at the memory.

He stopped.

"Sorry, I'm still getting the hang of my shoes," she lied. She couldn't explain that it wasn't the stilettos that had made her stumble, but the memory of that hot February night they'd conceived their baby.

A night that would never happen again, she thought wistfully. After tonight, he'd run away from her so fast that there would be flames left on the ground, like in a cartoon.

This time, a limousine waited for them. Collins, the driver, wore his formal uniform with a peaked cap as he held open her passenger door.

"Where is the ball this year?" she asked Darius.

"The Corlandt," he said, naming a venue that was nearly as famous as the Met or Frick or Whitney.

She gulped. It was even worse than she'd thought. As the limo took them uptown, she felt sick with dread. She looked out the window, frantically trying to build ice around her heart and get herself back into a place where she was too well armored to feel any attack.

But her newly scrubbed skin felt far too thin now. Wearing this beautiful dress, and being with Darius, she felt vulnerable. She felt visible. She felt raw.

Even though she no longer loved him, she still didn't want him hurt because of her. She tried to tell herself it would be for his own good, so he'd realize they had no future. But she couldn't bear the thought of what was about to happen.

All too soon, the limo arrived. Looking out at the crowds and red carpet and paparazzi, Letty couldn't breathe. Collins got out and opened their door.

Darius went first. There was a low roar from the crowds, watching from behind the cordons of the red carpet, at seeing Darius Kyrillos, the host of the evening and currently New York's most famous billionaire bachelor, get out of the limo, gorgeous in his tuxedo. As cameras flashed in the darkening twilight, he gave a brusque wave.

Looking at the photographers, Letty felt so weak she wasn't sure she could get out of the limo.

Turning back, Darius held out his hand to where she sat quivering in the backseat. He lifted a challenging eyebrow.

Shaking, Letty put her hand in his.

As she exited the limo, a low murmur started amid the photographers and press waiting outside the red carpet as someone recognized Letty.

Then it spread.

There was a gasp of recognition traveling among the photographers and crowd like a rumble of thunder rolling across the ground. The camera flashes went crazy as journalists and celebrity bloggers started screaming at her.

"Letitia Spencer!"

"Where have you been for the last ten years?"

"How does it feel now that your father's out of prison?"

"Do you feel guilty for your father's victims as you're coming to a ball in diamonds?"

"Are you two together?"

"Mr. Kyrillos, with all the city at your feet, why would you date a jailbird's daughter?"

Darius responded only with a glower as he arrogantly walked past them, Letty gripping his hand tightly. He led her past the reporters and inside the magnificent beaux-arts-style granite building. Only after she'd walked up the steps and past the imposing columns through the oversize door, and he'd shut it behind them, did she exhale. Immediately, he pulled her close. Letty closed her eyes, still shaking as she breathed in his strength, his warmth, his comfort.

"It's over," he said softly as he finally drew back, tucking back a dark tendril of her hair behind her ear. "That wasn't so bad, was it?"

"You think it's over?" She gave him a trembling smile. "It's only just begun."

Darius's expression darkened, but they were interrupted

as a famous white-haired society matron covered in jewels entered the foyer behind them. Her face brightened when she saw Darius. She immediately left her much younger date to come forward and give him air-kisses.

"Darius, how lovely to see you! Thank you again for hosting this important event." She simpered. "Though I think there will be many broken hearts when they see you brought a date—"

But as the matron turned to Letty, her smile froze. Her expression changed to shock, then outrage.

"Hello, Mrs. Alexander," Letty said bashfully. "I don't know if you remember, but I used to go to school with your daughter, Poppy. We were both debutantes at the—"

"Stop." The woman's eyes blazed. "Don't you dare speak to me." Looking back at Darius, she hissed, "Do you know who this girl is? What she's done?"

He looked at her coldly. "Of course I know who Letty is. We've been friends since childhood. And as for what she's done—I think you have her confused with her father."

The woman turned to Letty with narrowed eyes. "You have some nerve coming here. Your father stole money from nearly every person attending tonight." She looked at Darius incredulously. "And you are insane to bring her. Take my advice. Send Letitia Spencer straight out the door. Or you might find that you suddenly have no guests, and your charity will suffer. For what? So you can get that little tart in your bed?" She looked pointedly at Letty's belly. "Or perhaps you did that already?"

Letty's cheeks went hot. She suddenly felt like a tart, too, wearing this low-cut, formfitting pink dress that showed off every curve. Beneath the society matron's scrutiny, even her beautiful sparkly shoes lost their gleam, and suddenly just pinched her feet.

"It's only out of respect for those poor foster children that I'm not leaving here right now." The woman glared between them, then flounced away in her jewels and fluttering silk sleeves.

Letty was left paralyzed from the ambush.

"Don't listen to her," Darius said, putting his hand on her shoulder. "She's a witch."

"I don't blame her for being mad," Letty said in a low voice. "Her family lost a lot of money. Tens of millions."

"It obviously hasn't cut into her jewelry and plastic-surgery budget. Forget her. Let's go in."

Wrapping her arm securely over his, he marched her into the ballroom as cheerfully as a revolutionary leading a French aristocrat to the guillotine.

But it was no good. The rest of the evening was just as Letty had feared. As lovely and magical as the afternoon had been, the ball sucked the joy out of everything.

Darius insisted on keeping her by his side as he greeted his society guests, each of whom had paid thousands of dollars to attend this ball, ostensibly for the benefit of college scholarships for foster kids but mostly just to have a good excuse to party with friends and show off new couture.

Letty felt their hostile stares, though with Darius beside her, none were as brave or foolhardy as Mrs. Alexander. None of them said anything to her face. Instead, the cream of New York society just stared at her in bewildered horror, as if she had a contagious and fatal disease, then looked at Darius as if they were waiting for him to reveal the punch line of whatever joke had inspired him to bring a pariah like Letitia Spencer to the Fall Ball when he could have had any beauty in the city for the asking.

She heard whispers and felt their hard stares as she and Darius passed through the crowds in the ballroom. When he briefly left her to get drinks, she felt vulnerable, alone. She kept her eyes focused on the floor, trying to be quiet and invisible, as if facing wild animals. If they didn't notice her, they might not tear her to shreds with their teeth and claws.

It didn't work.

Within moments, three former debutantes blocked her like bouncers at a bar.

"Well, well, well." A skinny young woman in a designer gown gave her a hard-edged smile. "Letitia Spencer. This is a surprise. Isn't it, Caroline?"

"A big surprise."

Letty vaguely recognized the two women from her school, where they'd been a year older. They were looking at her now with the cold expressions of mob enforcers. She could suddenly imagine how her father must have felt right before that thug had broken his arm.

But the third woman stood a slight distance from the first two. It was Poppy Alexander. She and Letty had once been study partners, sophomore year. Poppy just stood there, looking pale and uneasy.

"Excuse me." Letty backed away. "I don't want any trouble."

"You don't want trouble?" The first woman's lip twisted scornfully. "How very amusing."

"Amusing," Caroline echoed with a sneer.

"You shouldn't be here."

"You're a disgrace to society."

"If you had any decency, you'd disappear or die."

Poppy stood silently beside her friends, looking faintly sick, as if she wished she were a million miles away. Letty sympathized with that feeling.

The first woman continued with a sneer, "You might think you're safe on Darius Kyrillos's arm, but…"

"Ah, there you are, Letty," Darius said smoothly, coming up behind them. "I brought your drink." Turning to the other women, he gave a charming smile. "Ah. Augusta. Caroline. And Poppy Alexander. How lovely to see you."

"Hello, Darius," they cooed with weak smiles, then departed, the first two with a final venomous glance at Letty, Poppy hanging her head, looking guilty and ashamed.

Emotions Letty knew well.

"Everything all right?" Darius murmured after they left.

She exhaled, blinking fast. "Fine. Just fine."

The night only got worse. It was past ten when the formal dinner was finally served, and Letty felt half-starved as she sat down beside Darius at the prestigious head table. But as she felt the glares from the four other couples at the table, she could barely eat a bite of salad or the lobster with white truffle cream. At any moment, she half expected one of the hedge fund millionaires or society wives might smash a three-hundred-dollar champagne bottle against the table and attack her with it.

That might have been preferable to the waves of unspoken hatred overtaking her like a blast of heat from all sides. During the unendurably long meal, Darius tried several times to start conversations with the others at the table. Each time, he succeeded. Until he tried to include her. Then the conversation instantly died.

Finally, Letty could stand it no longer.

"Excuse me," she breathed, rising from her seat. "I have to—"

She couldn't finish her sentence. Turning, she rushed past all the other tables and out of the ballroom. Going down the long hall, she found a ladies' bathroom, where she was violently sick. Going to the sink, she washed out her mouth. She looked at herself wanly in the mirror. She felt like she'd rather die than go back into that ballroom and see Darius trying to stick up for her.

Better for her to just leave quietly. Better for both of them.

After lingering as long as she could in the cool quiet of

the empty, marble bathroom, with the old-fashioned elegance of a more genteel era, she went out into the hallway.

She found Darius waiting for her, smolderingly handsome in his tuxedo, leaning against the wall with his arms folded and his jaw tight.

"Are you all right?"

He was angry. She could hear it in his voice. She stopped, barely holding back her tears. "Have you seen enough?" she choked out. "You're surely not enough of an idiot to marry me."

He came closer in the empty hallway, with its plush carpets and gold light fixtures. She tensed, waiting for him to tell her he'd obviously made a mistake, bringing her to his ball, and that there was no way he would marry her now or in fact ever wanted to see her again. She waited for him to give her what she'd wanted and set her free.

Except in this moment the thought didn't make her as happy as it once did.

He narrowed his eyes. "I didn't realize how bad it was for you."

She'd successfully fought back tears all night. But she could do it no longer. Not now, when the illusion of having a protector—even for a night—was coming to an end.

Letty took a deep breath, trying to ignore the lump in her throat, wiping her eyes before he'd see the tears. She tried to smile. "But now you know. So tomorrow I'll go to Rochester with my father. You can continue to be rich and famous and popular here. You can visit our baby anytime you want…" Something in his eyes made her voice trail off uncertainly. "If you even want to see our baby anymore," she whispered.

His eyes suddenly blazed with cold fury. "No."

"What?"

He gripped her arm. "I said no."

She tried to pull away, but couldn't. "What are you doing?"

"What I should have done the moment we arrived here."

He pulled her grimly down the hall, back toward the ballroom.

"No," she choked out, struggling. "Please. I can't go back in there. Don't make me…"

Darius was merciless. He dragged her back into the enormous ballroom, with its high ceiling and crystal chandeliers. He gripped her wrist as she limped behind him in the tight stiletto shoes and pink dress, going past all the big round tables, where a thousand people were now drinking after-dinner brandies and coffees and the men, at least, were eating desserts. Letty felt each ten-person table fall silent as they went by. She felt everyone's judgment. Their blame. Their hatred.

Ruthlessly, Darius pulled her through the ballroom, leaving people silent in their wake. As he walked past their own table, he grabbed his glass of champagne. Crossing the small dance floor, he dragged her up the stairs to the stage, where, still holding her wrist, he took the microphone at the podium. He cleared his throat.

Letty's knees were trembling with fear. She wished she'd never come here—wished she'd never taken a single risk—would have given twenty years of her life to be back at her tiny apartment, snug on the sofa with a blanket over her head!

"Good evening," Darius said into the microphone. His husky, commanding voice rang over the ballroom. A spotlight fell on him. "For those of you I haven't yet met personally, I'm Darius Kyrillos. Thank you for coming to my party, the event kicking off the New York fall social season, and thank you for supporting scholarships for kids in need. It's because of you that many deserving youngsters will be able to go to college or learn a trade."

A smattering of applause ensued; much less enthusiastic than it would have been if Letty hadn't been standing with him on stage. She was ruining everything, she thought unhappily. Even for those kids who needed help. She hated herself. Almost as much as she hated him.

Darius deliberately turned away from the microphone to give her a searching glance, and her stomach fell to the floor. *Here it comes*, she thought. *He's going to announce that he brought me here as a joke and have me thrown me out.* She was social poison, so he really had no choice but to distance himself. This was exactly what she'd expected.

She just hadn't expected it to hurt so much when it happened.

Darius's lips twisted. He turned back to the microphone. "Most of you know this beautiful woman on stage with me. Miss Letitia Spencer." There was a low hiss across the ballroom, a rumble of muffled booing. He responded with a charming smile. "Since we're all friends, I wanted you to be the first to know…I just asked her to marry me."

Letty's eyes went wide. What? Why would he say that? Was he insane?

"And she has accepted," he finished calmly. "So I want you all to be the first to wish us joy."

This time, the gasp came from Letty. Forget insane. Was he suicidal?

The low hisses and boos changed to ugly muttering across the ballroom, angry, obscene words that made Letty squirm. Instinctively, she covered her belly with her arms to protect her unborn baby from the cruel words.

But Darius's smile only widened as he put his large hand over hers, on her belly.

"We're expecting a baby, too. All of this has left me so overwhelmed with joy, I want to share it with all of you. Now. Some of you might know of her father's troubles…"

A white-haired man, unable to contain himself any longer, sprang up from his table. "Howard Spencer defrauded my company of millions of dollars!" he cried, shaking his fist. "We were only repaid a fraction of what we lost!"

A low buzz of rage hummed around him.

"Letty's father is a criminal," Darius agreed. "He abused your trust, and I know over half of what he stole is still unaccounted for. But *Letty* did nothing wrong. Her only crime was loving a father who didn't deserve it. That's why I've decided, in my future bride's honor, to make amends."

Suddenly, it was dead quiet across the tables.

Darius held his champagne glass high. "I will personally pay back every penny her father stole."

A collective gasp ripped through the ballroom.

The white-haired man staggered back. "But that's...*five billion dollars*!"

"So it is," Darius said mildly. He looked over the crowd. "So if your family is still owed money by Howard Spencer, I personally guarantee repayment. All in honor of my beautiful...innocent...unfairly hounded...bride." Turning back toward Letty on stage, he held up his champagne glass and said into the microphone, "To Letitia Spencer!"

As photographers rushed forward, Letty felt faint. Camera flashes lit up everywhere. There was a rumble of noise, of shouts and gasps and chairs hastily pushed aside as a thousand people scrambled to their feet and lifted their champagne glasses into the air.

"Letitia Spencer!" they cried joyfully.

CHAPTER SEVEN

IT WASN'T EVERY day a man spent five billion dollars on a whim.

Darius hadn't intended to do it. He'd had a different surprise in mind for Letty tonight: a black velvet box hidden in the pocket of his tuxedo jacket, which he'd planned to spring on her as soon as the evening was over and all her overblown fears had proved unfounded.

Instead, he'd realized how much she'd endured over the last ten years. Alone. While he'd been happily free to live an anonymous life and make his fortune.

Standing in the hallway, when he'd seen her come out of the bathroom looking shattered and as pale as a ghost, he'd finally realized the toll it had taken on her. And if this was how people treated Letty now, how much worse had it been ten years ago, when their rage had been white-hot?

He'd been forced to ask himself: If Letty had actually shown up the night they were going to run away together and told him about her father's confession, what would have happened?

Darius would have of course insisted she marry him anyway. After all, what did her father's stupid investment fund have to do with their love?

But as her husband, he would have been at her side throughout the scandal and media circus of a trial. He might not have received the critical early loan that enabled him to build his software, to hire employees, to lease his first office space. He would have been too tainted by association as Howard Spencer's son-in-law.

If Letty hadn't set him free, he might have been unemployable, unable to easily provide for his wife or children.

He might be living in that tiny Brooklyn apartment, too, struggling with the loss of his dreams. Struggling to provide for his family. Struggling not to feel like a failure as a man.

It was Letty's sacrifice ten years ago that had made his current success possible.

While he'd been triumphantly building his billion-dollar company, she'd lived in poverty, suffering endless humiliations for a crime that wasn't even hers. And she'd kept her sacrifice a secret, so he'd never once had to feel guilty about deserting her.

Even now, she continued to protect him. She'd warned him what would happen if he brought her as his date. And now he'd finally seen how the members of the so-called upper class had treated her all this time. He'd watched Letty bear their insults without complaint. And he'd realized her stigma was so bad that, in spite of his arrogant earlier assumption, his presence alone wasn't enough to shelter her.

He knew how it felt to be treated badly.

He'd once been the poorest child in his village, mocked as an unloved bastard. He was now the most beloved, feared man of Heraklios. He did pretty well in Manhattan, too. And London. And Paris and Rome, Sydney and Tokyo.

Money could buy everything from houses to souls.

Money made the man.

It astonished him that not everyone realized this. Some people seemed to think love was the most important thing. They were either fools, Darius thought grimly, or gluttons for punishment. He'd learned his own lesson well. The sick truth was that love only led to pain.

Love was a pale facsimile of money. Love begged.

Money demanded.

So when Darius had seen how badly New York society had treated Letty for all these years—these people who didn't have a fraction of her kindness or her loyalty or her heart—ice had seized his soul.

Especially when he'd realized that he'd treated her even worse. After a decade of ignoring her, he'd taken revenge for her so-called sins through cold seduction, insults and threats.

His jaw tightened. He would pay that debt.

Darius didn't love her. The part of his heart that had once craved love had been burned away. Love wasn't something he ever wanted to feel for anyone.

But there were other qualities Darius did believe in.

Honor.

Loyalty.

Protecting his woman.

So he'd settled the matter, once and for all.

Now Letty would be the most popular girl in the city. Every person who'd once treated her shabbily would be begging for an invitation to their wedding. Begging to be her friend.

At the moment of Darius's triumph, as he toasted her on stage, he turned to face Letty at the podium. Rough, raw desire surged through his body as he looked at her—his woman now, *his*—lush and pregnant and obscenely beautiful in that pink gown, which slid over her breasts and belly like a caress.

She stood unsteadily in those ridiculous stiletto heels, beneath the blinding spotlight, as a thousand people applauded from the darkness. People who had treated her like garbage just minutes before started chanting her name. Camera flashes lit up the darkness as reporters shouted questions.

"Miss Spencer, what's it like to be loved to the tune of five billion dollars?"

"When's the wedding?"

"When's your baby due?"

"How does it feel to suddenly be the most popular girl in New York?"

Letty looked at Darius with the expression of a terrified deer, and he realized she wasn't enjoying this as much as he was.

Turning back to the microphone with a smile, Darius answered for her. "The wedding will be soon. No plans yet. Our baby will be born soon, too." He looked past the reporters to the well-heeled crowd. "That's all. Thank you for your support! Enjoy your night. And since you're now all so much richer, don't forget to be generous to the scholarship fund—it's for the kids." Setting his empty champagne glass on the podium, he glanced at the full orchestra. "Let's start the music!"

"Kick off the dancing, Darius!" someone shouted from the back.

"Yes, the first dance to you and Letty!" someone else cried.

Darius led her down the steps from the stage, and as they reached the dance floor, the music started, a slow, romantic song he'd purposefully requested from the orchestra earlier because he knew Letty would remember it from that long-ago summer.

He was right. She stopped when she heard it, eyes wide.

Darius looked down at her with a crooked half smile. "What do you say? Will you dance with me, Letty?"

She looked around at all the people who had treated her with such contempt for the last ten years, now beaming at her as if they were best friends.

"Why are they acting as if they like me?" she said softly, for his ears alone.

"People love to talk about character and loyalty and love. They mean money." He allowed himself a grim smile. "Now the money's been paid, so they can love you again."

Letty's head snapped back to look at him. Her big hazel

eyes, fringed with dark lashes, were wide, as if he were a superhero who'd flown down from the sky. "Why did you do it, Darius? Why pay five billion dollars for a debt that isn't yours?"

The music swirled around them like a whirlwind. "Do you remember our old waltz?"

Her forehead creased. "Of course…" She looked back at the people yelling encouragement for them to dance. She bit her lip. "But not in front of everyone…"

"Now." Darius pulled her against his tuxedo-clad body. "Dance with me."

Letty's long dark hair was falling softly around her beautiful face to her shoulders, nestling against the diamonds sparkling around her neck. He'd already wanted her, but as he felt her body in his arms, and the crush of her belly and swollen breasts against his chest, he wanted her even more.

Just like that long-ago summer…

"Come on, Letty," he said in a low voice. "Let's show them all we don't give a damn."

He moved commandingly onto the dance floor, leading her in the first steps of the waltz he'd helped her practice for her debutante ball long ago, the spring of her senior year. They'd practiced the waltz over and over in the sunlit spring flower meadow on the Fairholme estate, overlooking the sparkling bay, as music sang from her phone.

They'd started out as friends and ended as something else entirely.

When she'd left for her debutante ball in Manhattan that May, looking beautiful beyond belief in her white dress, Darius spent the whole evening prowling the meadow in a rage, hating the Harvard boy who was her date.

He'd been shocked when Letty came back early, whispering, "I didn't want to dance with anyone but you…"

Darius had taken one look at Letty's joyous, upturned face surrounded by spring flowers, and then he, the chauffeur's son, had done the unthinkable: he'd wrapped her in his powerful arms and kissed her…

Now, as he swirled her around in that waltz, it was like going back in time. The audience standing on the edge of the dance floor clapped their approval. In this moment, in this place, Darius and Letty were the king and queen of the city, the pinnacle of all his youthful dreams.

But he barely noticed the crowds. There was only Letty. He was back in that meadow, a young man so sure of his own heart, so naively enthusiastic about his future, dancing with the beautiful princess he'd dreamed about, the one he could never deserve. And, oh, how he'd craved her to his very core…

Now, Darius pulled her more indecently close to his hard, aching body than any waltz allowed. She lifted her luminous gaze to his, visibly holding her breath. The electricity between them suddenly sizzled with heat.

He stopped dancing. Louder than the music, he heard the rush of his blood in his ears, the pounding of his own heart.

He needed her in his bed.

Now.

The music abruptly ended, and the ballroom exploded in applause echoing from the high ceiling. Without a word, Darius led her from the dance floor. He pulled her through the crowds, which parted for them like magic. Compliments and cheers followed them. Everywhere, people were apologizing to Letty for how badly they'd treated her. He recognized Poppy Alexander.

"I'm so sorry, Letty," the girl blurted out. "I was afraid to be your friend. I knew it wasn't your fault, what happened, but I was a coward…"

"That's all right, Poppy," Letty replied gently. She looked around at everyone else. "I don't blame anyone."

Darius thought about the dragon Poppy had for a mother, and he couldn't blame her for being scared. Until he thought of how bad Letty's life had been for the last decade, and he didn't think any of them deserved another minute of Letty's time.

He swept Letty away without looking back. He didn't care about anyone or anything right now, except getting her into his bed.

Darius pulled his phone from his tuxedo jacket pocket. By the time they exited the stately beaux-arts building, his limo was waiting at the curb. Collins leaped out and opened the passenger door.

The second they were in the backseat, and the door closed behind them, Darius pulled Letty roughly into his arms and kissed her.

Her lips were sweet as sin. She trembled, her curves melting against him. His whole body was hard with need. He had to have her.

"Sir?" said Collins from the driver's seat.

"Home," he said hoarsely. "As fast as you can."

Then he pressed the button that raised the barrier between front and back seats. Just those few seconds were agony. But he was not willing to share Letty with anyone. He'd shared her enough.

She belonged to him now. To him alone.

Once they had privacy in the backseat, he kissed her passionately as the limo moved through the sparkling streets of the lit-up city at midnight. But all he could see was her sensual beauty. All he could feel was the soft brush of her long dark hair, and her warm skin like silk beneath his hands. He pushed her back against the leather seat, devouring her soft lips, kissing her neck, running his hands over her full breasts overflowing the tight pink bodice of her dress.

He kissed her savagely, biting and sucking her lower lip. A gasp of need came from her throat as she returned his kiss with matching fire, gripping his shoulders through his tuxedo jacket. He kissed slowly down her neck as her head fell back, her eyes closed, her expression one of ecstasy.

When he saw that, it was all he could do not to take her, right here in the back of the limo. He was unconsciously reaching for his fly when he realized they'd stopped.

Resurfacing from his haze of desire, he saw the limo was parked beneath the porte cochere in front of his building. Just in time, too. He glanced at Letty, stretched back against the smooth calfskin leather seat. Her big hazel eyes were smoky with passion, her dark hair mussed, her pink dress disheveled. Another moment and he would have yanked up her dress and roughly pushed inside her.

That wasn't how he wanted this night to be, fast and brutish in the back of a limo. No. After the disaster of their first night together, when he'd taken her virginity then insulted her and tossed her out of the penthouse into the snow, he wanted this night to be perfect.

He would finally treat Letitia Spencer, the forbidden princess of his youth, as she deserved to be treated.

He would enjoy her as he deserved to enjoy her.

Thoroughly.

Reaching over, he smoothed the fabric of Letty's bodice modestly back over her breasts just as the passenger door opened behind him.

Taking her hand, he led her out of the limo and into the elegant lobby, where the doorman greeted him. "Good evening, sir."

"Good evening, Jones." Such civilized words. Wearing a tuxedo, Darius knew he must appear civilized on the outside. On the inside, he felt anything but.

Gripping Letty's hand, he desperately kept himself in check. Neither of them looked at each other as they went through the high-ceilinged lobby, past the front desk to the elevator. Civilized.

But as soon as the door closed behind them, they were

in each other's arms. He pushed her against the wall, kissing her hungrily, desperately.

She breathed against his skin, "I still can't believe you're doing this."

"Kissing you?"

"Giving five billion dollars away. Why did you do it?"

"Don't you know?" he growled, his lips against hers. "Can't you guess?"

Panting, she shook her head. "You hate my father…"

Darius's lip curled as he drew back. "I didn't do it for him."

"For your friends?"

"Those aren't my friends."

"For the other victims, then. All those hardworking people with pensions. Firemen. Nurses…"

"I'm not that noble."

The elevator door opened. The floor-to-ceiling windows flooded the penthouse with moonlight. Taking her hand, he led her inside. He could hear the tap of her stiletto heels against the marble.

She stopped, staring up at him.

"Then why?" she whispered.

"I couldn't stand to see you treated badly," Darius said huskily, "when all you've done is give your love and loyalty to someone who doesn't deserve it."

She bit her lip. "I know my father isn't perfect—"

"Perfect?" His jaw tightened. "He's a criminal—" He cut himself off, then said, "You're under my protection now."

She looked troubled. "Your protection—or your rule?"

"It is the same. I protect what is mine."

"Our baby."

His eyes met hers. "And you."

Letty stared at him, her eyes wide, as if she had no idea how to react. As if she had forgotten what it was like to have anyone properly look after her.

He wondered how long it had been since anyone had tried to take care of her, rather than the other way around. He suspected Letty always sacrificed herself to take care of others—especially that father of hers—while her own heart bled.

"But I'm not yours," she said quietly. "Not truly. We got pregnant by accident. I didn't think you were serious about marriage."

"I am."

"That commitment is serious, Darius. It means…forever."

"I know," he said.

She swallowed, searching his gaze. "I was sure after tonight you'd never want to see me again."

Taking her hand, he lifted it slowly to his lips. She seemed to hold her breath, watching as he kissed the back of her hand, breathing against her skin. Straightening, he held her hand tightly in his own. "I want to see you tomorrow, and every other tomorrow for the rest of our lives."

"Darius…"

"You will marry me, Letty," he said in a low voice. "You know it, and I know it. In your heart, you were always meant to be mine."

Marry him? For real?

How could she?

Even if Darius no longer hated her, he certainly didn't love her. And she was starting to fear she could love him again. Perhaps all too easily.

What hope could they have of happiness?

He'd never love her back. All he wished to do was possess her. He offered sex and money, and in return, he'd expect sex and total devotion. For her, those things went together. He wouldn't have just her body, but her soul.

So why was she still so tempted?

She shivered, caught between fear and desire.

"Are you cold?" he asked huskily, his eyes dark.

"No, I…I…" Hugging her baby bump, she gasped, "I need some fresh air."

He smiled. "Come with me."

Still holding her hand, he led her through the moon-bathed penthouse, and she thought dimly how she was getting in the habit of following where he led. But with his hand enveloping hers so protectively, she didn't want to do anything else.

She still couldn't believe what he'd done, announcing their engagement, defending her in front of all those people—and then telling the world he intended to pay billions of dollars of his own money to repay what her father had stolen.

She'd been dazed. Then she'd danced with him, the same routine he'd helped her learn so long ago, and she'd been back in that spring meadow, practicing the waltz not for the pimply-faced Harvard boy, who was the nephew of her father's lawyer, but for Darius, always for him, only for him. As they'd danced in the ballroom, she'd felt time melt away.

Darius was right. She was his. From the very beginning, Darius Kyrillos had been the only man she'd ever wanted. The only man she'd ever loved.

I don't love him anymore, she told herself desperately. She wouldn't let him buy her!

Darius led her up an elaborate staircase, then pushed open a glass door that led out onto a private rooftop garden.

Letty gasped at the beauty of the ivy-covered pergola decorated with fairy lights near a lit lap pool gleaming bright blue in the warm September night.

Above them, distant stars sparkled like diamonds across a dark velvety sky. Past the glass walls of the terrace, the night skyline of Manhattan glittered.

She kept her distance from the edge, afraid to go too

close. But Darius went right to it. He leaned against the short glass wall, totally unfazed and unafraid of plummeting seventy floors to his death. He looked out at the city.

Letty crept closer, her heart pounding. "This terrace is amazing."

"All the flowers remind me of home," he said simply. She wondered if he meant Greece or Fairholme, but didn't have the nerve to ask. She slowly turned her head, marveling at the lavish beauty of a rooftop garden that treated all of Manhattan as nothing but a backdrop.

"You're king of the mountain now," she said softly. "Looking down on a valley of skyscrapers."

Turning to her, he came forward. Then he abruptly fell to one knee in front of her astonished eyes.

Reaching into his tuxedo jacket pocket, he pulled out a small black velvet box.

"Rule it with me, Letty," he said quietly. "As my wife."

Shivering, she put her hand on her heart. "I already said…"

"You said yes when you thought I'd back out. This is a real proposal. I expect a real answer." He held up the black velvet box. "Letty Spencer, will you do me the honor of marrying me?"

He opened the lid. Inside the black velvet box was an enormous pear-shaped diamond set in platinum. It was the hugest, most outrageous ring she'd ever seen.

But that wasn't what made her lose her breath.

It was Darius's face. His dark, yearning eyes. As he looked at her in the moonlight, she saw the man who'd just bruised her with the intensity of his kisses. Who'd just defied all of Manhattan and paid five billion dollars for her. The man whose child she carried.

In his eyes, she saw the shadow of the younger man she'd once loved, strong and kind, with such a good heart. The one who'd loved her so fervently. *They were the same.*

Letty's heart skipped a beat.

It's an illusion, she told herself desperately. *He's not the same.* But as she reached out and brushed her fingers against the diamond engagement ring, it sparkled like the stars. Like the lights of this powerful city.

Like the smolder in Darius's dark eyes.

"It would destroy us," she said shakily, but what she really meant was *it would destroy me.*

Darius slowly rose in front of her, until his tall, powerful body towered over hers. Waves of blue light from the pool reflected against him as the warm wind moved across the water. Putting his hand on her cheek, he lowered his head.

"Say yes," he whispered. "Say you'll be mine."

His kiss was tender at first. She felt the rough warmth of his lips, the gentle hold of his arms.

Then his grip tightened. His embrace became hungry, filled with need. Spirals of heat twisted through her body, and she gripped his shoulders. Until he pulled away.

"Say it," he demanded.

"Yes," she choked out.

A flash of triumph crossed his starkly handsome face. "You will?"

She nodded, tears in her eyes.

"There will be no going back," he warned.

"I know." She tried to ignore the thrill that crept into her heart. Excitement? Terror?

Right or wrong, disaster or not, there was nothing to be done. What he'd said was true. She'd always been his. In many ways, this decision had been made for her long ago.

He slid the diamond ring over the third finger of her left hand. It fit perfectly. She looked down at it, sparkling in the moonlight. "How did you know my ring size?"

"It's the same ring."

She frowned. "What?"

"It's the same I bought for you ten years ago." His voice was low. "I had it set with a different stone."

The thought that he'd kept their original ring all these years made her heart ache. Whatever he might say, didn't that mean he might still care for her, at least a little?

Could love, once lost, ever be regained?

Looking at him with tears in her eyes, she breathed, "Darius…"

"You're mine now, Letty," he whispered, kissing her forehead, her eyelids, her cheeks. "You belong to me. Forever."

Then he kissed her lips as if those, too, were his possession.

Sparks of pleasure went up and down Letty's body, coiling low and deep inside her, and she felt his hands running down her bare arms, her sides, cupping her breasts over the pink dress.

She fell back against the ivy-covered stone wall. Above them, fairy lights swayed gently in the warm wind, the skyscrapers of Manhattan illuminating the moonlit sky.

Letty's eyes closed as he kissed his way down her throat. She felt breathless, like she was lost in a dream.

He kissed over the diamond necklace to her bare clavicle and the valley between her full breasts, half revealed above the low-cut bodice of her gown.

Picking her up, he carried her past the sweeping ivy into a half-enclosed room protected on two sides by walls, with a rustic chandelier hanging over a long table. Two leather sofas were arranged around a fireplace and well-stocked bar.

He flicked a switch, and the gas fire lit up. She saw Darius's face clearly in the flickering firelight as they faced each other silently. The soft wind blew against her hair, her skin.

Slowly, Darius removed his tuxedo jacket and dropped it to the flagstone floor. Coming closer, he unzipped her pink dress. She felt the brush of his fingertips, then the warm night air against her bare skin as her gown dropped to the floor beside his jacket. She stepped out of the fabric, wearing only the diamonds, a lace bra, panties and the wicked pink crystal stiletto heels.

He stepped back, looking at her.

"Incredible," he breathed in deep masculine appreciation, and she realized that, just as he'd promised, he was seeing her in the lingerie. She scowled.

"Do you always get what you want?" she said accusingly.

"I do," he said, caressing her cheek. "And now, so will you."

She licked her lips and felt a thrill of delight as his expression changed to raw desire. Reaching up, she saucily loosened his tuxedo tie, before tugging on it, drawing him closer for a kiss.

It was the first time she'd ever made the first move, and he growled fierce approval. Holding her tight, he kissed her back hungrily.

His hands caressed her naked skin, her arms, her shoulders, the small of her back. And suddenly she couldn't remove his clothes fast enough. His tie, cuff links, shirt. They all dropped to the floor.

His tanned body, laced with dark hair, looked like sculpted marble in the flickering firelight, all hard muscles and taut belly. She brushed her hand lightly against his chest. His skin felt like silk over steel. Biting her lip, she lifted her eyes to his.

"If I'm yours, Darius," she whispered, standing in front of him in the half-enclosed room, "you're mine."

Brushing back long dark tendrils of her hair, he pulled her roughly into his arms. His hard-muscled chest moved against her full, aching breasts and pregnant belly. The soft wind whispered against her bare skin as he unhooked her silk lace bra, and her breasts sprang free. He looked down at her body and gave a quick breath.

Pressing her breasts together, he cupped their weight in his hands before he lowered his head to suckle one pink, full nipple, then the other.

Shuddering with pleasure, she closed her eyes.

His hands stroked gently, reverently, down her body to her naked belly to her hips, still covered with the tiny silk panties.

Running his hand down her legs, he knelt before her and pulled off one stiletto, then the other, as she balanced against him, her hands gripping his shoulders. She remained standing—barely—as he caressed upward from her manicured toes, to the tender hollows of her knees, and higher still. She swallowed, holding her breath as he stroked up her thighs.

She closed her eyes, heart pounding as he pulled her panties down her legs. She couldn't move fast enough. He impatiently ripped them off in his powerful hands, tossing the flimsy silk aside.

"Those were expensive—" she protested.

He looked up, and the edges of his cruel, sensual mouth curved upward. "They served their purpose."

An icy fear suddenly crept through her heart as Letty wondered if she, too, might someday have served her purpose. If he might someday rip her apart, then discard her.

Then all her rational thought fled as, still on his knees, he gripped her hips and moved between her legs.

She felt the warmth of his breath on the most sensitive, intimate part of her body, as she stood naked with the warm night breeze swirling against her skin, as one of New York's most famous billionaires knelt before her in the firelight, beneath the ivy walls of a rooftop garden.

Holding her tight, he lowered his mouth between her thighs and tasted her with a soft moan. He licked her as if she were a melting ice cream cone in his favorite flavor, creamy and sweet. As she gasped, his rhythm intensified, until he worked her with his tongue, sliding sensuously against her. Pleasure exploded through her body almost immediately, and he gripped her hips, keeping her firmly against his mouth as her body twisted with the sudden intensity of pleasure that left her knees weak and sent spasms all over her body.

She was still dizzy in the heights of pleasure as he rose to his feet and drew her toward the sofa. He lay down first, stretching out naked against the black leather, hard and ready for her. She took a step, then hesitated, biting her lip.

"What is it?"

She tried not to look at how huge he was, his hard shaft jutting arrogantly from his body. She blushed, feeling shy. "Um, what do I do?"

He gave a low, lazy laugh, then pulled her over him.

"I'll show you," he said huskily.

He spread her across him on the sofa, her thighs over his hips, his arousal pressing low against her pregnant belly. He reached up, cupping her cheek. As he drew her down for a kiss, her long dark hair fell like a veil against his skin.

The kiss was tender at first. She relaxed into it with a sigh, her body curving over his as his hands roamed gently over her back, her arms, her belly, her breasts. Then his kiss deepened, turning urgent and fierce. Placing his hands on her hips, he lifted her up, positioning himself beneath her.

He slowly lowered her down on him, filling her, inch by delicious inch, in tantalizing slow motion.

She gasped as she felt him inside her, going deep, then deeper still. Her whole body started to tighten, more savagely than it had before.

Lifting her hips, he lowered her again, showing her the rhythm, until her body started to move of its own accord.

Closing her eyes with fervent intensity, she rode him, slowly at first, then faster. The pleasure built and built…

Her lips parted in a silent cry as joy burst like fireworks shaking through her body. She heard his low gasp as he, too, exploded, pouring inside her.

She collapsed, falling softly against him on the black leather sofa.

For long moments, he held her tenderly, as if her weight were nothing. Their bodies were still fused, slick with sweat, as he leaned up to kiss her. He felt so solid and strong beneath her. Like a foundation that could never be shaken.

She shivered in his arms. In the half-enclosed outdoor room, the September night was growing cool. But that wasn't the reason.

The idea of being Darius's wife had seemed like a recipe for disaster, if not outright doom. And so it would be, if she were tempted into giving him her heart, while in return, he gave her only money.

Letty looked down at the heavy diamond ring, now shining dully on her left hand.

If only Darius could again be the young man she remembered, with the kind nature and forgiving heart. She would willingly give him everything. Not just her body, not just her name, but her heart.

CHAPTER EIGHT

HE WAS A GENIUS, Darius thought as he woke in his bed the next morning with sunlight flooding in through the windows. He looked down at Letty sleeping beside him and smiled. A damn genius. Best five billion dollars ever spent.

And he would spend the rest of his life being thrilled, if it continued paying off like it did last night. The sex had been spectacular. And even more. Something had changed in the way Letty looked at him. He loved the mixture of gratitude and shy hope he saw in her eyes.

He kissed Letty's temple tenderly. She yawned, stretching like a cat.

"What time is it?" she murmured, her eyes still closed.

"Late," he said, amused. "Almost noon."

Her eyes flew open. "Oh, no! I'm late for—" Then she seemed to remember how much had changed in the last twenty-four hours, and that being late for work was no longer an issue. "Oh. Right." She bit her lip, blushing and looking so adorable that he was tempted to keep her in bed another hour.

It was incredible how much he still wanted her, when they'd made love *four times* last night—on the rooftop terrace, here in bed, and in the shower when they decided to wash off. Only to promptly get all sweaty again when they returned to bed.

Letty was meant to be his, Darius marveled. He'd never felt so sexually satisfied in his life.

And yet already he wanted more. How was it possible? He smiled down at her. "Hungry?"

"Starving," she admitted. "And thirsty."

"I can solve that." Rising from the bed, he got a white

terry cloth robe and handed her one, too. "Come out to the kitchen."

She gave a sudden scowl, and even that was adorable. "You didn't tell me you had staff staying at the penthouse. What if they heard us last night? What if they—"

"There are no live-in staff. I have a housekeeper who comes in four times a week, that's it."

She blinked in confusion. "Then who's going to cook?"

"I'm not totally useless."

She looked at him with unflattering shock in her eyes. "You can't cook, Darius."

"No?" His smile widened to a grin. "Come see."

She ate her words shortly afterward, sitting in the brightly lit kitchen at the counter, as he served her an omelet to order with tomatoes, bacon and five kinds of cheese, along with orange juice over ice. When she took the first bite of the omelet, her eyes went wide.

"Good, huh?" he said smugly, sitting beside her with his own enormous omelet of ham and cheese, drenched in salsa. Being a sexual hero all night definitely had built his appetite.

And hers, as well. If he felt like a hero, Letty was a sex *goddess*, he thought. Even now, he felt aware of her, just sitting companionably beside her at the counter with its dazzling view of the city through floor-to-ceiling windows. But he wasn't looking at the view. He was watching her.

"Delicious," she moaned softly as she gobbled it down, bite after bite. "We should serve omelets at our wedding."

He gave a low laugh. "I appreciate the compliment, but I don't see myself whipping up omelets for a thousand."

She froze. "A thousand? *Guests?*"

Gulping black coffee, he shrugged. "Our wedding will be the social event of the year, as you deserve. All of New York society will come and grovel at your feet."

She didn't look thrilled. She took another bite of omelet. "That's not what I want."

"No?" he said lazily, tucking back a tendril of her dark hair. His eyes traced the creamy skin of her neck, down to the smooth temptation of her clavicle and swell of her breasts above the luxurious white cotton robe. He glanced down to her belt, tied loosely between her breasts and pregnant belly. He had the sudden impulse to sweep all the dishes to the floor, tug open her robe and lean her back naked against the counter.

"A wedding should be a happy occasion." She shook her head. "Those society people aren't my friends. They never really were. Why would I invite them?"

"To rub your new status in their faces? I thought you'd glory in your return to status as the queen of it all."

"Me?" Letty snorted. "I was never queen of anything. As a teenager I never knew the right clothes to wear or understood how to play the society game. I was a total nerd."

He frowned. "I never saw you that way. I just assumed…"

"That I was a spoiled princess?" She gave him a funny smile. "I *was* spoiled, though not the way you mean. I always knew I was loved." Her face was wistful. "My parents loved each other and they loved me."

Revenge wasn't Letty's style, Darius realized. She never showed off or tried to make others feel bad. Even when she was younger, she'd always been most comfortable reading the dusty leather-bound books in Fairholme's oak-paneled library, baking cakes with the cook in the kitchen or playing with the gardener's kittens in the yard. Letty never wanted to be the center of attention. She was always more worried about other people's feelings than her own.

In this respect, Darius thought, the two of them were very different.

"And I had a real home," she whispered.

Memories of that beautiful gray stone manor on the edge of the sea, surrounded by roses, came to his mind. He said gruffly, "You still miss Fairholme after all this time?"

She gave him a sad smile. "I know it's gone for good. But I still dream about it. My mother was born there. Four generations of my family."

"What happened to it?"

She looked down at her plate. "A tech billionaire bought it at a cut-rate price. I heard he changed everything, added zebra-print shag carpeting and neon lights, and turned the nursery into his own private disco. Of course that was his right. But he wouldn't let me take a picture of my great-grandmother's fresco before he destroyed it with his sand-blaster."

A low growl came from Darius's throat. He remembered the nursery fresco, a charming monstrosity picturing a sad-eyed little goose girl leading ducks and geese through what looked like a Bavarian village. Not his cup of tea, but it was part of the house's history. "I'm sorry."

She looked up with a bright, fake smile. "It's fine. Of course it couldn't last. Good things never do."

"Neither do bad things," he said quietly. "Nothing lasts, good or bad."

"I guess you're right." She wrapped her arms around her pregnant belly. "But I don't want a big society wedding, Darius. I think I'd just like you and me, and our closest family and friends. I don't need ten bridesmaids. I just want one."

"An old friend?"

She smiled. "A new one. Belle Langtry. A waitress at the diner. How about you? Who would you choose as your best man?"

"Ángel Velazquez."

"Ángel?"

"It's a nickname. His real first name is Santiago, but he

hates it, because he was named after a man who refused to recognize him as his son."

"How awful!"

Darius shrugged. "I call him by his last name. Velazquez hates weddings. He recently had to be the best man for a friend of ours, Kassius Black. He complained for months. All that tender love gave him a headache, he said."

Letty was looking at him in dismay. "And you want him at our wedding?"

"He needs a little torture. When you meet him you'll see what I mean. Completely arrogant, always sure he's right."

"Hard to imagine," she said drily.

"So Velazquez. And my extended family."

Her eyes brightened. "Your family?"

"My great-aunt, Theia Ioanna, who lives in Athens. Assorted uncles, aunts and cousins, and the rest of my village on Heraklios, the island I'm from."

"Could we bring them all over from Greece? And of course we'll have my father…"

Darius stiffened. "No."

"No?" She frowned. "We could get married on Heraklios, if they can't travel. I've always wanted to visit the Greek islands…"

"I mean your father. He's not invited."

"Of course he's invited. He's my father. He'll walk me down the aisle. I know you don't like him, but he's my only family."

"Letty, I thought you understood." His jaw was taut, his voice low and cold. "I don't want you, or our baby, within ten feet of that man ever again."

"What?"

"It's not negotiable." Swiveling to face her at the counter, Darius gripped her shoulder. "I will pay back everything he stole. But this is the price." His dark eyes narrowed.

"You will cut your father completely and permanently out of our lives."

She drew back. "But he's my father. I love him—"

"He lost the right to your loyalty long ago. Do you think I want a con artist, a thief, around my wife…my child…my home?" He looked at her in tightly controlled fury. "No."

"He never meant to hurt anyone," she tried. "He always hoped the stock market would turn and he'd be able to pay everyone back. He just lost his way after my mom died. And he hasn't been well since he got out of prison. If you just knew what he's been through…"

"Excuses on top of excuses! You expect me to feel sympathy?" he said incredulously. "Because he was sick? Because he lost his wife? Because of him, you and I were separated. Because of him, my own father never had the chance to grow old! After he'd worked for him with utter devotion for almost twenty-five years. And that's how your father repaid him!"

"Darius, please."

"You expect me to allow that man to walk you down the aisle? To hold my firstborn child in his arms? No." He set his jaw. "He's a monster. He has no conscience, no soul."

"You don't know him like I do…"

Remembering her weakness where her father was concerned, her senseless loyalty at any cost, Darius abruptly changed tack. "If you truly love him, you will do as I ask. It will benefit him, as well."

"How can you say that?"

"Once I've paid all his debts, he'll never need to be afraid of someone breaking his arm again. He'll be treated better by his probation officers. By potential employers."

"He can't work. No one would hire him. He would starve in the street."

Revulsion churned in Darius's belly, but he forced himself to say, "I will make sure that does not happen. He can remain in your Brooklyn apartment and his rent will be paid. He will always have food and any other necessities he might require. But he must face the consequences of what he's done. He's taken enough from you, Letty. Your future is with me."

Pushing away the breakfast plates, he stood up from the kitchen counter and went to her handbag on the entryway table. Pulling out her phone, he held it out to her.

"Call him," he said quietly. "See what he tells you to do."

Sitting at the counter in her white robe, Letty stared at the phone with big, stricken eyes, as if it were poison. She snatched it up, and with an intake of breath, dialed and held it up to her ear.

"Hi, Dad." She paused, then said unhappily, "Yes. I'm sorry. I don't blame you for worrying. I should have… Ooh? You saw that?" She looked up and said to Darius, "Your announcement about repaying the five billion is already all over the news. Our engagement, too. Dad is thrilled."

"Of course," he said acidly.

"What?" She turned her focus back to her father. "Oh, yes," she whispered, looking up at Darius with troubled eyes. "We're very happy." She bit her lip. "But, Dad, there's this one thing. It's a big thing. A big horrible thing—" her voice broke a little "—and I hardly know how to say it…" She took a deep breath. "I won't be able to see you any-more. Or let you see the baby."

Darius watched her face as she listened to her father's response. Her expression was miserable.

He blocked all mercy from his soul. He was being cruel to be kind. Saving her from her own weak, loving heart.

"No," she whispered into the phone. "I won't abandon you. It's not…"

She paused again, and her expression changed, became numb with grief. Finally, she choked out in a voice almost too soft to hear, "Okay, Dad. All right. I love you, too. So much. Goodbye."

Tears were streaming down her face. Wiping them away, she handed Darius the phone. "He wants to talk to you."

He stared down at the phone in dismay. He hadn't expected that. He picked it up and put it to his ear.

"What do you want?" he said coldly.

"Darius Kyrillos." He recognized Howard Spencer's voice. Though the voice had aged and grown shaky, he could almost hear the older man's smile. "I remember when you were a little boy, just come to Fairholme. You barely spoke English but even then, you were a great kid."

Unwanted memories went through him of when he'd first come to Fairholme with a father who was a stranger to him, a lonely eleven-year-old boy, bereaved by his grandmother's death. He'd felt bewildered by America and homesick for Greece. Back then Howard Spencer had seemed grand and as foreign as a king.

But he'd welcomed the bereft boy warmly. He'd even asked his five-year-old daughter to look after him. In spite of their six-year age difference, Letty, with her caring and friendly heart, had swiftly become his friend, sharing her toys and showing him the fields and beach. While her father had given Darius Christmas presents and told him firmly he could do anything he wanted in life.

In an indirect way, Howard Spencer had even helped start his software company. As a teenager, Darius had been fascinated by computers. He'd taught himself to tinker and code, and soon found himself responsible for every tech device, security feature and bit of wireless connectivity at Fairholme. It was Howard Spencer who'd hired him as the estate's first technical specialist and allowed him to continue to live there. He'd even paid for Darius to study computer science at the local community college...

Darius felt a twist in his gut. Like...guilt? No. He rushed

to justify his actions. All right, so Spencer had encouraged him and paid for his schooling. Using stolen money from his Ponzi scheme!

"Yes, a good kid," Howard continued gruffly. "But stubborn, with all that stiff-necked Greek pride. Always had to do everything yourself. Letty was the only one you really let help you with anything. And even then, you always thought you had to be in charge. You never recognized her strength."

"Your point?" Darius said coldly.

He heard the other man take a deep breath.

"Take good care of my daughter," he said quietly. "Both Letty and my grandchild. I know you will. That's the only reason I'm letting them go."

The line abruptly cut off.

"What did he say?" Letty's miserable face came into view.

"He said…" Darius stared down in amazement at the phone in his hand.

He ground his teeth. Damn the old man. Taking the high road. He must be playing the long game. Trusting that Letty would wear him down after their wedding and make him relent. Make him forgive.

But Darius would never forgive. He'd die before he let that man worm his way back into their lives.

"Tell me what he said," Letty pleaded.

He turned to her with an ironic smile. "He gave our marriage his blessing."

Her shoulders slumped.

"That's what he said to me, too," she whispered.

So his theory was correct. Clever bastard, he thought grudgingly. He really knew how to pull his daughter's heartstrings.

But Howard Spencer had finally met someone he couldn't manipulate. The old man would end his days alone, in that tiny run-down apartment, with no one to love him. Just as he deserved.

While they—they would live happily ever after.

Darius looked at Letty tenderly.

After their marriage, after she was legally his forever, she would come to despise her father as Darius did. At the very least, she would forget and let him go.

She would love only Darius, be loyal only to him.

He wouldn't love her back, of course. The childish illusion that love could be anything but pain had been burned out of him permanently. But love was still magic to Letty, and he realized now it was the only way to bind her and make her happy in their marriage. For the sake of their children, he had to make her love him.

This was just the beginning.

"You did the right thing," Darius murmured. Pulling her into his arms, he kissed the top of her head, relishing the feel of her body against his, the crush of her full breasts and her belly rounded with his child. "You'll never regret it."

"I regret it already."

Leaning forward, he kissed the tears off her cheeks. He kissed her forehead, then her eyelids. He felt her shudder and pulled her fully into his arms. He whispered, "Let me comfort you."

He lowered his mouth to hers, gripping her smaller body to his own, and kissed her passionately. A sigh came from her throat as she wrapped her arms around him. He opened the belt of her robe and ran his hands down her naked body. Then with a large sweep of his arm, he knocked all the dishes to the floor with a noisy clatter.

Lifting his future bride up onto the countertop, Darius did what he'd wanted to do for the last hour. He made love to her until she wept. Tears of joy, he told himself. Just tears of joy.

* * *

Letty had never been the sort of girl to dream about weddings. At least not since she was eighteen, when her one attempt at elopement had ended so badly.

But she'd vaguely thought, if she ever did get married, she'd have a simple wedding dress, a cake, a bouquet. And her father would give her away.

This wedding had none of that.

Two days after Darius's proposal, they got married in what felt like the worst wedding ever.

Her own fault, Letty thought numbly, as she stood in front of a judge, mumbling vows to honor and cherish. She had no one to blame but herself.

Well, and Darius.

After her phone call with her father, Letty had been too heartsick to care about planning a wedding ceremony. Even Darius ruthlessly taking possession of her body on the kitchen counter hadn't cheered her up. Her heart felt empty and sad.

Darius had tried to tempt her with outrageous ideas for a destination wedding. "If you don't want a big society wedding, there's no reason to wait. The sky's the limit! Do you want a beach wedding in Hawaii? A winter wedding in South America? If you want, I'll rent out the Sydney Opera House. Just say the word!"

She'd looked at him miserably. "What I want is for my father to be there. Without love, what difference does the wedding make?"

The temperature in the room had dropped thirty degrees. "Fine," he said coldly. "If that's how you feel, we might as well just get married at City Hall."

"Fine," she'd said in the same tone.

So they'd gone to the Office of the City Clerk near Chinatown this afternoon, where they'd now been kill-ing time for three hours, surrounded by happy couples all waiting for their turn.

Letty felt exhausted to the bone. She hadn't slept at all the night before. Neither she nor Darius had even bothered to dress up for the ceremony. She wore a simple blouse and maternity pants. Darius wore a dark shirt, dark jeans and a dark glower.

Nor had it helped that the two friends they'd brought to be their witnesses had hated each other on sight. The constant childish bickering between Belle Langtry and Santiago Velazquez, who'd introduced himself as Ángel, had been the final nail in the coffin of Worst Wedding Ever.

It could have been so different, Letty thought sadly. If her father had been there, if she and Darius had been in love, nothing else would have mattered.

But there was no love anywhere on this wedding day.

As she and Darius had sat waiting, listening to their best man and maid of honor squabble, she couldn't stop tears from falling. Darius's glower only made them fall faster.

Their number was the very last to be called in the late afternoon. The four of them had gone up to the desk. As the officiant swiftly and matter-of-factly spoke the words that would bind her to Darius forever, Letty couldn't stop thinking about how she was betraying her father. The man who'd taught her to roller-skate down Fairholme's long marble hallways, who'd taught her chess on rainy days. The man who'd told her again and again how much he loved her.

"I screwed everything up," Howard had told her sadly when he got out of prison. "But I swear I'll make it up to you, Letty. I'll get you back the life you lost…"

He'd never once criticized her for getting pregnant out of wedlock. He'd just been delighted about a future grandchild. Even when she'd phoned him before the wedding, and told him she was marrying Darius, she'd felt his joy.

Though it had been abruptly cut off when she'd tearfully told him the rest of the deal.

Then he'd said quietly, "Do it, sweetheart. Marry him. It's what you've always wanted. Knowing you're happy, I'll be at peace."

Now, as she watched Darius speak his marriage vows, Letty's heart twisted. She blinked as she heard the officiant solemnly finish, "…I now pronounce you man and wife."

The whole ceremony had taken three minutes.

She dimly heard Belle clapping and hooting wildly as Darius leaned forward to kiss her. Some instinct made her turn away and offer him only her cheek.

His glower turned radioactive.

After signing the marriage certificate, their small party of four trundled out of the City Clerk's Office to discover the cold gray September skies pouring rain.

"Such a beautiful ceremony. I'm so happy for you," Belle sighed, obviously caught up in some romantic image that had nothing to do with reality. "You make a perfect couple."

"You're living in a fairy tale," Santiago Velazquez muttered. "They can obviously barely stand each other."

Belle whirled on him irritably. "Just once, could you keep your bad attitude to yourself?" Her voice was shrill. "I'm sick of hearing it!"

He shrugged, glancing at Darius. "You got married because she's pregnant, right?"

"Velazquez, don't make me punch you on my wedding day."

"See?" Belle crowed. "Even *Darius* can't stand you."

The Spaniard looked superior. "Just because I'm the only one who is willing to speak the truth…"

"The truth is that marriage is about love and commitment and a whole bunch of sophisticated emotions you obviously can't handle. So keep your opinions to yourself.

You might think you're being all deep, but talking like that at a wedding is just plain tacky!"

The Spaniard's eyes narrowed and for a moment Letty was afraid that the constant bickering between them was about to boil over into something truly unpleasant. But to her relief, the man abruptly gave a stiff nod.

"You are right."

Belle stared at him wide-eyed, then tossed her hair, huffing with a flare of her nostrils. "Course I'm right. I'm always right."

Letty exhaled as they seemed to drop the matter.

"Except for when you're wrong," came his sardonic response, "which is every other time but now, since you're obviously living in some ridiculous romantic dream world."

Belle glared at him, then whirled on Letty with a beaming smile. "Are you having a good wedding day, sweetie? Because that's what I care about. Because I'm not rude like some people. We learn manners in Texas."

"I have a ranch in Texas," the Spaniard rejoined. "And I learned an expression that I believe applies to you, Miss Langtry."

"The meek shall inherit the earth?"

He gave her a sensual half smile. "All hat, no cattle."

Belle gave an outraged intake of breath. Then she said sweetly, "That's a lot of big talk for a man with a girl's name."

He looked irritated. "You're saying it wrong. An-hel. And it is a man's name. In every Spanish-speaking country…"

"Aaain-jel, Aaain-jel!" she taunted, using the pronunciation that involved harps and wings. She blinked. "Oh, look, the limo's here."

Letty almost cried in relief.

"Finally," Darius muttered. The limo had barely slowed down at the curb before he opened the back door for his bride. Letty jumped in, eager to escape.

"Where are we going?" Belle said, starting to follow, the Spaniard coming up behind her. Darius blocked them from the limo.

"Thank you so much. Both of you. But I'm afraid Letty and I must leave immediately for Greece."

Belle frowned. "I thought you weren't leaving until tomorrow. We were going to take you out for dinner…"

"Unfortunately, we must get on the plane immediately. My family is waiting to meet my new bride."

"Oh," Belle said, crestfallen. "In that case… Of course I understand." Leaning into the back of the limo, she hugged Letty. "Have a wonderful honeymoon! You deserve every bit of your happiness!"

Belle was right, Letty reflected numbly as the limo pulled away from her friend still beaming and waving on the sidewalk. She'd get all the happiness she deserved after abandoning her father to marry Darius: none.

Letty stared out at the gray rain. Darius sat beside her silently for the hour and a half it took to drive through the evening rush-hour traffic to the small airport outside the city. As they boarded his private jet, he continued to ignore her.

Fine. Letty didn't care. She felt exhausted and miserable. Walking to the separate bedroom in the back of the jet, she shut the door behind her. Climbing into bed, she pulled the blanket up to her forehead, struggling to hold back tears. She closed her eyes.

And woke up in a different world.

Letty sat up with an intake of breath.

She was no longer on the jet. She found herself in a big, bright bedroom, empty except for a king-size wrought-iron bed.

Brilliant sunlight came through the open windows, leaving warm patterns against the white walls and red tiled floor. She heard laughter outside and conversation in an exotic language and the sweet singing of birds.

She looked down at the soft blanket and cotton sheets. Where was she? And—her lips parted in a gasp. She was wearing only her bra and panties! Someone had undressed her while she was asleep! The thought horrified her.

How had she gotten into this bed?

The flight across the Atlantic had been lonely and dark. She remembered crying herself to sleep on the plane. After her sleepless night before their wedding, she'd slept deeply.

She dimly remembered Darius carrying her, the warmth of his chest, the comforting rumble of his voice.

"So you're awake."

Looking up with an intake of breath, Letty saw her husband now standing in the open doorway, dressed more casually than she'd ever seen him, in a snug black T-shirt and long cargo shorts. Sunlight lit him from behind, leaving his expression in shadow.

"Where are we?"

"The island of Heraklios. My villa."

"I barely remember arriving."

"You were exhausted. Overwhelmed from the happiness of marrying me," he said sardonically.

"What time is it?"

"Here? Almost two in the afternoon." He motioned to a nearby door. "There's an en suite bathroom if you'd like a shower." He indicated a large walk-in closet. "Your clothes have already been unpacked."

"Are you the one who took off my clothes?"

"Just so you'd sleep more comfortably."

She bit her lip as she looked down at the bed. "Um. And did you…did we…uh, share this bed?"

His shoulders tensed. "If you're asking if I took advantage of you in your sleep, the answer is no."

She took a deep breath. "I didn't mean…"

"Get dressed and come out on the terrace when you're ready. My family is here to meet you."

Letty stared at the empty doorway in dismay, then slowly rose out of bed. Her body felt stiff from sleeping so long.

Going into the elegant marble bathroom, she took a hot shower, which refreshed her. Wrapping herself in a towel, she wiped the steam off the mirror. Her face looked pale and sad.

A fine thing, she thought. When she was about to meet his family. They'd take one look at Letty's face and assume, as Santiago Velazquez had, that she and Darius had gotten married only because of her pregnancy. Why else would someone as handsome and powerful as Darius Kyrillos ever choose a penniless, ordinary-looking woman like her?

He was taking a risk even bringing her to meet them. She could embarrass him, treat them disrespectfully. She could even explain how he'd blackmailed her into marriage.

Letty looked at her eyes in the mirror. She didn't want to hurt Darius. She just wanted him to forgive her dad.

Maybe she could start by treating his family with the same respect she wanted for her father.

Letty dressed quickly and carefully, blow-drying her long dark hair and brushing it till it shone. She put on lipstick, and chose a pretty new sundress and sandals from the closet. Her knees shook as she went down the hallway. A maid directed her toward the terrace.

With a deep breath, she went outside into the sunshine.

Bright pink bougainvillea climbed the whitewashed walls of the Greek villa, above a wide terrace overlooking the mountainous slopes of the island jutting out of the Ionian Sea.

Against the blue horizon, she saw the shaded forest green of a distant island. The whole world seemed bright with color: blue and white buildings, sea and sky, pink flowers, brown earth and green olive, fig and pomegranate trees.

She felt the warm sun against her skin, and pleasure

seeped through her body. Then she saw the group of people sitting at a long wooden table.

Darius rose abruptly from the table. Silence fell as the others followed his gaze.

Wordlessly, he came over to her. His dark eyes glowed as he lowered his head to kiss her cheek. Turning back to the others, he said in English, "This is Letty. My wife."

An elderly woman got up from the table. Standing on her tiptoes, she squinted, carefully looking Letty over from her blushing face to her pregnant belly. Then she smiled. Reaching up, she patted Letty on the cheek and said something in Greek that she didn't understand.

"My great-aunt says you look happy now," Darius translated. "Like a beautiful bride."

"How sweet… Did she see me before?" Letty asked.

"When I brought you in. She said you looked like death warmed over."

She stared at him in horror, then narrowed her eyes accusingly. "She never said that."

He gave a sudden grin. "She says our island has obviously revived you, all our sun and sea air. Plus, clearly—" he quirked a dark eyebrow "—marriage to me."

The elderly woman said something quickly behind him. He glanced back with an indulgent smile. *"Nai, Theia Ioanna."*

"What did she say?"

Darius turned back to Letty. "She said marriage to you seems to agree with me, as well." Looking down at her, he hesitated. "Our wedding was…"

"Horrible."

"Not good," he agreed. His dark eyes caressed her face, and he leaned forward to whisper, "But something tells me our honeymoon will make up for it."

Letty felt his breath against her hair, the brush of his lips against her earlobe, and electricity pulsed through her at the untold delights promised by a honeymoon in the Greek villa. In that enormous bed.

She tried not to think about that as he introduced her to the other people around the table, aunts and uncles and innumerable cousins. She smiled shyly, wishing she could speak Greek as one Kyrillos family member after another hugged her, their faces alight with welcome and approval.

One of the younger women grabbed her arm, motioning for her to take the best seat at the table. On learning she was hungry, other relatives dished her out a lunch from the tempting dishes on the table. Tangy olives, salad with cucumbers, tomatoes and feta, vine leaves stuffed with rice, grilled meats on skewers, fresh seafood and finally the lightest, flakiest honey pastries imaginable. After sleeping so long, and having no appetite yesterday, Letty was ravenous and gobbled it all up as fast as she could get it.

The women around her exclaimed approvingly in Greek. Darius sat beside her, smiling, his dark eyes glowing beneath the warm Greek sun.

"They like how you eat," he told her.

She laughed in spite of herself. In this moment, beneath the pink flowers and warm Greek sun, with the blue sea beyond, she felt suddenly, strangely happy. Finally, she pushed her chair away from the table, shaking her head as his relatives offered yet more plates. "No, thank you." She turned anxiously to Darius. "How do I say that?"

"Óchi, efharisto."

"Óchi, efharisto," she repeated to them warmly.

One by one, his family members hugged her, speaking rapidly, patting her belly, then hugging Darius before they hurried into the villa.

"Your family is wonderful."

"Thank you." He lifted a dark eyebrow. "By the way, some of them speak English quite well. They're just hoping if you don't realize that, you'll be inspired to learn Greek."

She laughed, then looked around the terrace at the flowers and sea view. "I'm feeling very inspired, believe me."

"They already love you. Because you're my wife." He put his arm along the back of her chair. "Not only that, you're the first woman I've ever brought home to meet them."

Her eyes went wide. "Really?"

He grinned, shaking his head. "For years, they read about my scandalous love life and despaired of me ever settling down with a nice girl." He sipped strong black coffee from a tiny cup. "Great-aunt Ioanna is delirious with joy to see me not only sensibly married, but also expecting a child. And she remembers you."

Letty's smile fell. "She does?"

"Yes."

"Does she blame me for—?"

"No," he cut her off. "She remembers you only as the girl that I loved and lost long ago. In her mind, that means our marriage is fate. *Moíra.* She believes our love was meant to stand the test of time."

Letty blinked fast. *Our love was meant to stand the test of time.*

Leaning forward, he took her hand. "You are part of the family. You are a Kyrillos now."

It was true, she realized. She had a new last name. When she updated her passport, she'd no longer be Letitia Spencer, the daughter of the famous white-collar criminal, but Letitia Kyrillos, the wife of a self-made billionaire. Just by marrying, she'd become an entirely different person. What a strange thought.

But maybe this new woman, Letitia Kyrillos, would know how to be happy. Maybe their marriage, which had been so bleak at the start, could someday be full of joy, as her own parents' marriage had been.

She just had to change Darius's mind about her father. It wouldn't be hard.

Like making it snow in July.

One of Darius's female cousins came back out of the villa and pulled on his arm, talking rapidly in Greek, even as she smiled apologetically at Letty.

"They need to move the big table," he explained. "To get the terrace ready for the party tonight."

"What party?"

"They wouldn't let us come all this way without making a big fuss." He grinned. "There's a party tonight to welcome you as my bride. Only family and friends from the village have been invited…"

"Good," she said, relieved.

"Which, naturally, means the entire island will be here, and a few people from neighboring islands, as well."

Her heart sank to her sandals at the thought of all those people judging her, possibly finding her unworthy of being Darius's bride. She whispered, "What if they don't like me?"

Reaching out, Darius lifted her chin. "Of course they will," he said softly. "They will because I do."

As the hot Greek sun caressed her skin in the flower-dappled terrace, the dark promise in his gaze made her shiver.

As his relatives bustled back out on the terrace, with maids following them, they started clearing dishes, wiping the table and sweeping the terrace.

Letty looked around anxiously. "Ask them how I can help."

He snorted. "If you think they'll allow either of us to lift a finger, you're out of your mind."

"We can't just sit here, while they do all the work!"

"Watch this." Pushing his chair back, Darius rose from

the table and said casually in English, "Hey, Athina, hand me that broom."

"Forget it, Darius," his cousin replied indignantly in the same language, yanking the broom out of his reach. "You sent my sons to college!"

"You gave me a job when I needed work," a man added in heavily accented English, as he lifted fairy lights to dangle from the terrace's leafy trellis. "We're doing this. Don't think you're getting out of it!"

They all gave a low buzz of agreement.

Looking at Letty, Darius shrugged. She sighed, seeing she was outmatched. His great-aunt was now, in fact, shooing them away with a stream of steady Greek, a mischievous smile on her kindly, wizened face.

Letty drew closer to him. "So what should we do with ourselves?"

Darius's eyes darkened as he said huskily, "We *are* on our honeymoon…"

She shivered at his closeness and at the tempting thought of going back to the bedroom. But she was distracted by the sweep of the brooms and the loud cries of the relatives and house staff bustling back and forth across the villa as they cleaned and set up for the party, all the while watching Darius and Letty out of the corners of their eyes with frank interest and indulgent smiles.

"I couldn't," Letty whispered, blushing beneath all the stares. "If we stay, I'll feel like we should help cook and clean."

"Then let's not stay." He took her hand. "Let me show you the island."

He drew her out of the enormous, luxurious villa, past the gate and out onto unpaved road. Looking around, she saw the rural rolling hills were covered with olive and pomegranate trees, dotted with small whitewashed houses beneath the sun. But there was one thing she didn't see.

"Where are all the cars? The paved roads?"

"We don't have cars. Heraklios is too small and mountainous, and there are only a few hundred residents. There are a few cobblestoned streets by the waterfront, but they're too winding and tight for any car."

"So how do you get around?"

"Donkey."

She almost tripped on her own feet. She looked at him incredulously. "You're joking."

He grinned. "I managed to put in a helicopter pad, and also a landing strip, at great expense, and it isn't even usable if the wind is too strong. Here we transport most things by sea." As they walked closer to an actual village clinging to a rocky cliff, he pointed to a small building on a hill. "That was my school."

"It looks like one room."

"It is. After primary school, kids have to take a ferry to a bigger school the next island over." As they continued walking, he pointed to a small *taverna*. "That's where I tasted my first sip of *retsina*." His nose wrinkled. "I spit it out. I still don't like it."

"And you call yourself a Greek," she teased. His eyebrow quirked at her challenge.

"I'd take you in and let you taste it, except—" he looked more closely at the closed door "—it looks like old Mr. Papadakis is already up at the villa. Probably setting up drinks."

"The whole town's closing—just for our wedding reception?"

"It's a small island. I don't think you realize how much pull I have around here."

Letty slowed when she saw a ruined, lonely-looking villa at the top of the hill, above the village. "What's that?"

His lips tightened, curled up at the edges. "That was my mother's house."

"Oh," she breathed. She knew his mother had abandoned him at birth. He'd never talked much about her, not even when they were young. "No one lives there anymore?"

"My mother left the island right after I was born, her parents soon after. It seems they couldn't stand the shame of my existence," he added lightly.

She flinched, her heart aching. "Oh, Darius."

"My mother moved to Paris. She died in a car crash when I was around four." He shrugged. "I heard her parents died a few years ago. I can't remember where or how."

"I'm so sorry."

"Why? I didn't love them. I don't mourn them."

"But your mother. Your grandparents…"

"Calla Halkias died in a limousine, married to an aristocrat." His voice was cold as he looked back to the ghostly ruin on the hill. "Just as I'm sure she would have wanted. The prestigious life her parents expected for her."

A lump rose in her throat as she thought of Darius as a child on this island, looking up at the imposing villa of the people who'd tossed him out like garbage. She didn't know what to say, so she held his hand tightly. "Did you ever forgive them?"

"For what?"

"They were your family, and they abandoned you."

His lips pressed down. "My mother gave birth to me. I'm glad about that. But I wouldn't call them *family*. From everything I've heard, they were a total disaster. Like…" He hesitated. But she knew.

"Like my family?" she said quietly.

He paused. "Your mother was a great lady. She was always kind. To everyone."

"Yes," she said over the lump in her throat.

"My *yiayiá* raised me. Our house didn't have electricity or plumbing, but I always knew she loved me. When I finally made my fortune, I had the old shack razed and built a villa in its place. The biggest villa this island has ever seen." Looking up at the ruin, he gave a grim smile. "When I was young, the Halkias family was the most powerful here. Now I am."

She noticed he'd never said if he forgave them. She bit her lip. "But, Darius…"

"It's in the past. I want to live in the present. And shape the future." Taking both her hands in his own, Darius looked down at her seriously on the dusty road beneath the hot Greek sun. "Promise me, Letty. You'll always do what's best for our family."

"I promise," she said, meaning it with all her heart.

Lowering his head, he whispered, "And I promise the same."

He softly kissed her, as if sealing the vow. Drawing back, he searched her gaze. Then he pulled her back into his arms and kissed her in another way entirely.

Feeling the heat of his lips against hers, the rough scrape of the bristles on his chin, she clung to him, lost in her own desire. He was her husband now. *Her husband.*

He finally pulled away. "Come with me."

He led her to the end of the dusty road, through the winding cobblestones of the small village of whitewashed houses. On the other side, they went through a scrub brush thicket of olive trees. She held his hand tightly as the branches scraped her arms, and they went down a sharp rocky hill. Then suddenly, they were in a hidden cove on a deserted white sand beach.

Letty's eyes went wide in amazement. The popular beaches of the Hamptons and even around Fairholme would have been packed on a gloriously warm September day. But this beach was empty. "Where is everyone?"

"I told you. They're at the villa, getting ready for the party."

"But—" she gestured helplessly "—there must be tourists, at least?"

He shook his head. "We don't have a hotel. The tourists are at the resorts up in Corfu. So we all know each other here. Everyone is a friend or relative, or at least a friend of a relative. It's a community. One big family."

No wonder this island felt like a world out of time. She felt her heart twist. Turning away, she looked around at the hidden cove with the white sand beach against the blue Ionian Sea and tried to smile. "It's wonderful."

"You're missing Fairholme," he said quietly.

She looked down at the white sand. "It's been ten years. It's stupid. Any psychiatrist would tell me it's time to let it go."

"I miss it, too." He grinned. "Do you remember the beach at Fairholme? Nothing but rocks."

"Yes, and the flower meadow where you taught me to dance."

"What about the pond where I tried to catch frogs and you always wanted to give them names and take them home—?"

Suddenly their words were tumbling over each other.

"The brilliant color of the trees in autumn—"

"Roller-skating down the hallways—"

"The secret passageway behind the library where you'd always hide when you were upset—"

"Your mother's rose garden," Darius said with a sudden laugh, "where she caught me that time I tried a cigarette. My first and last time—"

"And how Mrs. Pollifax scolded us whenever we tracked mud into her freshly cleaned kitchen." Letty grinned. "But she always gave us milk and cookies after we'd made it right. Though it took a while. You weren't very good at mopping."

"We always turned it into a game."

The two of them smiled at each other on the deserted beach.

Letty's smile slipped away. "But we'll never see Fairholme again."

Darius stared at her for a long moment, then abruptly started taking off his shoes. "The sea should be warm."

She lifted her eyebrows. "What are you doing?"

"I'm getting in." He leaned over to unbuckle her sandals. "And you're coming with me."

Barefoot, they went splashing out into the sea. Letty delighted in the feel of the water caressing her feet, then her calves and finally knees. She was tempted to go deeper into the water, to float her pregnant body in the seductive waves that would make her feel light as air. She took a few more steps, until the sea lapped the hem of her white sundress.

Splashing behind her, Darius suddenly pulled her into his arms.

As the waves swirled around them, he kissed her, and there was no one to see but the birds soaring across the sky. For hours, or maybe just minutes, they kissed in the hidden cove, between the bright blue sea and sky, beneath the hot Greek sun. He ran his hands over her bare shoulders, over her thin cotton sundress, as the salty sea spray clung to their skin and hair.

Waves swirled around them, sucking the sand beneath their toes, as the tide started to come in. The waves crashed higher, moving up against their thighs.

Finally pulling away, Darius looked down at her intently. She felt his dark gaze sear her body. Sear her heart.

"Letty, the house we grew up in might be gone," he whispered. "But we still have each other."

The lowering afternoon sun shone around the edges of his dark hair, making Darius shimmer like the dream he was to her.

And it was then Letty knew the worst had happened.

The doom and disaster. And it had happened more swiftly than she'd ever expected.

She loved him.

All of him.

The man he'd been.

The man he was.

The man he could be.

Since the February night they'd conceived their child, Letty had tried to convince herself that he'd changed irrevocably. That she hated him. That he'd lost her love forever.

It had all been a lie.

Even in her greatest pain, she'd never stopped loving him. How could she? He was the love of her life.

Glancing back at the lowering sun, Darius sighed. "Can't be late for our own party. We'd better get back to the villa." He glanced down at his shorts, now splattered with sand and seawater. "We might have to clean up a little."

"Yes," she said in a small voice.

"We'll finish this later," he said huskily, kissing her bare shoulder. He whispered, "I can hardly wait to make love to you, Mrs. Kyrillos."

As they splashed their way to the beach, and made their way up the shore, Letty stumbled.

He caught her, then frowned, looking at her closely. "Did you hurt yourself?"

"No," she said, hiding the ache in her throat, struggling to hold back tears. It wasn't totally a lie. She wasn't hurt.

But she knew she soon would be.

One day married, and her heart was already lost.

CHAPTER NINE

DARIUS NEARLY GASPED when he first saw Letty at the party that night. When she came out onto the terrace, she looked so beautiful she seemed to float through the twilight.

She wore a simple white maxi dress, which fit perfectly over her full breasts and baby bump. The soft fabric showed off the creamy blush of her skin and bright hazel of her eyes. Bright pink flowers hung in her long dark hair.

As the red sun was setting into the sea below the cliffs, three hundred people on the terrace burst into spontaneous applause amid a cacophony of approving Greek.

Darius's heart was in his throat as he looked at her. He was dazzled. He thought she'd put Aphrodite, freshly risen from the sea, completely to shame.

And the fact that he'd even have such a ridiculously poetic thought stunned him.

As she came closer, he cleared his throat awkwardly. "You look nice."

"Thank you," she said, smiling shyly.

He did not touch her. He was almost afraid to. She was simply too desirable, and after their hours of kissing on the beach, he did not know how much more temptation his self-control could take. They'd been married for over twenty-four hours, but had not yet made love.

The party was torture. It lasted for hours, testing his resolve. If it had been any other situation, he would have told everyone to go to hell and taken his bride straight to bed.

But this was his family. His village. He couldn't be rude to them or reject the warm welcome they gave his bride.

His whole body ached to possess her. He could think of nothing else. It was causing him physical pain. He was just glad he was wearing a long, loosely tailored jacket and loose trousers so the whole village could not discuss with amused approval his obvious desire for his bride.

The party was over the top, as only village affairs could be, with music, drinking and dancing. A feast had been lovingly prepared by his family and all the rest of the village. So many people rushed to Letty and started talking excitedly in Greek that she'd announced she planned to start taking Greek lessons as soon as possible. Some of his cousins immediately started cheering, and when Darius translated her words for his elderly great-aunt, Theia Ioanna actually stood on tiptoe to kiss Letty on both cheeks. His family loved her.

Of course they did. Letty Kyrillos was the perfect bride. She would be the perfect wife and mother. Now he'd gotten her away from her father, there would be no bad influences in her life.

Darius would be the only one to claim her loyalty. And the expression in Letty's eyes as she looked at him now—a mix of longing, hero worship and fear—did strange things to his insides. It made him feel oddly vulnerable, reminding him of the insecure, lovesick youth he'd once been for her.

No. He just desired her, he told himself firmly. He was appreciative that she was comporting herself as a proper Greek wife, with kindness and respect to his family. And he hoped—expected—that she would soon love him. It would make all their lives easier.

Darius did not intend to love her in return. He would never leave himself that vulnerable again. As the protector of their family, as a husband, as a father, as a man, it was his duty to be strong.

Letty's heart was her weakness. It would not be his.

His great-aunt went to bed at midnight, and the rest of the older generation soon after, but with the ouzo flowing and loud music and enthusiastic dancing, his cousins and many of the younger villagers remained well into the wee hours. It wasn't until the ouzo was gone and the musicians were falling asleep over their instruments that the last guests finally took the hint and departed, after many congratulations and kisses for the newly married couple.

Darius and Letty were finally alone on the terrace, surrounded by streamers and empty champagne glasses.

She looked at him, her eyes huge in the moonlight, the pink flowers wilting in her dark lustrous hair.

Without a word, he took her hand.

Leading her to their bedroom suite at the farthest end of the south wing, he closed the door behind them and opened the windows and sliding glass door to the balcony. The wind blew from the sea, twisting the translucent white curtains, illuminated by moonlight.

Turning back to her, he lifted her long dark hair from the nape of her neck and slowly unzipped her dress. In the hush of the night, it felt like an act that was almost holy.

Her dress dropped to the floor. She turned to him, her eyes luminous in the silvery light. Reaching up, she pulled off his jacket. She unbuttoned his shirt. He felt the soft brush of her hands against his chest and caught them in his own. She looked up at him questioningly.

A strange feeling was building in his heart. *Desire*, he reminded himself fiercely. *I desire her.* He kissed her hands—first one, then the other.

The wind blew against her hair, causing pink flower petals to float softly to the floor like a benediction. Without a word, he pulled her to the enormous bed.

This time, as they made love, there were no words beyond the language of touch. There was only pleasure and delight.

He'd thought he'd known ecstasy the night they'd made love over and over in his Manhattan penthouse.

But this was something else. It felt different.

Why? Because they were married now, and she was permanently his? Because she knew him better than anyone on earth? Because she'd truly joined his family?

Whatever the reason, as he made love to her on this, their first true wedding night, it felt sacred.

It felt like…

Happiness.

After they'd both joined and shattered like a supernova in each other's arms, Darius held her as she slept. As he stared at the ceiling, her words on the beach floated back into his mind.

We'll never see Fairholme again.

Her voice had been quietly despairing. As if she'd accepted bleak loss as her due.

Darius scowled. He didn't accept that.

He suddenly wanted to give Letty back everything she'd lost. And more.

Careful not to wake her, he rose from the bed in the gray light of dawn. Going out onto the balcony, with its view of the wild gray sea, he made a quiet phone call to his long-suffering executive assistant in New York. Mildred Harrison had worked for him for seven years, so she didn't even sound surprised that he'd be rude enough to call her so late.

"Pity you left New York right when you're the city's hero," she said drily. "Your picture is on the cover of the *Daily Post.* Apparently you're some kind of Robin Hood figure now, robbing from your own fortune to pay back Howard Spencer's victims."

"Glad I'm not there, then. We'll be back in two weeks, by which time I expect the papers will all be insulting me again. Anything else?"

"That Brooklyn apartment building has been purchased as you requested. Your father-in-law—"

"Never call him that again," Darius said tersely.

She cleared her throat. "Um, Mr. Spencer has been advised that he will be allowed to remain in the apartment for as long as he wishes, free of charge."

"Good," he said, already bored with the subject.

She paused. "There's something else you should know."

"Well?"

"The investigator following him says Spencer has been visiting an oncologist. Apparently he's sick. Maybe dying."

Darius's eyes widened. Then he gave a snort. "It's a trick."

"Mr. Green didn't think so. He managed to get his hands on the medical records. It seems legit."

"Spencer must have paid the doctor off."

"Maybe." Mildred sounded doubtful. "But if it were my father, I'd still want to know."

Yes, Darius thought. He looked back at the shadowy form of Letty sleeping in his bed. She would want to know. But there was no way he was telling her. Not when the old man was probably just trying once again to cause trouble between them.

At worst, Spencer probably had a cold and thought he could use it to get out of his well-deserved punishment. Darius was not going to let it happen.

"I won't have my wife bothered," he said shortly. "Spencer must have known he was being followed."

"As you say, Mr. Kyrillos."

He set his jaw. "I called you for another reason. I want to buy my wife a wedding gift."

"Beyond the billions you're already putting in trust for her father's victims? We've had a whole team of accountants coming through here, by the way, working with the Feds to determine accurate payments, including those for third-party clients. We're not really staffed for this…"

"You'll sort it out. And at the end, I'll send you and your husband to Miami for a week of well-deserved rest."

"Rome," she said firmly. "For three."

He grinned. Mildred knew what she was worth. He respected that.

"Three," he agreed. "But I need you to do something first. I want to buy a home."

"Your penthouse is too small?"

"I have a special place in mind. Find out what it would cost."

He explained, and she gave a low whistle. "All right, boss. I'll call you soon as I know. What's your ceiling?"

"Whatever it takes."

After he hung up the phone, Darius went back to the king-size bed he shared with his pregnant bride. Joining her under the blankets, he wrapped his arm around her as she slept. He heard the birds singing as, outside the window, the sun started to rise.

Holding Letty in his arms, he suddenly saw the reward for everything he'd done right in his life. He had Letty. He'd have the rest. Home. Children. Joy. All the things he'd stopped dreaming about long ago. He would have it all.

And nothing, especially not her criminal of a father, would come between them.

As their private jet began its descent through the clouds toward New York City, Letty felt a mixed sense of relief and regret.

She was glad to be returning closer to her father. Darius had assured her that Howard was fine and living rent-free in their old apartment with a stipend to supply his needs. "Your father is spending his days playing chess with friends down at the park," he'd told her irritably. She could only assume Darius had someone watching him, but she didn't even mind because she was glad to know he was all right. It felt so wrong never to see him, never to call him.

But at least now she'd know her dad was only a quick

drive away, if needed. And soon she hoped he'd be back in their lives for good.

The heart attack that had caused the death of Darius's father was a tragic accident. But surely he couldn't hate her dad forever? She loved Darius too much to believe that. Soon they would all be a family again.

And family was all Letty cared about. As she'd promised her husband in Greece, she would always put her family above everything else.

She already felt wistful for the tiny Greek island where she'd been immediately accepted into Darius's extended family. Their honeymoon had been the happiest two weeks of her life. She'd loved everything about Heraklios. The village. The beach. The vivid colors and bright sun. The villa. The people. Her eyes met Darius's across the airplane cabin.

The man.

He was sitting in a white swivel chair and had spent much of the flight typing on his laptop, with some idea he'd had for a new business venture. But as his gaze caught hers, she felt every bit of his attention. She always felt it to her toes when he looked at her.

Lifting a dark eyebrow, he teased, "We could still turn the plane around."

"I loved our visit," she said wistfully, then glanced out the window. "But it'll be nice to be back home." She paused, biting her lip. She knew she shouldn't ask, but she couldn't help it. "Now we're back in the city, maybe you could talk to my dad. Then you'd see his side…"

"Forget it," he said flatly.

"He never meant to hurt anyone, he—"

Darius closed his laptop with a thud. "Stop."

"Forgiveness frees the soul. You never know—" her voice sounded desperate even to her own ears "—*you* might have to ask someone for forgiveness one day!"

He snorted. "I don't intend to commit any crimes, so I think I'm safe."

"Darius—"

"No."

Disappointment filled her heart. Clenching her hands, she told herself she'd just have to be patient. She forced herself to take a deep breath and change the subject. "I loved spending time with your family. Maybe your great-aunt could come visit us in New York."

His expression relaxed and he smiled. "Theia Ioanna hates planes. She thinks of them as newfangled machines, a dangerous fad. She's waiting for everyone to come to their senses. But after our baby's born we could go back to Heraklios."

"I'd like that." Outside the window, the plane was descending through clouds that looked like white cotton candy. "In the meantime, I'm going to start learning Greek." She looked at him coyly beneath her lashes. "You'd like to teach me your native tongue, wouldn't you?"

His eyes darkened with interest. He started to rise from his seat, but as the plane broke beneath the clouds, the pilot announced over the intercom that they should buckle their seat belts for landing. Letty smiled.

Then she looked through the porthole window. "That's not Teterboro."

Now he was the one to smile. "No."

Staring down, she suddenly recognized the airport. Long ago, her family had landed here every time they went on a trip. She looked up with a frown. "Long Island? Is there a problem?"

"Wait and see."

After the plane landed at the small airport, the two of them came down the steps. A town car waited on the tarmac, and his driver and bodyguard swiftly loaded their suitcases from the plane.

"But why are we here?" she asked Darius helplessly in the backseat of the car a few minutes later as it pulled away from the airport.

"You'll see."

"You're really vexing."

His dark eyebrows lifted. "Vexing?" he teased, then moved closer as he whispered, "Is that what I am?"

Then he kissed her senseless in the backseat, until she was forced to agree rather unsteadily that he did have one or two good qualities, as well.

But she tensed when the limo turned onto the coastal road that she'd once known very, very well. Her suspicions were confirmed as they drove down the same country lane that she knew led to the massive 1920s beachfront estate that had once been her home. She turned on Darius angrily.

"Why would you bring us here?" she choked out. "Just to torture me? You can't see the house from the road." She felt a sudden ache in her throat as she looked out toward the gray-blue bay that led to the Atlantic. "The gate is guarded. That tech billionaire is serious about privacy. So if you're hoping to get a peek of the house, it won't happen."

"You tried?"

"A month after it was sold at auction. As I told you, I just wanted a picture of my great-grandmother's fresco. His guard did everything but set the dogs on me."

"That won't be a problem today."

Letty pointed at the road ahead. "See? I told you—"

Then her eyes went wide.

The gate was wide open. Their limo drove right past the empty guardhouse, up the wide driveway to the glorious windswept oceanfront manor that had been built by Letty's great-great-grandfather, a steel baron named Edwin Langford.

Fairholme.

Letty's breath caught in her throat as she leaned out the

car window, and her eyes were dazzled as she saw, for the first time in ten years, her beloved home.

Tears swelled in her eyes as she looked up at the gray stone mansion with its turrets and leaded glass windows soaring against the sky. Looking back at her husband, she breathed, "What have you done?"

He was smiling. "I've given you what you want most."

The limo had barely stopped before she flung open her car door and raced eagerly into the house. Pushing aside the stately front door—unlocked!—she hurled herself into the foyer where she'd played as a child.

"Dad?" she cried out. "Dad, where are you?"

Letty ran from room to room, calling his name, overwhelmed with happiness that somehow, while pretending he was never going to forgive her father, Darius had seen the desperate desire of her heart.

I've given you what you want most.

"Dad!" she cried, moving from one elegant, empty room to the next. Memories followed her with every step.

There she had played pirates with her father.

There she had slipped down the marble floor in socks as the two of them competed to see who could slide farthest and make her mother laugh loudest.

There she'd played with the gardener's kittens.

There she'd played hide-and-seek with Darius when they were kids…

There—every Saturday in summer—she'd tucked roses into the priceless Ming dynasty vase to make her mother smile.

But where was her dad? Where?

As Letty finished going through the main entrance rooms, she ran up the sweeping staircase toward the second floor. She stopped halfway up the stairs, realizing she was hearing only the echo of her own voice.

Her dad wasn't there.

Letty's shoulders sagged with savage disappointment. Turning back down the stairs, she saw Darius standing in the front doorway, watching her. The happy, smug expression had disappeared from his handsome face.

He said tightly, "Why do you think I would invite your father here?"

"You said—you said," she faltered, biting her lip, "you were giving me what I wanted most."

"This house." His expression now could only be described as grimly outraged. "Your childhood home. I arranged to buy it for you. It wasn't easy. I had to pay the man a fortune to leave before we arrived. But I wanted you to have all your dreams. Everything you'd lost."

Everything she'd lost...

Gripping the banister for support, Letty sagged to sit on a stair. Heartbreaking grief was thundering through her, worse than if she'd never gotten her hopes up at all.

She struggled to hide it. She knew she was being churlish. Her mother would be ashamed of her. Here Darius had given her the stars and she was crying for the sun.

She should be overjoyed.

Fairholme.

Letty took a deep breath, looking up at the high painted ceilings, at the oak-paneled walls. *Home.* She was really here. Darius had given her back the home that had raised generations of Langfords, her mother's family.

What an amazing gift.

Wiping her eyes, Letty looked at Darius and tried to smile.

His handsome face was mutinous.

She couldn't blame him. He'd gone to a lot of trouble and expense to give her this incredible surprise, and she'd been completely ungrateful.

Rising unsteadily to her feet, she walked down the stairs to the foyer where he stood with a scowl, his arms folded.

"Thank you," she whispered. "I love your wonderful gift."

He looked distinctly grumpy. "It didn't look like it."

Feeling ashamed at her bad manners, she wrapped her arms around his neck and kissed him.

"I love it," she said softly. "It's a miracle to be here."

Looking mollified, he accepted her embrace. "I've also hired Mrs. Pollifax to come back as our housekeeper."

"You have!"

He smiled, clearly pleased by her reaction. "Along with as many of the original staff who were available. Giving them a big raise, naturally. I've also established a bank account in your name."

"Whatever for?"

Darius gave her a sudden grin. "You obviously haven't seen the stripper pole the last owner put up in the library. I knew you'd want to oversee the remodeling personally. Perhaps the fresco can be repaired? I've instructed the bank to give you unlimited funds. Use the money however you please."

"For the house?"

"Yes."

"The baby?"

"Of course. And you, Letty. Anything you want, jewelry, cars, furniture. You don't have to ask me. Buy anything you desire."

Biting her lip, she blurted out, "Could I send some money to my father?"

She knew immediately it was a mistake.

His expression turned icy. "I weary of your constantly bringing up this topic. We have an agreement."

"I know, but—"

"Your father already has far more than he deserves."

"If I could only just see him, so I could know he's all right…"

"He's fine."

Letty searched his gaze, hoping for reassurance. "He's fine? You know for sure?"

He paused. Then he finally said, "Yes."

He wouldn't meet her eyes.

"I miss him," she whispered. She took a deep breath, reminding herself of everything she had to be grateful for. Taking Darius's hand, she pressed it to her cheek and looked up at him with gratitude. "But what you've done for me today, buying Fairholme back... I'll never forget."

For a long moment, the two of them stood together in the foyer, with sunlight pouring in through the open door. She breathed in scents she'd craved so long, the tangy salt of the ocean, the honeyed sweetness of her mother's rose garden. The salt and sweetness of a lifetime of memories.

"Thank you," she whispered. "For bringing me home."

He cupped her cheek. "You're worth it, Letty," he said huskily. "For you, I would pay any price."

Lowering his head, he kissed her, claiming her lips as he'd already claimed her body and soul. Words lifted unbidden to her throat. Words she hadn't tried to say since that horrible night in February. Words straight from her heart.

"I love you, Darius," she said softly.

He gave her an oddly shy smile. "You do?"

Smiling back through her tears, she nodded. Her blood was rushing through her ears, pounding through her veins, as she waited for what he'd say next.

Without a word, he kissed her.

As she stood in the Fairholme foyer, her heavily pregnant belly pressed between them as her husband kissed her so tenderly, miracles seemed to be spinning around her like a whirlwind.

They were married now. Expecting a baby. He'd paid off her father's debts. He'd just brought her home. She loved him.

And someday, he would love her.

Letty was suddenly sure. They'd already had so many miracles. Why not more?

Darius would soon forgive her father and let him back into their family. He was too good a man not to forgive, especially when it meant so much to her. It was the only thing he hadn't given her. That, and those three little words.

It was the same thing, she realized. When he forgave her father, that was how she would know that he truly loved her.

When he finally pulled away from their embrace, she looked up, still a little dazzled. "Is there really a stripper pole in the library?"

Darius gave a low laugh. "Come with me."

Taking her hand, he drew her down the long marble hallway to the oak-paneled library. When she saw the gleaming stripper pole set in the brand-new white shag carpeting, she burst into horrified snorts of laughter.

"I told you," he said.

"I'll get it removed. Don't worry. I'll make this house just like it was," Letty said. "Just like we remember."

"All those memories." He pulled her against his chest, his dark eyes intense as he whispered huskily, "But as I remember, there's one thing we've never done in this house."

And as her husband pulled her against him in a hot, fierce embrace, Letty knew all her deepest dreams were about to come true.

CHAPTER TEN

HOME. LETTY LOOKED around with satisfaction. Was there any sweeter word?

The remodel was finished just in time, too. The former owner's monstrous decor had been removed—the shag carpeting, the stripper pole, the "ironic" brass fixtures and all the rest of it—and everything at Fairholme had been returned to its former glory.

The sitting room felt cozy, especially compared to the cold November weather outside. A fire crackled in the fireplace. Polished oak floors gleamed beneath priceless Turkish rugs. The sofas and chairs were plush and comfortable, the lamps sturdy and practical. Family photos now decorated the walls.

Letty snuggled back against the sofa. Her husband was sitting at the other end, tapping away on his laptop, but periodically he would rub her feet, so she made sure they were strategically available. Earlier, they'd had a delicious hearty meal of lamb stew and homemade bread, her favorite meal from childhood, prepared by Mrs. Pollifax.

The housekeeper had just left, saying that she needed to go visit a friend at a Brooklyn hospital. She'd had a strange expression when she said it, causing Letty to reply with a sympathetic murmur, "Please take all the time you need for your friend."

"I just might," the housekeeper had replied tartly, "since his own family can't be bothered to go see him."

"Poor man," Letty had sighed, feeling sorry for him. She couldn't imagine what kind of family wouldn't visit a sick man in the hospital.

That reminded her of how much she missed her father

after more than two months of not seeing him or talking to him. Darius still refused to forgive him. But surely, after their baby was born, his heart would be so full, he would have a new capacity to forgive? To love.

Letty looked at her husband hopefully. With the departure of Mrs. Pollifax, and the rest of the staff in their outlying cottages on the estate, the two of them were now completely alone in the house. The room felt snug and warm with her afghan blanket, the crackling fire and Darius's closeness as outside the cold November wind blew, rattling the leaded glass windows.

She was getting close to her due date, and happier than she'd ever imagined.

The nursery was ready. She'd been overjoyed to discover that her great-grandmother's precious fresco hadn't been completely destroyed. A well-known art restorer had managed to bring a good portion of it back to life. The ducks and geese were far fewer in number, and the Bavarian village mostly gone, but the little goose girl no longer looked so sad. It was a joy to see it again, and though Darius pretended to mock it and roll his eyes as he called it "art," she knew he was happy for her.

The nursery was the most beautiful room in the house, in Letty's opinion, the place where she'd slept as a baby, as had her mother and her grandfather before. It was now freshly painted and decorated, with a crib and rocking chair and brand-new toys. All they needed was the baby.

"Soon," she whispered aloud, rubbing her enormous belly. "Very soon."

"Talking to the baby again?" Darius teased.

Holding up a tattered copy of a beloved children's book, she responded archly, "I'm just going to read him this story."

His dark eyebrows lifted. "Again?"

"The pregnancy book said…"

"Oh, have you read a pregnancy book?"

Letty's lips quirked. Her constant consultation of pregnancy books and blogs was a running joke between them. But as a first-time mother and an only child, she had little experience with children and was anxious to do it right.

"It's been scientifically proven," she informed him now, "that a baby can hear, and therefore obviously listen to stories, from the womb."

He rolled his eyes, then put his large hand tenderly on her belly. "Don't worry, kid," he said in a whisper. "I have something to read you that I know you'll find way more interesting than the bunny story."

"Oh, you do, do you?" she said, amused.

"Absolutely." Turning back to his laptop, he clicked a few buttons and then started reading aloud, with mock seriousness, the latest business news from overseas.

Now she was the one to roll her eyes. But she found Darius's low, deep voice soothing, even when he was describing boring tech developments. Sipping orange spice herbal tea, she nibbled on the sugar cookies she'd made earlier that afternoon. She'd been eating so much lately she felt nearly as big as a house herself.

But Darius didn't seem to mind. Her cheeks grew hot as she recalled how he'd made love to her all over the house. Even the bathrooms—those with showers, at least. Almost forty rooms.

"We have to make this house ours," he'd growled, and she'd loved it.

Now as she felt his gentle hand resting on her belly, she grew drowsy listening to his low voice reading news stories to their baby and punctuating them with exclamations when he felt the baby kick.

"Letty," Darius said in a low voice, "are you awake?"

"Barely." She yawned. "I was just going to head up to bed. Why?"

He was quiet for a long moment, then said quietly, "Never mind. It'll wait. Good night, *agape mou*."

The next morning, she kissed Darius goodbye as he left for lower Manhattan, as was his usual schedule Monday through Thursday. He'd set up an office for a new business he was excited about, to create software that would teach math and coding skills. Each day, Darius hired more employees, paying for their salaries out of his own pocket. There hadn't been any profits. "And there might never be any," he'd confessed sheepishly. But he wanted to make a difference in the world.

She'd never been so proud of him. He had a new spark in his eyes as he left Fairholme for his ninety-minute commute to the office.

Letty went up to the nursery, her favorite room, to fold all the cute tiny baby clothes one more time and make sure everything was ready. She'd had a dull ache in her lower back all morning. She went down to the kitchen, intending to ask Mrs. Pollifax if she knew of any natural remedy for back pain.

Instead she found the housekeeper crying.

"What's wrong?" Letty cried, going up to her in the enormous, gleaming kitchen. "What's happened?"

"My friend." The woman wiped her eyes with the edge of her apron. "He's dying."

"I'm so sorry," Letty whispered.

Mrs. Pollifax's eyes looked at her accusingly. "You should be. Since it's your own father."

Letty stared at her in shock. For a long minute, she couldn't even make sense of the words.

"I'm sorry—I can't be silent any longer," the housekeeper said. "Whatever caused you to be estranged from him, you're wrong to let him die alone. You'll regret it the rest of your life!"

"My father...?" Letty said slowly. "Is dying?"

Mrs. Pollifax's expression changed. "You didn't know?"

Shocked, she shook her head. "There must…must be some mistake. My father's not sick. He's fine. He's living without a care in the world…going to the park every day to play chess…"

"Oh, my dear." Coming closer, the housekeeper gently put her hand on Letty's shoulder. "I'm sorry. I judged you wrongly. I thought you knew. He collapsed a few weeks ago and has been in the hospital ever since. When I visited him yesterday, he didn't look well. He might have only weeks left. Days."

A loud rushing sound went through Letty's ears.

"No," she said numbly. "It has to be a mistake."

"I'm so sorry."

"You're wrong." Shaking off the housekeeper's hand, Letty reached for her phone. She dialed Darius's number first. When it went to voice mail, she hung up.

She took a deep breath. Her hands shook as she deliberately broke her vow to her husband for the first time. Her father had always hated cell phones, disparaging them as "tracking devices," so she called him at their old apartment number.

That, too, went to voice mail. But it was no longer Letty's voice on the phone greeting. Her father had replaced it with his own. For the first time in two months, she heard his recorded voice, and it sounded different. Fragile. Weak.

Terror rushed through her.

Her body was shaking as she looked up at Mrs. Pollifax. "Which hospital?"

The housekeeper told her. "But you're in no fit state to drive. I'll have Collins bring around the car. Shall I come with you?"

Letty shook her head numbly.

The older woman bit her lip, looking sad. "He's in room 302."

The drive to Brooklyn seemed to take forever. When they finally arrived at the large, modern hospital, Letty's body shook as she raced inside.

She didn't stop at reception, just hurried to the elevator, holding her heavy, aching belly. On the third floor, she followed the signs toward room 302.

Her steps slowed when she saw a man sitting in the waiting area. He looked up and saw her, too. She frowned. She recognized him from somewhere…

But she didn't stop, just headed straight for her father's room.

"Miss!" a nurse called anxiously as she passed the third-floor reception desk, barreling toward the corner room. "Please wait just a moment."

"It's all right," Letty said. "I'm his daughter." She pushed open the door. "Dad. Dad! I'm—"

But the room was empty.

Letty stared around in shock. Was she in the wrong room? Had she misunderstood?

Was he—oh, God—surely he couldn't be…?

"I'm sorry," a woman said behind her.

"You should be!" her father's gruff voice retorted.

With a sob, Letty whirled around.

In the doorway her living, breathing father was sitting in a wheelchair, glaring back at the dark-haired nurse struggling to push him through the doorway.

"You practically ran me into a wall. Where'd you learn how to drive?"

Letty burst into noisy tears. Her father turned his head and saw her, and his gaunt, pale features lit up with joy.

"Letty. You came."

Throwing her arms around his thin frame in the wheelchair, she choked out, "Of course I came. As soon as I heard you were sick. Then when I didn't see you in the bed, I thought…"

"Oh, you thought I was dead? No!" Glancing back at the nurse, he added drily, "Not for *some* people's lack of trying."

"Hmph." The nurse sniffed. "That's the last time I agree to help you win a wheelchair race, Howard."

"Win! We didn't win anything! Margery crushed us by a full ten seconds, in spite of her extra pounds. After all my big talk, too—I'll never live this down," he complained.

Letty drew back with astonishment. "Wheelchair race?"

"Admittedly not one of my best ideas, especially with Nurse Crashy here."

"Hey!"

"But it's what passes for fun here in the hospice wing. Either that or depress myself with cable news."

"It's totally against hospital protocol. I can't believe you talked me into it. Ask someone else to risk their job next time," the nurse said.

He gave her his old charming grin. "The race was a good thing. It lifted the spirits of everyone on the wing."

Looking slightly mollified, she sighed. "I guess I'd better go try convince my boss of that." She left the room.

Her father turned back to Letty. "But why are you crying? You really thought I was dead?"

She tried to smile. "You're crying, too, Dad."

"Am I?" Her father touched his face. He gave her a watery smile. "I'm just glad to see you, I guess. I was starting to wonder if you'd ever come."

"I came the instant I heard," she whispered, feeling awful and guilty.

Howard gave a satisfied nod. "I knew he'd eventually tell you."

"Who?"

"Darius. Sure, I promised I'd never contact you. But there was nothing in our deal that said I couldn't contact *him*. I left him a message four weeks ago, when I woke up in the hospital. I'd collapsed in the street, so an ambulance brought me here."

Four weeks? Letty was numb with shock. Darius had known for a *month* that her father was in the hospital, just an hour away from Fairholme?

Her father stroked his wispy chin. "Though I'm pretty sure he knew even before that. He's had me followed since the day you ran off with him. The guy must have noticed me going to my doctor's office three times a week."

She sucked in her breath, covering her mouth. Not just one month, but two? Darius had known her father was sick, dying, but he'd purposefully kept it from her?

Your father is spending his days playing chess with friends down at the park.

A lie!

Last night, when she and Darius had been cuddled by the fire, dreaming about their child, even then, her husband had been lying to her. While Letty had been eating cookies and drinking tea, her father had been spending yet another night in this hospital. Alone. Without a single word of love from his only daughter.

A cold sweat broke out on her skin. She trembled as if to fight someone or flee. But there was no escaping the horrible truth.

Darius had lied to her.

The man she'd loved since childhood. The center of all her romantic dreams and longings. He'd known her father was dying, and he'd lied.

How could Darius have been so callous? So selfish, heartless and cruel?

The answer was obvious.

He didn't love her.

He never would.

A gasp of anguish and rage came from the back of her throat.

"He never gave you the message, did he?" her father said, watching her. When she shook her head, he sighed. "How did you know I was here?"

"Mrs. Pollifax."

"I see." He looked sad. Then his eyes fell to her belly and he brightened as he changed the subject. "You're so big! You're just a week or two from your due date, aren't you?"

"Yes."

"I've almost made it." His voice was smug. "The doctors said I was a goner, but I told them I wasn't going anyplace yet."

Letty's body was still shaking with grief and fury. In the gray light of the hospital room, she turned toward the window. Outside, she saw November rain falling on the East River, and beyond it she could see the skyscrapers of Manhattan. Where Darius was right now.

Howard said dreamily behind her, "I was determined to see my grandbaby before I died."

She whirled back to her father. "Stop talking about dying!"

His gaunt face sagged. "I'm sorry, Letty. I really am."

"Isn't there any hope?" Her voice cracked. "An operation? A—a second opinion?"

Her father's eyes were kind. He shook his head. "I knew I was dying before I left prison."

She staggered back. "Why didn't you tell me?"

He rubbed his watery eyes. "I should have, I guess. But I didn't want you to worry and take all the stress on yourself like you always do. I wanted, for once, to take care of you. I wanted to repair the harm I did so long ago and get you back where you deserved to be. Married to your true love."

True love, Letty thought bitterly. Her stomach churned every time she thought of Darius lying to her all this time. The unfeeling bastard.

"It was my only goal," her father said. "To make sure

you'd be looked after and loved after I was gone. Now you and Darius are married, expecting a baby." He grinned with his old verve and said proudly, "Getting my arm broken by that thug was the best thing that ever happened to me, since it helped me bring you back together. I can die at peace. A happy man."

"Darius never told me you were sick," she choked out, her throat aching with pain. "I'll never forgive him."

Her father's expression changed. "Don't blame Darius. After all my self-made disasters, it just shows his good sense. Shows me he'll protect you better than I ever did." He looked up from the wheelchair. "Thank you, Letty."

She felt like the worst daughter in the world. "For what?"

"For always believing in me," he said softly, "even when you had no reason to. For loving me through everything."

She looked at her dying father through her tears. Then looked around the hospital room at the plain bed, the tile floor, the antiseptic feel, the ugly medical equipment. She couldn't bear to think of him spending his last days here, whiling away his hours with wheelchair races.

Her eyes narrowed. "Do you really need to be in the hospital?"

Howard shrugged. "I could have gone to full hospice. Other than pain meds, there's not much the doctors can do for me."

Her belly tightened with a contraction that felt like nothing compared to the agony of her heart. She lifted her chin. "Then you're coming home with me."

Howard looked at her in disbelief. "Back to that apartment? No, thanks. At least the hospital isn't cold all the time and someone brings me meals…"

"Not the apartment. I'm taking you to Fairholme."

His eyes looked dazzled.

"Fairholme?" he breathed. She saw the joy in his

wrinkled face. Then he blinked, looking troubled. "But Darius—"

"I'll handle him." Wrapping her arms around her father's thin shoulders, she kissed the wispy top of his head. Her father's last days would be happy ones, she vowed. He would die in the home that he'd adored, where he'd once lived with his beloved wife and raised his child, surrounded by comfort and love.

Letty would take care of him as he'd once taken care of her.

And, she thought grimly, she'd also take care of Darius.

She'd loved her husband with all her heart. Now she saw that all the sacrifices she'd made, all of her trust, had been for nothing. For an illusion. Darius didn't love her. He would never love her.

It was his final betrayal. And for this, she would never forgive him.

Darius walked into his office near Battery Park with a smile on his face and a spring in his step. He was late but had an excellent reason. He'd stopped at his favorite jeweler's on Fifth Avenue to buy a push present for his wife.

He'd read about push presents in a parenthood article. It was a gift that men gave the mothers of their children after labor and delivery, in celebration and appreciation of all their hours of pain and hard work. Since Letty's due date was so close, Darius had known he had no time to lose. He'd found the perfect gift—exquisite emerald earrings, surrounded by diamonds, set in gold, almost as beautiful as her hazel eyes. They'd even once belonged to a queen of France. With Letty's love of history, he knew she'd get a kick out of that, and he could hardly wait to give them to her. And even more amazing: when he did, their son would be real at last, and in their arms.

Darius realized he was whistling the same hokey lullaby that his wife had sung in the shower that morning to their unborn baby.

He loved Letty's voice.

He loved their home.

And he loved that he'd been able to blow off half a morning of work in order to get her a gift. It was supposedly one of the perks of being a boss, but at his last company, he'd been too grimly driven to do anything but grind out work. So he could build his fortune. So he could be worth something.

But even after he'd succeeded, even when he'd finally been rich beyond imagination, he'd been unhappy. He realized that now. He'd spent ten years doing nothing but work, and when he'd sold his company he'd felt lost. Money hadn't fulfilled him quite as much as he'd thought it would.

But now, everything had changed. Both in his work and his life.

He was building a new company. A free website would teach software coding, math and science skills, so others could have the opportunities he'd had, to get good jobs or perhaps even start their own tech companies someday.

His goal wasn't to build a fortune. He already had more than he could spend in a lifetime. When he'd paid out billions of dollars to Howard Spencer's victims, he hadn't even missed it.

Letty was teaching him—reminding him?—how a good life was lived.

Throughout their marriage, as Fairholme had every day become more beautiful, so had his pregnant wife. She was huge now, and she glowed. Every day she told him how much she loved him. He could feel it, her love for him, warming him like a fire in winter.

There was only one flaw.

One secret he was keeping.

And he knew it might ruin everything.

Darius's steps slowed as he crossed through the open office with the exposed brick walls.

Letty's father was dying. And Darius didn't know how to tell her.

He hadn't wanted to believe it was true at first. For weeks, he'd insisted it was all an elaborate con. "Call me when he's dead," he'd told his investigator half-seriously.

Then he'd gotten a message from Howard Spencer himself, saying he was in the hospital. Even then, for a few days, Darius had told himself it was a lie. Until his investigator had combed through the hospital records and confirmed it was true. Darius had no choice but to face it.

Now he had to tell Letty.

But how? How could he explain to her all his weeks of silence, when he'd known her father was dying in a Brooklyn hospital?

Darius still believed he'd done the right thing. He and Letty had made a deal at the start of their marriage: no contact with her father. There hadn't been any fine print or "get out of jail free" card if the man decided to die. All Darius had done was uphold their deal. He had nothing to feel guilty about. He hadn't just paid Spencer's debts, but also his living expenses and even his medical bills. He'd practically acted like a saint.

Somehow, he didn't think Letty would see it that way.

Darius dreaded her reaction. He'd halfheartedly started to tell her last night, but stopped, telling himself he didn't want to risk raising her blood pressure when she was so close to delivery. He didn't want to risk her health, or the baby's.

After the baby's born, he promised himself firmly. Once he knew both mother and baby were safe and sound.

She would be angry at first, he knew. But after she'd had some time to think it over, she'd realize that he'd only been trying to protect her. And it was in her nature to forgive. She had no choice. She loved him.

Feeling calmer, he walked past his executive assistant's desk toward his private office. "Good morning, Mildred."

Lifting her eyebrows, she greeted him with "Your wife is on the line."

"My wife?" A smile lifted unbidden to his face, as it always did when he thought of Letty.

"She said you weren't answering your cell."

Instinctively, Darius put his hand to his trouser pocket. It was empty. He must have left it in the car.

"Mrs. Kyrillos sounds pretty stressed." His executive assistant, usually stern and no-nonsense, gave him a rare smile. "She said it's urgent."

Letty never called him at work. His smile changed to a dazed grin. There could be only one reason she'd call now, so close to her due date!

"I'll take it in my office," he said joyfully and rushed inside, shutting the door behind him. He snatched up the phone. "Letty? Is it the baby? Are you in labor?"

His wife's voice sounded strangely flat. "No."

"Mildred said it was urgent—"

"It is urgent. I'm leaving you. I'm filing for divorce."

For a long moment he just gripped the phone, that foolish grin still on his face, as he tried to comprehend her words. Then the smile fell away.

"What are you talking about? Is this some kind of joke?"

"No."

He took a deep breath. "I've read about pregnancy hormones…"

Anger suddenly swelled from the other end of the line.

"Pregnancy hormones? *Pregnancy hormones?* I'm divorcing you because you lied to me. You've been lying for months! My father is dying and you never told me!"

Darius's heart was suddenly in his throat.

"How did you find out?" he whispered.

"Mrs. Pollifax couldn't understand how I could be such a heartless daughter to just let my father die alone. Don't worry. I've let her know that the heartless one is you."

He looked up, past his desk to the window overlooking the southern tip of Manhattan, and the Atlantic beyond it. Outside, rain fell in the gray November morning.

He licked his lips and tried, "Letty, I don't blame you for being upset—"

"Upset? No. I'm not upset." She paused. "I'm happy."

That was so obviously not true he had no idea how to react. "If you'll just give me a chance to explain."

"You already explained to me, long ago, that you wouldn't love me. That love was for children. You told me. I just didn't listen," she said softly. "Now I really, truly get it. And I want you out of my life for good."

"No—"

"I've brought my father to Fairholme."

Gripping the phone, he nearly staggered back. "Howard Spencer—in my house?"

"Yes." Her voice was ice-cold. "I'm not leaving him in the hospital, surrounded by strangers. He's going to spend his last days surrounded by love, in the home where he was married to my mother."

"It's not just your decision. I bought that house and…" He stopped himself, realizing how pompous he sounded. But it was too late.

"Right." Her voice was a sneer. "Because money makes the man. You think you can buy your way through life. That's what you do, isn't it? Buy things. You bought my virginity, and ever since, you've kept buying me. With marriage. With money. You didn't realize it was never your money I wanted." Her voice suddenly broke to a whisper. "It was you, Darius. My dream of you. The amazing boy you were." She took a breath. "The man I actually thought you still were, deep down inside."

"I'm still that man," he said tightly. "I was going to tell you. I just didn't want you upset…"

"Upset by my father dying!"

Darius flinched at the derision in her voice. "Perhaps I made a bad decision, but I was trying to look after you."

"And you assumed I would forgive you."

He felt shaken. "Forgiveness is what you do."

She gave a hard laugh. "How convenient for you. Only the idiots who love you have to forgive. But since you never love anyone, you never have to worry about that. You're free to hurt whomever you please."

She didn't sound like his wife at all, the kindhearted woman who greeted him every day with kisses, who gave so much of herself and asked for very little in return.

Except for him to forgive her father, Darius realized. That was the one thing she'd actually asked for. And the one thing he'd refused, again and again.

He, who was never afraid of anything, felt the first stirrings of real fear. "If you'll just listen to me—"

"I've had suitcases boxed up for you. Collins is taking them to your penthouse in Midtown. Don't worry. I won't stay here forever. You can have Fairholme back after…" Her voice was suddenly unsteady. "After. I don't want anything from you in our divorce. The baby and I will be leaving New York."

"You can't be serious."

"Poppy Alexander lives in Los Angeles now. She offered me a job a while back. I told her no. Now I'm going to say yes."

"No."

"Try and stop me. Just try." He could hear the ragged gasp of her breath. "You called my dad a monster. You're the real monster, Darius. Because you know what it was like to have your father die alone. That was the reason for all your vengeance and rage, wasn't it? That was the big reason you wouldn't let me see my dad. Well, you know what? My dad nearly died alone, too. Because of you."

The pang of fear became sharper, piercing down his spine. He licked his lips. "Letty—"

"Stay away from us," she said in a low voice. "I never want to see you again. Better that our son has no father at all than a heartless one like you."

The line went dead. He stared down at the phone in his hand.

Numb with shock, Darius raised his head. He looked blankly around his office, still decorated with his wife's sweet touches. A photo of them on their Greek honeymoon. A sonogram picture of their baby. He stared in bewilderment at the bright blue jeweler's bag on his desk. The push present for his wife, the emerald earrings once owned by a queen that he'd bought to express his appreciation and joy.

Above him, he could hear the rain falling heavily against the roof. Loud. Like a child's rattle.

And felt totally alone.

He'd known this would happen. Known if he ever lowered his guard and let himself care, he would get kicked in the teeth. Teeth? He felt like his guts had just been ripped out. For a second, he felt only that physical pain, like the flash of lightning before thunder.

Then the emotional impact reached his heart, and he had to lean one hand on his desk to keep his balance. The pain he felt then was almost more than he could bear.

Standing in his office, in the place he'd been happily whistling a lullaby just moments before, anguish and rage rushed through him. Throwing out his arm, he savagely knocked the jewelry bag to the ground.

Suddenly, he could almost understand why Howard Spencer had turned criminal when he'd lost his wife. Because Darius suddenly wanted to set fire to everything in his life, to burn it all down.

Slowly, as if he'd gained fifty years, he walked out of his office.

"Everything all right, sir?" Mildred Harrison said serenely from her desk. "Are you headed to the hospital for Mrs. Kyrillos?"

Mrs. Kyrillos. He almost laughed at the name. She'd never been his wife, not really. How could she, when she'd seen through him from the start?

You always said a man could be measured by his money.

He looked slowly around the bustling office loft, with its exposed brick walls, its high ceilings, the open spaces full of employees busily working on computers or taking their breaks at the foosball table. He said softly, "No."

His executive assistant frowned. "Sir?"

"I don't want it anymore." Darius looked at her. "Take the company. You can have it. I'm done."

And he left without looking back.

He spent the afternoon in one of Manhattan's old dive bars, trying to get drunk. He could have called Santiago Velazquez or Kassius Black, but they weren't exactly the kind of friends who shared confidences and feelings. Darius had only really done that with Letty. He told himself Scotch would keep him company now.

It didn't.

Finally he gave up. He was alone. He would always be alone. Time to accept it.

Dropped off by the taxi, Darius came home late that night to his dark penthouse. All the bright lights of Manhattan sparkled through the floor-to-ceiling windows. He saw nothing but darkness and shadows.

And three expensive suitcases left in his foyer. Suitcases Letty had packed for him when she'd taken his measure, found him completely lacking and tossed him out of their family home.

You think you can buy your way through life. That's what you do, isn't it? Buy things.

Slowly, Darius looked around the stark, impersonal penthouse at the sparse, expensive furniture. Everything was black and white. He'd bought this place two years ago, as a trophy to show how far he'd come from the poverty-stricken village boy he'd once been. A trophy to prove to himself that Letitia Spencer had made a fatal error the day she'd decided he wasn't good enough to marry.

This penthouse was not his home.

His home was Fairholme.

Darius closed his eyes, thinking of the windswept oceanfront manor with its wide windows over the Great South Bay and the Atlantic beyond. The roses, fields and beach. The sun-drenched meadow where he'd taught Letty to dance. Where he'd first learned to love.

Letty.

He opened his eyes with a slow intake of breath.

Letty was his home.

Even during their brief marriage, he'd experienced happiness he'd never known before. The comfort and love of having a wife who put him first, who waited for him every night, who kissed him with such passion. Who slept warm and willing beside him every night in bed.

More than that. She'd reminded him who he'd once been.

You didn't realize it was never your money I wanted. It was you, Darius. My dream of you. The amazing boy you were. The man I actually thought you still were, deep down inside.

Numbly, he looked out the two-story-high windows that overlooked the twinkling lights of the city.

Letty was always determined to protect those she loved.

Now she was trying to protect their child from him. Just as he'd once tried to protect Letty from her father.

You called my dad a monster. You're the real monster.

He leaned his forehead against the cold window glass.

Howard Spencer had been a good man once. He'd been a good employer to Darius's father and kind to everyone, including the scared eleven-year-old boy newly arrived from Greece. Then he'd changed after he'd lost his beloved wife.

What was Darius's excuse?

He took a deep breath, looking out bleakly into the night. Why had he been so determined to wreak vengeance on her father? So determined that he hadn't even cared how badly it might hurt Letty as collateral damage?

He should have told her the truth from the start.

He should have taken her in his arms. He should have fallen to his knees. He should have told her he was sorry, and that he'd do whatever it took to make it right.

Why hadn't he?

What the hell was wrong with him?

Darius had convinced himself he was justified for his actions, because he blamed Howard Spencer for his father's early, unhappy death.

Letty was right. He was a liar. And he'd lied to himself worst of all.

The truth was, deep in his heart, there had always been only one person Darius truly blamed for his father's death, and it had been too painful for him to face till now.

Himself.

He closed his eyes as a memory that he'd pushed away for over a decade pummeled him. But today, he could no longer resist the waves of guilt and shame as he remembered.

Eugenios had called Darius in the middle of the day.

"I've lost everything, son." His Greek father, usually so distant and gruff, had sounded lost, bewildered. "I just got a certified letter. It says all my life savings—everything I invested with Mr. Spencer—it's all gone."

Darius had been busy working in his first rented office, a windowless Manhattan basement. He'd only gotten three hours of sleep the night before. It was the first time the two men had talked in months, since Letty had dumped him and caused Eugenios to be fired and tossed from Fairholme. Just hearing his voice that day had reminded Darius of everything he was trying so hard to forget. A lifetime of resentment had exploded.

"I guess that pays you back for all your loyalty to Spencer, huh, Dad? All those years when you put him first, even over your own family."

Darius had been so young, so self-righteous. It made him feel sick now to remember it.

"That was my job." His father's voice had trembled. "I wanted to make sure I never lost a job again. Never felt again like I did that awful day we found you on the doorstep…"

The awful day they found him? Darius's hurt and anger blocked out the rest of his father's words as Eugenios continued feebly, "I had no money. No job. I couldn't let my family starve. You don't know what that does to a man, to have nothing…"

It was the most his father had ever spoken to him. And Darius's cold reply had haunted him ever since.

"So you had nothing then, huh, Dad? Well, guess what? You have nothing now. You ignored me my whole childhood for nothing. You have nothing. You *are* nothing."

He'd hung up the phone.

An hour later, his father had quietly died of a heart attack in his Queens apartment, sinking to his kitchen floor, where he was found later by a neighbor.

Darius's hands tightened to fists against the window.

His father had never been demonstrative. In Darius's

childhood, there had been no hugs and very little praise. Even the attention of criticism was rare.

But Darius and his grandmother hadn't starved. Eugenios had provided for them. He'd taught his work ethic by example. He'd worked hard, trying to give his son a better life.

And after all his years of stoically supporting them, after he'd lost his job and money, Darius had scorned him.

Remembering it now, he felt agonizing shame.

He hadn't wanted to remember the last words he'd spoken to his proud Greek father. So instead he'd sought vengeance on Howard Spencer, carefully blaming him alone.

Darius had thought if he never loved anyone, he'd never feel pain; and if he was rich, he'd be happy.

Look at me now, he thought bitterly, surveying the elegant penthouse. Surrounded by money. And never more alone.

He missed Letty.

Craved her desperately.

He loved her.

Darius looked up in shock.

He'd never stopped loving her.

All these years, he'd tried to pretend he didn't. Tried to control her, to possess her, to pretend he didn't care. He'd hidden his love away like a coward, afraid of the pain and shame of possible loss, while Letty let her love shine for all the world to see.

He'd thought Letty weak? He took a shuddering breath. She was the strongest person he knew. She'd offered him loyalty, kindness, self-sacrifice. She'd offered him every bit of her heart and soul. And in return, he'd offered her money.

Darius clawed back his hair. She was right. He'd tried to buy her. But money didn't make the man.

Love did.

Darius loved her. He was completely, wildly in love with

Letty. He wanted to be her husband. To live with her. To raise their baby. To be happy. To be home.

His eyes narrowed.

But how? How could he show her he had more to offer? How could he convince her to forgive him?

Forgiveness. His lips twisted with the bitter irony. The very thing he'd refused to give her all these months, he would now be begging for...

But for her, he'd do anything. He set his jaw. With the same total focus he'd built his empire, he would win back his wife.

Over the next month, he tried everything.

He respected her demand that he stay away from her, even after his friend Velazquez sent him a link to a birth announcement, and he saw his son had been safely born, weighing seven pounds and fourteen ounces. Both mother and baby were doing well.

Darius had jumped up, overwhelmed with the need to go see them in the hospital, to hold them in his arms.

But he knew bursting into her room against her express wishes would have only made things worse, not better. So he restrained himself, though it took all his self-control. He cleaned out a flower shop and sent all the flowers and toys and gifts to her maternity suite at the hospital. Anonymously.

Then he'd waited hopefully.

He'd found out later that she'd immediately forwarded all the flowers, toys and gifts straight to the sick children's ward.

Well played, he'd thought with a sigh. But he wasn't done. He'd contacted Mildred and she'd sent him via courier the jewelry bag he'd left in his office. He'd sent it to Fairholme, again anonymously.

A few days later he received a thank-you card from Mrs. Pollifax, stating that the earrings had been sold and the money donated to the housekeeper's favorite charity, an animal shelter on Long Island.

He'd ground his teeth, but doggedly kept trying. Over the next week, he sent gifts addressed to Letty. He sent a card congratulating her on the baby. On Thanksgiving, he even had ten pies from her favorite bakery delivered to her at Fairholme.

Pies she immediately forwarded to a homeless shelter.

As the rain of November changed to the snows of December, Darius's confidence started to wane. Once, in a moment of weakness, he drove by Fairholme late at night, past the closed gate.

But she was right. He couldn't even see the house.

After the pie incident, Darius gave up sending gifts. When she continued to refuse his calls, he stopped those, too. He kept writing heartfelt letters, and for a few weeks, he was hopeful, until they were all returned at once, unopened.

His baby son was now four weeks old. The thought made him sick with grief. Darius hadn't seen him. Hadn't held him. He didn't even know his name.

His wife wanted to divorce him. His son didn't have a father. Darius felt like a failure.

In the past, he would have taken his sense of grief and powerlessness and hired the most vicious, shark-infested law firm in Manhattan to punish her, to file for full custody.

But he didn't want that.

He wanted her.

He wanted his family back.

Finally, as Christmas approached, he knew he was out of ideas. He had only one card left to play. But when he went to see his lawyer, the man's jaw dropped.

"If you do this, Mr. Kyrillos, in my opinion you're a fool."

He was right. Darius was a fool. Because this was his last desperate hope.

But was he brave enough to actually go through with it? Could he jump off that cliff, and take a gamble that would either win him back the woman he loved, or cost him literally everything?

The afternoon of Christmas Eve Darius got the package from his lawyer. He was holding it in his hands, pacing his penthouse apartment like a trapped animal when his phone rang. Lifting it from his pocket, he saw the number from Fairholme.

His heart started thudding frantically. He snatched it up so fast he almost dropped it before he placed it against his ear. "Letty?"

But it wasn't his wife. Instead, the voice on the line belonged to the last person he'd ever imagined would call him.

CHAPTER ELEVEN

"IT's YOUR VERY first Christmas," Letty crooned to her tiny baby, walking him through Fairholme's great hall. She was already dressed for Christmas Eve dinner in a long scarlet velvet dress and soft kid leather bootees. She'd dressed her newborn son in an adorable little Santa outfit.

She'd asked Mrs. Pollifax to make all her father's holiday favorites, ham, plum pudding, potatoes, in hopes of tempting him to eat more than his usual scant bites. They'd even brought the dining table into the great hall, beside the big stone fireplace, so they could have dinner beneath the enormous Christmas tree.

Letty wanted this Christmas to be perfect. Because she knew it would be her father's last. The doctor had said yesterday that Howard's body was failing rapidly. It would likely be only days now.

Her heart twisted with grief. Her only comfort was that she'd tried her best to make his last few weeks special.

A lump rose in Letty's throat as she looked up at the two-story-high tree, decorated with sparkling lights and a mix of ornaments, old and new. Some of them Letty had treasured since childhood. And now they were back here, where they belonged. Funny to think she had Darius to thank for that. If he hadn't found her in Brooklyn and stopped her from taking that desperate bus ride out of the city, the ornaments would have been long lost to a junk dealer or the landfill.

Without him, she wouldn't be here now. Her father couldn't have come to Fairholme for his last Christmas, nor would her baby be here for his first one. It was because of Darius.

She missed him. No matter how much she denied it. No matter how she tried not to.

Every time some thoughtful gift had arrived at the house, she'd pictured how her father had looked in the hospital, so pale and alone. She'd remembered how Darius had taken her love for granted, and selfishly lied. She'd told herself she was done loving someone who could never love her back.

But as the gifts tapered off, and the phone calls stopped, and the letters stopped arriving in the mail, she hadn't felt triumphant. At all.

"I hate him," she said aloud. "I never want to see him again." She wasn't sure she sounded convincing, even to her own ears. So turning to her son, she held out one of the homemade ornaments. "Look!"

"Gah," the baby replied, waving his little hands unsteadily.

"You're so smart!" She let him feel the soft fabric of the dove against his cheek, then put it back on the tree before he tried to eat it. "Your grandma Constance made that," she said softly. "I just wish she could have met you."

Her six-week-old baby smiled back, Letty would swear he did, even though her father continued to rather annoyingly claim it was only gas. Letty knew her own baby, didn't she?

Even though Darius didn't.

The thought caused an unpleasant jolt. She'd thought she was doing the right thing to exclude him. She couldn't allow such a heartless man near her baby. Even if he *was* the father.

But Darius hadn't even laid eyes on their baby, or held him, or heard the sweet gurgle of his voice or his angry cry when he wasn't fed fast enough. Darius had already missed so much. Six weeks of sleepless nights, of exhaustion and confusion.

But also six weeks of getting to know this brand-new little person. From the moment her son had been placed in her arms at the hospital, Letty had felt her heart expand in a way she'd never known before.

Darius didn't know that feeling. He didn't know his son at all. Because of her actions.

Two weeks ago, her baby had been irritable and sleepless at midnight, so she'd wrapped him in a warm blanket and put him in the stroller to walk him up and down the long driveway, behind the gate. Then she'd seen a dark sports car driving slowly by.

Darius! She'd practically run to the gate, panting as she pushed the stroller ahead of her. But by the time she reached the gate, the car was long gone. For long moments she stared through the bars of the gate, looking bleakly down the dark, empty road, hearing only the waves crashing down on the shore. And she'd realized for the first time how empty the house felt without him, even with her father and her baby and all the household staff. She missed him.

No. I don't, she told herself desperately. And if she hadn't filed for divorce yet or hired an attorney, that was only because she just hadn't had the time. Taking care of a newborn, caring for her father and decorating for Christmas would be enough to keep anyone busy, wouldn't it?

Letty's lips twisted downward. She'd said things that would never be forgiven. She'd made her choice clear. She'd used his every olive branch as a stick to stab him with.

That car probably hadn't even been his. He'd probably moved on entirely, and if she ever heard from him again, it would be only via his lawyer, demanding custody. She stiffened at the thought.

Carrying her baby up to the nursery, she fed him, rocking him for nearly an hour in the glider until he slept and she was nearly asleep herself. She smiled down at his sweet little face. His cheeks were already growing chubby. Tucking him gently in his crib for his late afternoon nap, she turned on the baby monitor and crept out of the darkened nursery.

She closed the door softly behind her. Light from the leaded glass windows reflected against the glossy hardwood floors and oak paneling of the second-floor hallway, resting with a soft haze on an old framed family photo on the wall. She looked at her own chubby face when she'd been just a toddler with two parents beaming behind her.

Trying to ignore the ache in her throat, Letty started to turn toward the stairs. Then she heard low male voices coming from down the hall.

Her father's bedroom was the nicest and biggest, the room he'd once shared with her mother, with a view of the sea. He rarely got up from his bed anymore, except when Letty managed to cajole him into his wheelchair and take him down in the elevator for a stroll around the winter garden, or to sit in a comfortable spot near the fire, beneath the Christmas tree, as the baby lay nearby.

But the male voice Letty heard talking to her father didn't sound like Paul, his nurse. Who was it? Frowning, she drew closer.

"Yes," she heard her father say, his voice a little slurred. "Always a good kid."

"I can't believe you're saying that, after everything."

Hearing the visitor's voice, low and clear, Letty's knees went weak outside her father's door. What was Darius doing here? How had he gotten into Fairholme?

"You weren't so bad. Just prickly, like your father. Eugenios was the best employee I ever had. We used to talk about you. He loved you."

"He had a funny way of showing it." Her husband's voice wasn't bitter, just matter-of-fact.

Howard gave a laugh that ended in a wheeze. "In our generation, fathers showed love differently."

"Yet Letty always knew you loved her."

"I didn't grow up with your father's fears." Howard paused. "From the age of fifteen, he was your grandmother's sole support. When you came along, he lost any chance of a job in Greece."

"I know."

"His greatest fear was of not providing for you." Coughing a laugh, Howard added, "Maybe if I'd been a little more careful about that myself, I wouldn't have left my daughter destitute while I spent years in prison. It's only because of you that we're back home now. That's why I called. I'm grateful."

Darius's voice was suddenly urgent. "Then convince Letty to stay."

"Stay? Where would she go?"

"She says as soon as you're dead, she's leaving New York."

Howard gave a low laugh. "That sounds like her. Foolish as her old man. Can't see the love right in front of her eyes, has to flee her own happiness because she's afraid. Actually, now that I think about it, she sounds like you."

Letty's heart was pounding as she leaned against the oak-paneled wall beside the open door, holding absolutely still as she listened intently.

Silence. Then Darius said in a voice so low she almost couldn't hear, "I'm sorry I blamed you for my father's death all these years. The truth is, the person I really hated was myself. I said something terrible to my dad right before he died. I'll never forgive myself."

"Whatever it was," Howard said simply, "your father forgave you long ago. He knew you loved him. Just as he loved you. He was proud of you, Darius. And seeing that you were brave enough to come here today, I am, too."

Her father was proud of the man who'd treated her so

badly, who'd lied to her? Letty sucked in her breath with an astonished little squeak.

There was a pause.

"Letty," her father said drily, "I know you're there. Come in."

Her heart was in her throat. She wanted to flee but knew she'd only look foolish and cowardly. Lifting her chin, she went into her father's room.

His bedroom was full of light from the bay window. Her father was stretched out beneath the blankets, propped up by pillows, his nightstand covered with pill bottles. His gaunt face smiled up at her weakly, his eyes glowing with love.

Then, with a deep breath, Letty looked at the man standing beside the bed.

Tall and broad-shouldered and alive, Darius seemed to radiate power. For a moment, her eyes devoured his image. He was dressed simply in a dark shirt, dark jeans. His hands lifted, then fell to his sides as he looked at her, as if he had to physically restrain himself from touching her. But his dark eyes seared her. Their heartbreak and yearning cut her to the bone.

Her body reacted involuntarily, stumbling back as her heart pounded with emotion. Fury. Regret. Longing…

"What are you doing here?" she whispered.

"He's here to meet his son," her father said.

She whirled on her father, feeling betrayed. "Dad!"

"And I want him to stay for Christmas Eve dinner," he continued calmly.

She stared at him in shock. "No!"

Her father gave her a weakened version of his old charming smile. "Surely you wouldn't refuse your dying father his last Christmas wish?"

No. Of course she couldn't. She ground her teeth. "He kept me from you for two months!"

Her father stared her down. "Only a little longer than you've kept him from his son."

"I would like to meet him," Darius said quietly. "But if you don't want me around after that, I won't stay."

Trembling, she tossed her head defiantly. "Did he tell you the baby's name?"

"No."

"It's Howard." She lifted her chin, folding her arms. "Howard Eugenios Spencer."

To her shock, Darius didn't scowl or bluster. He didn't even flinch. He just looked at her with that same strange glow of longing in his eyes.

"That's not the name I would have chosen." Triumph surged through her as she waited for him to be sarcastic and show his true colors in front of her father. Instead, he just said quietly, "His last name should be Kyrillos."

Darius was upset only about the surname? Not about the fact that she'd named their precious baby son after her father—his hated enemy?

"Aren't you furious?" she said, dropping her arms in bewilderment.

His lips curved as he looked down at her father, then slowly shook his head. "Not as much as I used to be."

Darius came toward her. It took all Letty's willpower not to step back from him as he towered over her. It wasn't him she was afraid of, but herself. Her whole body was trembling with her own longing. Her need. She missed him.

But she couldn't. She'd made her choice! She wouldn't be married to a man who didn't love her!

"Please let me see my son," he said humbly. He bowed his head, as if waiting for her verdict.

"Let him," her father said.

Looking between the two men, she knew she was outnumbered. She snapped, "Fine."

Turning on her heel, she walked out. She didn't look

back to see if Darius was following her. Her hands were trembling.

All these weeks when she'd pushed him away, she'd pictured him as angry, arrogant, heartless. It was why she hadn't been tempted to open his letters—why would she, when she knew he'd only be yelling at her?

She'd never once imagined Darius looking at her the way he did now, with such heartbreaking need. But it wasn't just desire. He had an expression in his eyes that she hadn't seen since—

No! She wasn't going to let her own longing talk her into seeing things in his eyes that weren't there, things that didn't exist.

Pressing a finger to her lips, she quietly pushed open the nursery door and crept into the shadowy room, motioning for him to follow. Darius came in behind her.

Then, as they both stood over the crib, Letty made the mistake of looking at her husband when he saw their son for the very first time.

Darius's dark eyes turned fierce, almost bewildered with love when he looked at their sleeping baby. Tenderly, he reached out in the semidarkness and stroked his dark downy head as he slept.

"My son," he whispered. "My sweet boy."

A lump rose in her throat so huge it almost choked her. And she suddenly knew that Darius wasn't the only one who'd been heartless.

What had she done?

Blinded by furious grief at his lie about her father, Letty had actually kept Darius from his own firstborn son. *For six weeks.*

Anguish and regret rushed through her in a torrent of pain. Even if Darius could never love her, she had no doubt that he loved their baby. Especially as she watched him now, gently stroking their baby's small back through his

Santa onesie as the sleeping child gave a soft snuffle in the shadowy room.

She'd had no right to steal his child away.

"I'm sorry," she choked out. He looked up.

"You're sorry?"

Unable to speak for misery, she nodded.

Reaching out in the shadowy nursery, beneath the hazy colors of the goose girl fresco, Darius put his hand gently on Letty's shoulder, and she shuddered beneath his touch.

"Letty…there's something you should know."

Their eyes locked, and she saw something in his black eyes that made the world tremble beneath her feet.

Panic rushed through her heart. Seeing Darius make peace with her father, seeing him look so lovingly at their baby, had cracked open her soul and everything she hadn't wanted to feel had rushed in.

She'd painted him so badly in her mind. She'd called him a monster. And yes, he never should have lied about her father.

But when she'd said horrible things and threatened to take his child permanently away, he hadn't hired some awful lawyer to fight her. He'd done what she asked, and stayed away. Obviously at great emotional cost.

Now, she saw his sensual lips part, heard his hoarse intake of breath and knew whatever he was about to say would change her life forever. He was going to tell her he was done with her. She'd won. He'd given up. Now he wanted to talk like reasonable adults about sharing custody of their son.

She'd destroyed their marriage with her anger and pride. She'd told herself she'd rather be alone than married to a man who didn't love her. Now she suddenly couldn't bear to hear him speak the words that would end it…

"No," she choked out.

Turning, she fled the nursery. She ran down the hall, down the stairs, her heart pounding, gasping for breath.

She heard him coming down after her. "Letty!"

She didn't stop. Pushing off the stairs, she ran outside, into the snow.

Her mother's rose garden was barren in winter, nothing but thorny vines and dead leaves covered in a blanket of white. Letty's soft black boots stumbled forward, her long red dress dragging behind, scarlet against the snow.

But he swiftly caught her, roughly pushing her wrists against the outside wall of the greenhouse with its flash of exotic greenery behind the steamy glass. She struggled, but he wouldn't let go.

She felt his heat. His power. She felt the strength of her own longing for this man, whom she continued to love in the face of despair.

"Let me go," she cried.

"Forgive me," Darius choked out. He lowered his head against hers. She heard the heavy gasp of his breath. "You were right, Letty. About everything. I'm so sorry."

Her lips parted. She looked up at him in shock.

"*You're* sorry?" she whispered. "I kept you from our baby."

"You were right to kick me out of your life." He cupped her face in both his hands. "I blamed you and your father for so much. I blamed everyone but the person really at fault. Myself."

"Darius—"

"No." He held up his hand. "Let me say this. I don't know if I'll get another chance."

All around them in the silent white garden, soft snow began to fall from the lowering gray clouds. Letty's heart was suddenly in her throat. Now he was going to tell her that they were better off apart...

"You're right, Letty," he said in a low voice. "I did try

to buy you. I thought money was all I had to offer anyone. I thought I could selfishly claim your love, while being cowardly enough to protect my own heart. But I failed." He gave a low laugh. "The truth is, I failed long ago."

His dark eyes had a suspicious gleam. Surely Darius Kyrillos, the ruthless Greek billionaire, couldn't have tears in his eyes? No. It must be the cold winter wind, whipping against his skin.

"I loved you, Letty. It terrified me. My whole life, all I've ever known of love is loss. Losing you all those years ago almost destroyed me. I never wanted to feel like that again. So I buried my soul in ice. Then when I saw you again, when I first took you to my bed, everything changed. Against my will, the ice cracked. But even then I was afraid." Taking a deep breath, he lifted his eyes to hers. "I'm not afraid anymore."

"You're not?" she whispered, her heart falling.

With a little smile, he shook his head. He took her hand in his larger one. "Now I know the truth is that love never ends. Not real love. The love your father has for you and my father had for me. The love your parents had for each other." His hand tightened over hers as he said softly, "And even if you divorce me, Letty, even if you never want to see me again after tonight, I can still love you. And it won't bring me pain, but joy, because of everything you've brought to my life. You saved me. Made me feel again. Taught me to love again. Gave me a son." Stroking her cheek, he whispered, "No matter what happens, I will always be grateful. And love you."

His hand was warm over hers. With him so close, she didn't even feel the snow. Trembling, she whispered, "Darius…what are you saying?"

His jaw tightened. "If you still want to divorce me, you won't need a lawyer." He reached into his shirt pocket, where a single page was folded in quarters. "Here."

Opening the paper, she looked down at it numbly. She tried to read it, but the words jumbled together. "What's this?"

"Everything," he said quietly. "Fairholme. The jets. My stocks, bonds, bank accounts. It's all been transferred to your name. Everything I possess."

She gasped, then shook her head. "But you know money doesn't mean anything to me!"

"Yes, I know that." He looked at her. "But you know what it means to me."

Letty's eyes went wide.

Because she did know what Darius's fortune meant to him. It meant ten years of twenty-hour workdays and sleeping in basements. It meant working till he collapsed, day after day, with no time to relax or see friends. No time to even *have* friends. It meant borrowing money that he knew he'd have to pay back, even if his business failed. It meant taking terrifying risks and praying they would somehow pay off.

Those dreams had been fulfilled. Through work and will and luck, a poverty-stricken boy whose mother had abandoned him as a baby had built a multibillion-dollar empire.

This was what she now held in her hand.

"But I'm not just offering you my fortune, Letty," he said quietly. "I'm offering everything. My whole life. Everything I've been. Everything I am." Lifting her hand, he pressed it against his rough cheek and whispered, "I offer you my heart."

Letty realized she was crying.

"I love you, Letitia Spencer Kyrillos," he said hoarsely. "I know I've lost your love, your trust. But I'll do everything I can to regain your devotion. Even if it takes me a hundred years, I'll never…"

"Stop." Violently, she pushed the paper against his chest. When he wouldn't take it, it fell to the snow.

"Letty," he choked out, his dark eyes filled with misery.

"I don't want it." She lifted her hand to his scratchy cheek, rough and unshaven. Reaching her other arm around his shoulders, she whispered, "I just want you, Darius."

The joy that lit up his dark eyes was brighter than the sun.

"I don't deserve you."

"I'm not exactly perfect myself."

He immediately began protesting that she was, in fact, perfect in every way.

"It doesn't matter." Smiling, she reached up on her toes to kiss him, whispering, "We can just love each other, flaws and all."

Holding her tight, he kissed her passionately against the greenhouse, with the hot wet jungle behind the glass, as they embraced in the snow-swept bare garden. They kissed each other in a private vow that would endure all the future days of sunshine and snow, good times and bad, all the laughter and anger and pleasure and forgiveness until death.

Their love was meant to be. It was fate. *Moira.*

They clung to each other until he broke apart with a guilty laugh.

"Ah, Letty, I'll never be perfect, that's for sure," Darius murmured, smiling down at her through his tears. "But there's one thing you should know…" Cupping her cheek, lightly drawing away the cold wet tendrils of her hair that had stuck to her skin, he whispered, "For you, I intend to spend the rest of my life trying."

Spring came early to Fairholme.

Darius had a bounce in his step as he came into the house that afternoon with a bouquet of flowers. He'd had to work on a Saturday because it was crunch time developing the new website. But he was hoping the flowers would make her forgive the fact that he'd missed their new Saturday morning family tradition of waffles and bacon.

Darius had started that tradition himself, in the weeks he'd taken to focus only on Letty and their beloved son, whom they'd nicknamed Howie. After that, encouraged by Letty, he'd sheepishly called Mildred and apologized, then asked if there was any way she could try to reassemble his team at the office.

"The office is still in fine fettle," she'd replied crisply. "I've been running everything just as you requested. I knew whatever you were going through you'd soon come to your senses. I haven't worked for you all these years for nothing."

He choked out a laugh, then said with real gratitude, "What would I do without you?"

"You'll find out next summer," she'd said firmly, "when you send my husband and me on a four-week first-class cruise through Asia. It's already booked."

Darius grinned to himself, remembering. He was grateful to Mildred. Grateful to all the people around him, his employees and most of all his family, who saw through all his flaws but were somehow willing to put up with him anyway.

Money didn't make the man. He knew that now. What made a man was what he did with his life. With his time. With his heart.

His father-in-law had died in January, surrounded by family, with a smile on his drawn face. Right before he died, his eyes suddenly glowed with joy as he breathed, "Oh. There you are…"

"He saw my mother before he died," Letty told Darius afterward, her beautiful face sparkling with tears. "How can I even be sad, when I know they're together?"

Darius wasn't so sure, but who was he to say? Love could work miracles. He was living proof of that.

Now he looked around his home with deep contentment. The oak floors gleamed and fresh-cut flowers from the greenhouse filled all the vases.

Fairholme was about to be invaded by more of the Kyrillos family. He'd sent his private plane to Heraklios, and tomorrow, Theia Ioanna, along with a few cousins, would arrive for a monthlong visit. His great-aunt's desire to meet her great-great-nephew had finally overcome her fear of flying.

He relished the thought of having his extended family here. Heaven knew Fairholme had plenty of room.

Love was everywhere. Love was everything. His son was only five months old, but he'd already collected toys from all the people who loved him around the globe. His wife did that, he thought. With her great heart, she brought everyone together with her kindness and loyalty. She was the center of Darius's world.

"Letty!" he called, holding the flowers tightly.

"She's outside, Mr. Kyrillos," the housekeeper called from the kitchen. "The weather's so fine, she and the baby went for a picnic in the meadow."

Dropping his computer bag, he went outside, past the garden, where even though the air was cool beneath the sunshine, tulips and daffodils were starting to bloom. He walked the path through the softly waving grass until he reached the meadow where he'd first taught his wife to dance. Where she'd first taught him to dream.

He stopped.

The sky was a vivid blue, the meadow the rich gold-green of spring, and in the distance, he could see the ocean. He saw Letty's beautiful face, alight with joy, as she sang their five-month-old baby a song in Greek, swinging him gently in her arms as he giggled and shrieked with happiness. Behind them on the hillside, a blanket was covered with a picnic basket, teething toys and that well-worn book about the bunny rabbit. But now, as always, Letty was dancing. Letty was singing.

Letty was love.

Darius stared at them, and for a moment the image caught at his heart, as he wondered what he'd ever done to deserve such happiness.

Then, quickening his steps, he raced to join them.

* * * * *

CLAIMED FOR
HIS DUTY

TARA PAMMI

CHAPTER ONE

LEAH HUNTINGTON COLLAPSED onto the plastic chair behind her small desk, her knees buckling out from under her. The red stamp spelling out "REJECTED" on the application form blurred in front of her eyes. Her heart squeezed painfully as she fingered the flat sketches on her drawing board, the possibility of seeing her creation take form now evaporating like a puff of smoke.

Sweat ran down her back, the slow whir of the ceiling fan scraping against her nerves. She ran cramped up fingers over her neck, feeling the muscles tighten with tension.

Mrs. DuPont, the buying manager for a retail store, had given Leah only two months to create her first collection and all Leah had now were flat sketches. And as she had to do everything herself instead of contacting a factory like she did for the fashion house, every minute was important.

The most important of it being the funds she required to source raw materials… There were a hundred things she needed and it was all sitting in that bank.

She dialed the number for the bank manager she had spoken to just two days ago.

Her heart hammered painfully, thudding faster and faster, an ominous pounding she couldn't breathe past. There could be only one man behind this. Her stomach twisted as the bank manager coughed on the other end of the phone. His answer was curt, immediate as though he had been rehearsing the explanation, waiting for Leah to call.

They couldn't use the trust fund as security to approve her loan because—Leah could hear the hushed reverence in the manager's voice as he uttered the name—the trustee overseeing her fund had denied the use of the trust fund, *her trust fund*, as security.

Stavros.

Leah threw the handset across the room, every inch of her shaking. She kicked the chair aside, the impact of it jarring up her leg, every nerve cell in her humming with outrage.

How much more was he going to punish her? How long was she going to let him?

She picked up the phone again, her vision blurry now with unchecked tears. Her throat burned as she took a deep breath, her thumb hovering over the numbers on the handset.

She wanted to demand an explanation, she wanted to...

But what was the point? His secretary would politely tell her that he was not available. It was the same answer she had received over the last year every time she had tried to contact him. Even though they both lived in Athens, they might as well have been living on the opposite ends of the planet.

She bit her lower lip, her nails digging into her skin. A sob built inside her chest, fury rising through her like a storm that could swallow her in its clutches.

She had to put an end to this. She had to break free of the leash he bound her with, controlling her every step, every choice, while he enjoyed his life. She had let him do it for five years.

Five years of a sterile life, five years of being his prisoner—that she had accepted out of guilt and fear.

Scrubbing the tears from her cheeks, she pulled up the society feature she had purposely clicked away from this morning on her laptop.

Stavros's business partner and her grandfather's second godson, Dmitri Karegas, was throwing a party aboard his yacht.

Stavros and Dmitri were cut from the same cloth—breathtakingly gorgeous, built their empires from nothing under her grandfather Giannis's guidance, and considered themselves gods, their will law for the normal mortals they walked amongst.

Stavros hated parties with an intensity Leah had never been able to understand, but Dmitri would be there.

She just had to make sure the decadent playboy, who apparently was always surrounded by a group of willing women, noticed her presence aboard his latest toy.

Had to, somehow, gain his attention.

Her stomach clenched as she shoved the bedroom door open and walked toward the closet.

Every step toward it, every thought in this direction—was like walking to her own doom.

But Stavros had left her no choice…left her with no way out.

She dialed another number on her phone and booked a taxi. A shiver traveled over her spine as she viciously pushed the cotton tops and skirts in her closet away until she reached the end.

She pulled the gold silk dress, the one designer label she had kept, her fingers shaking violently as she realized how little fabric there was of the dress. Her back would be totally bare, which meant she had to go without a bra.

And it would leave most of her legs, her thighs bare too. So no underwear either.

Five years ago, she hadn't even blinked when she had worn it. Had thought it nothing to parade around with Alex and Calista, showing every bit of skin she could expose, barely looking decent…

And she had been almost twenty pounds heavier…

Just thinking of how she must have looked then made her cringe.

What the hell had the designer been thinking? What the hell had she been thinking?

She had been trying to please Calista, who had decreed she wear it that night… That's what she had been thinking.

Yet nothing else in her closet would do for tonight.

Of all the things to think about when her life was eternally stuck in this rut, when the very walls of this apartment were closing in on her…

Her palms were sweating as she pulled the dress to herself. The dress would fall scandalously above her knees, just about covering her buttocks.

It was the most outrageous dress she owned, the sartorial equivalent of a tramp and she had worn it the night Stavros had decided her fate. Fitting then that it was the one that would at least get her an audience with the man who was her jailor.

Every muscle in her trembled, and her mouth was coated with bitter fear as she walked into the bathroom and splashed water on her face.

He was going to explode, he was going to despise her even more, if that was possible. But she couldn't bear this… this isolation anymore.

She couldn't bear to continue like this. Something had to give.

Leah clutched the leather seat of the taxi, holding onto it a like a lifeline, the curious glances the cabbie threw her way doing nothing to propel her out.

She took a deep breath and looked out the dirty window. The marina was busy, a few of the yachts moored there highlighted by the setting sun. But even amidst the loud luxury, one yacht stood out, its gleaming white exterior splendid in the setting sun's light.

She took the bills out of her gold-lined clutch and handed it over. *This was it.*

She didn't let herself think, she didn't let herself even

look around over the next few minutes. Keeping her shoulders straight, head held high, she reached the security personnel guarding the planked entrance. Except for the glimpse of recognition in his gaze, the six-footer didn't budge a muscle.

Leah raised a brow haughtily, the gesture taking everything she had.

Yes, she had spent the past five years working as an apprentice in a mid-level fashion house, away from the spotlight, locked up in a bubble where no one knew who she was, where no one cared except that she didn't put a toe out of line.

She slept, she woke up, went to work, went back to her apartment, ate dinner and fell into bed again, while Stavros's minion, Mrs. Kovlakis, her housekeeper, watched her, made sure she didn't comit any further scandalous acts. But that didn't mean anyone had forgotten what she had done, or what Stavros had done to her as punishment.

Especially in this crowd that hung on to every word from Stavros's lips as if it was the Holy Bible. It felt like an eternity but only a few seconds passed before the man stepped aside. Taking his proffered hand, Leah stepped onto the deck, her guts twisting into a gooey mess.

For a few dazzling minutes, she forgot why she was there as she ventured further. Uniformed waiters passed around champagne. The party was in full swing on the deck, inebriated, sweaty bodies pressing against each other...

Excitement and an electric energy touched the air, and she swayed automatically to the music.

So everything she had heard of Dmitri's parties was true...and strangely the antithesis of everything Stavros was. So he wouldn't be here. But she needed to be recognized, which meant she had to grab Dmitri's attention, especially if he was busy ravishing his latest arm candy.

Smiling for the first time since this afternoon, she

walked toward the glittering glass bar that she had read about, planted herself on one barstool, ordered a cosmo and proceeded to get drunk.

Stavros Sporades frowned as his cell phone beeped for the tenth time in the last five minutes. He picked up the phone and smiled at Helene, loath to ruin their private dinner. It was the first time he was relaxing in a month and he guarded his downtime as fiercely as he did his work time.

He picked up his champagne flute and took a sip before clicking Yes.

Dmitri's drawling tone reverberated in his ears. "She's here. Aboard my yacht."

Stavros fell back against the seat in silent shock. Only one woman being aboard Dmitri's yacht would cause him to call.

Leah.

His blood pumped furiously through his veins. "Are you sure it's her?"

A mocking laugh met his ears. "It took me a few minutes to recognize her, but yes, it's her. She's drunk and dancing."

Drunk and dancing...

Instead of seeing Leah's face, he saw his sister Calista, unmoving and pale in death. He had tried so hard to find some kind of closure from Calista's untimely death, and yet, the anger and the powerlessness were just as raw, just as fresh.

Gritting his jaw, Stavros calmly pocketed his phone. Fury reverberated within, leaving his chest perversely cold. He made his apologies to Helene and exited the rooftop restaurant.

She's doing very well, Mr. Sporades, Mrs. Kovlakis had said about Leah, in her nasal voice on his weekly phone call. *Almost a changed personality, if you can believe.*

Had the woman been just telling him what he had wanted to hear?

Within minutes, his pilot landed them on Dmitri's luxury yacht.

He stepped onto the helipad, a corrosive anger roped with heart-pounding fear running through him. "Where is she?"

His gaze deceptively calm, Dmitri pointed to the dance floor on the lower deck. "I could have had the security personnel grab her, but I think that would have made the situation worse."

Stavros nodded, unwilling to meet his oldest friend's eyes.

His control was barely teetering on the edge as it was. He didn't want to be thankful for the fact that it could have been worse, much worse than Dmitri's yacht.

He didn't want to feel grateful that it was just alcohol, not drugs.

Cristos, he didn't want to set eyes on the woman he had married as punishment and penance.

He didn't want to set eyes on Leah.

Even in the drunken haze caused by the three cosmos she had consumed, Leah knew the exact moment Stavros had reached the dimly lighted dance floor.

The hairs on her neck shot up, her stomach plummeted. An unbearable cold claimed her skin even though the breeze from the sea was warm. She shook her head slowly to clear the fog and looked up.

The famous, specially commissioned, glittering glass bar that was the prize of Dmitri's yacht showed a hundred reflections of Stavros. Narrowly sculpted face as if a sculptor had been asked to keep austerity at the front of his mind, the sharp, long bridge of his nose that was arrogance embodied, the cruel slash of his wide mouth that instantly reminded her of that one punishing kiss, and the tawny, long-lashed eyes…

And the hatred blazing in them when he met her gaze

in the glass—a hundred flickers of fire that could scorch her in so many ways.

Nausea bubbled through her and Leah stumbled.

Shaking uncontrollably, she wrapped her fingers around the nape of the twenty-something guy she had been dancing with for the last quarter of an hour. Although it was more him holding her boneless body up.

Thankfully, the stranger's face was blurry to her. She didn't want to remember anything from this night tomorrow. She moved her feet slowly in rhythm with the beat of hip-hop blaring around them. His hands moved over her hips, hesitated, then moved back up over her back, before embracing her.

Her stomach quivered, the faint whisper of something as mundane as comfort warming her insides.

How pathetic had her life become if the man's thin body comforted her?

Willing herself to ignore the cloud of black thunder she could sense around her, she dragged in a raspy breath. Softly ominous whispers emerged through the din and music, the sweaty, swaying bodies parting without his uttering a word. It was as if even the air in that lower deck was suspended in the face of the thundering storm.

She pulled herself up and kissed her companion's smooth, almost boyish jaw and whispered *sorry*.

It wasn't the poor guy's fault that he had no knowledge of who she was or he wouldn't have dared to touch her. Would have sidled away from her, treating her like a pariah as the rest of the crowd had done once Dmitri had walked by, his gray gaze devouring her with unhurried interest. Once they had all realized she was Leah Huntington Sporades, prisoner and possession of Stavros Sporades, not to be looked at or even spoken to, especially by another man.

Because, Alex, her one friend who hadn't turned away from her, who had tried to contact her even after Calista's death and her marriage, had ended up in jail on some trumped-up charges Stavros and that equally arrogant Dmitri had fabricated out of thin air.

The depth of her hatred for Stavros left her shaking uncontrollably.

A steel band wound around her waist and jerked her away from the stranger. Maybe he was even a teenager, she thought, feeling old and tired at just twenty-four.

She fell against a solid, hard frame with a soft thud that knocked the breath out of her.

Unlike the man she had been dancing with, Stavros was all hard, unforgiving muscle that sent her body into shock at the contact.

Long fingers held her arms in a grip this short of hurting and turned her, the heat emanating from his body hitting her like a wave of the sea.

Blinking, Leah raised her gaze and then shied away immediately.

Coward, a voice mocked her inside but she didn't care.

The soporific effect of the alcohol she had consumed stunting the hatred that buzzed her blood, she went like a doll incapable of independent motion as he picked her up and threw her over his shoulder.

The jutting bones of his shoulders dug into her rib cage, her breasts crushed by his muscular back but Leah refused to let even a whimper emerge.

The world tilted upside down and a tear seeped through despite her efforts. The quiet hush that preceded them was like the calm before the storm…

She had done what she had wanted to do.

She had made a spectacle of herself, she had Stavros's attention.

Except nothing could numb her to the blistering contempt that had flashed in his gaze in the split second she had looked into it.

She squeezed her eyes shut and gave herself over to the haze in her head.

* * *

Leah jerked and breathed in great gulps as ice-cold water drenched her from all sides. She yelped and scooted back on her bum but there was no escape from the chilly spray. Her breath came in quick, short bursts, her lungs struggling to pump it out.

Another hard surface at her back thwarted her attempt at escape and she gave up, shuddering.

Reaching out with her hands, she touched cold marble. Her gaze flew open and she blinked to get the water out. The gold silk plastered to her body offered no protection against the cold. Shivering, she looked around, the chill sinking into her blood, raising goose bumps over her skin.

With shaking hands, she pushed her wet hair out of her face, her mascara running in black rivers down her fingers. So much for waterproof.

Blew out a long breath through her mouth and tried to make sense of her bearings.

She didn't need to turn to see Stavros standing there, watching her with malicious satisfaction. Could muster not a bit of surprise at what he had done.

Even through every nerve in her flinched at the cold, Leah could still feel his wrath, the heat of his anger. She stretched her arm, still shaking and turned off the glinting silver faucets.

Suddenly, all she wanted to do was curl up in the marble tub and close her eyes. Her body sank into the tub as if her muscles had no rigidness anymore.

"Get out of the tub." The quiet command landed on her like a slap, jerking her back to the purgatory that waited for her.

And the man who wanted to punish her for the rest of her life.

Even after years, she had no strength to face Stavros, couldn't face…

No, she wouldn't feel sorry for herself. Not after all that she had done today to just see him.

Clutching the marble, she pulled herself up to her legs.

Seconds piled on as the shaking in her legs subsided and the luxuriously spacious bathroom stopped swaying in front of her.

Blinking at the glare of light from a crystal chandelier overhead, she took in the dark oak floors and the blue sea outside the window.

Instead of the din, so nerve-racking that she swayed, utter calm reigned.

On shaking legs, she stepped out, dripping water everywhere. Her shoulders shook with the effort it took to keep standing.

A towel came straight at her with a resounding, "Cover yourself."

She buried her face in the plush cotton, taking the few seconds of privacy it afforded to shore up her defenses. But the contemptuous note in his tone pricked, as if a needle had punctured her skin and drew blood.

Fighting the urge to stay behind the towel, she straightened her spine and threw the towel back. "I'm wearing a dress, thank you. It's your fault if it reveals more than it covers," she said, brazening it out.

The plush cotton landed on one arrogant shoulder and she saw those broad shoulders tense. Felt his perusal as if he had laid those big hands on her...

Which was the strangest, scariest thought she had to have ever had.

"I see that you still don't know what is good for you then, Leah."

Gathering her wet hair in one hand, she squeezed the water out. Forced an indifference she didn't feel in the least. Because the reality of her reaction to him was too scary. "More like an allergic reaction to you. I'd rather catch pneumonia and die than be saved by you."

He reached her suddenly, a wall of fury and contempt that narrowed her very world to him.

Fear and confusion and so many things that she had battled over the last decade deluged her.

The overhead monster lighting illuminated his stark features—a sharper slap to her senses than the ice-cold water, but it was the tawny eyes that knocked the breath out of her.

Calista.

Calista had had those same eyes, except they had been kind, quick to smile, always in search of the next thrill, luring men into her orbit like a spider did with her web.

Her gut twisted into that insidious, painful knot that crept into her when she didn't make a conscious effort to turn her mind to something else, something other than Calista and that night.

It didn't help. Nothing did. But amidst the shock of seeing him again, something else penetrated through with an insidious clarity as he neared her.

Set against the severity of his face, the lush lashes and the glittering eyes stood out like an oasis in a desert. Rendering the man impossibly gorgeous, darkly stunning.

His scent was alien, yet alluring.

Leah breathed in a lungful before she could stop, a feverish shiver taking hold of her limbs that had nothing to do with her wet dress.

"Stavros, I—"

Long fingers crawled up her nape into her scalp, tilted her up, while the other hand clasped her jaw loosely.

He studied her every feature with such thorough appraisal that her insides turned into gooey pulp.

No one had even touched her in so long…it had to be why she could feel his touch like a brand on her skin… why such heat was pooling under her skin and rushing to the fore.

Why she wanted to sink into his rough touch more than she wanted to breathe…

Until she realized what he was doing.

He was checking if her pupils were dilated, wondering if she was high.

She stared into his glittering gaze, noted the concrete set of his jaw. Saw a shadow of something in his face that hurled the words past her throat. "I'm not high, Stavros." It came out as a whisper, an entreaty, and Leah recoiled at that pleading tone.

When he didn't relent, she grabbed his wrists. Every cell in her rose to attention as the whorls of hair there tickled her palm, as a shot of electricity sparked in the air.

"I remember the last time you said those words…" He sounded as if he was far away, in another place, another time.

Leah jerked his hand away, the heat from his body potent in its draw. Her skin tingled, every muscle in her rearing to get closer to him to soak up that deceptive warmth. She would freeze to death before she sought anything from him. "I'm telling the truth, Stavros."

I have never touched drugs, she wanted to scream, like she had the night when Calista had died. But he hadn't even acknowledged her teary words.

His teeth bared in an entirely cold smile. "Ditching your security detail, lying to Mrs. Kovlakis, appearing on Dmitri's yacht of all places—which is infamous for its wild parties, and knocking back drinks, forgive me if I don't take your word for it."

How unfailingly polite he was… He had done that before too, even as he had ruined her life.

You can either marry me or you can go to jail, Leah. The choice is yours.

"It got your attention, didn't it?" she said, realizing too late she had given herself away. Not that she had meant to keep it a secret.

CHAPTER TWO

"What?"

Stavros loosened his grip on Leah, struggling to get himself under control, struggling to get his neurons to fire again.

Guilt roiled through him, a heavy pulsing weight in his gut, something he had managed to subdue into a dull ache. But one look at Leah was enough to unman him again.

He took a step back as a sharp scent combined with the scent of her skin teased him softly, the cold from her arms clinging to his fingertips.

Frowning, he muttered a curse.

For the first time in his adult life, he lost the razor-sharp concentration that had made him a force to be reckoned with in the business circles of Athens. For several seconds.

"What did you say?"

She glared at him. "You, Stavros. You were the prize in this tacky show. If you had returned a single phone call, if you had read even one of my numerous emails to you... So, of course, I had to lower myself to your standards, didn't I?"

"My standards?" He was beginning to sound like an idiot and yet, it seemed his brain's higher functions had fractured.

An ominous thud started somewhere in the regions of his heart. His gaze swept over her with a swift greed he had no chance of curbing. The gold silk dress was almost the color of her skin that had a golden tone that no amount of spray tan could manufacture.

The result was that the dress moved sinuously against those high breasts, dipped at her waist, painting an erotic picture of almost nudity that had knocked him for sixes when he had first spied her at the bar.

Any traces of the curvy, awkwardly brazen girl he had married were gone. Instead, the woman who stood there— the delicate contours of her face rendering her infinitely fragile, her body bordering on scrawny, which made her breasts stand out even more—was a complete stranger.

"This is what you expect of me, isn't it? So I delivered. And here you are, in front of me, for the first time in five years as if I had conjured you with a spell."

A spell, as preposterous as it sounded, could be the only thing that could explain how dumbfounded he was.

Her long brown hair was plastered to her scalp and sprayed her face with drops of water when she rubbed it roughly. And every move was touched with an elegant sensuality that, he knew, was more innate than manufactured.

He had handled her so roughly just now, blinded by fury and fear. And any time he felt that unbalanced, his temper took a nasty dive, as his sister used to call it. "You look like... What the hell have you done to yourself?" he said, his control snapping.

She didn't even flinch, although he saw her lashes flicker down for a second. Her oval face was so thin and fine-boned that her light brown eyes were like dark, murky pools in it. Her arms were thin, too, but at least there was muscle tone to it.

Her hand curving over her hip, her tarty dress clinging to her wet skin, her teeth chattering in her mouth, she thrust one bony hip out in a seductive little moment. "What? You don't like my utterly fabulous and thin body? Your prison sentence has had at least one perk, Stavros. I lost so much weight that even the models parading through the fashion house keep asking me for tips. I can't count the number of times Marco has asked me to do a shoot, told me I would be a natural…"

It was the utterly uncaring, blind privilege in her words that broke the haze from Stavros's eyes. She was manipulating him, working herself under his skin like she always did, and yet he could do nothing to stop her.

From the moment he had laid eyes on her, Leah had been nothing but a spoilt, selfish, pleasure-seeking brat who didn't know the value of what she had or the people she hurt around her.

So she looked different. It didn't mean anything except that she had another bow in her arsenal for causing trouble. The first thing he needed to do was to get that… body covered up.

He grabbed her wrist, realized how fragile she was, and loosened his grip. Dragged her with him to Dmitri's bedroom.

"Wow." Her unconcerned exclamation boiled his blood anew.

He stilled on the way to the wardrobe, her stretched out body on Dmitri's vast bed sending the most insane urge to pull her off it.

Cristos, something was wrong with him.

For several seconds, he stared blindly at the rows of neatly arranged Savile Row shirts. Wondered what he was doing in there.

"Dmitri does know how to party and live in style, doesn't he?"

With a curse, he grabbed a shirt and threw it at her just as she pulled herself up. Her legs, long and toned, with black leather strips from her three-inch sandals winding round and round to her calves, glimmered against the dark red of Dmitri's sheets.

"Let me get this straight. You dressed like a ten-pound hooker, got drunk and plastered yourself over that boy to get my attention? And it has nothing to do with the fact that a normal, alcohol- and drug-free life was getting to you?"

The shirt he threw came flying back at him, missing him narrowly. He turned and stilled.

The goose bumps on her skin stood out, her eyes huge in her oval face.

"I've been trying to get in touch with you for a year. If you had the decency to speak to me, I wouldn't have had to do anything so drastic. It's the first time I've touched alcohol in five years. Not surprisingly, I'm not driven to drink anymore."

For all his self-discipline over the last few years, he couldn't stop looking. He couldn't stop devouring every small bit about her like he couldn't stop breathing.

Her nipples pebbled against the flimsy dress, her breasts, unsupported by a bra, heaving with her harsh breathing.

She looked like a red-blooded man's wet dream, and he was in no way impervious to the effect.

No!

This was Leah, a chain of duty and reminder of his failure around his neck. He had absolutely no interest in her except to keep her safe.

With ruthless will that had directed that he marry the woman responsible for his sister's death, he cut that line of thought.

"Meaning I drove you to drink?" When she remained resolutely mute, he took another clearing breath. He couldn't get this riled up over her. "Good for you. But I'm sure some habits are harder to kick than others. Like finding a scapegoat to hide your weaknesses behind."

She flinched. He saw her swallow and turn away.

Hated the vicious satisfaction her pale face gave him. This was why he had avoided seeing her for so long.

With her mere presence, Leah reduced him to a hurtful, raging bastard with no control, ripped off any semblance of closure he deluded himself into achieving.

"I didn't make a spectacle to discuss my shortcomings with you." Said in that flippant voice that he had heard so many times.

But her whole body shook with the breath she dragged in. Curved like a bow, her pink mouth looked inviting. Like it was made for mindless kissing.

He studied it with rising fascination, the relentless drag of guilt and anger he felt in her presence dulled by something new, something far more dangerous.

He pushed a hand through his hair, wondering what was getting into him. "You have my attention now, Leah. Tell me, what is that you want?"

"You've proved to the whole world what an honorable man you are by marrying the disreputable Katrakis heiress. You've kept your word to Giannis. You've punished me for five years for my sins and more. Now…please, cut the leash on my life, Stavros."

Her gaze held steady when he looked up, the fluttering pulse at her neck the only sign of her desperation. She linked her hands in front of her, and for a moment, Stavros couldn't help but be impressed by her determination to keep a lid on her temper.

It was like watching a volcano trying to contain the lava within.

"Did you think for a second what you did would completely defeat your goal, Leah? How could finding you drunk and plastered over someone persuade me to let you go? Within the month, you will be back to it all, the drugs, the parties. And I can't let that happen."

Every drop of blood fled from her face. "You cut me off from the entire world. You cut me off from my friends. You have your goons watch over me night and day. You… And that's fine too.

"But…you've been ignoring my emails, your hateful secretary is forever deflecting me. You…you can't just take me on as a responsibility and then…just lock me up. I'm not a possession to safeguard. You left me no choice."

"There are always choices. It's a pity that with everything you have in the world, you never learned to make the right ones."

"I'm not interested in discussing the past or the present." If she did, she would crumple to the floor in a helpless heap. Like she had been for the first couple of months after Calista had died. "All I care about is myself and my future."

"Of course." His jaw tightened. "So you have nothing to say to me, nothing to ask?"

She shook her head. "I have a hundred things to organize for my collection. I'm already behind. All I want is a phone call authorizing the release of the…"

He prowled toward her in a slow gait that sent her heart thumping like a bass drum.

"You haven't seen me, or anyone for five years. Aren't you even remotely curious, Leah?"

"About what?" she managed to whisper, under the thrall of his mesmerizing gaze.

With a smooth flick of his wrist, he tugged her and she fell into him with a gasp. Every muscle in her body sighed at the contact with his hard one. A little more pressure and he had her locked in his arms with their faces only inches apart. Leaving her with no choice except to look into the anger that turned his eyes into dark gold. "About how your grandfather is doing, you ungrateful little brat." At her gasp, his hold tightened further, this short of hurting. Sinuous heat burst in her belly and Leah struggled. "Is it too much to hope you would care about the man who took care of you when your father died?"

With a grunt, Leah pushed him back, hating the fact that he had muddled with her head with so little effort. She couldn't let on how rattled she was by his presence, how out of balance she felt when he touched her, even innocently.

She breathed in roughly, gritting her jaw so tight that

she would need to see a dentist soon. There should have been smoke coming out of her ears too. "First of all…I'm not sixteen anymore so stop calling me a brat.

"Secondly, not that I have to explain myself to you, I know how Giannis is doing. I speak to his nurse every day."

She instantly regretted her words when she saw the disbelief in his gaze.

Turning away from him, she walked to the mini fridge in the corner, needing the time away from his scrutiny to compose herself. Grabbed a bottle and gulped the water down so fast that her throat burned at the chill.

And yet she could feel the heat pooling under her skin as he watched her from the other side of the room, could feel an unnamed charge building up in the room…

This slicing awareness of him, this reaction to his nearness…it was intolerable and utterly frightening. Stavros had only wreaked destruction on her life—why didn't her body understand that?

"You haven't visited him once in five years."

Her chest ached at the thought of seeing Giannis. God, how she wanted to see that kind smile… Even through his heart attack and triple bypass surgery five years ago, Giannis had survived. She wouldn't risk it by seeing him now.

"My relationship with Giannis is none of your business."

His mouth stretched into a smile, the straight upper lip losing its severity in the process. "I'm making it mine."

"And I'm saying 'No more.' I have spent five years living a life you dictated, Stavros, down to the food I ate, the clothes I wore, the people I spoke to. Whatever you think needed fixing in me, it is fixed now. I want to lead my life, I want to build a career…" Frustration filled her throat with tears. "What more do you need to be convinced that I can lead my own life?"

"Not getting a phone call from Dmitri that you are

drunk and plastered over some boy would have been a start."

"I told you why I did that. If I hadn't, you would have gone another decade without answering my phone calls." She hated that her every action was being driven by him. That even in her own mind, she had no freedom. And it could not continue.

"I have spoken to a friend of mine. Philip is a lawyer." She stepped back from him, willing herself to stay strong. "I'm aware of my rights, Stavros. There are a hundred different reasons that could be cited and accepted by the court for a divorce."

"A divorce?"

"Yes. I want a divorce. I want to never see you again. And I'm sure the thought of being rid of me forever fills you with happiness. So give us both what we want."

A small smile touched his mouth but didn't reach that compelling gaze. Again, Leah had a feeling that it hid so much she didn't know. "You have rights and lawyers. But it could take years if I didn't agree, Leah. We could be celebrating a ten-year anniversary before we even get through the preliminaries."

"Is this what I have become for you?" Leah grabbed the edge of the desk to hide the trembling of her hands, a scream building away in her chest.

Hot tears prickled behind her eyelids. "Someone to punch, something to punish eternally so that you can feel better about what happened to Calista? Believe me, I wish it had been me that ended up dead that night and not her. But you know what? Wishing doesn't make anything come true."

Because even though she had never touched drugs in her life, she had enabled Calista that night. And that guilt choked her.

For the first time that evening, or maybe in forever, he

looked so shocked that Leah would have celebrated it as a victory if not for the gnawing in her gut.

Slowly, he recovered, those long lashes hiding his expression. "I have never wished that you had died instead that night, Leah."

She didn't want to believe him. But Stavros was never less than honest.

Of course he wouldn't have wished Giannis Katrakis's granddaughter's death. His control, not only over his actions, but even his very thoughts had always disconcerted and fascinated her in equal measure.

He lived by such a stringent code of his own rules, and applied it to everyone around him that no one could really hold up to it.

Not Dmitri, not Calista and definitely not her.

Recovering from the memory, she shook her head. "Right. You didn't wish my death because who else will you take out your sadistic side on if I were gone?"

"You call the last decade of your presence in my life sadism. I call it masochism."

She knew, *had always known*, what he thought of her. But hearing it in his own words... Her fingers pressed into the glass in her hand, the urge to throw the glass, water and all, at his head bubbling up inside her.

His amused gaze followed her shaky movements. "Try it."

The utter satisfaction in his voice got through to her like nothing else could.

He expected this of her. He expected a juvenile tantrum and she had already catered to him today and for years. Every time he had warned her to not do something, she had done that and more. Had lashed out against him from the moment she had landed in Greece.

Hating Stavros, especially when he had continuously given her ample reasons, had been easier than dealing with the grief and fear inside her.

No more, Leah.

There was power in that choice, power in saying she wouldn't give him the satisfaction of being right about her anymore.

Instead, she took a deep breath, reminded herself why she was here. It would be great if Stavros released those funds to her. But she had known it wouldn't be that simple.

Any other man would have sent the woman he thought responsible for his sister's death to the other end of the world.

Instead, hours after he had buried Calista, he had bound her to him in the most sacred of bonds.

She didn't even care about the divorce. The mockery of her marriage had never meant anything to her. All she wanted was to succeed, to give her life meaning, to take the joy she had always found in designing and creating to the next step.

"What do I have to do that you will release those funds?"

"Will you do anything I ask of you?"

Something in the silky tone of his voice—a flicker of interest maybe, nudged her into panic zone again. "My personal life is my own. Even with the shackles you bound me with, I have friends who mean something to me. If you order me to cut ties with them, I won't.

"Last time you cut off my friends from me and gained control over my life, I was…I was too…"

"Too high to even notice what was going on around you?"

She hadn't even gone on the anti-anxiety medication that had been prescribed after her dad's death, hadn't wanted to numb the grief of his death.

But it was pointless to defend herself when he had already passed judgment.

"I know how much you resented my responsibility from the moment I stepped off that plane. It doesn't have to be like that anymore."

Walking around the desk, he reached her side, and Leah fought the automatic impulse to step back, to keep some distance between them.

With his Greek-god good looks and smoldering arrogance, Stavros had always made her feel like the proverbial ugly duckling, made her feel even more awkward than she already had, surrounded by her grandfather's high-class society friends.

It seemed like a thoroughly unwelcome awareness took the place of her anxiety now. The faint stubble on his tight cheeks, the perfectly etched curve of his mouth...

The collar of his dress shirt was open, showing his olive skin. Holding her breath in, she pulled her gaze to his.

Every nerve in her body thrummed as he neared her. At thirty-three, he was a decade older than her. So why couldn't he have grown a paunch and become bald? Couldn't fate or whatever it was up above give her a break at least in this?

Couldn't he have been a little less gorgeous?

"If you have waited five years, what's three more months for a divorce? Or is this Philip more than just a lawyer?"

"Philip is only a friend. And if you want to continue satisfying your twisted sense of duty...fine."

Stavros watched in rising fascination as she closed her eyes and pulled in a long breath.

Shame filled him as he took in her slender frame. He hadn't seen her once in five years. He hadn't even made a call. Had just left her to Mrs. Kovlakis's care.

It had been unbearable to even look at her after Calista's death.

Theos, he had been so angry with her...

He had granted her request to apprentice at the fashion house, and yet, he hadn't really done his duty, had he? Marrying her to protect her from fortune hunters that had always surrounded her like vultures, to protect her from her own reckless lifestyle, as he had promised Giannis, had only been the first step.

He had let grief and anger distract him. It had been easy to forget about her, easier even to tolerate her presence in his life from a distance.

A possession to safeguard?

She was right—it had gone on too long. He had resented his future with her for long enough.

"I've learned all I could at the fashion house. I have made some good contacts, and I would like to leave it now."

Tension swathed him as she interrupted his thoughts. He should never have left her alone for so long, shouldn't have given her this chance to go on the offensive.

"Leave and go where?"

"Ideally, I would love to go to New York City. But it—"

"New York and your inheritance—I can see where this is going."

"—will be like starting all over," she continued, glaring at him. "I have made some good contacts here—buyers at retail stores, models who like what I have come up with so far. So I decided against it. But I do need to take the next step now. The fashion industry moves so fast that waiting until the few people that like my designs forget me will harm any future I have in it."

"What is the next step?"

Sudden energy filled her eyes. "I'm going to take a chance and start freelancing, do custom orders for now. Right now, I have interest from a woman who buys for a small retail store in London."

"Going out on your own, especially in your field, is a risky venture. Shouldn't you continue at the fashion house?"

"I have been making clothes all my life, Stavros. I have worked there for seven years and except for being allowed to give input on a senior designer's creations, I don't have any growth there."

"But you don't know anything about running a business."

"You grew up on some itty-bitty farm and Dmitri... what was he...a drug runner or a pimp? I forget... The point is both of you knew less than squat when Giannis brought you here."

He continued staring at her, his silence wreaking havoc on her breathing.

"I need to take this shot. And I need money up front for all the costs. I can't access my trust fund unless you stop controlling it, unless you step down from your role as..."

"Ahhh..." He smirked and Leah wished she could get away with slapping the hateful man. But one wrong breath now and he would never listen to her again.

"That's what this is all about. Money."

"Yes, money," she added, mimicking his sarcastic tone. Easy for him to look down upon her when he had gazillions of it. "Money that my father left me and has nothing to do with you or Giannis or my mother or the bloody Katrakis dynasty's inheritance."

"Fine."

Was that it? So easy? Leah let out a long breath. Excitement fizzed through her. She would call her contact at the textile factory as soon as she got out. She would have to finalize and place orders for the raw materials, would have to hire someone to help with the sewing, would have to order equipment...

"Show me a proposal for this alleged business you want to start. If I find it sound," he said, stressing how improbable he found the very idea, "I will invest in it myself."

Anger and hurt ripped through Leah, leaving her trembling all over. Her chest was so tight that it was a miracle she could breathe.

She wanted to smash the expensive porcelain vase on the side table next to her, she wanted to let the scream building away in her chest loose, she wanted to...

"I don't want your investment. I don't want anything from you. I want my money. I want this...my career—I need this to be about me, Stavros, something I love doing, something I can take on without fear. Something I give all of myself to."

"I should have made my intentions clearer to you far sooner. You were right, I shouldn't have let it go on for so long. But now that you are here, I will correct the situation immediately."

Her heart lurched into her throat, cutting off Leah's breath. Whatever it was that he meant, it wasn't going to be remotely what she wanted. "What do you mean?"

"When I gave my word to Giannis that I would protect you, even from yourself, I didn't mean it temporarily, Leah. I meant the *until death do us* part. Whatever way that death might come for you. So let's get two things straight."

He looked like someone had carved his features in stone, removed every ounce of emotion from it. "This lawyer friend of yours... he should know better than to tangle with my wife.

"Secondly, you'll move in with me."

"What? Why?"

"Because it's high time we started our life together.

"And as for your career, we will get a fashion house, London or Milan or Paris, whatever you choose, to launch a line for you. As my wife, you will lack for nothing."

CHAPTER THREE

LAUNCH A LINE from a top design house in the world? Lack for nothing as his wife?

His wife?

He had to be joking; he had always liked making her miserable!

You cannot see that boy anymore, Leah...

No more trips to New York...

Giannis allows you far too much financial freedom but not anymore...

Leah met his gaze and everything within her stilled.

Stavros Sporades didn't give his word or make a promise easily. When he did...

Fear struck her so hard that her knees shuddered under her.

He instantly moved forward to catch her but Leah jerked away from him. "Don't come near me," she whispered.

She grabbed the door to stop from sliding to the floor in a puddle. She wanted to scream her denial but what left her mouth was a soft gasp.

He would never forgive her, or himself, for Calista's death, never even give her a chance. Would punish them both for the rest of their lives.

And to even contemplate being his wife in the true sense of the word...

Perversely, she felt a chilly calm inside instead of a boiling rage. "When I decided to come here today, I didn't even care about whether I was married to you or not. I didn't care about being so lonely all these years…friends I knew once living their life to the fullest… I lived it as if I deserved to be punished. But now…I won't quietly accept your word this time.

"I'm going to file for divorce, Stavros."

A tic played in his jaw, the only thing that betrayed his even gaze. He looked insurmountable, like a boulder intent on crushing her. "Lawyers and court proceedings cost money."

That patronizing tone set her teeth on edge. "I will sell myself if I have to, to pay for it. Within the week, I will move out of that flat, will be handing in my resignation at the fashion house. The moment I step out of here, I'm going to call Philip and tell him what I plan to do."

He moved to block her path, his gait predatory. "I'm not your enemy, Leah."

Panic pushed a hundred different flight routes in her head, one more desperate than the next. "No? Because God help me the day you decide that you are. If your goons even lay a finger on me, I will go to the media and start talking about how you have treated me over the last five years. I'll tell them I've been nothing but a glorified prisoner.

"I'm sure they would love to hear that saintly Stavros Sporades is nothing but a sadist."

"I do not care what the media calls me."

Nausea pooled in her mouth. "They will, of course, dig through the whole story again about that night and Calista."

If there was fury before in his eyes, now there was nothing but the bitterest loathing for her. And seeing as she felt the same inside, that she despised herself for how far she was taking this, his loathing couldn't touch Leah.

For once, his opinion of her couldn't hurt her, as twisted as it was.

"If he even hears a whiff of it—" a vein throbbed in his temple and his hands fisted at his side "—Giannis, who…

has done nothing but love you, he will be destroyed to see the Katrakis name dragged through mud. You will kill him with your stupid stunt, and my grandparents…they can't bear to think of Calista's death anymore."

"But you already know that I don't care about anyone but myself, don't you?" she bluffed, swallowing the bile that rose through her.

She couldn't betray the depth of pain that she held at bay every day thinking of her grandfather, of knowing he was close by but not seeing him.

Guilt ate through her insides. But she had no recourse except to threaten Stavros like this. She forced a smile, her cheeks hurting at her continued pretense. "If you don't want me to drag the Sporades name and the Katrakis name through mud, you will have to agree."

She opened the door and looked at him again, feeling truly afraid for the first time. She had gambled on the one person that she loved with all her heart. She could never hurt her grandfather. Even speaking about it like this was cutting her in two. But she had to make sure Stavros would believe her capable of it. "You will have to release those funds and you have to cut the strings you hold over my life. The choice is yours, Stavros."

"I thought I knew the depths of selfishness you could sink to, but you always manage to surprise me, Leah."

Desolation filled her at the utter resignation in his voice. That he believed her bluff didn't fill her with relief or gratitude however. Only painted a picture of what her life would be like with him.

And thinking of being caught in a circle of hatred and hero worship, she didn't have to try to sound like she didn't care. "What's new about that, Stavros? And who knows? Once I'm out of your life, you might even thank me for it."

Without stopping for even a breath, she rushed out of the bedroom and through the corridors, her legs barely holding her up.

She made it to the main deck before she collapsed onto the floor and clutched her knees. Leaning her head against her knees, she fought to corral her uneven breathing.

The very real possibility of Stavros still not believing what she had threatened sent a shaft of fear through her.

Her nape prickled as she heard someone approach, and instantly, she straightened her shoulders. She couldn't afford to let him see her like this… He would know that she had been bluffing. And she would be worse off than she had started today.

Breathing hard, she composed herself and looked up.

His hip lolling against the bar counter in casual elegance, Dmitri watched her with gray eyes. "Hello, Leah."

Shuddering, Leah swallowed the hard knot in her throat. She couldn't break down now, not when Stavros was so close.

A daring mockery in his gaze, Dmitri extended a hand to pull her up.

Leah grabbed his hand and pushed herself to her feet.

His hands were callous but didn't leave her shaking like Stavros's grip had done. His mocking gaze didn't compel her to react nor did his arrogant perusal leave her off balance and breathless. She didn't feel compelled to be better than she was, or to give up in frustration because nothing would ever change, as she did with Stavros.

She didn't feel anything except questionable warmth at seeing a familiar face.

Why Stavros of all men? Was she that much of a sucker for pain?

"I can see that you're—" Dmitri's gaze swept over her "—looking astonishingly well, so I'm not going to ask how you have been."

Set against Stavros's lacerating contempt, there was a slumbering, almost comforting quality to Dmitri that had always put her at ease. Looking into the bottomless depths of Dmitri's eyes now, she wondered how much of that warmth was a deceptive facade.

"Come, I'll take you home. Stavros will thank me for stopping *his precious wife* from getting arrested for indecent exposure."

Leah shivered, only barely stopping herself from covering her chest with her arms. Hearing herself referred to as Stavros's wife, even the mention of that bond that tied them together made her queasy inside, and Dmitri knew it.

Straightening her shoulders and resolutely holding her arms down, she glared at him. "Then he shouldn't have dumped me in that monstrous tub of yours."

His laughter swathed her. Leah ducked, just enough when he threw an arm to pull her to him.

"I'm not playing your games, Dmitri, so back off."

His eyes warmed up even more. The few times she had come into contact with him, he had at least had a kind smile for her, whether real or fake.

Familiar trust awoke in her, something inside her desperate for a friend after Stavros's stinging scorn.

Unless it was part of his game to get her to trust him and pump her for information so that he could take it back to Stavros... She sighed, feeling immensely tired and lonely.

"I have missed your sharp tongue all these years."

"Wish I could say the same, but I don't have your gift or charm for lying."

Reaching her, he hooked her arm through his and herded her toward the steps. "Let's not pretend about your talents. At least not with me."

Swallowing her fear, Leah dragged her feet. Dmitri saw far more than he let on. As different as they were, his friendship with Stavros was as inviolate as their devotion toward Giannis.

Donning that mask of reckless ignorance, Leah faced him. "I have no idea what you're talking about but I can find my own way, thank you."

"I heard your conversation, Leah."

"Then you're as uncivilized as they say."

He stared at her with unblinking eyes. "I had the yacht empty in five minutes but I couldn't leave. I was afraid of what you both would do to each other," he drawled silkily.

Every time she had seen Giannis with either Dmitri or Stavros, she had felt a yawning chasm in her chest knowing she could never share something like that with her own grandfather. And that it was her choice.

"It doesn't concern you, Dmitri."

Grabbing her arm, he turned her. "You're playing a dangerous game with Giannis's life, Leah. This is not like one of those antics you used to take up just to make Stavros furious."

That he had always seen through her ploys unnerved Leah. "All I want is my freedom, Dmitri, a chance to live my life. You get that, don't you?" she threw back at him, remembering bits and pieces of what Calista had told her about Dmitri's life before Giannis had plucked him off the streets of London.

"Try a different way then. For once, try to change the dynamic between you two, Leah."

"How?" she whispered, her voice breaking. "He's left me no choice. In that moment—" she pointed to the ominously quiet lower deck, her heart pounding in her chest "—it started as a bluff. But I… I don't know what I'm capable of anymore."

"Stavros and you are intent on destroying each other."

"Me destroy Stavros? All the power, all the cards are in his hands, Dmitri. As always." And the worst part was that she had given it all to him with her irresponsible behavior.

All she had today was the wretched power to hurt Giannis. And Leah was terrified that she would use that power. Desperation turned her words into a pitiful entreaty.

"If you count Stavros as your friend, if you really care

about Giannis's well-being, then convince Stavros that I don't need his brand of protection anymore. Please, Dmitri."

Two days later, Stavros and Dmitri were sparring in the ring in the ultra-sophisticated, custom-built gym attached to Dmitri's Athens apartment.

It had started when Stavros had suggested Dmitri could work his way out of a temper instead of losing it when Giannis had brought him to Athens years ago, morphed into a way for them to resolve arguments when they struggled to keep up with the rigorous, grueling schedule that Giannis set for them.

A habit they had carried into adulthood.

But today, Stavros was the one who felt bloodthirsty, like he was coming apart at the seams.

After two days in which he had been supremely unproductive, he still hadn't been able to master his reaction to seeing Leah.

You already know that I don't care about anyone but myself, don't you?

Her words rang through him, her glittering gaze and her vibrating body etched into his brain.

The brazen curve of her mouth, the reckless shrug with one hand on a bony hip, her dark brown hair drying in curls around that angelic face... *Cristo*, he still couldn't believe that...*boldly stunning* creature had been Leah.

Leah, who had jumped like a live wire when he had touched her without meaning to...

Leah, who, even at a naive sixteen, had somehow always pushed all the wrong buttons in him...

Leah, who was, even now, insidiously unfurling the iron fist with which he ruled his...

No!

Moving his right foot forward, Stavros swung his left hook with a vicious fury. The thwack of his knuckle against

Dmitri's jaw, and the hiss of his exhale, followed by the filthiest curse words reverberated in the quiet.

Shock flashed in Dmitri's eyes.

That Stavros had gone on the offense when it had always been about letting Dmitri work through one of his tempers, who learned to use his fists on the streets of London amidst gangs, spoke to his ragged control.

"Ding, ding," Dmitri mocked, dark amusement in his gaze. "Point for *Leah Huntington Sporades*."

Gritting his jaw, Stavros shot him a filthy look.

Massaging his jaw with one hand, Dmitri reached for a bottle of water with the other. "In all the years that we have known each other, you have never gone on the offensive. Today's win has to go to her."

Knowing how cunningly perceptive Dmitri was, Stavros decided to leave. It had been a miracle in itself that Dmitri had—showing what Giannis would have called uncharacteristic wisdom—left Stavros alone after Leah's latest stunt.

He didn't want to discuss Leah, with him of all people.

Dmitri's jaw was already black and blue, and for once, Stavros enjoyed the result of his loss of control. "Put some ice on it."

Dmitri stopped him with a hand on his arm. "You're pushing it too far, Stavros."

"Leave it alone, Dmitri." He knew exactly what his friend was talking about.

Moving around him, Dmitri blocked his path. "You went above and beyond what Giannis asked of you. Wash your hands off."

Giannis, to whom he and Dmitri owed their entire world, had asked for only one thing in return after becoming their salvation when they had been nothing but uneducated thugs.

And Stavros had failed spectacularly at it. "Have you forgiven yourself for everything you have ever done? Or failed to do?"

All emotion seeped out of Dmitri's face, leaving an uncaring mask in its place. "Do I look like I have been punishing myself for the last decade?"

Stavros made a doubtful sound of assent in his throat. "See you next week."

"Giannis asked you to protect her, Stavros, *ne*?" His breath hung in his throat as Stavros waited. "But what I saw two days ago… He should have entrusted me with Leah. I would have seduced her within the day, made her fall in love with me and then cast her aside after a week. She would have learned her lesson.

"But you—"

Stavros curled his hand around his friend's throat, fury filling every vein. The thought of Dmitri seducing and throwing away Leah made him crazy like a rabid dog he had once put down as a teenager. "She is not one of your party bunnies, Dmitri. She's…she's Leah."

His breathing loud to his own ears, Stavros stilled. Dmitri watched him with hooded eyes, not even trying to shake off his grip. They both knew what he had been about to say.

She is my wife.

When had he become so possessive of Leah? When had she gone from a chain around his neck to something that could incite him like this?

"To see Stavros Sporades's ironclad control unravel like this… But even a man made of stone would have noticed that gorgeous body. Leah could always get under your skin so easily," Dmitri continued, frowning, "but now, she has another weapon to wield against you."

"*Enough, Dmitri!* I don't interfere in your life nor pass judgment on it."

"But Leah is not just any woman. If you're doing this just because you suddenly have the hots for your little wife—"

"Some days, I don't know whether to call you friend or foe."

Dmitri didn't even blink. "You are the most honorable man I know, Stavros. Until I met you, I didn't know what it was. There are days when I still don't. But Leah's threat concerns Giannis. You need to make a decision soon."

"I already made one. Five years ago."

"Then why have you left her under someone else's care, kept her at a distance? Either she's truly your wife or you're through with her.

"You can't hang both your lives in limbo as if it was some sort of penance."

A chill seeped into his skin despite the fact that he was sweating. Stavros let Dmitri go. "What if she hasn't changed? What if she…"

"Give her a chance at least, Stavros. To prove you right or wrong."

It was Dmitri that finally left the room.

Everything Dmitri had said was stuff he had already been over a thousand times.

The moment Dmitri had called him, guilt had clung to Stavros.

All his life, he had tried to do his duty by his grandparents, by Calista, by Giannis. He hadn't let his own fears or wants matter. He had always done the right thing. He knew what he had to do now, knew Leah deserved a chance. And yet, he wavered, for the first time in his life.

Never had his mind or body been so out of sync as it was now.

Five years ago, he had let his anger detract him, and now the intensity of his want for her was a weakness he had never had to deal with before. He wiped his face and looked at himself in the mirror.

He had let nothing but his responsibilities, his sense of duty, guide him his entire life.

Nothing was going to change that, not his reckless, selfish, brazen wife of all people in the world.

CHAPTER FOUR

Standing at the small balcony that offered a view of the colorful Athens evening ahead, Leah looked out.

She had been running for the past hour, the one thing that had always grounded her. Yet, all she felt like was running away, and this time, not looking back.

The panic-fueled urge was like an itch under her skin, a fire in her nerves.

It was a quarter past five and already the cafes and eateries were filling up with locals and tourists alike. Laughter and excited phrases in Greek swirled up through the air. It was a sight that had brought her a smile countless number of times after another long, lonely day. Today, it couldn't dispel her anxiety even a little bit.

Sighing, she went back inside. The pristine white walls that she had refused to adorn with even a single photo closed in on her and she started pacing.

Why hadn't she run away before now? Why hadn't she walked away from Stavros and this…pitiful thing between them that was a marriage, and not looked back?

Had she been so lonely to cling to this familiar world even knowing that she could never be close to her grandfather in the way it mattered? Had even Stavros's punishment been better than facing a life alone in the world?

She would never forgive herself for the part she had played in it, but, to this day, she had no idea that Calista had been using. Had no idea that hiding Calista's involvement in everything Stavros had abhorred about Leah would go that far.

Had no idea what it was about Stavros that made the worst parts of her manifest so well.

Impulse and fear making her movements jerky, she reached her closet and pulled out a shoulder bag that had collected dust from sitting unused for so long. Grabbed a few clothes and threw them in the bag.

For two days, she had waited calmly, taking Philip's advice to not do anything rash. Had waited for the explosion from Stavros to come. Had barely slept a wink, was driving herself crazy.

She couldn't wait to see if Stavros would take her bait. She would have to cut her ties, beginning with this flat and her job.

Just as she grabbed her phone, it pinged and the name Stavros popped up on her screen.

Leah dropped it with a gasp, her heart jamming in her throat. Perspiration condensed on her forehead as she stared down at the phone on the dull carpet.

It pinged again, jolting her out of her haze. She swiped it open to the text.

Come down to the café in ten minutes. I have an offer for you.

An offer? Could she trust him? Had she finally got through to him?

Will scream if I see your 'security guys.'

She waited, her breath hanging in her throat.

Enough drama, Leah. Come down or I come upstairs.

The thought of Stavros invading her private space, as much of a jail as it was, sent her fingers flying over the phone.

Fine, see you in a bit.

Feeling more hopeful than she'd been in months, she was about to step into the shower when it pinged again.

Leah...Dress appropriately.

Leaning against the bathroom wall, she made an utterly juvenile face at the phone. The small space thundered with the boom of her heart.

Stavros was here because he had bought her bluff. It wouldn't do to let on how petrified she was inside, to let him set the tone for this conversation.

It was like a mask she had to wear and the more she did it, the more it felt like she would become that uncaring, selfish person that he had always despised.

He had said ten minutes.

By the time he spied her crossing the street from her building to the café, it was well over half an hour. In true Leah form, she had also blatantly disregarded his last text.

The peach-colored silk blouse pressed against her body, neatly delineating the globes of her high breasts as a gust of wind blew across the street. He saw her shiver and grab the edges of the long-sleeved cardigan together.

Heat uncoiled under his own skin, a soft, sinuous gathering of something molten.

The silk blouse was paired with an even more flimsy pair of shorts that showcased her long legs. The glint of a toned thigh muscle, the way her wavy brown hair swept into a high ponytail swung with her long-limbed stride as she walked toward the café in her knee-high leather boots turned more than one male head.

She walked with the innate grace of an athlete, confident in her own skin. There was nothing of the Leah he had married and not because she had grown into her beauty. It was like a fire burned within, one that made her something to behold.

Was it truly as she had claimed and about her career? Or was it a man? Every cell in him went on high alert at the thought.

The last man Leah had been close with had been a crook of the first order—Alex Ralston, who was in jail even now for possession and distribution of drugs.

"When will you learn that defying me only wrecks your own life, Leah?" he said, dragging her down to the seat next to him.

Crossing her legs in a languorous gesture, she curved her pink-glossed mouth in a too sweet smile. "When will you learn that you cannot order me around, Stavros?"

As silky soft as her skin had been to the touch, her pulse had been pounding a thousand beats a minute. She was nervous. And yet, she was doing everything she could to not let him see it.

He waved away the waiter that arrived at their table with a beaming smile for her.

She waved him back with a friendly smile. When he glared at her, she sighed.

"*I am* hungry, Stavros. I rarely, if ever, eat out so I'm going to pretend you enjoy my company and make the most of it."

He waited in silence as the young waiter appeared again. Watched in mounting fascination as she ordered three appetizers and two entrees in fractured but perfectly accurate Greek.

"I'm not eating," he said dismissively as the waiter left.

"I know. It's Friday evening and you'll have dinner

with Helene Petrou, ex-lover and—" a curse flew from his mouth "—current *friend*."

Leaning forward in an elegant move, he pinned her gaze. "How do you know about that?"

"Philip has his resources."

"So your little lawyer asked you to casually throw that into the conversation?"

"Actually, quite the opposite. He told me not to even betray the fact that I knew anything about her," she said with that blunt and reckless honesty.

Stavros settled back slowly.

Leah had zero self-preservation. How was he supposed to believe that she could look after herself?

"Then why did you?"

"I don't want to wage a war against you, Stavros. It's… my last choice. I bring it up because I was…shocked to hear her name after so many years. That you see her apparently on a weekly basis."

"Shocked to learn that I keep in touch with a woman I admire?" he said, choosing his words carefully.

Looking anywhere but at him, she nodded. The fine sheen of color in her cheeks snagged his attention.

Brazen, reckless Leah was uncomfortable?

"I remembered that Calista…she talked so much about you guys. That you were made for each other," she said, her gaze wandering off into the distance.

The look in her eyes was a compelling blend of pain and ache that Stavros had never seen before. Did she truly mourn Calista that much? "Leah?"

She blinked and then curved her mouth. But the artifice of the action wasn't lost to him. "You would be free. To be with her."

"You want me to be with Helene?" he said, shocked.

"Yes." She took a sip of water, her gaze lingering on him. "Of course, I would prefer it if you were as miserable as you've always made me, but if your happiness is the price of my freedom…then so be it."

"That's very magnanimous of you, Leah." The whole conversation was twistedly perverse. "I'm surprised you remember her. Or anything from that time."

His dig bounced off her. "Her resume is far too impressive to forget. Businesswoman, fashion icon, former model and the best of all, the one who could stand up to Stavros Sporades's infinitely impeccable standards for a woman."

He stared at the almost cynical twist of her mouth, something in her tone grating at him. "You have quite the opinion about her."

"Of course, I do. I was obsessed with…" Coloring, she trailed her gaze away from him. "How successful she was at such a young age."

He had a curious feeling that it wasn't what she meant to say. If he compartmentalized his abhorrence for everything Leah represented and his unwise awareness of her every move, he could admit that Leah was funny and resilient as hell.

The more he pondered that, the more he realized how true it was.

Despite losing her father suddenly in a car accident and being thrust into an unfamiliar world that Giannis and he lived in, he had never seen her morose or down.

That same selfishness that he abhorred also lent her a strange strength. It was as if she stood behind a veil that separated her emotions, her very self from the people around her.

"So was all that food to please the waiter?"

"Where are your manners, Stavros?"

"All my finer qualities disappear like a mist when it comes to you, Leah."

"I was running this afternoon. So *all* that food is for me."

Stavros nodded, understanding the toned litheness of

her body. "What happened to walking out the flat and the job? To letting your little lawyer loose on me?"

He saw her still for a second before she turned toward him. "I... Philip advised me to not do anything rash."

"And you listened." Which meant she trusted him, which meant Stavros needed to know everything about him.

The waiter brought the food and she grabbed a fork. A satisfied sound erupted from her mouth, drawing the gaze and attention of more than one man sitting at the neighboring tables.

She looked up from her food suddenly and blushed. "So what is your offer?"

"I'm proposing a compromise."

"Nothing you ever suggest is a compromise. It will be your will, only couched in deceptive words. You did the same thing to..."

At the sudden glint in his gaze, Leah fiddled with the fork and looked away.

"To whom?"

Her shrimp suddenly tasted like sawdust in her mouth. Leah swallowed it down with a sip of her water. "To me and Calista, of course, countless times. Anything she proposed, you forbade it."

Like the time when she had wanted to study art in Paris one year, and when she had wanted to travel to New York with Leah. Like the time when Calista had wanted to start bartending at a nightclub where her friend had worked.

And when he refused her, one of Calista's rages would begin. Just the memory rattled Leah on a deep level. Calista had had a temper but she had hidden it so thoroughly from her brother.

"For instance?" he added softly, and Leah blinked. "You looked so pained just now, tell me what you were thinking, Leah."

The inherent command rankled Leah, and yet, beneath

it, she sensed his eagerness, his curiosity. That there could be more to Stavros than rules and duty…it threw her.

He had only been in his twenties when she had arrived in Athens, and yet, all she remembered about Stavros was his incredible sense of responsibility and duty toward all of them.

For the first time, she wondered what drove him to it.

Her curiosity tempered her response. "Why do you want to know?"

He blinked now, as if he couldn't believe that she dared question him. No, it wasn't that. Dumbfounded, she watched as he struggled to put his thoughts into words. "I… Even though I gave her everything she could ever want, I never understood—" something in her loosened as he visibly swallowed "—why Calista chose to follow your lead, how I failed to protect her."

The anguish in his gaze sent memories and impressions hurtling through Leah. Her shoulders shook. "I don't know—"

"Not that I expect you to know the answer, when you're the one who led her to drugs."

Her head jerked up.

Arrogant implacability wreathed his features. As if he had realized who he was talking to. As if there could be nothing but contempt between them.

"No, of course not," she whispered, buffeting herself against the immense hurt his words caused. Leah put her fork down.

Despite all her grand plans and ideas for adventures, Calista had never even lifted a finger in the house. Whereas Leah, whose mother had died giving birth to her, had always done more than her share to help out her dad even from a young age.

My saintly brother has servants for that… It had been her favorite thing to say when Leah would suggest cleaning up or cooking sometimes.

She had been sixteen and afraid and grieving in her own way. How much of her understanding of Calista would hold up today? For a minute, it seemed she and Stavros had found something common in their grief over Calista.

But no, the past was done. She had to look forward to the future.

Collecting herself, Leah looked up at him. "Tell me what I have to do."

He studied her for the longest time. Each falling second twisted her gut. "Live with me for three months and prove that I can trust you."

"No." The table rattled with the force of her movement.

"This is the only way I will even consider it."

"What do you expect me to do these three months?"

"Convince me that you're serious about this fashion design career, that you won't drain your inheritance on some trumped-up business."

"The vote of confidence in your tone is really inspiring."

That hardness in his eyes didn't budge. "I'm giving you a real choice. If you fail, our marriage stands. You'll be my wife in every sense for as long as one of us is alive."

A violent tremble started at the base of her spine and spread upward and outward. The happy voices around her buzzed as if they were noise feedback. And in that space between them, a charge built up winding and changing with every breath they took.

Leah struggled against it, rationalized against it. He met his lover every week. He could not be attracted to her. Nor she to him.

This charge was antagonism that had gone unaddressed for so many years, hatred and resentment and their struggle against this very fate that was spilling over into something else. Maybe it would be true if she believed it enough, she thought desperately.

Because thinking of Stavros in this way—when even

her juvenile crush on him had always left her feeling inadequate, was the last thing she needed in life.

Through sheer will, she forced herself to break his gaze, to focus on the fact that he was giving her a real chance. That Giannis would be far removed from their deal was positive.

"If I do prove that I'm everything that is virtuous and sweet and biddable and completely without personality?" His scowl deepened and since needling Stavros was the only thing she had control over in the sinking confusion of her world, she continued, "I'm just a little bit worried that you might not want to give me up then."

His laughter clanged in the open café. It was a sound Leah had so rarely heard that she stared at him, her breath caught somewhere in her throat.

That lean chest rumbled as if he couldn't contain it. From the long column of his throat to the sharp grooves in his sliced cheeks…he was gorgeous to behold.

It seemed the café froze around them to take in the sight.

A woman at the next table stilled with her coffee cup halfway to her mouth, her gaze eating him up. Still laughing, he pushed back the thick lock of jet-black hair that fell onto his forehead.

And the solid gold band on his finger glinted in the streetlight.

The twinkle of the metal struck Leah in the chest as if it were an arrow.

The wedding band… He was wearing his wedding band?

The ring she had slipped onto his finger while tears had pooled in her eyes. The ring that had bound her to him in the holiest of bonds and yet was nothing but a shackle…

Why did he wear the damned ring? Had he worn it that day aboard Dmitri's yacht?

Had he worn it over the past five years?

Anxiety rippled over her, like a flurry of ants had skittered over her skin.

Just like her, the woman's gaze also fell on the ring and then shifted to encompass the both of them. Leah felt her curiosity like a prickle, could see her trying to calculate where Leah fit into Stavros's life.

Nowhere, Leah reminded herself. That he wore that ring was probably nothing but a reminder of his duty to Giannis.

Did he keep it on when he made love to the regal Helene? What would it be like to be the woman he respected, he adored, the woman he promised his utter devotion to? Would his passion run just as deep as his sense of duty?

"Even in the most unlikely chance that I find you that irresistible…" Utter mockery resonated in every word, crashing her down. "I will sign the divorce papers, release your inheritance. You'll be free."

Three months with Stavros…

"The freedom to live my life as I want is my basic right. I shouldn't have to prove anything for it nor should I have to threaten…nor do I have to do despicable things."

"So you're not completely without conscience?"

She refused to answer that when he was the one who had pushed her to it. "You're not the lord of my life."

"Apparently, I am. And you lost all rights to your own life when you threatened it by living so recklessly." His very stillness as his gaze burned with frustration was disconcerting. "*Theos*, Leah…Calista died and Giannis almost did because of the heart attack you gave him. How can you sit there and defend yourself?"

"I can defend myself because…" Clutching the metal edge of the table, Leah breathed deeply. His accusation was unfair, so wrong, and yet, the guilt it brought was no less suffocating.

And to dig into the past, to tell him the truth would mean exposing herself to a man who tolerated no weakness, knew no fears.

Would he laugh at her as he had done just now or pity her?

So she gave in. "Fine. I'll do as you demand and earn that right back."

Silence met her acceptance.

He hadn't expected her to give in so quickly. Did he think it was an admission of guilt?

His arrogance that he knew everyone and the best for everyone had riled her from day one. Not once had he tried to figure out what or how she had felt. He'd only made assumptions, and then ordered her around.

He dropped some bills on the table, and extended his hand for her. "Let's pick up what you need for a few days. The movers will bring the rest of your belongings later."

Panic ran free in her gut as Leah shook her head. "No. I…I can't just pack up everything I need in ten minutes. I need a few days."

She couldn't just move in with him in a matter of hours. She needed to get used to the idea first. Needed to get her head screwed on right.

He checked the glinting Rolex on his wrist and then looked back at her. "I'll have someone come by to give us a hand. In the meantime, we can get started."

"You're actually, physically going to help me pack?"

"Is that a problem?"

"Yes, of course it is," she sputtered, refusing his outstretched hand. "I don't want you in my…I just… The flat is a mess, and you'll instantly judge me and tell me I shouldn't be allowed to live by myself or some such nonsense."

The hateful man had the gall to smile at her. To actually smile, showing his perfectly even teeth and the dimple in one cheek that should have made him look effeminate yet only added to that austere masculinity.

"What if I tell you that housekeeping is not a criterion I'll count?"

Desperation coated her throat. "I…I'm not comfortable with others touching my personal stuff."

"Neither am I about welcoming you to my estate…"

With his hand at her elbow, he made it imperative for her to stand up. "I won't touch anything. You can pack and I'll supervise."

"You'll lord it over me, you mean?" she said, using sarcasm to hide the trembling beneath.

In all the years she had known him, he had, in turns, aggravated her, captivated her and in the end, had ended up ruling over her life. And that was when there was no direct relationship between them.

How was she supposed to survive through three months of living with him?

CHAPTER FIVE

SHE HAD BEEN lying blatantly, *of course*.

Stavros didn't know what shocked him more. The fact that she would tell such a white lie about something so trivial or the reality of her lifeless, joyless flat.

It was as if she had intentionally designed herself a sterile prison cell, had punished herself.

Everything inside him recoiled that she had lived like this for five years. Why? Why live as though she was punishing herself when she had argued with him so furiously that she wanted it to end?

Had Calista's death scared her so much? Had it really changed her?

There was not a single thing out of place in the living room, or the small kitchen, or in the glimpse he had caught of her bedroom. She had everything she required.

The cupboards were full of silverware; a plasma television adorned the wall in the living room, yet was coated with five layers of dust.

There were no decorative items, no knickknacks. Just the bare essentials wherever he looked. The walls were a pristine white exactly as he had remembered from five years ago, when he had inspected the building and the flat, a week after they had married.

It screamed of loneliness, detachment.

Leah was a firestorm and it seemed only a ghost of that girl lived here.

The first year and a few months into the second after she had come to live here, he had had things delivered to her. Boxes of clothes and shoes, handbags and other accessories Helene had told him a young woman would require. He had even sent her things that had once belonged to her mother, found when he and Dmitri had gone through Giannis's old estate after his heart attack...

But she had sent every box back, stubbornly refusing to accept any of it, and so he had stopped trying. Even the box with her mother's things.

He had, conveniently, shrugged off his duty toward her. To the point of ignoring her very existence.

His gut twisting into a tight, unforgiving knot, he followed her into her bedroom. There was a nightstand next to the bed. A tissue box, some pencils and loose paper, and a tiny photograph of her father, he assumed from the same brown eyes, were on it.

Stretching on her toes, she pulled a bag out of her closet that was already half full. Turned around and stilled as he stayed at the entrance.

"I have someone bringing up boxes. Not that it seems you need any."

"The work room has lots of stuff I need."

He nodded and waited, his thoughts in an unprecedented jumble.

"I don't have to stay in your house for this...this test of yours, Stavros. I could just continue here."

He prowled into the small room, feeling on edge. He was angry at himself, he realized slowly. And he was angry at her. It was irrational, and yet he couldn't loosen its grip over him.

"Why not?" The taunt in his words shamed him.

The brown of her eyes transforming into a dazzling color, she glared at him. Her pulse at the neck fluttered belying the anger in her eyes. "Because I don't think it's a good idea.

"You can't stand me, for sins I know and some I don't. And I...you're arrogant, you're a hypocrite and I..." she said with that standard animosity she seemed to reserve especially for him. Yet he heard the quiver beneath those words.

She was trying so hard to hide her awareness of him. So hard to fight it.

The Leah that he knew, *that he thought he had known*, had never fought anything she felt. Gave in to every juvenile urge, every self-serving impulse until she crashed and burned.

And had dragged Calista down with her.

This effort now...it sparked a curious fire in him just as much as the fluttering pulse at her neck did.

He came to her bed and leaned against it, blocking her. "So that you could continue to live in this hole like some damned martyr?"

A silk skirt in hand, she turned that gaze to him again. "It is what you chose for me."

"I never meant for you to live like a prisoner. I sent you everything you needed."

"To do what with?" Throwing the skirt and a couple more things into the bag, she zipped it up vehemently. "I have no friends, Stavros. No family..."

"You rejected the one you have for years. You still do," he couldn't help but point out, a gnawing frustration in his gut.

She didn't even flinch as she continued. "Even the staff at the fashion house, people I have been working with for five years, they treat me with this—" he saw her swallow and a wave of tenderness, shocking and acute, rose inside him "—nauseating combination of dislike and affected regard.

"I don't know if they think my designs are really good or if they are just saying that because I'm Leah Sporades, the wife of the textile magnate of Greece, a shame he hides from the world.

"You married me even though you despised the sight of me. You…you kissed me in front of the media that day for the express purpose of warning away my friends, the entire world. You might as well have branded me like they do livestock."

"Leah—"

"No, Stavros…I was nineteen. I lost the one friend I had, Giannis had just had a heart attack…"

"Whom you still refuse to see," he cut in.

Do not give up on my Leah, Stavros. Please…she is very fragile…

Fragile was the last thing he had ever thought of Leah… She had barely ever sat down for five minutes with him, yet even surrounded by tubes and equipment, she'd been all Giannis could think about.

Every inch of her slender frame vibrating with anger and pain, she clutched the lapels of his shirt. "…and in the next two days, you took my entire world away from me. You locked me up here and promptly forgot about me.

"Did you ever feel even an ounce of shame that you co-erced a nineteen-year-old into marriage?"

Stavros felt her words dig into him like the serrated edge of a blade, drawing blood.

For five years, he had ignored her very existence, had let her live like this, had informed Giannis again and again that Leah was well…

How had he committed such an unforgivable mistake? "Answer me."

"No, I don't regret it. I would have done anything to save you from that drug-induced-drink-all-night-reckless-party life."

No denial rushed out of her this time. Instead, she closed her eyes and bent her head to his chest. The raw intimacy of the gesture flayed him, reaching a part he didn't know he possessed.

Her shoulders pushing at his chest, the scent of her coating the air he breathed, her lithe form was so tempting. He wanted to wrap his arms around her, he wanted to bury his mouth in… Feeling like an iron anvil was sitting on his chest, he clasped her wrists to push her away.

Instead, the pad of his thumb moved over the plump vein of its own will.

Her breaths came in a slow rasp until, suddenly, she looked up. His lungs burned for air as her fingers laced around his, as a blunt nail raked the center of his palm, her molten brown gaze clung to his lips.

Something so desperate and wanting flashed in her gaze that Stavros dropped her hand.

It was so unlike Leah that a shiver raked down his spine.

Jerking away from him, she drew a deep breath. "Deal with the consequences of what you did then," she said, moving her hand over the room. "Alleviating your guilt about this…it's not my responsibility."

It was the most adult thing she had ever said to him. And just like that, his world tilted an infinitesimal inch.

A world in which Leah was right and he was wrong. A world in which he had let himself be led by pain and resentment until he had neglected his duty…neglected the vow he had made to Giannis.

"You're right. It's not."

"What?"

"I said you're right," he said willingly, the bright wonder on her face drawing it out of him. "What I did that day had consequences that I didn't own completely."

"Am I actually hearing this?" Her brows rose into her hair, her mouth opened in a long O. Mirth overflowed in those eyes, making her look absolutely stunning. *"Boom!"* The scent of her skin swirled around him, drugging him so insidiously that his blood became sluggish. "Did you hear that, Stavros? I think the sky just exploded…"

He stole another greedy look at her. And like a snake

waiting to strike, the most incredible urge to press his thumb against the lushness of her lower lip, struck him.

He collected himself slowly and stepped out, wondering if this sinuous desire for her was his true penance.

"Show me your workroom," he said, over his shoulder.

Her workroom knocked the breath out of Stavros.

It was as though a veil, the veil that separated Leah from the rest of them, had been lifted. A tentative smile on her face, she walked around touching things here and there in the chaotic room, eons different from the Leah who usually glared at him with such hatred.

Sunlight poured in streams into the high-ceilinged room, exposing the beams. Everywhere he looked, there was color, such a vivid contrast to the rest of the apartment that it took him a few moments to actually see it.

Two racks hung around the back, with evening gowns in different degrees of completion. An old sewing machine lay on a table in the other corner. One whole wall was covered with sketches made in pencil, illustrations, even cutouts from fashion magazines.

Swatches of fabric were pasted on another wall. Reams of it spilled over from a rickety shelf in the corner—satin and silk and cotton, pretty much every fabric he knew of in his ten years in the textile industry.

Something tightened in his chest.

"The retail buyer that you were talking about, what is she interested in?"

"I'm putting together a collection of evening wear for her—cocktail dresses, formal gowns, and the prize of the collection will be one bridal dress."

"That's quite a workload for one designer..."

"Slash seamstress," she finished, fingering the sheer fabric of one unfinished dress.

"You're going to..."

An utterly confident smile dawned on her face. "Actually cut and sew the dresses, yes. I custom-design and sew every dress myself and that's what I would like my brand to be. When the buyer was talking about what she would like, what she liked about my previous designs...I could see the concept from start to finish."

Color flushed her skin.

He walked around and touched the cut bodice in ivory silk. "Has she seen the flat sketches?"

She shook her head. And he saw the surprise in her eyes that he knew the term. "We have had two discussions around it."

"Leah, it's a huge risk to create an entire collection for one woman's tastes at this stage."

She tilted her jaw aggressively. "You gave me your word not ten minutes ago." Her lithe frame vibrated with her growing panic.

"And I will stand by it. But I'm also a businessman and in case, you have forgotten, I run a group of textile factories that export all over the world. All I'm doing is pointing out the pitfalls, as I would do with any business I want to invest in. Creatives have a tendency to run the business into the ground with their half-realized dreams."

"But I'm not creating exactly what she wants. More like my vision of what she has in mind." She turned to him, a frown on her face. "Anything I tried to design with some freedom at the fashion house ends up changed for the brand of the house. I want this collection to be mine. And I need cash upfront for all the raw materials."

He nodded. "I want an expense report including quotes from all the vendors you'll be sourcing the raw material from. I want every penny accounted for."

"I will send you my spreadsheet."

"You have one already?"

"Surprised, aren't you? I've been having problems with one vendor based in Brazil though. He keeps upping the price of the cotton I need from him."

"I can help with that," he said, the fire in her eyes stunning him. "Do you plan to hire another seamstress?"

"Not at this point."

"But it's too much work for just one person."

"I don't want anyone else involved in this…in my first collection."

"Fine," he said, noting that the stubborn streak of independence was still there. Also that whatever advice he gave now, she wouldn't heed it. "You'll have the money within the hour. I will be gone next week, and during that time—"

Walking back into the kitchen, she pulled a bottle of water from the fridge. "I'll be watched by your housekeeper and your new security head. Poor Dmitri, along with his arm candies, will be reduced to babysitting duties. Although, I don't mind him."

"No?" The question left his mouth before he knew he had thought it.

"Dmitri?" An almost dazed kind of smile glimmered in her expression. And he cut the irrationally possessive thought her expression evoked before it could form fully. "Of course not. He was always kind, even when Calista…" Sudden tension dawned in her gaze and she looked away from him.

"When Calista what, Leah?"

She cleared her throat and started again but resolutely kept her gaze away from him. "This one time, we snuck into his room and stole a bottle of whiskey. Only he caught us…"

"Whiskey, Leah?"

"We were just goofing around, Stavros. We were seventeen."

"My father was an alcoholic who stole from his own parents, sold our house just so that he could drink, and drove my mother away. Calista wasn't supposed to even touch that stuff."

Shock flared in her gaze, widening those beautiful eyes.

Only then did he realize how much he had betrayed. "I had no idea, Stavros."

"What did he do, Leah?"

"Oh, he told us we could drink the whiskey—" color stole into her cheeks and she wouldn't meet his eyes "—as long as we were also going to join him for a threesome after."

"*Cristo!* Of all the things to say to—"

As if expecting his reaction, Leah sighed. "We dropped the bottle where we stood and we ran, Stavros. Dmitri was used to…he knew how to deal with us."

Unlike you, her unsaid accusation screamed.

He had a feeling Dmitri definitely understood Leah far better than he did. A mistake he had to rectify…

If Giannis had asked me… He pushed away the scenario provoked by Dmitri's taunting remark from his head and focused his mind on practicalities.

"Leah…fashion design is extremely hard to break into. On a given day, there are tens, if not hundreds, of designers launching new labels. And I don't know whether you actually have any talent for this."

"I know that. All I'm asking is a chance to do it, to access the resources that I do have."

"And when—" he checked himself as she threw that trademark glare at him "—*if* you fail in this venture?"

"Then it will be my failure. All mine. Just as the success would be. It will be something I have put my heart and joy into, something that doesn't scare me."

"I thought nothing scared you, Leah."

She offered him a perfunctory smile, and Stavros realized how much he didn't know about the girl he had thought his bitterest penance.

CHAPTER SIX

A WEEK LATER, Leah walked over the white sandy beach on Stavros's estate on one of the tiny islands along the Aegean coast. Stavros's "house" turned out to be a hundred-acre estate close to the sea, a ten-minute helicopter ride from Athens that had thrilled her quite a bit.

Even with Stavros studying her curiously the whole time.

She had lived in Athens for so many years and yet she had known nothing about the little slice of heaven that was the island he called home.

Nestled amidst two tiny hills, the mansion was stunning in its simplicity. No glittering glass bars like Dmitri's yacht, or a lifeless steel-and-chrome affair, which was lately the trend with billionaire homes.

The manor was made entirely of stone, with cathedral ceilings framed by exposed beams, whitewashed walls, a pool and a wine cellar. It was full of soaring spaces and light, stunning in its simple lines.

Austere, private and yet so breathtaking, the exact reflection of the man who owned it, it was an authentic slice of rural Greece. But even when it was only the wind chimes that punctured the silence, even when it was just the staff keeping her company as it had been at the apartment, Leah felt anything but lonely.

There was something very peaceful about the estate and the people surrounding it.

She smiled now about how worried she had been about

being confined in a house with him. About seeing Stavros wherever she turned. Not only did the house boast seven bedrooms and attached baths, but Stavros, when he returned from Katrakis Textiles, she realized, worked in the estate.

Although if he had looked smolderingly arrogant in his suit, he looked painfully handsome in light blue jeans and a white polo shirt.

The sounds of the helicopter blades had jolted her from her bed the first morning. Still in her cotton shorts and sleeveless T-shirt, she had run to the attached balcony, spurred on by what, she still didn't know.

Dressed in a white dress shirt that draped lovingly over his broad frame and plain khaki trousers that looked way too sexy, he had been about to step in.

Except he had turned and looked at her, the breeze ruffling his hair.

Her heart thudding, her mouth dry, Leah had broken his gaze and gone back in.

Now returning from the beach, she waved at workers heading home to the small village from the vineyard, which she had been surprised to learn was operational. Several guesthouses were dotted across the grounds in addition to a horse farm.

When she had laughingly asked Stavros which one Dmitiri preferred when he visited, she had gotten a black look in response.

It was as she passed a couple, probably in their fifties, that she remembered another little tidbit. Stavros and Calista had been from a little village that surrounded Stavros's estate. His grandparents, she knew, still lived there. Even though their grandson was a household name in all of Greece.

Feeling nauseous at the thought of how brazenly she had threatened to go to the media and how his face had blazed in contempt, she pulled in a long breath and broke into a run.

From the moment he had showed her around the estate, she had loved running through the trails cleared through lush acreage. In just the past week, she had found a trail that touched the horse farm and rounded through the orchard.

She turned the winding bend around it and came to a skidding halt near the glittering pool that was by the house.

The evening sun kissing the bridge of his nose and his cheekbones, Stavros was sitting at the poolside table.

A tall jug of the customary lemonade that she requested every day and a selection of fruits and assorted cheeses were on the glass-topped table between the two loungers.

His head was thrown back against it, and his eyes were closed. Her breathing still raspy, Leah stilled. Her gaze lingering on the corded column of his throat, the planes of his sculpted face, at the way his long lashes almost kissed those sharp cheekbones...

It was something to see the man in repose like that, to study him without his contemptuous gaze peeling layers off her. And the way her breath hitched and her gut folded, the frenzied clamoring of her heartbeat to the very sight of him, it was telling.

For the past week, she had seen the stamp of the man in the thriving estate.

In the tired but happy workers on the vineyard, in the affluent praise the villagers bestowed on him, in the way some of the women's eyes had widened when they had realized who she was, the reverence in their tone when they addressed her as Thespinis Sporades...

The responsibility of bearing that name, the reality of being the woman Stavros would respect and know *and want*...it sent shivers down her spine.

The usual white dress shirt he wore was unbuttoned, showing dark olive skin. His cuffs, folded back, displayed his muscled forearms, to the veins extending from his wrist and down... The sight of those powerful thighs, encased in tight blue jeans, made her remember how hard and corded they had been against her own…made her wonder how they would cradle her if she…

Heat, that had nothing to do with her running, pooled under her skin. The stretchy fabric of her Lycra top rasped against her nipples, the soft hem of her shorts rubbing against her inner thighs…

She was breathing like she had run another few laps, her skin so overheated that dunking into the pool was so inviting. Just as she found her willpower and took a step, she heard her name.

Turning slowly, she saw his fingers laced against his chest, faint color bleeding into those cheekbones.

His eyes were still closed when he said, "Did you have a good week, Leah?"

He sounded hoarse, uneven. Very unlike him. *Had he felt the way her gaze devoured him in that motionless state?*

How could just looking at him fill her blood with this molten wanting?

"Come, sit here and tell me how it was," he said softly.

While she still stood there stupidly, hovering between drugged inertia and fluttering panic, his gaze opened slowly. Traveled over her with such a thorough intensity that she could almost believe he had been dying to look at her.

In the seconds-long perusal, Leah knew he had noted everything about her, including her heightened color. Hoped he would put it down to the fact that she had been running.

She ran her palm over her forehead, wondering if she was feverish. Because that's how she felt. Could a harmless, adolescent crush turn into a full-fledged obsession, she thought sarcastically. "I'm sweaty. I need a shower," she finally responded, and began to walk away.

"Rosa told me you like to swim after your run. Don't change your routine on my account. Or am I one of those incredible things that scare you, Leah?"

It was so on target that her denial shot out of her mouth like a missile in a defensive tone. "I'm not afraid of you."

His brows rose questioningly. Then he smiled, a real flicker of warmth lighting up those tawny irises.

She could deal with Stavros hating her, questioning her worth, and thinking the absolute worst of her. This... strangely speculative mood he seemed to be in, she couldn't.

No way was she going to put on her bikini and parade in front of him. She would probably self-combust if he so much as looked at her, even innocently. "I ran far more than I intended today. I'll skip the swim," she said, turning around.

"How do you like the estate?"

She was so wired up into his every breath, every nuance that her foot slipped on a wet patch.

He was out of the chair and by her side in a flash, his hand around her waist. The side of her breasts squished against him, her midriff knocked hard against his. All of her breath jarred into her throat, her muscles groaning at the impact. He was so hard and hot...

"You are unhurt?"

"I'm fine." She pushed the words out, feeling so out of control that tears prickled behind her eyes.

What was the matter with her? Where was this desperate awareness stemming from?

He was silent next to her, his large hands still resting on her hips. She didn't have the guts to turn and meet his gaze.

The idea of seeing the same awareness in his drove her out of her skin. The idea of seeing nothing but a patient indifference made her skin crawl.

With the guise of reaching for the lemonade, she withdrew from his touch. "It's remote and a little out of sync with the twenty-first century, don't you think?"

For the first time in years, she had felt completely at home, had forgotten the pain of the past and the endless, lonely future stretching ahead of her. But she had nothing to fight her reaction with, if not with her lies. Nothing except to continue the animosity between them that she didn't even know the origins of anymore.

"Remote, yes. Out of sync with the rest of the world, no."

She looked at him over the rim of her glass. "Perfect for you though—stark, severe and forbidding."

"That's exactly what Dmitri says when he visits. Says he can't stand the relentless silence." He smiled. "So you do not like it then?"

She frowned, wondering why he was asking. "I just… I prefer something a little flashier and more hip, like Dmitri's yacht. Or that infamous bachelor pad of his in the business district of Athens." When had lying become this easy? She had been to Dmitri's flat once and it had been a soulless, colorless monstrosity of steel and chrome. "This is a bit too isolated for my taste."

"Is it?"

She swallowed the lump in her throat at the thought of leaving here. But if this was how she was going to react to seeing him after a week, she couldn't imagine what she would do if she saw him daily. "Hmmm."

A little knot tied his brows and cleared again. Something she had never seen danced in the depths of his gaze.

He was going to relent. He was going to send her back to that dinky flat, back to the dragon, Mrs. Kovlakis. A breeze could have knocked her down at how desperately sad the thought made her.

Dark gaze unmoving from her, he finished her drink. She looked down, rattled by the intimacy of the gesture. He put the glass down slowly and wiped his mouth while she waited on edge. "I think I will choose not to believe you, *agape mou*."

The endearment ripped through her. It meant nothing to him but weaved an intimacy that she didn't know how to counter. "What…what do you mean?"

"You are lying." The announcement reverberated around them in the vast space. He didn't sound angry though. "I probably have been arrogant enough in the past to take everything you said on face value. Even made it easy for you to manipulate me, *ne*? The why of it, I have not learned it *yet*." A promise, that he would find out sooner or later, resonated in his tone.

"I think you love the estate. I barely took my jeep out when I got stopped so many times today. Everyone already knew your name, everyone had tales to tell about you. Rosa," he said, coming closer, "even said she had never met such a hardworking and lovely young woman."

Leah frowned, as if trying to keep her shock out of her face. "Of course, I was forced to be nice to her. Your housekeeper is an evil genius that bewitched me with that decadent dark coffee and servings of baklava."

"The important question is how many things have you lied about?" he continued, as if uninterrupted.

Her skin paled, leaving such a frightened look in her eyes that Stavros jerked her around to him.

Was that unwise desire that widened those beautiful eyes real?

Was the pain in her eyes when she spoke of Calista real?

The whole week that he had been gone, he had found himself running through every encounter he had ever had with Leah.

Wondered why she had done so many things he had forbidden her to do, wondered how someone who could be so rejecting and disrespectful of Giannis again and again could also turn around and mourn for his sister, Calista, for so many years.

She had lied about the apartment. She had lied today about liking the estate, a seemingly inconsequential thing that threatened nothing that she held dear.

A keening frustration spread through his veins. Like there was a pit full of dangerous truths that he had never faced and Leah held the key to it all. He forced a smile to his mouth and pressed his hand to her back.

She instantly stiffened and he gritted his jaw, fighting the shockingly strong urge to assert his right like an uncivilized thug.

Right then, it seemed he cared very little about duty, or what was right. All he wanted to do was touch her, to feel like this stranger who told him nothing but lies, that selfish, reckless girl he had married, was really present.

Right then, he wanted to claim something, a part of her, even an emotion, an expression, that no one else knew but him.

Right then, he wanted to be a self-serving bastard like Dmitri and assure himself that she would respond, even against her own surprisingly strong will, when he touched her. That she couldn't pretend, fake, or lie to him in that.

It was as if suddenly there was a beast inside him that wanted to do as it pleased, that was railing against the cage after a lifetime of doing what was right.

And it was Leah that did these things to him.

"So your lawyer friend visited you on Wednesday."

Resignation flattened the curve of her mouth. "His name is Philip." He was only a few inches taller than her, and standing a step below her, his eyes were level with her mouth.

What would she do if he touched those lush lips with his?

Would she fight him and scratch him like the alley cat she had always pretended to be? Or would she sink into his kiss as that desperate desire in her eyes suggested?

Which was the real Leah?

"He was in a foul temper because I came away with you without taking his advice. Not knowing how autocratic you can be, he thinks I gave in too easily."

Stavros wanted to figure her out, put her in a category and move on with life. He didn't want this curiosity, didn't know how to arrest this indulgent self-awareness that she incited in him.

"I think he sees his piece of pie from your fortune dwindling away."

She walked around the table like a cornered prey. "Because he befriended me with nothing but an eye toward what I'm worth?"

"Yes. Your fortune always attracts those kinds of men."

A sigh escaped her, but she wasn't spitting in fury as he had imagined. As if he were the despot she could hate again. "And of course, you know everyone and their intentions best."

"No, I know Philip Cosgrove better than you do. He has had two broken engagements—one with an American candy heiress and the other with a princess from a minor South American nation. He has also been having an affair with a client."

Hands on hips, she looked like a wildcat. "You had him investigated?"

"You should know the truth about him."

"Truth about his personal life? He's a friend and my lawyer, Stavros. Not my lover. If he was going to be one, I'm sure he would have volunteered that information. And even if he didn't, it's my decision to make."

The thought of Leah with any man...he wasn't prepared to ponder his reaction to that. "Now you know what decision to make."

"About whether I want to screw him or not?" she said crudely, even as color darkened her cheeks. "You don't have the right to police me on who I sleep with."

"Discussing my rights and privileges when it comes to you is not a conversation you will like, *agape mou*."

"No, I won't. Because you're a hypocrite. Do you tell your lovers that you have a wife you hide as if she were a stain on the very fabric of your life, Stavros?" Her fingers clutched his hand and pulled it up, a startling tremble in it.

The contact jolted through him. "Do you take it off when you undress your lover? Do you—"

"I don't have to tell them anything," he whispered, dragging her against him. She was stiff against him, yet just the drag of her body set his muscles curling with need.

Ever since she had entered his life, there had been no escape from the shackles his own sense of honor bound him with.

Strange then that he had resented it and fought it for so long.

Was it because, as he had always known, Leah would never be the kind of wife he had imagined for himself— someone calm and dependable like Helene? Even then, had he known that she would incite him to this kind of reckless, unwise need?

"Anyone who's someone knows I have a wife. Which also means I don't have to fend off women with marriage on their mind…"

She stared, unblinking. Her nostrils flared. "You're… disgusting."

It was addictive to play her own game with her, so compelling to watch the different expressions pass through her eyes. In that moment, there were no lies she could tell him. In that moment, the connection between them was as explosive and destructive as the wildfire that had wrecked through the surrounding acreage a few years ago.

A fire that was going to need feeding soon if he didn't it to want it to consume him, as it had already begun to… if he didn't want to lose all sense of right and wrong.

And what was wrong with wanting his own wife in his bed? Maybe if he gave in to the fire, he could function normally again.

"You wanted to know," he goaded her.

"No, I didn't. I was just trying to make a point."

"You sounded like a nagging, jealous wife. Just what I wanted my marriage to be."

All color fled from her face, leaving her gaze stricken. Tears pooled in her eyes. And the sight of those big brown eyes brimming with moisture punched him in the gut.

"*Theos*, Leah—"

"I hate you. I hate that you're keeping me here. I hate that you have so much power over my life and that you use it at every turn to put me in the wrong. And I'm such a pathetic coward that I still stand here, day after day, hoping that you will change your mind. I forget that all you want is to punish me, and yourself, for what happened to Calista.

"That's all this is, isn't it? Duty, righting a wrong... nothing touches you beyond that."

She cast another desperate glance at him, swiped her hands roughly over her eyes and walked away.

Her words sliced at Stavros rendering everything she said about him a lie.

It did hurt, he realized with a strange new awareness. What she said about him mattered because he hadn't meant to hurt her today. *Christos*, he had never meant to hurt Leah.

He had been powerless about her influence on Calista, he had despised her willful rejection of Giannis's love, he had resented that she had sealed his fate the moment she had walked into his life but he had never meant to hurt her.

Not even the day when he had spoken his vows to her utterly petrified form.

Yet, it seemed it was all he had ever done.

That Leah could be vulnerable when it came to him, instead of making him powerful, felt like a curse.

Giannis had saved him from a life of misery and poverty and yawning emptiness and all he had done in return was make his granddaughter's life miserable.

He wouldn't forsake his duty, but neither did he want to hurt Leah anymore.

Leah leaned against the wall in her workroom, shame ringing in her ears. She couldn't believe she had betrayed herself like that. She didn't even care that he had investigated Philip or about what he had found.

But when he had called her a *nagging, jealous* wife, it was as if she could see their future like that...as if he would never see her true self. As if he would never know the real her.

Standing up, she reached for a jug of water. Poured herself a tall drink and guzzled it down.

It couldn't matter this much, not when she would be gone soon.

She couldn't be so vulnerable to him, couldn't get so emotional. The only way to accomplish that was to accept him this way. He would watch her, hover over her, dictate her life *forever*, if she wasn't careful now.

She would give up a little now for the long run.

It wasn't as if the news of Philip's past engagements affected her.

For as long as she had understood herself, only one man had always stubbornly occupied the space in her head. And still, only one man could set her heart racing, only one man could make her hate herself that she wasn't smarter or calmer or even stronger, that she wasn't a match for him in any way.

For the next week, Leah barely slept. The retail buyer, Mrs. DuPont, set up an appointment to see what Leah had for her so far. The conversation that followed, where Leah explained to her that she was now living at Stavros's estate and her reaction to the fact that she was *that Textile Magnate's wife*, had been extremely awkward. As if suddenly Leah's worth as a designer had changed. Whether for good or bad, Leah had no idea.

Once she had heard from her, Leah had finished the sewing on the first three dresses.

Unaccountably nervous, she had snarled at Stavros yesterday for making it all so complicated.

The evening after Mrs. Dupont had called, a seamstress had arrived at her workroom. Her mouth falling open in awe, she fingered the turquoise sheer silk of the cocktail dress, had said in broken English that she loved sewing, and would Mrs. Sporades please give her work.

Having neatly been maneuvered into it, Leah had nodded. Now, she was glad she had given in to Stavros's tactics. Anna was not only talented but also enthusiastic. Having arranged the three dresses on a rack, Leah endlessly tidied the workroom, her stomach a tangle of nerves.

She had risked a lot to be able to make this ready for Mrs. DuPont, to arrive at this stage of making her dream come true.

And yet, it was Stavros's challenging gaze that stayed at the forefront of her mind. The strength of her desire to show him that she was talented, hardworking, that she had what it took to succeed, only grew.

She was determined to make him see her as his equal, in this at least.

Leah would have had her meeting with the retail buyer this afternoon.

The small nugget jolted through Stavros's subconscious like he had set up a reminder chip in his brain to go off every hour. All through his day, through numerous meetings, he found himself thinking of her, of how nervous she had been last night, of how he had seen her work long hours, only remembering to eat because Rosa threatened her.

In the last two weeks, he had found that he couldn't fault her dedication or hard work. And the night before last, learning that she had once again skipped her dinner, he had gone into her workroom.

He had found himself on her doorstep, stunned into silence as Leah commanded Anna to turn around slowly.

Being almost as tall as him, Anna was the perfect model to showcase a knee-length sheath dress in red silk.

Simple yet chic, it touched Anna with sophistication she hadn't possessed before.

Suddenly, he was extremely glad that Giannis had pushed him and Dmitri to start their work at his textile factories on the sewing floor.

In two weeks, he had learned how dedicated and hardworking she was, and in that moment, Stavros had no doubt of her talent.

It was after six by the time the helicopter touched down at his estate. A curious eagerness buffeted him like the wind from the rotor blades.

He headed directly for her workroom, seeing the light on as he approached the house.

He found her at her drawing table, one hand around her nape, turning her head this way and then other. And then her face flopped down onto her table, her shoulders trembled, and a loud, rattling sigh escaped her.

The depth of frustration in that sound startled him.

She straightened up again, tore off sheets from her sketchpad, crumpled them and tossed them.

He must have made a sound, because she suddenly turned then. "I'm so sorry, Anna, but I won't have any work for you in the near—"

In the few seconds before she realized that it was him, Stavros saw it. Distress and disappointment, which slowly cycled to wariness for him.

She slid off the high stool, holding herself stiff. "I thought it was Anna."

"How did it go?" he said, his eagerness to know unprecedented.

Folding her arms defensively, she shrugged. He saw her swallow, look away, and turn toward him again.

When she met his gaze again, she looked ready to battle him. "You were right," she said with bitterness coating it. "She didn't like a single design. You'll be happy to know—"

"You think I would be happy that all your backbreaking work came to nothing?"

She had the sense to look ashamed. *Theos*, she truly believed him to be a sadistic monster, didn't she? Had he ever given her reason to believe otherwise?

"How so?" he asked, noting the lines of strain around her mouth.

Now, she looked stunned. "What do you mean?"

"Why did she reject them? Did she give a reason?" When she still stared at him blankly, irritation touched him. "I'm trying to have a conversation, not attack you," he burst out.

"She thought they were far too high-end for her store, way too sophisticated and bohemian for the clientele that comes to her boutiques. *Too geared toward the jet-setting club like your husband's* were her exact words."

Whatever she had shown her, Mrs. Dupont had refused to budge from her stance. Disappointment settled on Leah's shoulders like a heavy cloak. Had she risked everything for nothing?

"So what is your plan of action next?"

She pulled her attention back to Stavros, sharply aware of his potent presence in her small workroom. In every conversation they had ever had about her work, his interest had been genuine, and suddenly she felt like an ungrateful bitch. Grabbing the notebook, she showed him the notes she had scribbled earlier. "I did what you said I should do in the first place. Had a lengthy discussion about her expectations." That he asked so politely made her failure even more real. "So it's back to the drawing board for me."

He took the book from her and flipped through the notes. "Didn't you leave the fashion house because you wanted to give your own vision a try?"

It had been the foremost thought in her head since Mrs. DuPont had left. "Yes, it was. But it also means walking away from a sure customer, and continuing to trust my vision."

Leaning by her side, he crossed his ankles. The long stretch of his legs in front of her, his tapering waist, the breadth of his shoulders…his masculinity was a striking contrast against her silks and dresses.

"Tell me… all the ideas you discussed today, do they excite you enough to want to risk everything like you did with me?"

Sucking in a deep breath at how effectively he shot to the heart of the matter, Leah shook her head. Talking strategy with him was the last thing she had expected.

He threw the book on the table and turned to her. "Then it is as simple as saying no, and forging ahead."

"But—"

"I saw Anna wearing that red dress and I believe that you're talented, Leah. Add to that, a rich husband who's willing to feed you and supply you with endless fabric. Trust your gut and go for it."

Stunned into a monosyllabic response, Leah stared after his retreating form hungrily, all of her crushing disappointment from the day leaving her in a whoosh. Every muscle in her body ached and yet she felt like there was a renewed fire in her.

And it was thanks to the man she had deceived and hated for years.

CHAPTER SEVEN

LEAH SMOOTHED DOWN the fabric of the beige, supremely boring satin silk she was wearing and suppressed another sigh. The dress, picked by the stylist and coming with a hefty designer tag, wasn't ugly per se.

But the classic fitting bodice and the flaring skirt were not at all her style. With her hair pulled back from her face and the cashmere wrap, she felt thoroughly unlike herself. The heavy diamond choker lay against her throat like a dead, cold weight that could siphon off every bit of warmth from her skin.

Blinking, she looked at Stavros sitting on the other side of the wide cabin, his arrogant head bent to his laptop.

She unbuckled the seatbelt and paced the length of the long cabin all the way to the rear and back.

Her back ached from all the work she had done the past few weeks, once she had received the delivery of all the raw material she had ordered.

In the evenings, she had had meetings every day of the week, some arranged by her, some by the man who, it seemed, would never relent in his duty.

She had met with a graphic designer, a contact she had made working at the fashion house, who was designing her website; a seamstress who had come in from the village because, like Anna, she had heard what Leah did and begged to work on them with her, because she loved dressmaking; and with an attorney that Stavros had arranged to take care of trademarking her label and setting up a company in her name.

Tears had filled her eyes when she had eyed the paperwork with her name on it.

Leah Huntington Sporades—Head Designer.

Her father would have been so proud of her. Giannis, if he knew, would be so proud of her. Even more so, because he had started Katrakis Textiles as a small retail merchant decades ago. But seeing him would mean getting close to him and she couldn't risk that.

Stavros had stood witness to all of it, a silent specter in the room as the platinum-tipped pen had slipped from her hand a couple of times when she wanted to sign the papers. Lost in the magnitude of the moment, she had felt grateful for his hand on her shoulder.

"Have you picked a name for the label?" his question had boomeranged in the silence, testing her strength.

Calista and she had made so many plans. She had been the one who had pushed Leah into stretching her wings, given her confidence that her designs were brilliant. Had worn the dress Leah had designed to her eighteenth birthday party and had dazzled the world in it.

Holding the logo she had come up with with the help of a graphic designer—an elaborately stylish L and C tangled up together, she whispered, *"Leah & Calista."*

His silence beat down on her as she braced herself against his censure.

All her hopes and happiness tied to that name, she couldn't feign defiance. Couldn't muster any defense against his intrusion into what was a monumental moment for her. Would have crumbled into pieces if he had pushed her.

But he had said nothing. Neither praise nor judgment.

Only studied her with a strange light in his eyes until the room had swelled and collapsed around them, echoing with her lies and his questions.

The waiting lawyer had finally cleared his throat and Leah had looked away.

After that day at the pool, Stavros and she had fallen into a surprising routine. Every evening, when he returned from work, he would come into her workroom and they would discuss his business and her work like two polite strangers reading from a script, carefully steering away from any number of topics.

And the elephant in the room, that sharp and growing awareness of each other, roamed free.

At least she had made a lot of progress in the week. And by the end of the day, her back hurt, her fingers ached, and she fell into bed exhausted.

To Leah, it felt like the calm before the storm. But she was determined to continue the peace for as long as he was determined to keep her future hanging in the balance.

So when he'd walked into her workroom yesterday morning, his skin tanned in the glorious Greek sun, and declared that she needed a break after a grueling week, she had readily assented, even if the thought of going away somewhere with him filled her with all kinds of tension.

Had not even blinked when he had told her that they would be attending a small party, would be staying away for a week and that he'd arranged a stylist for her.

He had stood there, as solid and magnificent as ever in a white shirt and tight jodhpurs and riding boots, sweaty and sexy and insanely real, waiting for her to argue and throw a fit.

She had rubbed a hand over her chest, as if she could appeal to her heart to stop its frenzied clamoring. Delusional really, that she still thought she could beg, force or control her body when it came to Stavros.

Did he hate how she dressed? The stinging question had come to her finally. But she had nodded and thanked him, like the dutiful Leah he wanted her to be.

So here she was, on his private jet this time, ensconced

in sheer luxury. Thick cream carpet that swallowed her, spacious rear cabin with a huge king bed, and the man who was turning her inside out, as always.

Sighing, she locked her fingers in her lap when all she wanted was to sweep her fingers into the elaborate updo the stylist had twisted her hair into.

The weight of her thick hair piled into that unceremoniously tight knot pressed against the back of her head and neck. Tension piled into her shoulders.

When the stewardess arrived and inquired after her, she requested sparkling water and aspirin.

"You do not feel well," he stated in that final tone of his.

In a movement that was as graceful as it was quick, he reached her side of the aircraft. His seat was not attached to hers yet he was far too close.

She remained stubbornly silent, determined to win the war against herself.

"You've been fidgeting uncontrollably for the past hour."

"If I'm disturbing you, I—"

"*Theos*, Leah. For once, just answer my question."

"I… I don't like this hairstyle or this dress. They make me feel like…" Closing her eyes, she leaned back against her seat. God, she couldn't have sounded like she was ten years old if she had tried harder.

"Like what?" his tone hovered between resigned amusement and curiosity.

She took the water and aspirin from the stewardess and swallowed it while it watched her.

"Answer me, Leah."

Fighting the urge to burrow into herself like a turtle, she said, "I look like your version of me."

"My version of…" He looked stunned. "Explain."

"In this dress and jewelry, I am Leah Sporades, the demure and dutiful wife of respected billionaire Stavros Sporades. There's nothing of me in this. It is all you."

He froze and it seemed air and sound, the very matter around them froze along with him. "I do not understand."

"That stylist you hired, she—" she forced herself to breathe "—this is what she presented me with."

Frowning, he ran his gaze over the straps and over the tight ruffles of the bodice.

Her skin warmed up as if she was a flower and he was the very sun she craved. Leah tightened her fists to stop from covering herself.

He cleared his throat, his nostrils flaring. "I agree that it is not your usual…style."

She nodded, wondering why she couldn't have just shut her mouth. Why some stupid, irrational, brazen part of her always insisted on putting herself in his line of fire. Why, even as she hated his overbearing interference, she recklessly courted it.

"You are saying that this stylist, that someone in my staff picked, chose…this *demure, dutiful little outfit*," he repeated her words, "based on how I want my wife to be presented to the world?"

"Yes."

He lounged in his chair, his expression thoughtful. "Why did you give in then? You won't even breathe air if it means following my orders."

"You commanded an army to help me get dressed for a party. Like any sane person would, I assumed that you hate how I dress. Just as you hate how I breathe, talk and generally conduct my life."

"I don't hate how you dress. You do, somehow, own and wear the flimsiest articles of clothing of I have ever seen…"

"*That is* my style as a designer—light and dreamy bohemian pieces," she sputtered, affronted.

"…and will probably expire either because of the sun or the cold one of these days, but you always look sexy and sophisticated."

Little pinpricks of heat awoke all over and her gaze flew

to his. He stared right back, as if daring her to challenge his accurate and somehow intimate observation of her style. Or maybe his right to comment on it.

The moment stretched and morphed into something else, a strange heat filling the cabin.

Accepting defeat under the thundering boom of her heart, Leah looked away. She cleared her throat and fingered the fabric of her dress.

"For all my sins, *thee mou*, I did not dictate how you should be dressed."

She looked up. "Then she, like everyone else in the world, rightfully believes that you are ashamed of me and decided that her job was to make me somehow worthy of you."

"Do not push me, *yineka mou*." The glitter in his eyes pushed Leah into keeping mute. "Tell me why you relented, Leah."

She looked away, squirming under his leisurely scrutiny. "I'm being dutiful, cooperative…"

The words trailed on her lips as he started laughing.

It swelled in the decadently silent cabin, crept inside her, filling every yearning space with itself. Scraped against her senses, like a physical thing meant to incite that relentless clamoring in every cell again.

"When you laugh, you almost look human," she blurted out.

"As opposed to an alien?"

"As opposed to a man whom I've never seen to be anything but rigid, autocratic, and driven by duty and responsibility. When was the last time you did something because you wanted to do it and not because your lofty sense of morals said you should do it? Something that's totally crazy but feels unbearably good? Something that devours you until you have it?"

Lazy interest flickered in his face. Little pinpricks of

desire uncurled within her. "What and when was the last time you did something like that?"

Her throat dry, Leah licked her lips. "I ate half a cheese-cake that Rosa baked for me last night. It was heavenly."

That tawny gaze fell to her mouth. And lingered. "Wanting to do something with an utter madness is usually a sign of why you shouldn't."

Leah could very well imagine that mouth, beautifully carved and yet cruel, pressing on hers, could feel the liquid desire skitter across her skin.

"Living like that, with no thought to the future or the people around has lasting effects, *pethi mou*. It's a choice that has consequences beyond one."

"Like what?"

He shrugged, something shuttering in his expression.

"How is it that Dmitri and you are such close friends and he didn't corrupt you at all?" Leah asked.

"Maybe I'm incorruptible."

The cocky rise of his brows goaded her on. "Maybe," her heart beat so loud, "the right temptation to corrupt you hasn't come along."

The challenge simmered in the air. But terrified as she was, Leah wouldn't look away. Something about that hard, unyielding arrogance of his shattered her usual defenses, drove her to one risk after the other.

Being in his company made her forget all her fears, she realized with a staggering self-awareness.

Suddenly, he caught her hands and dragged her forward on the seat. Only his hands touched hers, and yet she was aware of every inch of her skin.

"You have been working all kinds of hours this week."

"Don't sound so surprised." She searched for something to concentrate on instead of his tight clasp. "Anyway, so do you."

"Yes, but mine is not grueling, backbreaking work like yours. Rosa tells me you take frequent breaks to stretch and run, so that's good." He turned her hands around in his, as if testing the weight and fit of them against his. Slowly resting them back in her lap.

"So you do admit that I know how to take care of myself?"

"I never disagreed that you have the faculty for that. Whether you choose to use it or not…" Uncharacteristic hesitation danced in his face. "Leah, I ordered an army because I thought you would enjoy being pampered for a day. Thought you would like dressing up, have a chance to catch up with others like you. You did say my estate was in the middle of nowhere."

Warmth swelled in her chest and spilled over. Nothing she said to herself to contain it helped.

She was like the pathetically adorable little puppy that whimpered and promised forever for a little bit of attention and kindness.

Did she thank him for it or did she brazen it out with an inappropriate remark? In the end, she did neither. Just nodded and stood up, suddenly feeling caged in her own skin.

She wanted to, *needed to*, hate Stavros. And seeing this side of him was slowly but surely eroding the entire foundation of her life.

"What kind of party requires that we stay there for a week?"

"Katrakis Textiles is celebrating its fiftieth year anniversary. Tonight's grand celebration is to honor everything Giannis has accomplished in the past fifty years. And then we will spend a week with him."

Katrakis Textiles—Giannis's legacy for Dmitri, Stavros *and* her. "I want no part of it."

"I don't believe you."

Trembling with panic, Leah locked her hands by her sides, the urge to pound at him rising again.

"I'm not lying about this. Dmitri and you are welcome

to it. Now if you could please tell your pilot to turn around and head back to your estate—"

He didn't even blink. "I won't. Maybe I forgot to mention it, but this is one of the conditions you have to meet for your freedom, Leah."

Her throat felt like it was made of glass. "You can't do this."

Rising from his seat, Stavros planted himself in her way. He frowned, taking in the trembling of her shoulders, the real flare of panic in her eyes. "Leah, what's going on?"

Her chin tilted up, her gaze slowly focusing on him again. Jaw gritting, she squared her shoulders. "I don't want anything to do with Giannis or his legacy. He…rejected my mom without looking back just because she fell in love with my dad. He didn't even come when she died, he never accepted my dad."

"He was heartbroken that he had driven your mother away, Leah. And she…she was just as stubborn as him."

"He loved you and Dmitri more than he ever loved her or me. He took me in because he had no choice after my dad died."

"He tried to make amends for his mistakes."

Leah shook her head, forcing the words to come. "He did what he failed to do with my mom, to me. He…he ruined my life by bringing you into it. He took away my freedom by forcing you to marry me."

"He did not force me, Leah. I owed him everything in my life. I would have made any sacrifice he…"

She recoiled from him as if he had struck her.

Christos! She was a complex puzzle he would need to spend a lifetime to understand.

Beneath the reckless defiance, beneath her constant animosity for him, did Leah want his approval?

"Of course," she said, her voice trembling. "The great Giannis Katrakis who's made kings of his godsons, plucked them from poverty and obscurity…and the honorable Stavros Sporades who would do anything for him, to the point of marrying his obnoxious granddaughter…and whose life has been ruined by it?

Mine.

"I'm not an instrument in achieving redemption for Giannis or for you to show your gratitude."

"You don't understand how much he longs to—"

"And you do? You understand feelings and fears, Stavros? Even Calista's death…all it means to you is a failure… Do you ever miss her? Did she ever mean anything to you other than being a responsibility?"

Tight grooves appeared by his mouth, his stunning face white beneath his dark skin. He looked haunted. "I took care of her since she was a crawling toddler. I—"

"*You took care of her, you protected her, you bought her clothes and jewelry*, but did you ever love her? Does Giannis mean anything to you other than a debt to repay? Am I anything but a penance for your supposed failure? God, it's like your heart is nothing but stone."

Pure fury wreathed his features and yet, he didn't scare Leah. All she wanted was to hurt him for pushing her to this.

First her father, then Calista—they had left her shattered, inconsolable, alone. Yet, somehow she had managed, she had found something she loved and started pouring her heart and soul into it.

She couldn't risk getting attached to her grandfather, she couldn't survive another loss.

"Everything you have ever done has been self-serving, and you dare to question me?" he shot back.

"Yes, I dare. You have no fears, no doubts, nothing that holds you back from what you think is right. Don't pretend like he means something to you."

"Giannis is the father I never had. He's been a better mother to me than the one who walked out on us. He has been my family, my friend; he's everything to me. He came for me based on a small promise my drunkard father roped him into making for some age-old village tradition. If he hadn't kept his word, I wouldn't have known kindness or honor. I would have spent my life in poverty and misery. So yes, I would do anything if it means it would bring a smile to his face."

His outburst stunned Leah, the ache in those words irrefutable, rendering her bitter accusations a lie. That he had suffered neglect at the hands of his parents, that there was so much depth to his determination toward his duty, it shook her from within.

The silence rang with his fury, his movements caged and restless.

He ran a hand over his eyes and exhaled, suddenly looking extremely tired. A haunted look wreathed his features. "I don't care if you think he ruined your life. All he ever intended was to keep you safe, even from yourself.

"So you will not only act how Giannis Katrakis's granddaughter and heiress should tonight, you will also spend the next few days with him, and you will tell him how grateful you are for everything.

"If you know what's good for you, and I think that is one thing you know very well, you will obey me."

CHAPTER EIGHT

LEAH LOOKED OUT from the huge balcony that gave a view of the lush acreage surrounding her grandfather's house.

The estate was covered with huge marquees. Multi-colored fountains were lit up in the grounds, buffet tables groaning under the weight of delicacies and dishes. Soft music filtered from unobtrusive speakers nearer the house.

Laughter and greetings in Greek floated up from the crowd of two hundred or more guests, piercing through the melancholy that gripped her. In the half hour or so she had spent down there, she had only heard goodwill for Giannis and praise for Stavros and Dmitri.

It seemed her grandfather couldn't have chosen better men to continue his legacy. She was the outsider, the curiosity, the unknown, and being among people who had known her mother, the fact hurt. Yet she had no one but herself to blame.

When she had stepped out of the limo on Stavros's arm, it was as if the entire world had come to a standstill. Thundering silence had reigned as she had walked through the parting crowd, her gaze both searching for and bracing for the sight of her grandfather.

He's taking a break, Stavros whispered in her ear and her breath left her in a ball. Her knees would have buckled beneath her if he hadn't held her up against his solid frame.

An hour later, here she was waiting for Giannis, everything she had done over the past decade rushing up toward her.

She hadn't been in her grandfather's house for almost eight years now, having chosen to live with Calista at Stavros's house even before he had tied her to him. The grand house was as lifeless as Stavros's house had been full of peace.

Her grandfather had been so open and loving of her when Stavros had brought her home. Just fifteen, she had been grief-stricken, too shattered by her father's sudden death to respond to Giannis with anything more than single-word responses. But he hadn't given up on her. He had bid Stavros to bring Calista along next time. And just as he had predicted, Calista had been a welcome storm in her life— fun, reckless, daring, and somehow, she had understood Leah's grief.

Except Leah had never imagined it would be Calista that she would lose.

Crippled by Calista's loss, stunned by Stavros's decision, she had refused to even look at Giannis. If she didn't love him, if she didn't hug him as his arms sometimes ached to, if she didn't pin all her love on her kind grandfather who told her thrilling tales about a mother she had never known, she wouldn't have to live through another loss.

If she didn't love him, there would be no pain when he was gone. Even when Giannis had recovered from his heart attack, she had refused to see him.

Stavros was right. She had truly become selfish. A coward who cared about nothing but protecting herself from pain.

Something broke her reverie and she turned around.

Stavros standing slightly behind him, for support she knew, her grandfather stood under the archway, his brown eyes hungrily studying her. "Come close so I can see you." His voice, soft and coarse, reverberated in the stillness.

Tugged as though by invisible cords, she took a few steps. Her heart thudded in her chest.

"You look so much more like her now, so much like my beautiful Ioanthe. Welcome home, Leah."

And just like that, every defense she had put in place, every wall she had erected around her heart, came tumbling down.

Tears overflowing onto her cheeks, half blinded by the emotion engulfing her, Leah stumbled toward him. Wrapped her arms around him with no regard to his frail body, with no thought other than to lose herself in his unconditional acceptance. On the periphery, she heard Stavros's soft curse.

Giannis was so thin and insubstantial that if not for Stavros anchoring them, she knew she would have toppled them down. "I'm so sorry," she whispered, a haunting void in her gut.

How cowardly she had been to deny herself his embrace, his love?

Her grandfather held her with a tight grip. The remembered pine scent of him made her tremble. "Shhh…do not cry, *thee mou*."

When she became aware of her surroundings again, Giannis was sitting in a chair and she was kneeling in front of him, the stone floor digging into her knees. Overwhelmed by shame and grief, she hid her face in his knees while he kept his hand over her head, whispering endearments. Even in the turmoil she was in, she knew Stavros had left them alone. Breathing loudly, she swiped her fingers over her cheeks and looked up.

"I'm a coward. All I ever cared about was protecting myself."

He shook his head and smiled, tucking her hand into his. "You are here now."

She wouldn't be if not for Stavros. But with all her old

fears swirling beneath the joy of seeing her grandfather, Leah couldn't be grateful to Stavros. Not yet.

Leah's soft cries haunted Stavros as he paced room after room, trying to find her. More than two hours had passed since he had left her with Giannis and rejoined the party, his thoughts in a whirl.

When Giannis had brought him to this very mansion years ago, it had taken him a month to learn the layout of the house. Now he cursed it.

His nurse had just informed him that Giannis had returned to his bedroom an hour ago. Which meant Leah could be anywhere.

A sense of failure haunted him, a gnawing in his gut just as in the days after Calista had died. Had he pushed her too far tonight? Why had she cried as though her heart had been breaking?

Her reaction to seeing Giannis shook Stavros on levels he couldn't grasp.

He finally found her in the dark music room, a shadow sitting in silence. Ioanthe used to play piano here, he remembered Giannis telling him fondly.

Stepping inside, he flicked the switch on and light from the overhead crystal chandelier flooded the room.

His chest swelled with a sudden surge of emotion as his gaze found her on the chaise longue, her legs tucked under her, her dress billowing around her.

"I wouldn't comment on the wine bottle, or my dress or how I live my life just now, Stavros." She flicked him a wary glance, guilty color streaking her cheeks. A bottle of red wine sat on the vanity table, a half empty glass in her hand. "I'm painfully alive, so that should be good enough for you."

His breath came out in shuddering exhale, old fear lurking just beneath the surface.

Her hair had come undone from the severe style she

hadn't liked, framing her face in disarray. Her eyes looked a little swollen and that laughing, mocking, sensuous mouth was pinched at the corners. Face scrubbed of makeup and huddled against the dark red upholstery, she looked achingly innocent, and lonely. And *afraid*, he thought frowning.

"Are you hiding from me, Leah?"

Her sigh rattled in the silence. "Would it help my case if I said I was?"

Irritation flickered inside him. Couldn't she tell him even such a tiny truth?

Even the proper, demure dress had lost its war against her. Crumpled and stained at the hem where she must have been kneeling while one strap hung half down her arm, it bared her neck and the upper swell of one breast. The diamond choker glittered against her slender throat.

A relentless peal of hunger began to simmer through him. His fingers itched to trace that delicate collarbone, his mouth tingling to press against the pulse hammering at the base of her throat.

But even as desire ran rampant in his veins, it was the underlying thread of tenderness that unsettled him. He should have been happy that she had done as he had asked, that she hadn't hurt Giannis as she had…*hurt him? Wounded him?*

You are made of stone.

How had her words found such purchase in him? Another new awareness that only Leah could elicit, another new territory that she pushed him into…

Theos, what was wrong with him?

Tucking his hands in the pockets of his trousers, he leaned against the doorway.

"You don't look like my version of you anymore. You look like…you. Even that dress…I think you have bent it to your will, Leah."

"I'm glad to hear that," she said, sounding anything but. "Aren't you done pulling my strings tonight?"

The dare in her tone would have made him smile if

he could have believed it completely. If he hadn't heard the quiver she worked hard to suppress. If he hadn't seen such ache and longing ravage her fragile face when she had seen Giannis.

Still, he played along, unsure of her mood. Even more dangerous, unsure of his own intentions. "Have you still not learned not to challenge me, Leah?"

She looked down into her drink and he had a feeling she wanted to hide from him. That she didn't want him to see her like this at all.

"I'm telling you to leave me alone, Stavros." She confirmed his suspicions. "I'm telling you that I feel as reckless and deranged as you have always called me. I'm telling you to not dissect my actions today and pronounce judgment."

Even as her tone rose, she still didn't meet his eyes.

Had he made it so hard for her to show him anything but that selfish facade? Was he truly such an unfeeling monster then?

Had he always been like that?

He had worked so hard at his grandfather's small farm, trying to pitch in for his father's negligence, afraid that they would throw Calista and him out on the streets.

He remembered a strange calm the night his grandmother had said his mother wasn't coming back; he remembered not shedding even a tear when he had found out that his father was dead. All he had thought of even that day was how he would shield Calista from it.

For as far back as he could remember, it had been about the little girl that had followed him around from the moment she had been able to walk, hugging him, kissing him, and coming to him with tears when she had a bruise, knocking the breath out of him.

She had had such trust in her eyes that he hadn't known, literally, what to do with it. Hadn't known how to return those hugs, hadn't known what he could say to her. So instead he had done what he could.

He had protected her, provided her with everything he possibly—

Theos, no!

The thought that had always brought such comfort to him now flayed him, digging in, making him flinch in pain.

Do you actually miss Calista? Did you ever love her?

Had Leah been right in her cruel judgment of his feelings for Calista too?

After he had lost Calista, he had felt angry, confused, unbalanced. His failure poisoned his very thoughts, so he shoved them away and focused on his actions instead.

Protecting Leah, and punishing himself and her, had provided him with perverse relief.

Now, her words taking root inside him, he felt raw.

He should leave her, every instinct warned him. He should walk away when all she was capable of was piercing him with her acerbic words. He should be done with her, set her free and not look back.

And yet, he couldn't have walked away if his very breath had depended on it.

Beneath his duty toward Giannis and his sense of responsibility toward her, even beneath his unnerving attraction to her, something very strange had begun to flutter in him for Leah.

He was in awe of that feeling as much as he was wary of it.

"What else do you intend to put me through in this test of yours, Stavros?"

Everything about what he had seen tonight troubled him. "Leah, was your hatred of me reason enough to keep away from Giannis?"

The wariness slowly dissipated as she held his gaze and finished her drink. Something new dawned in her glittering gaze—a satisfaction, and his breath rattled. One long leg stretching in front of her, her stance loosened. Her slender shoulders squared, her nostrils flared.

"I would let you think that if I thought it would hurt you. I would do anything right this moment if I thought it would make you bleed."

He found himself walking toward her, found himself straddling the lounger to face her. It was as though the combination of pain and fury in her eyes tugged at him.

She looked glorious, infinitely breathtaking.

She had already somehow pierced him, the truth lingered on his lips. The thought of that vulnerability, of sharing that much with her made his gut clench.

Clasping her cheek, he lifted her to face him, his pulse pounding in his veins. The sound of her sharp breath was like a balm to him. "Are you so thirsty for my blood then, *pethi mou*?"

"Yes."

Her resounding answer sent a shiver through to his very bones. It was as though seeing Giannis had peeled off that facade of hers.

"Are you satisfied, Stavros? Have I risen in my worthiness in your eyes?"

The thunderous roar of his heart, the curling heat in his muscles made it harder for him to whisper the one question that had been battering at him all day. He felt as if a huge truth was within his grasp, as if the real Leah was within his reach. And in that moment, he would do anything to have it.

To have her, to know her, to feel her...

If he had her, would the strange turmoil inside him stop?

"When has my opinion of you begun to matter, Leah?" he whispered softly, the words burning on his lips.

He felt her instant recoil in the stillness of her form, in the way the very air around her seemed to suspend and freeze.

A violent energy burst from her limbs. Lifting the hem of that heavy, voluminous dress away from her legs, she faced him. A flash of a toned thigh met his gaze and he looked away guiltily, the depth of his hunger for her shredding his control.

Her hair whipped around her face, the swish of her dress adding to the harsh exhales of her breath.

The uncaring mask back in place, she mocked him with that practiced glare in her eyes, with that biting edge to her tone. By hiding from him what he so desperately wanted to see.

"You know what, Stavros? Scratch that answer. I don't care whether I could hurt you or not. I don't give a damn about you. I did what you asked of me, I made sure Giannis is happy. I played the part of an heiress and his loving granddaughter to the hilt. Which means I'm one step closer to achieving my freedom. *That's* what I care about.

"Tell me what will make the next month go faster so that I can see the back of you. Tell me what is next so that I never have to talk to you ever again."

A dangerous fire burst in his belly.

How dare she put on this mask again? How dare she deny him even the merest hint of the real her? How dare she sink under his skin and yet deny him the same satisfaction?

How dare she turn him into this man teetering on the edge of his control, and walk away so blithely?

Before she could get to her feet and escape, because he had no doubt that she was about to escape, he clasped her wrist and tugged her down.

She fell onto her haunches, her shoulders knocking against his chest. For the first time in his life, Stavros gave in to every irrational urge, every desperate want. "What are you afraid of, Leah? Me or yourself?" he taunted.

Primal satisfaction pounded through him, the increasing frenzy of her movements telling him he had hit the mark. "I'm not afraid of you," she said, twisting her upper body to get away from him. Ended up torturing him further with the slide of her body against his.

"Then face me, Leah," he whispered, driven by some

reckless urge to prove that his opinion mattered to her, that he mattered to her.

Just as she was beginning to matter to him...

She couldn't let him touch her, she couldn't let him kiss her.

If she let him touch her tonight, if she let him hold her tonight, something inside her would break. She would pour out the whole wretched truth, she would blurt how lonely she had been...

If she let him see the real her, she would have no shield, no armor against him. And even in the fragility of her emotions, Leah knew she couldn't let Stavros close.

"Why are you acting like this?"

Her arms ached with the effort it took to hold herself so stiffly in the circle of his body; every inch of her hurt to stay unaffected in the warmth of his rough embrace.

"Like a man acts with his wife?"

She fought back stupidly hot tears, knowing that she didn't stand a chance against that claim.

When she pushed against his wrists again, he grabbed her hands this time. Laced her fingers through his and pulled her forward. Her hip touched his rock-hard thigh and she bit down on her lip.

Giving up her struggle, she leaned her forehead against his shoulder. "What do you want from me?"

"All I've ever wanted is the truth, *pethi mou*." His fingers circled her nape with a possessively delicate touch. Her heart thudded as if it would thunder out of her chest as she raised her head. Molten heat filled his eyes. "But you won't give me that. So, I will claim what I can of you."

Somehow she shook her head, even mesmerized by how low and silky he sounded, by how astonishingly expressive his face was.

How had she always seen only one facet of Stavros?

There were so many sensations—the rough texture of his hands against hers, his bruising grip on her wrists, the sudden heaviness of her breasts as they jutted against him, the beckoning hardness of his thighs against her hips—she should have expired from so much sensory input. It was as though her body was one pealing, pulsing mass of sensation…

He was everything she ever wanted and yet she couldn't give in. "I don't want this. I…"

"In this, you're not a good liar." He placed a finger on the pulse at her neck, feral satisfaction filling his gaze. "Your pulse betrays you…your darkening eyes betray you." With every word he said, his accent became thicker, her breaths came faster. "Even your mouth betrays you…" His long fingers framed her cheeks, pulling her closer.

Her hips nudged his thighs apart, and the hottest sensation zigzagged through her. His thighs were so hard and powerful, his touch possessive and potent.

How was she supposed to resist him when he looked at her like that?

"I will not be your wife soon. I won't—"

He smiled then, and the sinful curve of his mouth, the dark laughter in his eyes undid the last layer of her willpower. "Now, tonight, in this moment, you're still mine, *yineka mou*. One kiss for all the trouble you have caused me, Leah, one kiss for everything you deny me…"

He had turned her life upside down, and now he was doing the same to her heart.

Even as he staked his claim, he didn't take the kiss. Long lashes hiding his gaze, his arm around her waist a heavy weight, he paused. But sinking under a deluge of emotions, Leah stared, transfixed, at the bow shape of his leanly sculpted mouth, felt need trump every fear.

Covering the last millimeter, she pressed her mouth to his. His savage growl shocked her as much as the incinerating texture of his lips…

His mouth was hot and hard, and a million sparks exploded under her skin.

With erotic strokes, he left her no air to breathe, gave her
no room to think. Sensation exploded as he slanted his lips
this way and that, his fingers in her hair holding her immo-
bile for him. Teeth bit into her lower lip and punished. When
she moaned, he softly blew at the spot before nipping again.

One hand slid over her hips, moved possessively over to
her buttocks and then pulled her closer until she was straddling him. But not close enough for her to feel the part of
him that she wanted to...

Even that, he controlled.

Her breasts felt full and aching as he crushed her against
the wall of his chest with a palm at the base of her back.
She panted, her breath balling up in her throat. Trembling,
she ran her fingers over her mouth, and her cheek where
his stubble had scratched her skin.

That mouth that could lacerate her with words, God,
it could weave such erotic magic...those hands that had
dumped cold water on her, they could evoke such heat
in her; the cradle of his arms, it made her feel so alive...

He didn't kiss softly, he didn't seduce, he didn't cajole.

He wrung the response out of her as he did everything
else with her. Impinging his will on her senses, imprinting
his hard muscles over her soft ones... The way he ruled
her life, the way he decided what she needed.

She could have spent the next hundred years wedged
against his hardness, lost in his kiss, delirious with the
pleasure he brought her. But not let him tell her what she
needed, not accept what he deigned to give her.

No!

In that, she couldn't let him decide her fate, couldn't
let fear rule her.

Determined to give him a fight, determined to demand
her due, she pulled her mouth away from his, trailed it
along that hard jawline, buried it in the crook of his neck.
Tasted the salty tang of his skin. An insistent pull began at
her sex, and she moaned against his bristly jaw.

His grip loosened in her hair, his other hand loosely anchoring her against him as she caressed him roughly, learned every muscle and sinew.

She touched him everywhere, reveling in the tensile hardness of him. Traced up his rock-hard thighs, up toward his groin. And her palm found his erection—hard and long and so utterly arousing... Her breath jerked in her throat.

She had done this to Stavros. The harsh rhythm of his breath in her ears, that incredible stillness of him around her...

Goaded by a clamoring instinct, she shaped him with her palm, moved her finger down the length of him, a shiver spewing in her own muscles.

A guttural sound fell from his lips as he bucked against her hand. It lasted an infinitesimal breath but she knew he had almost surrendered then, that he had lost his rules, his very control then.

Only a second but it was still a victory.

He clasped her wrist in a vise-like grip. She looked up at him and smiled, feeling dazedly powerful, painfully glorious.

In this moment, with him...any pain would have been worth it.

Dark color filled his cheeks, his gaze haunted, agonized. "Why do you push me to the very edge, Leah?" His accent was coarse and uneven as he breathed the words into her temple. "Why do you fight me, deny me every step of the way?"

"Did you not like how I responded, Stavros?" she said shivering, and for a second, he clasped her in his warmth. If he had showed her tenderness...no, this was better. "You forced me to...to respond, just as you force me into everything. That kiss was about domination, not desire, not about taking tenderness."

He studied her, his own gaze curiously empty. "And if I had asked?" Shaking his head, he stepped away from her.

As if he didn't want her answer. When he met her gaze again, his expression was shuttered. "You're not wearing your ring."

"It's somewhere in my jewelry."

"As long as you're still bound to me, you will wear it."

She stared in stunned silence.

"It would please Giannis too. And that matters to you, doesn't it, Leah? So I don't have to worry that you would talk about our little deal with him."

"And when I'm...when I win our deal?" she forced the words out through the knot in her throat. That she would never see him again was like a lead weight in her chest.

"You will not abandon him, I know that." Retribution, if she did, rang in his tone. "And I will continue to take care of the one man who means the world to me."

Stavros left Leah without looking back, the image of her swollen mouth and dazed eyes burned into his brain forever. If he stayed another minute, he didn't know what he would do.

He was unknown to himself the way he had reached for her, the way he craved her. In that moment, he had so desperately needed to claim something of her. Shuddering with frustrated desire, he wondered if she had given him anything that he hadn't taken, wondered why it mattered so much, now.

One of these days, he would be releasing her from their marriage. He knew it as surely as the taste of her still floated on his lips.

Yet, instead of anticipating his freedom, all he suddenly knew was a keen urgency.

To understand Leah, to steal a part of her for himself even as she denied him.

CHAPTER NINE

WHY HAD HE kissed her?

The question haunted Leah endlessly.

What had driven her into giving in so easily?

If she closed her eyes, she could still hear his harsh breath, his softly spoken words…

Her fingers shook and her scissors slipped on the fabric. With a frustrated cry, Leah threw the scissors across the room and fingered the silk gently.

The sheer tulle she was cutting for the underskirt of the wedding gown was the most expensive fabric that she had ordered for her collection. At least, the amount of cloth she had ruined was minimal.

Carefully, she folded the fabric and tucked the tissue wrapping around it. She wasn't going to get anything that needed focus done today.

More than a week had passed since the night of the party. The next evening, Stavros had left. She had had a feeling he had left because of the kiss.

There was something new—an intensity to his gaze now when he looked at her.

Walking to the rack, she took a cocktail dress in deep red. Threading the needle, she sat down on the couch and began piping the hem.

She was glad she had persuaded Stavros to have most of her materials packed and sent to her grandfather's estate. Her grandfather tired easily and without her work to keep her busy, she would have driven herself mad thinking of Stavros the whole time.

The sheer arrogance of the man, the clinical coldness with which he had made her respond—she had whimpered like a dog, for God's sake… Even that couldn't stop her from trembling every time she remembered the feel of his rough mouth, the bite of his teeth into her lower lip, the way his large hands skimmed and molded her body…

It had been her first kiss and it had been an exercise in… What? A war of wills? A balm to his ego? Or had he been as powerless as her?

Frustration carved through her.

She wanted to hate him, she did hate him for that cold resolve…but he also made her feel so alive. Lost in his kiss, drowning in his arms, there had been no place for fear, no place for hiding.

Nothing but living…

When he looked at her with such glittering desire in his tawny eyes, when he looked at her as if she could unlock something inside him…it was so easy to believe that he saw her as an equal.

Which was the stupidest thing ever given that he was with his lover in Athens attending a charity event right now… He was probably back in her bed too, she thought nastily and gasped as she pricked her finger with the needle.

The good thing was how much work she had gotten done and the time she had spent with Giannis.

After an excruciating couple of days, Giannis had finally taken pity on her and asked her to show him a dress from her collection. He had pronounced her dress beautiful and her, an extremely talented designer who would take the fashion industry by storm. Making dresses was in their blood, he had said with pride. While his praise had been extravagantly effusive, it had still filled her with warmth.

So every day, she took breakfast and lunch with him, then accompanied him on a short walk around the house.

Sometimes, they played a board game that he taught her, and sometimes, they discussed her designs. They carefully kept away from talking about Stavros and the state of her marriage.

After being afraid for so long, after training herself to not get attached to him, forming such a strong emotional bond should have been hard to do in just a few days. But spending one of those yawningly long Greek afternoons chatting with Giannis, or just sitting together in comfortable silence, or the times he would nap and she would sit with her sketchpad on the back terrace, had become incredibly precious to her.

Her grandfather was irreverent, naughty, and kind.

As the sweltering days gave way to cooler nights, her fears melted away and like the leaves slowly changing color, an incredible sense of joy pervaded her. It was so alien that she had taken to staring at herself in the mirror, wondering if it made her look different.

As her cell phone chirped, she realized it was time for lunch with Giannis.

The time that Stavros had stipulated she spend with Giannis was rapidly coming to an end, and suddenly, saying goodbye to her grandfather, even temporarily, was the last thing Leah wanted to do.

Stavros was avoiding her, she knew as surely as her heart thumped when he called every evening and asked about Giannis.

Something had changed between them that night, whether for good or bad, she didn't know.

Her footsteps clicking on the outer courtyard, Leah sighed. She could hate him all she wanted for forcing her to this, but she wouldn't have had this wonderful week with Giannis if not for him.

Leah joined Giannis at the table laid out on the back patio that offered an unending view of the shoreline. The raised porch provided shade from the Greek sun. Reaching Giannis, she kissed his papery cheek and sat down.

The small table groaned under the weight of a colorful and mouthwatering array of dishes. "I didn't know that we were having a feast today," she said, spreading her napkin on her lap. "I would have skipped breakfast and run a few more miles."

"Eat," Giannis said. "No man likes his woman so thin that it could hurt him if he embraces her."

Popping a piece of a juicy, thick-crusted pie into her mouth, Leah shook her head. "Since no man is actually intent on embracing or otherwise expressing love for your granddaughter," she continued in that same irreverent tone, "no worries there."

It had become a bit of a game this past week between them, about who could say the most outrageous thing. The smile disappeared from Giannis's face. "He is your husband, child. Are you denying him rights?"

Leah coughed, choking on the flaky piece of pastry. Recovering, she took a sip of frosty lemonade. "I don't want to ruin the afternoon by talking about it."

"Your mother is gone. Calista is gone. I learn from Stavros that you keep to yourself. Maybe talking to an old man will help, *ne*?"

His overtly sweet tone made her smile. "I do not want to talk about his rights, or how subservient I have to be because I'm his wife, grandfather."

"You want a modern marriage. I understand. But I have concern for you. You are very lonely. I see it in your eyes."

She was lonely, she had been for so many years now. That's why she had capitulated so easily to Stavros's touch.

She could almost fool herself into believing that.

"Leah?"

Leah didn't have the heart to push his concern away. It was so strange that she couldn't be angry with Giannis when he was the one who gave Stavros all the power over her, yet she could hold a grudge against Stavros himself.

Somewhere along the line, it had become a shield, she realized. A shield that was slowly beginning to get holes. That's what had changed.

Her grandfather clutched her fingers and she returned the pressure, feeling a sudden thickness in her throat.

"What Stavros and I have…it's too complicated. How can I think of him as my husband or anything else respectful for that matter if he continues to treat me like a child?"

"It is his nature to protect the people he considers close."

I'm not close to him, the juvenile taunt rose to her lips. She didn't care that she wasn't, she decided resolutely.

"I have a feeling that's all he knows how to do. He…I have never seen him laugh, never need anyone. Never seen him vulnerable." And yet, he had looked so different that night they kissed, almost vulnerable…to her touch, to her words even. "He was probably born fully formed with a set of rules about how life should be lived, in his hand."

Something flickered in Giannis's gaze and Leah swallowed the rest of her words. "Stavros does not ask, or take anything for himself. Only gives."

There was such truth in her grandfather's words that Leah stilled. She had never seen him ask, or demand anything for himself. It had only ever been about her, or Calista or Giannis, or even Dmitri sometimes. But never about himself.

Still grappling with that, she made her voice casual and gripey again. "For all I know, he does not need anything like normal people do. He will probably order the cook to not serve me if he learned I eat my dessert first."

A twinkle appeared in Giannis's eyes. "You speak like this to him?"

When she nodded, he laughed, the flimsy sound bursting out of him. It shook his frail frame, and alarm crashed through her. Sensing her anxiety, he sobered. "Laughing

with you is good for me. I still believe in the rightness of
your marriage. You are precisely what Stavros needs in his
life. And you—" something too close to the truth lingered
in his eyes "—him. I wish you would give it a real try. You
will find him to be an honorable man."

Beneath his rigidness, beneath his tunnel view of the
world, she hated to admit, Stavros's actions had always
been driven by good intentions.

What would it be like to trust him with her fears? What
would it be like to give herself over to him? To really give
their relationship a try? To be the woman he shared himself with?

Feigning a nonchalance she was far from feeling, she
looked at Giannis, who watched her curiously. She had
seen the questions in his eyes, had seen him hesitate. And
suddenly, she couldn't bear to go away with Giannis not
knowing the truth.

Abandoning her food, she clasped his hand. "I didn't
take drugs that night. I have never touched that stuff in my
life. I know I have pained you but I…"

A catch in her throat, she pinned her forehead to his
hand.

How could she put her irrational fear into words?

The sound of a soft tread, the way her skin prickled,
she instantly knew.

Without turning, she let go of Giannis's hand and leaned
back in her seat.

Stavros was back.

He believed her.

The realization stopped Stavros in his tracks. As powerful as the sun beating down on him, as simple as the
feeling in his gut.

Just as she would never have gone to the media with her
story, would never have dragged Giannis and him into a
dirty scandal to facilitate a divorce.

She had been bluffing that day.

And he had fallen for it.

He had believed every lie Leah had ever told him, had spun his own theory of how she had led Calista astray, that, somehow, she had convinced his naive sister to try something dangerous...

But if Leah hadn't been the one that had pushed Calista to it, then what had happened? That Leah had lived while Calista had died of a drug overdose that night, he had chalked it up to pure chance.

But it wasn't.

Whatever choice she had made that night, his sister had made it of her own accord.

His head pounded with the questions it let loose; his entire world tilted.

Had he not really known Calista either?

"Come, Stavros," Giannis beckoned him with a smile before he could disappear with his shifting thoughts.

Stavros looked up, zeroing in on Leah with a stinging hunger.

On her way to the other side of the table, she stilled without looking at him. Her fingers slipped on the serving spoon, the sound clanging in the patio.

Slowly, she moved her head and met his gaze. The impact of it rocked through him, the picture she presented ripping through the semblance of control he had fooled himself into achieving over the past four days.

An off-shoulder, black, cutoff blouse showed a strip of her back, indented by the line of her spine, an outlandish article of clothing if he had ever seen one, and yet it suited her to perfection, with the long, gray skirt that billowed around her legs.

A soft breeze pushed it against her legs, outlining the lean, toned length of them.

Heat thrummed in every pore, his arousal painfully instantaneous.

He wanted to see if she was just as silky everywhere, he wanted to see that glorious hair, right now piled atop her head and falling from it, spread against his pillows, he wanted to feel that mouth against every inch of him...

Leah affected him like no other woman ever did, or could. Whether it was because she was his wife or because she was inherently Leah—beautiful, demanding, lively— he wouldn't know.

All he knew was that she was destroying every assumption he had made of her, inching toward her goal, once again, changing his life irrevocably.

But he couldn't let her go, not until he knew the truth about Calista. Not until he knew everything there was to know about Leah.

Not until he had tasted that luscious mouth one more time.

Just this once, he would reach for what he wanted, he would take what he craved and damn his sense of duty.

The strangest expression glittered in Stavros's eyes. Her gaze followed the corded length of his thighs as he chose the chair wedged against hers. The memory of how hard and welcoming he had been beneath her suffused her face with warmth. Hoping they would think it was the sun, she smiled pleasantly for Giannis's benefit.

Giannis slowly got up from his chair, and both Stavros and she rose from theirs. Grabbing his walking stick, he waved them off. "It is time for me to rest. You both sit," he said with such a teasing twinkle in his eyes that Leah sighed like a deflated balloon.

How would Giannis face it when Stavros finally set her free? Would Stavros tell him?

The moment Giannis was out of sight, she stood up too, the very joy she had found this morning evaporating under her own conflicting emotions.

His fingers clamping her wrist, Stavros looked up. "Stay, Leah…*please*."

The edgy request warned her not to argue.

Increasingly aware of the high-pitched chirp of a bird in the olive groves, the rustle of leaves, and the painful thud of her own heart, she studied him under the guise of bravely facing him.

As always, he was dressed in formal clothes but the shirt was unbuttoned, and his hair looked like he had messed it up quite a bit.

From the arch of his eyebrows to the straight line of his nose, from the way his mouth tilted up on one side when he smiled to the blunt nails of his long fingers, he was painfully familiar to her now…a desperate longing awoke in her, to trace that austere face, to taste him in tenderness, to just once meet him as his equal without lies and fears.

"How is your collection coming along?"

Blinking, she searched for an answer. "Very well. I finalized the design on the last dress. I'm terrified that it might not be as breathtaking as I think it is."

"The wedding gown?"

The smile came naturally then. "Yes. I have to do the cutting on it. I've been taking the fabric, laying it all out and then just staring at it for hours… I can't afford to…"

"You're nervous?" he said with such genuine warmth that she flushed.

"It's the prize of my collection but it means so much more to me. A wedding dress, as much as it has become a symbol of status and wealth and showing off in these days, it means a lot to a woman, right? It's the one day she gets to be what she longs to be all her life."

Somehow, he had moved closer to her. Her hand lay in his loosely, the pad of his thumb tracing the top of it gently. "What is that?"

"Beautiful, special, loved." Pulling her hand away from him, she smiled to herself. "No matter what age, that day, she is the center of the whole universe for this one man... that day, it's a new beginning, a fresh start, a promise she cherishes that her life will hold meaning to someone else. It's the first day of a whole new way of life, of the most important, intimate relationship she's ever going to have... and the wedding dress... it symbolizes all those hopes and dreams she's ever cherished."

Sensing his stillness, she turned and saw the lacerating pity in his eyes.

It was like the most vulnerable part of her, the part she even hid from herself, had been ripped open.

Shutting her eyes to stop the heat building behind, she saw what he remembered.

She had married in a ghastly cream silk dress that had been too tight on her chubby body. With a stone-faced Dmitri as witness while Giannis lay in a hospital bed. Drowning in guilt over Calista, numb that she always seemed to be saying goodbye to loved ones, terrified about what Stavros intended, and hating herself...

That bleary day had been about punishment and penance, about duty and fear. Just as the moment after when he had pressed his mouth to hers, had been.

Even then she had been eager for his kiss, had clung to him in her shame when he had put her away from him, and wiped his mouth.

"At least, that's the statement I want this collection to make, you know." Her blasted voice wouldn't stop quivering. "Like you said, it's a career saturated with so many fresh faces that you can disappear in a second... You have to be able to put a new spin on your collection, present it almost like a story so that your consumers will fall in love with it, and that's how—"

Clasping her chin, he turned her toward him. From casual to a vehement intensity, his expression changed in mere seconds. "Don't, *agape mou*."

Still, she tried to pretend. "You probably find this intensely boring."

"Do I not deserve the truth even in this, Leah?" Resting on his haunches in front of her seat, he took her hand in his. The tenderness in his gaze unraveled her defenses. "Do not lie about something that is so important to you, do not cheapen what truly comes from your heart. Not this..."

"I..."

"Did you once dream like this too? Was marriage that important to you?"

Her throat raw, she nodded. "I believed in the sanctity of it once, yes. My father...I never knew my mother and I always used to get this sense that a part of him was gone with her. He loved me but his heart...it was with her. When you grow up seeing love like that, you believe in its power. You start hoping for it even when you know..." She shrugged, loath to betray herself even more.

"I'm sorry for ruining your dreams, Leah," he said with such withdrawal, that it was Leah who held onto him this time. "You were a dangerous combination of recklessness and... I had to protect you from fortune hunters and—"

"Myself, of course." But there was no real bite to her words.

She could not lie and absolve him of any of it. Despite wanting to hate him, she even understood why he had done it, but his apology touched something inside her. "I wanted a lot of things. But life happened. I'll be fine, Stavros."

He nodded and rose to his feet. "What will your collection be called?"

"New beginnings."

"I do not know about dresses..." he said with such a straight face that she laughed, "but the passion I hear in your words, I am sure it will come through in what you do, *ne*?"

"You think so?"

"I believe that it will."

He said it with such confidence that a snippet of conversation she had heard between him and Giannis came back to her. Her grandfather had been asking Stavros about his contacts with major design houses and Stavros had been patiently explaining who would be open to launching a new label with a fresh designer.

Pushing her chair back, she stood up, her stomach in knots. "Your belief in me is encouraging, but I can't forever be ensconced safely in this world that Giannis and you have created for me. I can't let you and him launch a label for me using your contacts and the might of..."

"If you meant your apology, if anything has changed in how you see me—" she could feel heat rising in her cheeks, but she continued stubbornly "—you'll stop arranging my life in cahoots with him."

"He wants to do it for you because he cares—"

"Becoming successful because I'm the Katrakis heiress or Stavros Sporades's wife will forever ruin my joy in this. Will you do that to me again, Stavros?

"Please... allow me the freedom to succeed or fail on my own merit. Tell Giannis to stop with this launching my label nonsense."

"If you haven't realized it, your grandfather has a will of iron—"

"And you can convince him that you could walk on water, so get him to back off."

Smiling, he nodded. "Anything else?"

She hesitated, which in itself, held Stavros's attention instantly.

"After that imperious command, what can be so hard, Leah?"

"I have been researching various fashion events and programs around the world and there's one in Athens tomorrow night that caught my attention."

"Ahhh...that's why the uncharacteristic call to my office."

She let his comment pass. "It's like a co-op event, to

be exact, an incubator for fashion design. No big labels or famous designers. Instead your… *Helene* and a group of fashion icons like her provide a stage for up-and-coming designers to showcase their talents. My application is ready. But I…"

He waited patiently.

"The entry fee is pretty hefty. Even with that, anyone who gets picked has to actually come with a recommendation from one of the event coordinators."

Wariness and pity filled his eyes and Leah blanched at it. "Helene is one of those rare women who won't take you on to do me a favor, Leah. In fact, recommending you to her will only lessen your worth in her eyes."

She shook her head, wondering if he would always think her less than capable, less than what she was. Did she have anyone but herself to blame if he did?

And why, in God's name, did the thought hurt so much?

"No, all I want is an introduction to her. My collection, at that point, will hopefully speak for me and garner her recommendation. Even if she doesn't like it, I will still get some exposure to the industry folks." Even as she confidently made her case, another tension filled her.

Just admitting the fact that Helene knew Stavros in a way Leah never would, made her want to throw up.

How could he mention the other woman so glibly? Where was his honor now, she wanted to demand. But to ask would be to show that she cared. That she spent entire afternoons wondering how he justified breaking his vows to her so boldly.

Was she so completely and irrevocably only a responsibility that he didn't think he was cheating on her?

Standing up from his chair, he extended a hand to her. "I'm sure I can convince her to give us ten minutes before the show begins." He stood tall and broad and incredibly handsome in front of her. His gaze was on her mouth; he was thinking about their kiss, she knew. Because it was impossible not to think about it. "But I need something from you in return, Leah."

The soft intonation of her name stole her breath.

He had changed toward her if he was asking and not commanding. And whatever the reason, he was even more irresistible and dangerous now.

The judging, dominating Stavros, she could hate. This insightful, approachable Stavros…she didn't stand a chance.

Spending a few days with Giannis and amassing a lifetime of memories was one thing. But tangling with Stavros, who would demand everything she had to give and more, who would bare her body and soul…she couldn't risk the pain of knowing him and then losing him.

"What," she finally managed.

"I will ask you some questions before the event. If I get a truthful answer, I will introduce you to Helene."

"Anything else I can do instead?" The moment the words were out of her mouth, she wanted to snatch them back.

He only stared at her with that intensity again. "If you won't tell me the truth, then how about a kiss?"

"You've already proved that I…I can't resist you. There is no reason for you to kiss me anymore."

He pushed a stray tendril of hair back from her forehead. And she stood very still in the wake of sensations that small touch aroused. "There is a reason."

"What?"

"That I wish to. It is only when I kiss you that I know you, Leah."

Warmth pooled in her belly, every word out of his sensuous mouth a caress and a promise. "What happened to that phenomenal willpower of yours that had the rest of us quaking in our boots?"

Laughter—hearty, gorgeous, and spine-tingling, enveloped her. "In this case, I have decided not to employ it.

"You can see Helene, Leah, but you shall have to give me your truths or your kisses. The choice is yours."

How very neatly he had trapped her, how very stupid she had been in challenging fate when she had said Stavros knew nothing but duty. His words now were honeyed, so damn seductive that her heart thudded. "What if I asked you questions?"

"But I have never lied to you. However, if you ask me a question and I do not tell the truth, you are free to kiss me, as much as you want to."

"Thanks but no thanks," Leah managed to say, past the whooshing of her heart.

Turning away from him, she ran back to the sanctuary of her workroom, wondering what had suddenly unleashed this facet of Stavros.

Her wedding gown wasn't done, but she had three other dresses she could take with her for tomorrow. Swiftly, she removed the dresses from their plastic bags and looked them over for anything to fix.

Countless hours later, she wrapped them back in the hanging bags and zipped them up.

Her heart thudded as she pulled another dress, a dress she had made for herself almost a year ago. The design had literally begged to be borne onto paper, and she had finished it in less than a week.

It was simply cut yet daring, a dress that would say all the right things about its designer. In the end, she decided to brave it out and wear it tomorrow night.

Brave because tomorrow night was going to be dangerous in so many ways that she wanted to turn the time back to a couple of months ago when it had been just her and the apartment and her blistering hatred of him...

Whatever truth he was hunting, it wouldn't be anything she'd want to tell. Which left her to face his kisses...

Running a comb through her messy hair, Leah stilled. A glimmering energy in her gaze, her pulse beating with a frenzied clamor, she looked like a stranger.

She looked almost happy.

CHAPTER TEN

HE WAS GOING to lose in his own game, Stavros decided ruefully as Leah walked down the steps of the house the next evening.

A game the likes of which he had never before thought of.

He was still amazed at how easily Leah made him laugh, tease, even think of absurd scenarios just for a chance to touch her.

Thin, almost flimsy straps at her shoulders held up the black dress. The hem of the dress, startlingly white, ended high above her knees in the front but fell to her ankles at the back.

Animal-print pumps showed toned calves when she walked down the steps.

All in all, the dress was simply elegant. Or so he thought until she moved, waiting against his Maserati.

A flash of creamy thigh greeted his greedy gaze. The clinging material outlined her braless breasts when she took another step. A sudden breeze highlighted the tips of her nipples as she neared him.

Pure, liquid lust hit him hard, and every muscle in his body tightened, readying for pleasure.

Begging, at this point, if he was honest.

Smoky shadow and dark red lipstick turned her face from pretty to siren… Thick glorious waves framed her fragile features… Her cheeks were pinkened by the time she stood in front of him…

Was that his perusal that had done this to her? Would she tell the truth when he asked or would she prefer to be kissed?

Cristos, he would never even want truth this way. All he would want was to kiss her again and again.

Because he didn't know what was the right step anymore. He didn't know where his duty ended and his need for her began...he didn't know if he was making reparations for the mistake he had made or if he just wanted to see her smile for his own selfish reasons...

For the first time in his life, Stavros was lost, didn't care about right or wrong. Only how startlingly alive he felt when he was with Leah.

"Hey," she said, reaching him.

He nodded, still absorbing the effect of her smile. She looked excited, almost happy, and he felt like he had done something right for the first time in so long.

She pointed to the top of the stairs. "So I packed up some of my collection...will you help bring it to the car?"

Inordinately pleased that she was flustered at seeing him, he halted her with a hand on her arm. "You look gorgeous."

She blinked, and then looked at him almost shyly. "Thanks, it's one of my own designs."

"It's insubstantial, sophisticated and outrageously sexy. I figured out that much."

By the time they had arrived at the venue, Leah couldn't sit still, much less think straight. And the pleasant conversation with Stavros, the way his gaze lingered over her mouth for a fraction of a second longer every time she turned toward him, it was like she was being pumped with a bit of electricity.

The powerful Maserati crawled to a stop at a centuries-old hotel and a uniformed valet immediately ran up to them.

The locks turned on with a click on the doors. Frowning, she turned toward him. "What is it?"

"Time for my first question, *pethi mou*."

"What...now?" The intensity in his expression sent tingles up and down her body. "Stavros, I'm going to show my collection to a group of intimidating professionals who make or break designers on a whim. This is not the time for some silly game that I lose whichever way—"

"Why? Do you have so much to hide?"

That shut her up promptly. "Fine," she said, bracing herself for a lacerating question.

"My estate, what did you truly think of it?"

"Austere and isolated, like you." The lie was so automatic, so swift that only after hearing it in the lush interior of the powerful vehicle did she realize that she had said it.

His gaze instantly fell to her mouth. "Liar."

In a movement that was like slow motion, he wrapped his hand around her nape and slanted his lips over hers. The gear shift dug into her side, her torso was twisted to the side, but the hot taste of Stavros's mouth...it numbed her to everything else but him.

There was no soft seduction in this kiss, no gentle erosion of her senses. No intent to dominate or control...only to take pleasure...

He pressed and licked, sucked and stroked, made love to her mouth with such raw passion that Leah couldn't breathe.

Gasping for breath, moaning in the back of her throat, she wrapped her fingers around his nape. A blistering heat spread through her, pooling at her sex as his large hand caressed her knee, climbing up her thigh...

His mouth trailed wet heat over her jaw. Sucked at the pulse at her neck. An arrow of sensation went straight to her sex and she squirmed in frustration. "God, please..."

Those devilish lips opened against her skin and she

felt his smile. "I would like nothing but to continue, *gae-lika mou...*"

Her forehead flopped against his shoulders, her lungs burning for breath. "Fine, I lied. I...love that estate. It's the most beautiful, most peaceful place I have ever seen in the world. Even Giannis's estate cannot compare against such simple, stark beauty."

His silence reverberated in the interior, the remnants of lust making the tawny irises wide. "Now I wish I had shown you my bedroom."

Their gazes collided and Leah shifted in her seat, unbearable to be in her own skin. The rub of her thighs when she crossed her legs, the rasp of her dress against her nipples, every inch of her sparked with awareness. It was like the powerful car they were sitting in. She was all revved up by that kiss and yet, there was no relief.

All evening, this was what he was going to do to her. No wonder he had looked so damn interested in taking her.

How, despite all her efforts to the contrary, was it that Stavros always ended up with all the power? "You're enjoying torturing me like this, aren't you?" she whispered.

The locks on the door opened with a click. "It's very little compared to the torture you put me through all these years, *pethi mou.*"

Having nothing suitable to contest that with, Leah stepped out of the car on legs that could barely hold her up.

Her dress bags draped over his shoulder casually, Stavros caught her. "Smile, Leah. The world's not going to know what's hit them when they see your creations."

With her hand over his arm, she stopped him. There was nothing but sincerity in his expression. "I would not jest over something that is so important to you, Leah."

No, he wouldn't, she realized. Whatever he decided her fate to be in the end, she would always have his support in this too.

God, how had she always been the one with such tunnel vision? How easily she had chosen to hate him, had chosen to see only the surface of him?

"How can you be so sure that I will succeed?"

"All these years, you have hidden so many things from me, and even from yourself, maybe? But when I enter your workroom, I feel all your energy, your passion. I see all of you, Leah. Such pure passion—" his gaze flicked to her mouth "—people can't help but fall in love with it."

Throwing her arms around him, Leah kissed his cheek on an impulse. The fact that a man of such willpower and discipline as Stavros believed in her dream just made her day perfect. That a man like him belonged to her, at least for tonight, it made her blood pound.

Stavros handed over Leah to Helene and accepted a glass of champagne from a waiter. The expression on Leah's face when they had entered the huge, buzzing auditorium, her exclamations as she noticed and pointed out one fashion icon after another, it had been a delight to see.

The soft touch of her lips on his cheek, he could still feel it. Her mouth had been such heaven under his and knowing that all he had to do was push his hands under that hem, that he could bare her and feast his eyes on her...it had taken him everything to bite down the urge to make love to her right there in the car.

The banquet hall where they were serving pre-show drinks and hors d'oeuvres was overflowing with designers and actresses and fashion icons, one more gorgeous than the next. And yet it was Leah his gaze followed hungrily as she flitted through the long hall, her dress sinuously draping her lithe curves.

After a while, he walked through the crowd, found her and introduced her to some more people he knew. A bittersweet feeling filled him as she introduced herself as Leah Huntington with a wary glance at him.

But, whatever his own seesawing feelings when it came

to her, he found he couldn't begrudge her the need to be herself, tonight of all times.

She returned to his side in the auditorium a quarter of an hour before the runway show was about to begin.

Her brown eyes glittered with a joy he had rarely, if ever, seen. "Now that it's too late, I'm so beginning to see the benefits of being your wife." Her words were rushed, falling over each other. "Damn, you have some pull, man."

He was as committed to his vows as he had ever been, if not more. He arrested the words, remembering how hurt she had been when he had mocked their marriage once.

And that he was utterly serious didn't bear thinking about.

He grabbed a plate from a passing waiter. "Would you like to eat something?"

She didn't wait for his reply. Reaching him, she grabbed his hand and directed the little flaky pastry into her mouth. Licked the tips of his fingers, her pink mouth closing around one. Lust hit him so quickly that he was achingly hard within seconds.

It was like a haze fell over his senses and all he could see, all he could hear was Leah. Grabbing her wrist, he pulled her behind a long column. Took her mouth in a feral kiss. Cupped her breast, covering her possessively as he had wanted to do all evening.

The rasp of her rigid nipple against his palm made him growl in the back of his throat. He dug his teeth into her lower lip. Her whimper of pain even as she clung to him stopped him. Breathing raggedly, he wondered how easily she undid him.

She glared at him. "You didn't ask a question."

He smiled, her confusion making her even lovelier. "Do not lick a man's fingers, sucking them into your mouth and then expect rationality, Leah."

Cristo, what was he doing with her?

He would, he *could* stop at a kiss, he had thought when he had come up with this game. Now, he didn't know anymore.

"Oh…" she licked her swollen mouth, and the innocent gesture sent his blood flowing south. "I will remember that when I'm tempted to lick a man's fingers next time."

The molten fury that flashed in his gaze before he willed it away made Leah want to scream in joy.

He didn't have all the power. They both had it over each other, she slowly realized.

There was something between them that denied rational explanation, that devoured self-control.

"I'll ask the question now."

Brows raised, he nodded. "Ask soon, or you will miss the show."

The simply elegant Helene's polite face had stayed with her. His friend or lover or whatever the hell she was, the woman hadn't betrayed surprise or shock or any emotion even by the flicker of a perfectly drawn eyebrow. Had talked to Leah as if it was any other fashion designer trying to break into the industry.

His kiss still stinging her lips, her will pretty much nonexistent, falling into bed with Stavros was like a fate rushing at her like an express train. If he hadn't stopped any of the times, if he willed it, she couldn't resist him, she knew.

And she refused to let him make all the rules.

"How do you…how does this work with you kissing me like this and with Helene? Are you guys taking a breather while you sort me out? What happens if you decide you want to…?"

"Yes?"

Her meager grasp on her own emotions slipping bit by bit, she shivered. Damn it, she had been so happy today and she knew it was largely because it featured him. "Don't make me say it, Stavros."

"Say it, Leah."

"Does she not mind if you…if you have sex with me?"

"Do you want to, Leah…have sex with me?"

Her spine tingled at just hearing that. "That's not the point."

"Then isn't the question moot, too?"

Frustration pumping through her, she pushed into his space. "You promised me truth, Stavros. If something happens between us before I leave, if…will you make one set of rules for me and a different set for yourself?"

His hands climbed up over her back, cradling her against him. "You hide from your own truth every day, Leah… Can you handle mine?"

"Yes."

"I told you that day aboard Dmitri's yacht that I meant my wedding vows. I have never broken them. I have not touched Helene or another woman since I married you. And I won't. Not as long as I wear your ring, as long as I'm your husband."

Her ring, her husband…

Her grip slacking, Leah fell back, and would have hit the ground if he hadn't caught her. The entire axis of her life shook, shifted and she could do nothing to stop it. "You're lying, you have to be…"

His silence jarred against her nerves.

Stavros never lied. Stavros always kept his word. Stavros lived by a code of duty and honor that was everything to him.

And she…she didn't want to lose her will to a man like that. She didn't want to be measured against him and fall short. Because, her fear would always trump everything else about her.

"It has been five years, Stavros. No man can—"

There was no nuance in his expression. "But I'm not any man, Leah." He didn't proclaim it like an achievement, he didn't dismiss it like it hadn't cost him anything. He stated it like a foregone fact.

"My word to Giannis means something to me. My vows to you mean something to me. It's true that I neglected you, did not treat you like a wife, but our marriage, it was a commitment I made intending to keep. So I waited. I waited for you to grow up. I waited for you to change. I thought I had to…"

"Fix me to be worthy of you?" she said, anger coming to her defense.

"No, I thought I should give us both time…" Something gripped his features and Leah knew that he knew it. "But then you didn't need to be changed, *ne*?"

So many years, she had wished she had had the courage to tell him the truth. That he would, for one second, see the real her. And yet now that he did, she felt naked, terrified.

The sudden silence in the long hall made her heart thud so much louder in her ears. The show had begun.

"I'll miss the show," she said, moving away. But he pulled her back. Trapped her between the pillar and his body.

"Tell me about Calista."

Her gaze flew to him. "Stavros, I—"

His hand under her chin tilted her up. "I deserve to know the truth, Leah. If you have never used drugs, that means you didn't introduce her to them."

She closed her eyes, holding back tears. "No." His silence drove her to open them again. "I went to every party you forbade me from, I drank even though most of the time I couldn't even keep it in, I flirted with boys who didn't care an iota about me because it would enrage you, I spent money only because you said not to, but I…I never touched drugs. I didn't even know that crowd…" She stopped, once again, skating the line of lies. "I didn't know where she even got it…God, if I had…"

The confusion, the guilt in Leah's eyes far too real, Stavros didn't need to ask her why she had never told him the truth before.

Because he wouldn't have believed it. He had been so blind, he had been in so much pain that he had shut everyone out. Only his failure had mattered, not the why of it.

He had so conveniently blamed Leah for it, absolving Calista of any fault.

"Then why do you carry such guilt in your eyes?"

"Because I loaned her that money a couple of days before. I was so angry with you for cutting my trip to New York short. I…hated you so much. So when she said that she needed cash, that you would never agree to give her so much, I gave her every last penny."

She flopped against him, her body shaking. Feeling as if there was an anvil on his chest, Stavros wrapped his hands around her.

Calista had borrowed it from Leah, knowing that he would not like it, probably even aware that he would take it out on Leah. *What had she been thinking?*

He hadn't known his sister then. It hung like a boulder around his neck, choking his breath. Leah had been right in this too.

Leah couldn't speak for the pain in Stavros's gaze, in his sudden withdrawal.

She had hated Stavros for being so tough on her and Calista, but Calista hadn't once mentioned her unhappiness or her problems to him.

With him, Calista had almost been a different person. Loving, smiling, obedient…as if she had just slipped into a different skin.

Now she wished she had gone to Stavros and blurted it all out.

Calista had been troubled, she realized that now. Maybe even depressed.

With hindsight, she wondered how much of that had fueled her own antagonism toward Stavros, because it had been so scary and powerless to see Calista like that. She had been mired in her own pain about her dad's death and Stavros had been a convenient target to lash out at. And yet she hated having to tell the truth now, hated this power that she had over him.

She didn't want to cause Stavros any pain.

He was rigid, he was stubborn and arrogant, but God, he had loved Calista in his own way. He had tried so hard to keep Leah away from her because he had thought her a bad influence on her. He had given Calista everything except…except listening to her.

But how could she tell him that now? How could she tell him that Calista had already been in trouble long before Leah had come into her life? That Leah had followed Calista's lead always?

The man she knew now, he still dominated, even used her attraction but hadn't she pushed him to it by dangling the truth in bits and pieces?

Calista was gone. There was nothing to be done now. There was nothing to be achieved by digging into the ugly truth.

So, she swallowed all the other truths back, bolstered her own courage and looked into his eyes.

Managing a smile, she squeezed his hand. "She was not unhappy, Stavros. I think, just restless. She…she definitely hated your rules as much as I did." She forced a smile to take the bite out of it. "But she…loved you."

He remained silent. And Leah wondered if he knew that she was quaking inside. When she had lied to him before, it had been to protect herself. This time, it was to protect him.

"I think that night whatever she took…it must have been a one-time thing. Something she thought she would try and then walk away. I'm so sorry that I gave her that money."

"You were barely nineteen, Leah. And I…made it so hard to come to me with anything, *ne*? I found fault with you at every turn, I curbed all your freedom, and then I—"

"Why?" The question barreled out of Leah.

By his actions toward her, his efforts to again and again control her, change her, he had made it so easy to hate him, so easy to hide the truth about Calista from him.

She had wanted to not care about anyone ever again in her life, had pulled the act so well that Stavros had believed all of it.

He had started a war between them, and Leah was the one who had kept feeding it. To better hide her attraction, to better fight whatever risk he presented to her emotions, she realized now. "Why did you always hate me so much?"

"I didn't hate you."

"In the beginning, I thought it was because Giannis brought me here. Because you resented my being the heiress to such a vast fortune. Which, it turned out was a big joke. You were the one, along with Dmitri, who turned Katrakis Textiles into a multimillion-dollar business. So what was it, Stavros?"

His expression shuttered instantly. "It was wrong of me, Leah. Isn't that enough?"

"No, it's not. I have a right to know. I…"

"You just…your actions—your neglect of Giannis, they reminded me of someone. But it was no excuse to—"

"Of whom?" Leah couldn't let go. Not when she was finally so close to understanding him.

"Of my father. All he cared about was himself, his next drink and how he would gain it. My mother, instead of kicking him out, instead of caring for her kids, walked out without looking back. Neither Calista nor I mattered. They left us with our grandparents who weren't equipped to raise us. All they had was a small farm. I managed fine. But Calista…

"She would watch for her at the gate for so many hours…and then one day, we got news of my father's car crash." He rubbed his face. "I remember thinking that it was a blessing for her." His mouth twisted into a bitter curve. "He died and all I could think was Calista wouldn't suffer anymore."

That said so much about his own state of mind. "And then Giannis came for you?"

"Yes, my grandfather wrote to him about my father's death. I fought so much to bring her with us. But he said he had failed with his own daughter and that he couldn't bear to fail again. I—" such pain impinged on his features that a lump formed in her throat "—I...promised her I would come back for her. And I did... It took me two years to convince Giannis. Two years to go back for her."

"What was she like when you went back?"

He frowned at her sudden question. "Why?"

"Never mind," she replied, faking nonchalance. But her head hurt, and her chest felt so tight.

My brother—I can't disappoint him, Calista had admitted once to her. Had she been afraid he would not come back? Had she been afraid to show her true self to him?

"Leah, why—"

Sinking her hands into his hair, she pulled him down for a kiss. His hands on her waist, his taste on her lips, made her feel she was owned by him. She wanted to take away his pain, to ease the confusion in his eyes every time he talked about Calista.

Drowning in his taste, she could forget all the truths bearing down upon her, she could swallow the truth forever.

His arms tightened around her while his mouth continued its passionate assault.

Just as all the other times, he was the one who finally stopped. The heated rush of their breaths mingled as he rubbed a gentle finger over her mouth.

"What was that for?"

"I have no more truths to tell. The show, I don't want to miss it, Stavros."

"Go," he commanded, a thoughtful look in his face.

"But we are not through, Leah." All kinds of promises lingered in his words.

And Leah fled.

She muddled through the darkness of the auditorium and found her seat. Up-tempo music blared as the runway dazzled with one magnificent creation after the other.

But it was mostly lost on her. He didn't join her in the adjacent seat, and Leah, still shaken by everything they had talked about, was glad for a reprieve.

Now, she wished she hadn't asked. She wished she hadn't seen that vulnerability in his eyes. That she hadn't seen the ache when he mentioned his parents.

She wished she didn't know how committed he was to his vows.

Wished she didn't understand what made Stavros the way he was. She wished she had never started on this path at all.

Because understanding Stavros meant wanting Stavros with a cloying, all-consuming madness.

Already, she saw admiration, respect in his eyes when he looked at her, she saw that flash of curiosity when she evaded his questions.

If he showed such commitment, such respect for the vows he had made to the selfish, immature girl she had been, what would he be like if she shared her fears, if she followed her heart and gave this relationship of theirs a chance?

Because, suddenly, she wanted to be that woman more than anything she had ever wanted in her life.

CHAPTER ELEVEN

WHEN LEAH HAD woken up that morning in her sun-kissed bedroom, she had already known it was a new kind of day.

Despite her efforts to protect herself, which she saw clearly now, it seemed Stavros actually saw her, the true her.

He knew that she hadn't ever touched drugs in her life. He knew that a career in fashion design meant the world to her. He knew that Giannis meant a lot to her.

It had been almost two in the morning when she had finished meeting with everyone she wanted to see. And all the while, Stavros had loomed large in her mind.

Both emotionally and physically tired and strung out by Helene's positive initial reaction to her designs, she had fallen asleep within moments after he had started the powerful engine.

It had been the best night of her life.

She felt like she was standing in front of him without a shield for the first time. It was a moment of both power and fear, for he could so easily bind her to him always, he could so easily make her…

Pushing her hair away from her face, Leah walked to the window. Fueled by that growing need to see him, she showered and dressed in a sleeveless yellow blouse and a long, flowy skirt. Braided her half-wet hair into a plait, pushed her feet into comfy flip-flops and made her way down.

She was at the last few steps on the winding staircase

that opened to the main foyer when the deafening silence finally registered.

His collar undone, his cuffs rolled back, Stavros still wore the same shirt as last night.

His hair was unkempt and his pallor a ghostly white under that olive skin. His nostrils flared as he saw her at the steps; something slithered across his face but he held her gaze, almost as if willing her to only see him, as if making her oblivious to the rest of the world.

And he was such a commanding figure that it almost worked.

Except she had lived half her life with moments like this, with that gut-twisting fear that something always went wrong when she found happiness.

Nausea pushed its way up her throat.

She gripped the balustrade so tight that her knuckles turned pale against the dark sheen but she forced herself to break his gaze and look beyond him.

Dmitri emerged from her grandfather's room, his features ravaged. A half-empty bottle of scotch dangled from his hand, and his eyes were bloodshot. He looked at her, blinked, and then walked away without another glance.

He looked like he was coming apart at the seams, the complete contrast to Stavros's frozen withdrawal, to the tight ropes with which he held himself.

"What happened?" Her words were loud, almost a scream in that dignifiedly morbid silence. She flew off the steps when he didn't answer.

Launched herself at Stavros like a crazy dog. Like an immovable wall, he absorbed all her rage, all her blows as she pummeled at him. "What happened, Stavros? Tell me or I will—"

Pulling her into him so hard that the breath was knocked out of her, Stavros hugged her. Hugged her so tight her chest hurt with the effort to breathe, her head was dizzy...

until all she could focus on was getting air into her collapsing lungs.

Only then did he loosen his hold on her. Tucking a finger under her chin he pushed it up to meet his gaze. "I'm sorry, *pethi mou*. Giannis is gone, Leah."

Leah flopped onto him, the words stealing into her with a sickening thud. "No…" she whispered, futile tears filling her eyes.

"Look at me, *galika mou*," he pleaded with such tenderness that she did.

Clasping her cheeks, he looked into her eyes. "He passed with a smile on his lips, Leah. He said he loved you, that he…he was so happy that you spent the past few days with him. I have never seen such peace in his eyes in all the years I have known him. You brought such joy to him."

"Why didn't you wake me? Why didn't you at least let me say goodbye?" She pushed away from him, bitterness and anger and pain all roping together. "He was my grandfather. You and Dmitri…I had just as much right to be with him."

The pads of his thumbs caught her spilled tears. "He insisted that I did not disturb you, Leah. Said you were not fond of goodbyes."

A sob rising through her, Leah ran back upstairs without another glance at Stavros.

He had known. Her perceptive grandfather had known how scared she had been, he had known what it had cost her to reject him again and again…

In just a few weeks, Giannis had become such a huge part of her life and now, he was gone…Leaving her alone again to mourn him.

And for once in her life, Leah didn't want to be alone, didn't want to be ruled by fear. For once, she wanted to reach for the man she desperately needed. She wanted to lean on his strength, she wanted to take everything he would give of himself, everything she had always been too scared to ask.

* * *

It was almost evening when Stavros entered Giannis's house again that day. He came to a halt in the vast foyer, the image of Leah standing at that last step, her expression of such fear and pain, the first thing he saw.

He had never seen her like that. Never heard that desperation in her tone. Over the last couple of weeks, he had accepted the fact that he had been wrong about Leah on so many levels. Yet he realized tonight that he had been no closer to truly understanding her.

She had desperately wanted him to say anything other than what he had, he knew. And the force of his own need, of his own desire to offer her anything but the hard truth, it had knocked him where he stood.

He wanted to wipe away those tears, he wanted to protect her from that grief, he wanted to…and all of it, it had nothing to do with duty.

The silence tonight was so different from all the other nights. He had done everything he possibly could to do all that Giannis had asked of him. All the arrangements had been put in place for the funeral to happen in a few days.

He was about to call for his housekeeper, instruct her to check up on Leah when she emerged from his office, rubbing her eyes. The yellow top that had looked so bright this morning was rumpled. Her hair was tangled all around her and dark circles hung under her eyes.

"Leah, were you waiting for me?"

Grabbing her hair away from her face, she pulled it tightly at the back. "Yes."

The innocent action thrust her breasts up and he swallowed his hunger.

Cristo, this was not the time for his control to shred. He was literally shivering with need.

It had been easy to offer comfort this morning. Yet now, he couldn't move, couldn't form a coherent thought. The shock of losing the one man who had ever tried to understand him, who had tried to care for him hit him hard in that moment. And he felt curiously weak, as if a strong gust of wind could knock him down.

He must have swayed because suddenly Leah was almost bowed back trying to support his weight. Her breasts rubbed against his side, her scent kicked him in the gut.

Her eyes were molten pools of concern and vulnerability as she held onto him. "You look like you are ready to fall apart. Have you sat down for a minute since last night?"

Putting her away from him, Stavros searched for his fragmented willpower. "I just need some sleep. What did you want?"

Would she ask to leave tonight? What would he do if she did?

The three months were almost up. After seeing her with Giannis these past two weeks, after talking to her about Calista, he had questions about himself.

He was drowning and he so desperately needed the very woman he had doubted.

"Nothing important. Come, I'll walk you to your room."

He smiled then, the weight on his chest lightening. "You, *pethi mou*?" She looked so lovely that his eyes hurt. "You will break in two if I so much as lean on you."

Her hands on her hips, she mock-glared at him. "I'm not as weak as I look, Stavros. If your *studly, macho ego* rails at accepting help from me, that's fine. But when was the last time you had something to eat? I can make something if you like."

"You're offering to cook for me?"

"Well, I can't make a three-course meal but I can manage a grilled cheese sandwich."

It was a tempting offer. Everything about her was tempting. And tonight, he was hanging on by the end of his rope.

"I'm not hungry," he said morosely, unbuttoning his shirt. She followed the movement with such wide eyes that his fingers slipped on the damn buttons. Rubbing a hand over his gritty eyes, he gave up on it. "Go to bed, Leah."

"I don't think I could sleep tonight." A shudder racked her. "I never do on such nights." The resignation in her words brought his head up. For someone so young, she had seen too much death, he realized with a pang.

They both had, a perverse thing to have in common.

She looked so vulnerable, right then, her oval face small. The urge to take her in his arms was so strong that he had to fist his hands. "There's nothing I can do for you tonight, Leah."

"No, I don't want anything, I…I didn't see you again all day and whenever I called, I was told you were busy."

Because he had instructed his secretary to not put her calls through. "I had too many things to take care of."

Wrapping her arms around herself, she nodded. "I just wanted to make sure you were okay, Stavros. And to apologize."

"Why?"

"I'm sorry for going off at you like that this morning. I'm sorry for always attacking you."

He forced a smile. "I can take it, Leah."

"It's just that…I forgot how much Giannis meant to you too."

Raising his hand, he stopped her. "Leah, it's not needed."

"Yeah?" she said with a depth of sadness. "Okay. Anyway, once I stopped crying and managed a shower, I went looking for you. Dmitri came back and wouldn't leave even though I promised I was okay. You sent him, didn't you?"

Today of all days, he didn't trust himself to be near her. That pain of hers, it had unlocked something inside him. And until he understood what, she was better left alone.

When he shrugged, she continued. "Dmitri said you hadn't said a word all night. And that you probably won't over the next few days or maybe even months. That your silence…it was the most nauseating thing in the world. That for months after Calista died, the only words he had heard from your mouth were the vows you made to me that day."

Anger roared out of him. "Bloody Dmitri needs to learn to keep his mouth shut."

"You'd rather I continue to think you as unfeeling as you make out to be, Stavros?"

"This is not your burden to bear, Leah. I have no expectations of you—"

Hurt etched into her mouth. "You will turn my life upside down because I need to be protected, but I can't even wonder what's going on with you?"

"I do not need to be protected, Leah."

"You have never wished you could unburden yourself with someone, that you could share your joy or pain or..."

"No. For as long as I can remember, I never had the indulgence to do so. If I hadn't shoved all that pain and grief away and handled things, life would have stopped for me and Calista. The way forward was the only thing left." All his life he had been alone in moments like this...and there had been far too many of them.

Had he reached his edge now?

"Well, I don't accept that. Today, of all days, when we have both lost the man who did everything he could to bind me to you, I won't accept it. This relationship he forced on you—"

"For the millionth time, he didn't force it on me." In the roiling confusion he felt, perversely, that he couldn't bear to hurt her. Not anymore. He couldn't bear for her to think he resented her in his life anymore.

Right now, she felt like the only thing that was anchoring him to his sanity. Right now, all he wanted was to take what she was offering. Right now, he wanted to lose himself. In her.

"It was not just for my benefit. He told me that, Stavros. He said you needed me just as much as he thought I needed you."

Stavros closed his eyes and dealt the blow that he knew would hurt. "But we found out that he was wrong, didn't we, Leah? It turns out you didn't need me to lock you up in a cage, you didn't need me to steal away any joy from you for five years, turns out that I was wrong about you every way... And by that same token—" he had to say it, he had to believe it, because the alternative was just unthinkable for a man who possessed no capability for emotion, knew nothing but duty "—I don't need you in my life either. It was just an old man's dream, Leah."

"Don't you dare say that!" she screamed at him, her body vibrating with rage. "Don't you dare...not tonight, Stavros."

"Leah, walk away, *pethi mou*," he warned her, past the hard lump in his throat.

It felt like he wouldn't be able to breathe for the tightness in his chest if she came any closer. It felt like the grief running through him would consume him, *and her*, if she came any closer. It felt like he wouldn't stop when he should if she came any closer.

But his stubborn, reckless wife didn't heed his warning. She never did.

"But what he said to me won't leave me alone, Stavros." Reaching him, she clasped his cheeks, stared into his eyes as if she could read into his soul.

There was nothing for her to see, nothing for her to learn. The chill that had been curling around the edges all last night and today pervaded through.

"He...loved you so much..." She ran her fingers over his mouth, her touch reverent and possessive at the same time. "When I first came to Greece, he told me so much about you that I hated you for what you had with him... and then there you were, wherever I turned, so austere, arrogant, hating me back... Any time he talked about you, his eyes lit up and this fierce pride came into his eyes, he said you only gave—" she leaned her forehead against his lips now, a long exhale racking through her "—that you... never ask anything for yourself."

Her hands vined around his midriff. "I don't want to be alone tonight. And I definitely won't leave you alone, even if you don't say a word to me."

And Stavros lost the battle against himself.

Had he even stood a chance against her from the moment he had seen her on Dmitri's yacht, he wondered.

He grabbed her wrists to push her away, to reject her embrace as every finely honed instinct warned him to. Raking her fingers over his skin, she pushed at him, until he relented. Laced their fingers together. Pulled at him until their joined hands bound her to him.

And then she took his mouth with hers, like a wave he couldn't beat down, engulfing him.

The taste of her filled him with pleasure, infused him with electricity, flew into all the open, aching places inside him.

"I'm so sorry for your loss, Stavros. You...meant so much to him. You looked after him better than his own family did."

Those words destroyed the last bit of his will, her slender body pressed to his was his undoing.

Jerking her up against his body, he covered her mouth with his. Such hunger emanated within, such need knocked at him that he devoured her soft mouth. Digging his hands into her hair, he nipped and licked, he bit and stroked, he let himself drown in her.

She gave in with a soft gasp, opened her honeyed warmth to him. The taste of her, the sound of her breathless gasps filled him up.

After five years of celibacy, he didn't have the remotest control over himself. After a lifetime of not needing anyone, the need she brought out in him, the pain she brought out in him, he had no defense against it.

* * *

His kisses were drugged, his caresses setting her on fire, his touch tearing open a chasm of longing inside her. Surrounded by his warmth, drowning in the masculine scent of him, Leah felt like she would never be alone again.

As long as Stavros continued to kiss her like this, there was no fear in her life.

There were no lies or games or duty or even the bonds of marriage between them now.

All there was was this desire in all its eviscerating and humbling honesty. In this, finally, they were equals. In this, finally, he was a man she couldn't breathe without knowing in the most intimate way and she, she was the woman who had ripped the civilized facade from him.

A sobbing protest rose through her when he tugged his mouth away from hers. The sound of his harsh breathing was little comfort. But he lifted her up until she wrapped her legs around him.

"Hold tight, *thee mou*," he commanded, his eyes so lust-glazed, his voice so rumbly that a shiver snaked up her spine.

She buried her mouth in his neck, hiding the sudden shyness that rose through her. She didn't want him to see it and stop, she couldn't bear it if he walked away because he thought she was afraid.

She was not afraid. At least not of what he would do to her. Only of the intensity of her want for him. She was afraid that whatever he did would only be the beginning of an intense yearning.

He returned to her mouth with a blistering passion that she had wanted for so long. Buried his mouth in her neck and sunk his teeth into her skin. Her legs wrapped around him, her skirt riding up to her thighs, she jerked against him, when he sucked at the soft flesh. Then he found her mouth again, nipped her lower lip this time.

Throwing her head back, she moaned loudly, pain and pleasure infusing in her very blood. And then he licked that very spot.

He carried her as if she weighed nothing, his long fingers cupping her bottom.

Heart thundering in her chest, Leah opened her eyes as she heard the thud of a door closing.

He had brought them to his office. The moment her bottom touched the oak desk, his hands reached for the hem of her blouse.

Her breathing coming so hard that it should have been a loud rattle in the room, Leah looked down. His hands disappeared under the yellow silk of her blouse. Those hair roughened wrists against her midriff, the bulge in his trousers…it was the most decadent sight she had ever seen.

"*Theos*, you're gorgeous," he groaned just as his fingers tugged her bra down with frenzied movements. And then his abrasive palm covered her breast.

"Oh…" Leah slid a little on the desk as he rubbed her aching nipples. Every time he pulled it between his fingers, her sex pulsed.

Pushing into his hand, she forgot what she had been about to say. Just his touch was sending her over the edge. Both his hands covered her breasts now. Pulling and kneading, while he murmured words she didn't understand in Greek.

"Please, Stavros…" she said, mindless in her search for release already.

All of a sudden, his curse ripped through the air and he pulled away from her.

Frustrated desire wreaking havoc on her, Leah struggled for her breath. Her breasts left alone, felt heavy, her nipples knotting with need.

"Why would you stop," she said, pushing back tears. He was so hard and warm and she was already afraid she would never want to leave. But how did she walk away from this hot magic he weaved? From how wanted and needed he had made her feel?

"Is this punishment too, Stavros?"

"Leah, look at me, *pethi mou*."

She raised a dazed gaze to him, ready to beg him to not stop. But he didn't stop. His mouth took hers in a ravishing kiss… Their tongues dueled and sucked with a frantic desperation, teeth scraped against each other until they were both panting.

"I have no protection, Leah," he murmured against her mouth finally. "I dare not risk—"

"I'm on the pill," she said in a small voice. "You dragged me to the gynecologist and stood outside her door, remember?" A flush overtook his cheeks and she milked the moment for all its worth. "It was the most humiliating moment of my life but—"

His hand covered her mouth. "No more words, *ne*?"

She pressed a kiss to the center of his palm and nodded. Continued tracing the hard mound of it to the thick veins in his wrists while her other hand explored his body.

Pushing her hands higher, he pulled her top off. Leah could hardly take in the sensations piling over her when he muttered a hoarse "Take off your bra."

In another blink, he tugged her skirt down her legs.

She sat in front of him, her breasts heavy and aching, her nipples turning into painful knots and a thong that showed more than it covered.

"*Theos*, you're going to be the death of me, Leah."

For long seconds that felt like an eternity, he only looked at her. Pulled her calf up until her foot was resting over the table, exposing the heart of her in such an indecent way that she resisted.

The hunger in his face was possessive, all-consuming, his grip over her calf unrelenting. "No, don't hide. Leah, never hide yourself from me."

Palm down, he touched her everywhere, from her shoulders bones to the valley between her breasts, from her abdomen to finally the one spot that ached for his attention.

When he covered her mound with his hand and pressed with the pad of his finger, Leah jerked, a spasm of spiraling pleasure gripping her belly.

His dark hand covering her wet warmth...fire flew in her veins. "I can smell your arousal, Leah," he whispered at her ear and she hid her face in his chest even as she reveled in his raspy voice. "That I make you feel like this...it drives me crazy in my own skin."

With a hand in her hair, he tugged her back, his grip just a little short of bruising. Dragged his mouth over her neck, leaving a trail of heat. "Every gasp you make, every moan that escapes you...tonight, they are mine. You, *pethi mou*, are all mine."

Staring into his eyes, Leah dragged him down for another kiss. "As you're mine," she whispered against his mouth.

She had never seen that blistering need in his eyes, never seen those commanding eyes darken like that.

Two fingers moved arrogantly over her nipple, plucking and rubbing while his gaze stayed on her face.

The heat with which he watched her made her feel even more exposed than her nakedness. That she would know what it felt to be possessed by him, that he would know her like no other man ever had, it filled her blood with thrill.

"Touch me," he commanded.

Still being plundered mercilessly by his mouth, Leah obeyed. If this was how alive she felt in his arms, she would be his willing slave, she thought, tucking her hand under his shirt.

He was so hot, the washboard stomach instantly clenching under her fingers, the shuddering exhale of his breath drenching her...he was as far gone in this madness as she was.

When she moved her hand down, and traced his arousal

with shaking fingers outside his trousers, he thrust his hips into her hand.

Such carnal need touched his arrogant features that Leah felt like a victor.

Leaving her breasts, he traced her rib cage, drew sensuous circles around her navel, impatiently pulled her thong off.

When he fingered her folds after what seemed like an eternity of waiting, Leah shivered violently. When he said, "Widen your legs," with such possessive intent, a feverish tremble claimed her.

When he pushed a finger, then two into her wet heat followed by a string of curses, she whimpered and dug her teeth into his shoulder.

The slick glide of his fingers was intrusive, yet addictive, his touch was alien and it felt as if she had been waiting for it, her entire life.

All of her being pulsed at her sex, on the erotic movements of his fingers as they disappeared into her aching folds, on the way he pulled her into the heat of his body…

"You are so responsive, Leah, I could do this all day long," he uttered, his other hand moving up to cover her breast again.

"I couldn't, Stavros, please…" she begged, the ever-spiraling tension too much to bear.

His fingers slicked in and out of her on a relentless tempo, stroking the fire along her nerve endings into an inferno.

She was gasping, sinking and sobbing, and she wanted more.

His hot mouth, trailing wet heat over her skin, reached her breast. With a groan that aroused her as much as his touch, he licked the aching nipple. Stroked it and played with it and did everything except what she wanted.

"Stop torturing me," she said in a voice that sounded alien to her own ears.

She felt his smile against her mouth. "Say 'please, Stavros,'" he whispered against her skin. He sounded drunk, guttural.

Joining in his game, she let go of the last layer of inhibition. She refused to beg however. Refused to bend to his will when she could demand what was hers... "Put your mouth where I want and I will put my mouth where you want it," she dared.

His curse reverberated in the dead silence, seconds before his mouth closed on her nipple.

Sensation upon sensation beat over her. Her fingers sinking into his hair, she held him at her breast. Every time he closed his mouth over her nipple and sucked, a thousand little tremors began in her lower belly.

He raked the highly sensitized point with his teeth slowly, as if he was savoring every second of it and Leah came with a scream that shattered the hot silence.

Everything inside her splintered into a thousand shards as the tremors piled on and on in mind-numbing pleasure.

Even as her voice turned hoarse with her continued gasps and screams, even as her breath left her lungs entirely, he didn't let go. His fingers continued their assault, wringing every last pull of her muscles, turning her into a mass of shuddering sensation.

When he let go of her, she flopped onto him, damp and hot and shivering, her limbs incapable of independent motion.

She heard the rasp of his zipper, followed by the quiet swish of his trousers falling and somehow, managed to look up.

The streak of color in his tight cheeks, that muscular chest falling and rising, the washboard abs, and his erection, thick and corded, lying against his belly... He was a vision, a sight she thought she would never see.

A new friction began to build between her thighs. "Wow," she said, reaching out to touch him.

The velvety weight of him was nothing like she had imagined.

Tawny irises dilated to dark pools as she wrapped her hand around it.

Tiny tremors pulsed through her sex as she rubbed the soft tip, and she marveled at her own body's reaction to him. He hissed out a breath as she tested the weight and feel of it. Cursed as she fisted him and moved up and down in a movement as instinctual as breathing.

"I'm ready to keep my word now," she said boldly, intent on tasting him, intent on driving him as mad as he had done her.

A dark smile warmed his gaze. "Yes?"

She nodded.

"I have not tasted you either, *ne*?" he said with such carnal intent that she instinctively clutched her thighs together.

But he jammed a rock-hard thigh in between. Her sensitive core rubbed against that hard thigh and a whimper escaped her.

Tugging her head back, he ravished her mouth until her lips stung. Every inch of her vibrated. "This madness, it is only beginning, *pethi mou*. Another night, we will taste each other."

He was so velvety hard in her hand and the need to know how he would feel inside her, the need to know Stavros in this raw moment…

"Do not look away, *Leah*. I want to see every expression on your face, I want to hear every sound you make."

One hand moved over her body in long, lingering strokes, over her breasts, over her stomach, and then, in one thrust that breached her virginity, in one movement that changed her forever, he entered her.

CHAPTER TWELVE

THE PAIN THAT streaked through Leah's eyes, the jagged whimper that fell from her swollen mouth arrested Stavros when he would have thrust deeper inside her. The walls of her sex were so tight around his rigid shaft, the friction so unbearably good that he had to bite the inside of his cheek to stop.

The taste of his own blood finally punctured that haze.

Slowly, as if he was waking through a fog that owned his senses, he tried to shake off the fever that clung to his skin and muscles. The dawn of truth on his lust-riddled brain was slow, excruciating.

Cristos, she was as untried in body, as innocent as she had been of all the wrongs he had attributed to her.

Another horribly wrong misstep on his part.

He had taken her so roughly, on his bloody desk of all places! For five years, he had lived like a monk and now, pushed inside her like an animal…

Shame and fury roped together inside. He wanted to pound his fist into the desk. The only thing that stopped him was the thought of scaring her.

Sweat beaded on his brow. Marshaling his thoughts by the skin of his teeth, he looked down at her. Her pinched lips, the white pallor of her cheeks…it was like a lash against his skin.

"Looks like more lies, *little wife*," he snarled.

Color returned to her cheeks and with it, that reckless

defiance that had given him sleepless nights. Like a bloody switch, he hardened even more inside her. "You assumed everything about me," she replied, her fingers digging into his shoulders.

Every inch of him felt the heat of her fingers, of her breath feathering over his skin.

He was so aroused, his body so out of his control that he closed his eyes and willed his breath to calm down. Holding her hips, he slowly pulled out, the slick slide of her walls too much temptation to resist.

She stole her hand under his shirt, searching, caressing, possessive. Like she owned him. Like he hadn't just breached her virginity like a marauding animal. Like she knew her way around a man's body.

No, his body, he corrected himself, as the feathered strokes of her fingers wreaked hell on his better intentions.

She had and she would only ever know his body, came the utterly useless and distracting thought.

Her soft fingers reached his buttocks and she dug her nails in. Sharp and hard. She pushed closer with her bottom until her breasts rasped against his chest. Pleasure burst forth in his belly and the back of his thighs and he pushed into her wet heat, despite himself.

He pulled at her hair roughly, trying to grab her attention. "Stop it," he whispered, fighting the heat building inside, the need clamoring at him to just let go. "I don't want to hurt you. *Theos*, Leah, I just…" He felt something in him clench tight against her, as if she could wreak infinite hurt on him. "I could not bear it if I hurt you anymore."

"Stavros…won't you look at me, please."

The pleading, persuasive tone would have pulled him into hell.

He opened his eyes and was lost instantly.

Her eyes glittered with raw emotion, and once again, he found himself stunned at how much she could feel, how much Leah risked despite all her lies.

In a sensuous movement that was born more of need than finesse, she brought her mouth to his. Slowly, softly, seduced him with long kisses and lingering strokes. Set her tongue to his mouth and made love to him like he had never experienced before.

Her breath was a harsh whisper against his mouth. "You will hurt me if you stop now. I started this knowing what I wanted, I started this because you finally saw me as your equal. Not a thing to be protected and controlled. Right?" When he remained silent, she buried her face in his neck, a catch in her throat. "From the moment you stood there at the airport to pick me up, all haughty, forbidding, so contemptuous—"

He groaned. "You tried to run away to Paris while Giannis waited on tenterhooks for you in Athens."

"—I had such a crush on you. I have had dreams that you would look at me like you did tonight. Please, Stavros. Tell me that I didn't imagine that look in your eyes. Tell me that you're doing this because you want me and not because you feel sorry for me or because it's your duty."

Tenderness joined fiery desire now. Tilting her chin up, he caught the tear that ran down one soft cheek. The sight of that lone tear undid him as nothing ever had. A fist could be squeezing his chest for the tightness there. "My want...for you, my need knows no reason, Leah... That I do this when I should be..." He searched for the words to say it right, searched his own feelings, as raw and strange as they were. "You make me selfish, Leah. You make me angry, and sad, and laugh and...just so unbalanced. You sink under my skin, *pethi mou*, and I can't breathe for wanting you."

Such a smile dawned on her lips that the beauty and joy in it made his breath catch.

Her shoulders tense, she slowly thrust her hips forward. "It doesn't hurt..." When he glared, she added, "...that much." Wrapping her hand around his nape possessively, she leaned in. "Give me this tonight, Stavros. Please. Give us both what we want."

That raw, unabashed request coming from that perfect little mouth was enough to shred his will.

He thrust his tongue into her mouth, falling deeper and deeper into her spell. "Tell me if it becomes too much," he commanded. "I will stop, Leah." *Even if it killed him.*

She nodded, like a good little dutiful wife when the cunning minx was anything but.

Palming her breasts, he rubbed her nipples, and the tight points curling his muscles into a new frenzy.

"You like it when I do that." She moaned into his mouth, a smile curving her lush mouth. "I could do it all day, *pethi mou*, caress your breasts, suck your nipples until you... come just from that."

With every word he said, he started moving again. And her heat welcomed him, sending a current of need through his nerve endings. "Tell me what you feel," he said, continuing to kiss her, tease her nipples with his fingers.

"No more pain," she said against his shoulder.

He thrust in again, slowly but forcefully. Reminded himself to speak again through the delirious heat enveloping him. "Now?"

"It feels achy...full...incredibly hot..." she half sobbed.

"Hold on tight to me, *thee mou*," he whispered, and pulled all the way out.

She whimpered, like a kitten denied her treat. "I feel empty now," she said, meeting his gaze, unbuttoning his shirt.

He thrust back in again, heat curling through his muscles as she slapped those long fingers over his chest. Scraped a flat nipple with her nail. "Now?"

"Oh God, Stavros..." a guttural groan escaped her.

Grabbing her hips, he locked her against him as he built up a rhythm. His climax was rushing at him, hard, explosive. Spots were beginning to dance behind his eyes.

His pulse raced, his lungs burst. Every thrust brought him closer to the edge and he couldn't contain the momentum, couldn't control his pace.

Desperation took the place of finesse, animal lust destroyed concern for her.

"Leah…I can't slow down now, *pethi mou*."

"Don't." She opened her mouth against his chest, and he jerked. Pleasure hung around on a serrated edge as she dug her teeth in, harder. "I want all of you, Stavros. I want everything you give."

Clutching her bottom, he tilted her and thrust again.

"I want to die, now. It's so much," she moaned.

"Look down," he commanded, raking through the sheer lust to find an iota of control, determined to push her to the edge one more time.

She did. A raw groan fell from her mouth.

"Touch yourself, *galika mou*." The desk shook with his thrusts, blood whooshed in his ears.

Shock flashed in her eyes. "No. I…can't. That's… just…" Her innocence tugged at him even as she undid every one of his rules with her innate sensuality.

Christos, this need for her would not stop here, would never stop consuming him.

He licked the rim of her ear, and pleaded, as he had never done before. "Imagine that it is me touching your wet heat, imagine it is me licking you there… Do it for me, Leah. *Please*."

Color streaking her cheeks, she met his gaze. "You would like it?"

"It would be the most erotic sight I would ever see."

Her mouth trembling, she snuck her hand between their bodies. Her long finger reached between them slowly. "Go on…"

Her head went back, her back arched as she stroked herself.

Stavros groaned, pumped into her, hard and fast, pleasure drenching him in sweat, robbing his breath from him.

"Come for me, Leah."

For once, in his life, the firecracker that his wife was, complied.

Pleasure burst in his veins, in his blood, in his muscles as Leah came with a long, drawn-out groan and her contracting muscles pulled at him.

His climax knocked his breath out, and his mind blanked out as he broke apart into a thousand pieces and got back together again.

Theos, he had waited because it had been the right thing to do, because his honor wouldn't let him cheat on his wife even if he didn't live with her. But, he had never expected it to be this life-changing, mind-numbing experience with her.

Leah was in his blood now, a craving in his gut. He would never have enough of her. Of her lithe body, of her glorious smile, of her sometimes infuriating words.

He had never known this exhilaration as he did with Leah, he had never felt so alive. He had never felt so needy as he did with her. He had never wanted to change, never wanted to risk his emotions as he did with her.

He had never wondered what else he had been missing out on as he did with her.

Running his hands over her shaking form, he hugged her to him. She was so fragile. And yet he felt like he was the one who was risking everything. "Leah, say something," he whispered into her scalp.

"Hmmm?" she said, lazily snuggling into him.

"You are all right?"

Her mouth opened against his chest. "I want more of you, more of this."

Laughter burst out of him. The tightness in his chest relented as she vined her arms around his waist, opened her hot mouth against his shivering muscles and kissed him. He let out a long breath, unmanned by her tenderness.

"We're only getting started, *pethi mou*," he said, enfolding her in his arms.

Over the next few weeks, Leah was so busy that she didn't have a moment to sift through the storm building through her. The night that Stavros had made such explosive love to her, she had asked if they could return home to his estate while they had been in the shower.

It was an intimacy Leah had cherished as much as the sex itself. Every little moment with Stavros, she realized, taught her more about herself.

He had stopped midway, his hands incredibly gentle as they washed her. After he had carried her to the en suite bathroom of his bedroom, turned on the shower and demanded to know if she was hurting anywhere. Had looked so vulnerable when he had said he didn't usually behave like a rutting animal.

How he believed that she could think that of him when he had honored the vows he had made to her, she didn't know. But his concern had touched her on a fundamental level.

The first thing the next morning, they had returned here. Once the servants had unpacked for her, and he had carried her from her bedroom to his, declaring in that arrogant tone that she wouldn't sleep anywhere else but his bed, only then had she realized that she had called it home.

But that's what his estate felt like to her.

Home.

She had been accepted to present at the Independent Fashion Week in New York in September. When she had told him after Helene had called her personally, he had smiled at her, fierce pride glinting in his eyes, and told her that he wasn't the least bit surprised.

After a few meetings with Helene and another fashion

director, the scale and the scope of her collection was even more than she had dreamed. She had added four more designs to it.

She was on such a constant high, on a ride that only kept going higher and higher that she didn't want to stop even for a moment to see where it was that she was going or how long she would be able to sustain that momentum.

She worked twelve, fourteen hours to finish her first collection, which was turning out to be better than she had ever imagined. Models came in almost every day now for trials, she had two assistants helping her with the final touches, gowns that were being resized and resewn, and then pressed once finalized…

At the end of the day, she fell into bed exhausted. She put off questions about the future. She ran around the estate, she worked with such feverish compulsion that Stavros had one day locked her in his bedroom after she had almost collapsed in her workroom.

But even through the frenzy of the creative drive that gripped her through the day, the best parts were at night.

Intense, hot, turning-her-inside-out nights with Stavros.

It was as if they were both determined to assuage a hunger of a lifetime every single night. It didn't matter what time he flew back from Athens, it didn't matter that sometimes her own work kept her past midnight, he brought her to his bed at all manner of times.

Sometimes, they would both be too exhausted to do nothing but sleep wrapped up in each other, and he would wake her after the edge of sleep was gone. Sometimes, he woke her up in the early morning and was moving inside her before she was completely awake.

He was insatiable, possessive, his touch incredibly addictive.

The one time he had stayed overnight in Athens, a strange panic had gripped her. Suddenly, it was as though she had lost her anchor. She had woken up to the sounds of rotor blades the next morning, her breath painfully hovering in her throat. Had waited for him to come to her.

Morning had given way to noon, and then to a gorgeous sunset. He was busy, he had sent a message when she had inquired.

Even loathing that she was losing some unknown battle of wills, she had gone looking for him once the estate had settled down for the night. She had found him in his office, in the middle of a conference call, his gaze settling on her with a possessive hunger. Yet, he hadn't moved.

She had had the strangest feeling that he had kept away on purpose. As if it was a test he was conducting. As if he wanted to prove something to himself.

An experiment she had no interest in, she had realized, a test she had lost even before it had begun. How dare he deny her after he had made her addicted to him?

So she had teased him when he had made no move to interrupt the call.

Brazen and bold, she had slowly stripped every single piece of clothing from her body even as he was still on the video call. He had looked at her with darkening eyes, daring her to continue.

Of course, she had never been able to resist a dare, especially when it came to riling, or in this case, arousing Stavros.

He had even held out for a few minutes.

Her skin on fire, her body craving him, she had refused to back down. She had touched herself, her breasts first, rolling her aching nipples between her fingers, imagined it was those rough fingers of his. Like he had begged her to do that first night.

Dark color streaked his cheeks, and the pen he had been holding to make notes had clattered to the ground. But still, he hadn't given in.

Her throat had felt like parched paper, her grasp on her emotions tenuous at best. She had become a slave to his will. Even worse, she had become a slave to her own need for him.

Throwing her hair back, as she had seen one of the models wearing her own creation do, she had strutted farther into the room. He had lasted another two seconds before he had minimized the screen, marched to her, picked her up, called her his doom, and taken her against the wall, even as the call was going on.

All the while his mouth had covered hers, swallowing her moans and finally the sound of her climax. There had been no finesse to his raw thrusts, there had been nothing of his will left by the time he had climaxed, his skin damp to her touch.

She had won that day. But the fear that she wouldn't another day, another moment, gathered like a black cloud. Because as invested as he was in their madness, she knew he was retreating. As if she and his desire for her, they were a rope that was slowly binding him and he...he was struggling against it.

He refused to discuss the state of their little deal. Every time she tried to talk of the past or the future, he evaded her or worse, seduced her. And the coward that she was, Leah let him be. Settled for the warmth of his arms, for the heat of his caresses, for the fiery intensity of his passion.

"Are you happy?" she had asked him one morning when he had brought her breakfast in bed.

He had covered her body with his, taken her mouth in such a tender kiss that it had brought tears to her eyes. "I don't know about happy," he had said against her mouth with that trademark honesty. The question seemed to have thrown him, but lost in the magic his mouth weaved, Leah hadn't cared. "But I've never felt more alive, *agape mou*."

There was something disconcerting about that answer, she remembered thinking.

Almost a month passed by like that. And from the dreamy, drugged state, something else emerged. A tiny sliver of fear for the future. Of what she was letting happen, of what it was going to hold for her and Stavros.

For a few weeks, she had been hinting about going to Paris for a small fashion event that Helene had mentioned. It was like puncturing the bubble they seemed to exist in, but she pushed the matter anyway. Sooner or later, they would have to emerge from it and for her part, she wanted him to acknowledge their relationship outside of his estate.

Finally, the night before the event, he had given in. Surprised her by joining her the next evening. And any thoughts she had that their relationship would change evaporated in the week they had been in Paris.

Leah dragged him on a tour of the beautiful city and shopping while he dragged her back to their luxurious hotel suite on the Champs-Elysées every time the mood struck him. Which was much too often, she had complained once laughingly.

But she hadn't denied him, not once. She was just as addicted to him as he seemed to be with her.

They had been in Paris a week when, one evening, someone knocked quite rudely on the outer door of their suite.

Leah laughed, and hid her face in Stavros's chest while he continued to lick and kiss her breasts with no thought to the caller. Soon, she was as lost as he was when he lazily pushed into her and struck a slow, mind-numbing pace toward release. The elegant side table, whose design she had only remarked on earlier, bumped against the wall as his thrusts became harder and faster.

"What you do to me, Leah," he whispered, leaning into her.

She kissed his sweat-beaded brow when he suddenly stilled.

And Leah heard it—the sound of footsteps coming closer toward their bedroom.

In a movement that was both blurry and genius— because she couldn't even move a finger, Stavros was off her and pulling on his sweatpants. Had just covered her naked form with a sheet when the double doors burst open.

Arrogantly leaning against the wall, Dmitri surveyed them, the wickedest grin curving his sinful mouth. Heat bloomed over every inch of her as that dark, slumberous gaze took in the state of their undress and their still uneven breaths.

Stavros's curse, filthy and loud, should have colored the room blue before he dragged her behind him. "Forgotten your manners again, Dmitri?"

Such blistering scorn filled his voice, yet Leah, peeking from behind his shoulder, only saw it bounce off Dmitri's amused smile. Being the complete opposites they were, Leah had never understood their friendship. Only that it was inviolate.

"Of all your dresses, I think this suits you best, *pethi mou*," Dmitri offered with an outrageous wink and Leah couldn't help but smile.

A growl emanated from Stavros and her gaze flew to him. It was a savage sound she would never associate with him of all the men in the world. His passion was insatiable, never-ending but he hid it under such a civilized facade that she couldn't believe it the first few days.

He did, and made her do, the wickedest things in bed—which she did with the same spiraling hunger as he did, but outside of bed, outside of sex, he was still far too private.

She knew that, in the past month, Dmitri had wanted to see them, more than once. Wanted to join them either for a dinner, or even for a lazy afternoon at Stavros's estate. But he had said no every time in that arrogant tone of his. Hadn't even bothered to make an excuse.

It was almost as though he didn't want Dmitri to see them as a couple.

Was he still ashamed of her, she wondered now, trying to stave off the hurt it caused. *Or did he think it a tempo-*

rary madness that he didn't want to share with his clos-est friend?

"I wouldn't have had to disturb your connubial bliss," Dmitri drawled completely unaffected by Stavros's rising temper, "if you had not done the disappearing act on me. I had to half seduce your location out of your poor secre-tary. Very uncharacteristic of you, Stavros. Your staff is petrified that you might be dying."

Stavros turned to her. "Do you want to get dressed, Leah?"

"She should hear this. I wouldn't have barged in just for anything, Stavros."

"What is it, Dmitri?"

"Alex Ralston showed up on my yacht today. My secu-rity tried to grab him but they weren't successful."

Suddenly cold, Leah shivered. Throwing his arm around her, Stavros pulled her into his warm body.

Alex had been Calista's on-and-off boyfriend. "Alex… you sent him to jail after Calista…"

"We found that he was the one selling drugs that day. He had a long record of possession and substance abuse," Dmitri replied while Stavros remained stubbornly silent.

"I thought you did that because…" The words trailed off Leah's lips as she realized how absurd she sounded.

Alex had been the one who had given them to Calista? Charming, easygoing Alex? And in contrast, Stavros had seemed such a monster in her head.

"Get dressed, Leah. Let me talk to Dmitri alone."

She was so much in panic that she didn't even say a word. Something flickering in his eyes, Dmitri hugged her, sheet and nakedness and all.

After all these years, what did Alex want now?

CHAPTER THIRTEEN

STAVROS HAD BEEN expecting something to strike at the haze in which he had been living for the past month. Something that would wake him up from the dreamlike state he had been functioning in with Leah. Something so painfully real, so achingly raw, it was bound to end.

He expected the novelty of making love to her to wear off. He expected the high of being around her, the high that came with her laughter, with her irreverent humor, with how easily she gave of herself and how possessively she demanded of him, to end at some point.

He expected the amazing light and joy that had pervaded him, even as he had tried to tether and control it, to fizzle out.

Because life didn't work like that, did it? At least, not his.

It didn't carry so much joy, so much laughter, so many emotions that had overthrown him the last month. It never had such gnawing hunger, such desperate need to grasp what he could, such panic-ridden drive to control it so that he didn't become its slave.

But he didn't think it would come in such a way. He hadn't thought it would rip his heart out like this and leave him gasping.

That it would wreak on him an avalanche of hurt and inadequacy and pain.

He had thought Dmitri uncharacteristically foolish to even indulge Alex Ralston's demand to talk to Stavros.

Yet, he had just disconnected the call with Alex, a video call that the thug had insisted on.

Nausea whirled in his gut at the things Alex had said about Calista. It was like hearing stories about a stranger, not his sister at all.

All he had known of Calista had been a front, a lie. A lie that had been neatly supported by Leah for so many years. Because Leah had known it all.

And in the sinking morass of his grief, that betrayal cut the deepest. Leah had known and hadn't whispered a word to him. Even when he had asked it of her.

"Stavros?" Dmitri nudged him.

"Locate him, Dmitri." He stood up with such force that the desk rattled. "He can't go to the media with this. *Theos*, this is Calista... I don't want her name besmirched like this."

"I will stop him. Stavros...it's not your fault. Calista... whatever Ralston told you about her, you couldn't have known. You did everything you could to help her."

"I should have known. All along, she had so many problems and I..." A growl escaped his throat.

"Have you ever thought that some of us are beyond help, Stavros? Too broken to be fixed? Giannis said she was just a child when your mother walked out. Whatever Calista needed, you didn't have it."

"She needed to be loved, Dmitri. And I couldn't do it. I didn't know how. Not then, not now."

He was the one in pain, and yet Dmitri looked pale. He kept shaking his head as if he could see into Stavros's head. "Her behavior is not your fault."

"I wish I could forgive myself as easily as you, Dmitri," he said, hating himself, hating Dmitri for being so understanding.

He couldn't numb the gnawing in his gut as the truth solidified. He had never had what it took to begin with.

Was that why he had clung so tightly to doing what was

right? Because he hadn't possessed, hadn't ever known, his heart?

Beneath Leah's betrayal, beneath the shock of learning his sister's truth, only one thing remained.

You are made of stone.

How right Leah had been... If he had ever known it once, he didn't remember. He didn't know if he had buried it deep so that his parents' indifference, their negligence didn't hurt.

He had never understood Calista, never saw past the facade his sister presented because he had never understood her fears, her pain, her joy. Every time she had mentioned their parents, every time she had expressed her confusion, he had only pushed her to move on, had brushed her away believing that they were better off without them.

Because he hadn't wanted to dwell on it, because it would mean acknowledging all the wrongs they had done to them, it would mean letting them be a part of who they were.

Again and again, he had closed himself off to her grief, her pain. Until she had decided that he would never understand? Until she had decided, *like Leah*, that he didn't have the capability to understand? The capability to love?

In the end, his parents had robbed him of everything.

Even if he forgave Leah's lies, what did he possess to give her? How long before she would realize the truth? How long before she realized that he had never known and would never understand love?

That he would never know how to give it and take it.

It was two hours before Stavros returned to their suite, two hours in which Leah had become half-crazy wondering what was going on. One look in his eyes, and her heart skidded to her gut.

"Pack your bags. You're catching a flight to New York in a few hours."

"What? The fashion week isn't for another fortnight..."

He stood only a foot away, yet it could have been a thousand miles. Why wouldn't he look at her?

"It is better for you in New York rather than here with Ralston around. Apparently, he's very much interested in hearing how I've mistreated you."

"But all my stuff is…" She stopped, his words slowly registering with her.

His cell phone rang and he looked at her finally. "I will ensure that Rosa packs up your stuff with utmost care."

Rosa was going to pack her stuff, she was going to leave for New York…

Leah stared at the empty space he left behind for a few seconds. The shock slowly blunted, bringing in its wake utter panic.

Throat dangerously close to tears, she found him in the study that offered a breathtaking view of the Eiffel Tower.

He was on the phone, listening, but his gaze stayed on her face. And that's when Leah noticed the white pallor to his skin.

She would have welcomed his blistering contempt, or even his lacerating fury. But the resignation in his gaze… As if he had lost something precious. As if he had finally given up.

The minute he disconnected the call, she stepped inside.

"If he comes for me, he has to get through you, doesn't he?" she demanded, anger coming to her rescue. She wouldn't let him treat her like this again. Not after the last month.

He looked up, a bitterness curving his mouth. "I'll be busy trying to stop him from taking the story to the media, from turning my life and Calista's…and yours into a cash cow."

"What?" she said, fear spewing into her words now.

"If you go to New York, you'll be free to do as you please. I know how much you don't like being told what to do. I'll make sure Ralston doesn't follow you."

"Why does it sound like you're sending me away?" She sounded desperate, pitiful, but she didn't care. It seemed she had no armor left.

He stood up from the chair, his every movement precise, his skin tautly pulled over those sharp features. There was nothing anymore of the man she had known this last month. The man who had smiled, laughed, kissed her, the man who had looked at her as if he would drown if he didn't possess her one more time, nothing.

It was as if he was pulling himself back, word by word, second by second, until he became that Stavros she hated again.

Her gut twisting, she walked around the huge desk until he was forced to look at her. Placing her hands on his chest, she asked, "What did I do this time?"

He grabbed her wrists to push her away. But she didn't let go. She would never hold him again if she let go, the fear clamored through her. "Tell me what's going on, Stavros. Or I swear I'll…" she broke off on a sob.

"You'll what, Leah? Tell a new lie? You have won." He became stiff, like he was a statue who possessed no feeling, no weakness. "I'll sign the divorce papers, release your inheritance as soon as possible. You are just Leah Huntington again." His gaze moved over her features with a hunger she knew he would deny. For all his withdrawal, she had the strangest feeling that he wasn't untouched. That he was struggling just as she was.

Or it was the delusion she really wanted to cling to, she thought pitying herself.

"There's nothing binding you to me or to Katrakis Textiles now."

Her breath whooshed out of her in a painfully long exhale. Legs shaking beneath her, Leah grabbed the table. Tears pooled in her eyes and spilled over. Just breathing became a chore. "You're punishing me again…"

"Punishment, *pethi mou*? No. I'm finally freeing us

both. Giannis is gone, and you've proved beyond doubt that you can take care of yourself, *ne*? What is left of our relationship, if it could be called that, if we take away my duty and your lies, Leah?"

"The last month—"

"Last month has been nothing but sex. Five years of celibacy and you…it would mess with any man's head, even a stone like me."

That he would reduce the last month like that, that he would cheapen what they had shared so easily…she couldn't even breathe.

Fear stole coherence from her. Slowly, she thought back to how the dreadful afternoon had begun. "What did Alex say?"

"Threatening to go the media with a colorful story about Calista and her monster of a brother who neglected her and then married the heiress… The pictures he has of her, the horrible things he's threatening to say about her…" Restrained violence simmered in him as he moved away from her. As if he didn't trust himself to be near her. "The parties, the drinking, the men… *Cristos*, I didn't know my sister at all, did I? And you knew it all along." He turned toward her again, accusation and pain in his eyes.

"She begged me not to tell you, Stavros. Every time you found us at some party, she would beg me to leave her out of it. She asked me to cover…just once more. When she saw you, when she was with you, she…she wanted to be perfect. She was desperate to not lose you. Desperate to not lose your love. She was afraid that you would…"

"All your arguments with me, if you had thrown it once in my face that she was the one—"

The calmer he got, the more she panicked. "I didn't realize how bad it had gotten until that night. Stavros, I was immature, foolish. I told you, I didn't know that she was using. I feel sick to my stomach when I think I could have helped, when I could have—"

"What about the last few weeks, Leah? What about when I begged you for the truth about her? What reason could you possibly have to lie after all these years? Were you afraid that I would punish you for her actions? Even after these few weeks, were you just looking out for yourself?"

Her heart hammered away in her chest, her knees trembled beneath her and all she wanted was to be held by him, to see him smile, to do whatever she could to remove that betrayal, that pain from his eyes.

And just like that, the truth struck Leah. In that dark-paneled study in a majestic hotel in one of the loveliest cities in the world, with Stavros looking at her with utter resignation, it came to her.

She was in love with Stavros. A few months ago, she would have cackled hysterically at the prospect. And yet, had she ever truly stood a chance against the man she had discovered him to be?

Despite all the wrongs done to him as a child, he had done his duty. He could cajole and love and support as fiercely as he followed his duty, he could care, even though it was through actions and not words...

Calista had been so wrong in not trusting him, in doubting his love, so painfully unknowing of her own brother... But Leah understood him finally, she knew what a complex and honorable man her husband was.

And knowing Stavros meant loving Stavros, loving his generous heart, his sense of duty, even his rigidly autocratic dictates.

Why else had she risked everything she had always been scared of, this past month, how else would she have thrown herself into this madness with such relish... "After all these years, I didn't think the reasons for Calista's death mattered anymore. Not when I was finally..."

"When you were finally getting what you wanted," he finished and utter fury filled her.

She gasped as it unfurled inside her, this new feeling, sinuously breathing courage into her very veins, filling her with a tremendous energy.

Reaching him, she refused to let him dismiss her so easily. "When, *finally*, you saw me for what I was, and let me see what kind of a man you were. I thought I should leave the past where it was. I thought…I could have—"

"Your wants, your needs—it's all about you, isn't it, *pethi mou*?"

"For years, it has been, yes. All I thought of since stepping in Athens was protecting myself from pain, from ever having to mourn another loved one again. But not anymore. For the first time in my life, I lied, not for myself, but for you. I lied to protect you, to spare you from this pain of knowing Calista's reality.

"I lied because I…care about you. I lied because, somehow, you gave me the courage to live without fear, I lied because you made it impossible to not love you."

His skin pulled into a taut mask, he looked as if she had dealt him an invisible blow. Everything in her scrunched into a painful ball as Leah realized that her words, somehow, had only hurt him even more.

"Say something, Stavros," she said desperately.

"I didn't realize until today how ill-suited we are for each other, *pethi mou*. Even if I continue this charade in the name of Giannis, it won't be long before we rip each other into shreds. Before there's nothing but pain left."

The bridge of his nose, the sculpted planes of his face, the stubble that was already coming in…it hurt to look at him. "Is that any worse than what you're doing now?" A shuddering gasp left her. "Somehow, I doubt that you can get any more cruel, any more heartless, Stavros."

"Then you know why our farce of a marriage needs to end," he finally said after what felt like an eternity of hell. "You have your freedom. Goodbye, Leah."

* * *

For the first time since Giannis had brought him to Athens years ago, Stavros did not return to work after Leah left.

He let Dmitri's calls go unattended, told his assistant to cancel everything indefinitely, heard from his head of security that a particularly treacherous board member, a distant cousin of Giannis who had always resented that Stavros and Dmitri were the topmost shareholders on the Katrakis board, was planning a coup to take over.

Rumors swirled about that Dmitri and he had fallen out, causing the stock for Katrakis Textiles to sink.

But Stavros, try as he did, still clinging to his wretched sense of duty, couldn't give a damn. He and Dmitri had slaved night and day to build it into a multimillion dollar industry for over a decade, given it their all because they had wanted Giannis's legacy to mean something…because they had both wanted something to anchor their lives.

And yet, he did not care if it all crashed and burned. All he wanted to do was shrug off the world and retreat. And he did.

Yet, wherever he turned, there were signs of Leah at his estate.

From the workers at the vineyard to the seamstress who asked if Leah was taking New York by storm, from the trails she had loved running through to the small, inconsequential things she had left lying around the house, like her iPod. She was everywhere.

She was under his skin, in his every breath, she had somehow become an irrevocable part of himself.

The peace he had found on his estate, the rules he had set in place all his life, everything was shattered. He felt empty within and he hadn't even known that he had something so precious.

It was as if Leah had breathed life into him, showed him what it was to laugh, love and live.

For days, he let himself remember every bleary moment

from when his mother had left to when his father had died, and he grieved for Calista. Grieved for the innocence he had never had. For days, he sat in the study in his estate, wandered into Leah's empty workroom.

And slowly, her words gained strength in him, shifted and morphed his very view of himself.

For the first time in my life, I lied, not for myself, but for you, Stavros. I lied to protect you, to spare you from this pain.

I lied because I...care about you. I lied because, some-how, you have given me the courage to live without fear, I lied because you made it impossible to not love you.

Leah loved him, she had protected him. When had any-one ever thought of him like that?

The Leah that wouldn't leave him alone the night of Gi-annis's death, the Leah that had so innocently and full of hope, asked him if he was happy, the Leah that had teased and aroused him with such stark, possessive need...that Leah who refused to let him deny what they both wanted, needed when he had worried that it was becoming an ob-session, a madness, the Leah that had held him tightly, when in the aftermath of making love to her he had con-fided that he didn't remember how his mother looked, the Leah that had believed in the sanctity of marriage...

That woman was worthy of a fight, was worthy of a man he could be.

She had made him love for the first time in his life, she made him care, had made him live for himself, made him want with such gnawing hunger.

Had given him a taste of happiness, of pain, of ache, of loss.

She had made him feel everything he had shied away from his whole life. And he wanted to live like that again. He couldn't go back to being an automatic machine.

Shaking at the very chill in his bones, he leaned his forehead against the glass door looking out into the estate.

In a moment of utter desolation he had admitted to Giannis that night that he had been wrong about Leah, that he had ruined her life. Even facing death, Giannis had smiled, had said that Leah needed him, that he, Stavros, was a man worthy of her... Those words pushed through to the fore, crushing his self-doubt.

Maybe he hadn't deserved Leah five years ago.

But now, facing his own incapability to love Calista as she had needed, and accepting that, despite his every effort, his parents had somehow damaged him, forgiving himself for not loving Calista as she had needed, he deserved Leah now.

He deserved to be happy, he deserved to think about himself after a lifetime of thinking about everyone else.

Suddenly, Stavros couldn't live without telling Leah that, couldn't bear that she was thousands of miles away. Not when he loved her so much.

CHAPTER FOURTEEN

HER COLLECTION AT the Independent Fashion Week in New York had gone better than Leah could have imagined in her wildest dreams. Her designs had been called modern, colorful, yet sophisticated. Just last week, with Helene's advice, she had invested a load of money into creating a lookbook that incorporated line sheets, one that gave buyers and fashion magazine editors a view into her brand.

After a crazily hectic two weeks, she had returned to Athens. When she had knocked at Mrs. Kovlakis's door and requested the keys to her old flat and the dragon had simply handed them over, she had been both shocked and relieved. One look at the news and she found Dmitri and Stavros and herself at the front and center of it.

Hiding and barely eating, she had slept for a week. All of a sudden, she would find herself awake and looking at her phone, before she realized she was waiting for his call.

Had he so thoroughly washed his hands of her? Had she truly meant nothing to him?

She had cried until she had been disgusted with herself, moped around the flat until one afternoon, Dmitri had almost broken the door down when she hadn't heard his knocking.

He had taken her out to lunch, plied her with food until she had eaten enough for a month, inquiring if she needed anything.

Did he send you? she had asked, pitifully desperate.

No, he had said with unflinching honesty. *You've truly proved yourself to him.*

Words she would have embraced before now seemed like punishment.

At which point, she had cried and he had sighed and hugged her, and point-blank asked her if she meant to spend the rest of her hard-won freedom like a howling puppy, if she meant to spend the rest of it as the discarded wife of Stavros Sporades, hiding from the world.

Hating him and loving him for it, she had decided enough was enough. After fighting Stavros tooth and nail, she refused to let him win, refused to let herself become a shadow.

She had her whole life in front of her. She had decisions to make about where she would operate, about staff to hire, preparations to make for the winter collection, about her finances and how much of her inheritance she could invest in her business and how much she needed to save for a rainy day. She couldn't live in some distant, unfamiliar corner of the world because Stavros was here.

The freedom to make her own choices, once she had begun, was heady, exhilarating.

More than one designer house approached her with offers to join them. Loath to compromise her creative vision, she refused all of them in a bold move.

Just as she finally embraced the fact that she was a shareholder in her grandfather's textile companies, that she was part of his legacy.

She had walked into the legendary Katrakis offices in downtown Athens and attended her first board meeting, her heart threatening to rip out of her chest at the thought of facing Stavros.

That Stavros was absent and she was present created a stir that had made Dmitri smile wickedly. Whispers and innuendoes abounded large, about Dmitri, about Stavros, about her. And the worst of all, about the state of her marriage to Stavros.

It had taken everything she had possessed to get through the day. Especially after she received a message from Stavros's assistant that he would like to meet her before she left on her trip to Milan the next day. The requisite paperwork would be sent to her lawyer if she could provide a name, she had been told.

Nausea rising in her throat, Leah had headed straight to the ladies' room.

That was that then. He was going to divorce her. After five years, the bond between them would be broken. He would be free of her and she…of him. He would not be hers, even for a moment, ever again.

That night she went to bed, an ache in her gut.

She dreamed of him, intense, vivid dreams that woke her from restless sleep, breathing hard and aching, damp with need, inconsolable that he would never hold her again.

Violently furious that after demanding that she show him the real her, he had not believed the biggest truth she had ever told him.

He didn't deserve her, she decided, the lie hollow to her own ears.

Leah arrived at Stavros's office thirty minutes after ten, having finally fallen into a fitful sleep in the early hours of the morning. Her head hurt, her muscles ached from having thrashed so much.

So when she grabbed the handle and pushed the door open, she was feeling particularly bloodthirsty, as he put it once.

There was no one in his office room. Her heels clicking on the marble floor, she walked around. Her nape prickled and she turned.

Standing at the entrance to his private suite, Stavros studied her.

He looked as he always did, arrogant, implacable, larger than life, except for the haunted look in his eyes. He wore jeans that molded those powerful thighs and a gray shirt that stretched against the muscled expanse of his chest.

He was so achingly gorgeous, so painfully beautiful that her throat closed up. She just stared at him hungrily for several minutes.

"I found the land you were looking at to build a factory."

Leah flinched at the sight of him, at his raspy voice, at his blank expression. That was the first thing he said to her? Not even hello?

"I don't need your help," she said flippantly. "Where are your lawyers?"

"We don't need them."

"Then why did you summon me here? Why not just sign the papers and be done with it? Or have you gotten addicted to me begging you for things like cash, sex and the minimum courtesy that you believe me?"

Something slumberous glinted in his gaze. "I don't remember you begging me for sex."

"Maybe because it held no meaning to you except for relief after five years of…" He prowled toward her with such dangerous intent that she stopped talking.

"I remember every moment, *pethi mou*. I just don't have a memory of you begging me for it. All those nights, and days, *not once*." A dark current tinged his words as if he was very much fantasizing the prospect of it now. "You teased me, you taunted me, you seduced me…and I just gave in every time, your willing slave."

"I'm leaving," she said, his strange mood making her weak everywhere.

He blocked her way. "Dmitri told me that you attended the board meeting. That you caused quite a stir. A walking powerhouse, that's what he called you."

She sent a silent thanks to Dmitri for hiding the ugly crying from Stavros.

"Are you surprised? I will not slink away from what is mine like a coward anymore. I will sit on the Katrakis board, I will launch my label from Athens. I will not hide as if the fiasco of our marriage is my fault.

"I won't let you browbeat me into anything I don't want to do ever again."

He looked tortured, his mouth pinched. "Forcing you to marry me was the biggest mistake I have ever made, *thee mou*. I can't believe—"

She had no idea that she had thrown herself at him. That with her weight and fists she had pushed them farther into the rear room of his private suite. Pain, and ache and a bone-deep hunger, everything deluged her.

Tears flew freely down her cheeks as she continued attacking him.

How dare he call knowing her a mistake? How dare he hurt her when all she had wanted was to protect him? How dare he be so heartless when she cared so much about him?

"Do you, *agape mou*?" he whispered when she hit him in the gut and she realized she had been screaming the words at him. "Do you care so much, Leah?"

She wouldn't say it again, wouldn't beg for his love when it had to be hers, when it was what she deserved.

"Leah, *pethi mou*, look at me," he begged continuously, yet she couldn't stop.

She was so afraid that he would disappear if she stopped, so afraid that she would wake up and realize it was a dream. That she would be achingly alone again.

"I'm sorry, *yineka mou*," he whispered, without even trying to stop her. "I'm so sorry that I sent you away. I'm so sorry that I didn't listen to you."

"You're a heartless bastard and I should hate you," she said, with another push and then they were falling into the bed.

"*Theos*, no more than I hate myself, Leah," he said on a ragged whisper.

Her breath jarred out of her as Leah landed on top of him. Fear and relief gave way to something else as her mouth lodged in his neck and his arousal pressed against her belly. Moving of their own accord, her legs straddled him, until his hardness pressed against her heated core. Her thighs shivered with the repressed need to ride him.

Her hands in his hair, Leah lifted her head and looked into his eyes.

Their harsh breaths thundered in the silent room, joined by the whisper of the satin sheets.

"I want you to sign those papers and get the hell out of my life. I want to never see you again."

"I can't," he said, sounding almost regretful.

"I do hate you," she said again, every inch of her desperately craving what he could give.

Only him. Always, only Stavros.

She closed her eyes to lock away the tears and touched her mouth to his.

Familiar and intense, the taste of him made her shiver violently, sent a jolt of electricity through her very veins. She continued kissing him softly until her heart was beating a loud tattoo against her chest, until tears blocked her throat again.

Until all she could touch, breathe and feel was him, until she could be sure that he was here, with her.

"I will never divorce you, Leah. I will never set you free."

What new madness had he thought of now?

Rolling away from him, she began to slide off the bed. His hand on her ankle, Stavros pulled her back onto the sheets in a deft movement. Struggling to get free, she squealed. And gasped when he covered her body with his.

His weight pressed her into the bed, stealing her breath. Clutching her eyes closed, Leah fought the craving that burst within her belly like a fire. Her arms literally ached to hold him, her body on fire to be possessed by him.

"I have missed you so much, *agape mou*," he said, shuddering harshly.

She felt his mouth probe hers softly, slowly, as if asking for permission. Holding her wrists at her head with one hand, he pressed little kisses on the seam of her lips, his warm breath drenching her.

In a needy, hoarse voice that unlocked every last fear in her, he punctured the kisses with words in Greek.

"Please, *pethi mou*. Let me in." He swiped at her mouth with his tongue, his body pressing into hers. "I would drown if you would not let me kiss you, Leah, I would stop breathing if you gave up on me now. My life is no life without you in it. Until you brought it to me, I have not known love. Do not take it away now, Leah."

And the tender gesture, the unvarnished love in his words undid her. Twining her arms around his neck, Leah gave in. He kissed her as if he were truly drowning, with desperate desire.

Lips scraped against teeth, limbs tangled, breathing was secondary as the fire between them consumed them.

"Tell me that I haven't lost you already. Tell me that you will teach me how to love you, Leah. *Theos*, it is all I want."

When she remained silent, he whispered, "I love you, Leah."

The declaration rang around in the silence, and slowly Leah opened her eyes. The truth of it shone in his eyes, rendering him acutely vulnerable. It was a look she had never thought to see on Stavros's face.

"You sent me away without a thought to me. I couldn't believe how cruel you were, how much it hurt," she said, her mouth trembling. "How easily you could break my heart, reject my love…"

"The news about Calista devastated me, I thought I could never love you like you need to be loved… I stomped on my own feelings, Leah."

"But you do know, Stavros. You don't say it in words,

you won't share your thoughts, but your actions…they speak so much. You are incredibly giving, caring, even if you drive me up the wall with your arrogance."

He traced a finger over her mouth, such tenderness in his eyes that Leah couldn't breathe. "I will never stop loving you, nor will I ever give you up. I—"

She ran shaking fingers over his brow, pushing back his hair. "When I'm with you, I'm unafraid. All I want is to take risk upon risk, all I want is to live and love you."

"Then let's do it, *pethi mou*."

Burying her face in his neck, Leah nodded, her head dizzy with euphoria, fear beating a tattoo. He pushed them both off the bed and brought her to the edge of it. While she shivered all over from the intent on his face, he knelt in front of her.

Looked at her with such love in his eyes that fresh tears fell on her cheeks.

"Will you marry me again, Leah?" he asked against her lips. "Will you…choose to spend the rest of your life with me, *pethi mou*?"

Leah buried her mouth in his throat, swallowed the tightness in hers. "Yes, Stavros. I'll marry you… Tomorrow, if you can arrange it."

"No, not tomorrow," he said, tugging her face up to his.

"Why not? Are you having second thoughts already?"

The ache in his eyes undid her. "I…want you to have the wedding you've always wanted. I want to take you out a few times. I want to do all the things you might have wanted to do before you married… I want you to take all the time you want…and until then…" He looked into her eyes and the love she saw there sent her heart to bursting.

She shook her head, instantly understanding how his mind worked. Scooting closer to him, she straddled him and they both groaned. "No… I can't sleep without you by my side. I can't bear it if you—"

"You will see me every day. When I make love to you again, you will have chosen to be my wife this time."

Something in his tone told her how important this was to him. That she marry him, that she become his wife because she loved him. "Three months," she moaned, tugging his lower lip with her teeth. "Let's set a date for after three months and no later. I don't have your patience or your willpower…"

He took her mouth in a hungry kiss that set fire to her claim… "Willpower, *yineka mou*? Waiting for you to walk toward me in your wedding dress…that's the only thing that will keep me going."

EPILOGUE

Three months later

STAVROS HAD NO idea that three months could feel like an eternity. *Theos*, he must have been insane to set the rule he had because touching Leah and kissing Leah without taking her had been an exercise in torture.

But in the same breath, he was also extremely glad that they had waited. Because Leah was worth every smile, every ache, every moment he had spent thrashing in his bed because he missed her with a bone-deep hunger.

On a beautiful October evening, he waited with his breath hovering in his throat while a hundred guests looked on.

Giannis's mansion and grounds had been decorated lavishly and he stood under an archway in the garden. Lilies in beautiful arrangements spread their fragrance while the sky glittered a brilliant blue.

Most of the guests had come to see his beautiful bride, the new designer that had shaken the fashion world with her designs—models she had worked with the past couple of months, half the population from his estate, workers from her factory, all because of Leah's generosity of spirit, her kindness, the depth of her commitment and loyalty.

And finally today, the magnificent woman was going to be his in a bond born out of love and laughter and joy. His heart ached as he remembered how much Calista would have loved to see Leah and him like this…

And there she was, on Dmitri's arm, walking toward him with sure steps.

His heart threatened to jump out of his chest when he saw her.

She had told him she was going to wear her own creation—the first wedding gown she had ever designed.

She looked utterly fragile and so beautiful that he stared hungrily, desire fisting tight in his gut.

Her long hair was combed away in a stylish ponytail, pearl earrings that had been a gift from Giannis at her ears, and the dress she wore was a demure creation in lace and sheer silk that didn't bare an ounce of flesh.

The modern, no-frill design hugged her slender body, leaving her arms bare, highlighting the long line of her thighs and legs.

Had she made the outfit more modest because of him? Did she think he wouldn't like it if it was one of her outrageously sexy, insubstantial creations?

Had he made her doubt his love again?

But one look into her gorgeous, shining eyes and all his doubts perished like so much dust.

They shone with such happiness that he felt a tightness in his chest relent.

They had spent the last three months touring for fabrics, laughing, and teasing each other, learning each other and falling in love all over again, and breathlessly waiting for this day.

He felt his entire world sway and tilt at the love he saw in those eyes, at the way her luscious mouth trembled.

She kissed Dmitri's cheek and he handed her over to him.

Gripping her fingers with his, he pulled her closer, the scent of her hitting him right in the solar plexus. "I love you, Leah," he whispered in her ear, without waiting for the priest to begin.

Her breath caught, she ran shaking fingers over his cheek as if she needed to check that he was all there.

"I can't wait for tonight," she finally whispered, and pulled back, a wicked twinkle in her eyes.

It was only later that Stavros finally noticed the back of Leah's dress. Specifically when the photographer had asked her to turn around and smile over her back.

Her gaze holding his, she turned slowly, a coy smile curving her mouth.

Heat pounded his blood, desire hitting him like a tsunami.

Her back was bare, dipping precariously low to the curve of her buttocks, except for a row of white buttons drawing a tempting line down her spine, holding the sheer illusion panel together...

Just the sight of that smooth, bare skin sent heat searing across his own.

He could love her for years to come but his wife would always surprise him, he realized with a smile.

Joining her, he ran his fingers up her spine, a fever overtaking his muscles.

"Ready for your wedding night, *yineka mou*?" he asked, pressing a kiss to her jaw.

She trembled and turned into his arms. "Do you like the dress?"

He nodded, and picked her up. A hundred cheers went up around them as he walked toward the entrance to Giannis's house. "I love it. But I apologize in advance."

Her hands tightened around his nape. "For what?"

"For ripping those delicate buttons. That's the only way to get it off you, isn't it?"

Her smile reached into the depths of his heart. He carried her over the threshold and took her mouth in a hungry kiss. "Now you're mine forever and forever."

"And you are mine," she whispered, before claiming his mouth again.

* * * * *

TAKEN BY HER GREEK BOSS

CATHY WILLIAMS

CHAPTER ONE

FOR Nick Papaeliou, the evening was beginning to take on a bizarre, surreal air.

For starters, he was not a man who enjoyed public scenes. He liked to exercise control over every aspect of his life, not least his emotions. And yet, what had happened less than an hour previously? His girlfriend, now relegated to the position of ex-girlfriend, had drunkenly initiated a confrontation that had heralded the demise of their relationship. Of course, he had known for a while that he would have to break off with Susanna, had heard the warning bells begin to ring when her hints had moved from the general arena of *proper relationships* to the more specific one of *wanting to climb off the merry-go-round and settle down before her biological clock began really ticking.* But had he listened? No. The intention to finish with her had hovered on the periphery of his consciousness, but he had been in the middle of a highly complex deal and he had stupidly relegated it to the back-burner.

And then the party tonight. Not just the usual boring model bash to which he had grudgingly agreed to go, knowing that it would be the last with her, but a lavish, private dinner hosted by a fashion-designer couple with a passion for social climbing.

The wine had flowed freely and how true it was that alcohol loosened tongues.

He thought back with distaste to Susanna, the tears, the shouting, the pleading—all conducted in front of an audience of roughly forty people.

Naturally he had left, with every intention of heading back to his penthouse apartment in Mayfair where he would be able to forget the nightmarish previous two hours in front of his laptop computer. It would have been the preferred conclusion to an aberrant evening, but…

He looked sideways at the young woman sitting in the back of the taxi alongside him. Here he was. Waylaid by a fresh-faced blonde who had been waitressing at the party and had coincidentally been leaving at the same time as he had.

He had found himself joining her for a coffee at the café close by and over his cup of strong black coffee, with his defences momentarily lowered after his bruising public bust-up with Susanna, had engaged in the rare pastime of sitting opposite a beautiful woman to whom he was not in the slightest bit attracted and actually listening to what she had to say, even though much of what she had told him amounted to a story he had heard a thousand times. The beautiful young woman whose dream was to be an actress. Optimism was written all over her youthful face and flowed around him in waves in her excitable conversation and earnest body language.

God, she had made him feel jaded. When he had told her, as kindly and as tactfully as he could, that he was off limits, he had felt, literally, a hundred years old.

How long, he had wondered, could he continue living the bachelor lifestyle? His father had died when he was still a young man in his twenties and his mother had followed him eight years ago. Was that why? Lack of parental pressure to do the expected thing and father the obligatory two point two kids? Or had his single minded and meteoric rise through the ranks provided him with everything wealth and power could buy while, perversely, creating a world into which no one was allowed to take up residence for any period of time?

He honestly didn't know. What he *did* know was that Lily, the part time model who made ends meet however she could while still believing in her dreams, had stirred an unexpectedly almost paternal interest in him.

Which was why, he now contemplated, he was in this taxi with her, having agreed to accompany her back to her place for a nightcap, amused at her palpable horror when he told her that he should really be going back to his place to do a bit of work.

'No one works on a Saturday in the middle of winter at midnight!' she had exclaimed, shocked, and he had almost laughed at her naïveté. She thought, he knew, that she was doing him a good turn in making sure that he had some company after his unpleasant incident at the party, to which she, as everyone else, had been witness. She was also, and he could see this in her wide blue eyes, in awe of him. As most people were. It was something he had become accustomed to taking for granted although, at least in this case, he was pretty sure there was no hidden agenda. She didn't want anything from him and that was refreshing.

The taxi, having wound its way through a myriad deserted streets, all identical in their never-ending rows of unlit terraced houses, finally drew to a stop and, to his further amusement, Lily refused to let him pay, even though she would certainly know him for the billionaire he undoubtedly was.

'It's not much…' she apologised, fumbling in her bag for her front door key.

Nick murmured something suitably polite as she finally

opened the front door, but really she was absolutely spot on.
It was a house in an area that might, possibly once, have been
considered a fairly decent location, but which the passing
years had rendered shabby and depressingly uninviting, and
stepping inside only served to cement that first impression.

Nick hadn't been to a place like this for a very long time.
He had dragged himself up by his bootlaces, worked like a
slave so that he could accumulate the necessary qualifications
that would enable him to escape a life of mediocrity in the
Home Counties, where his father had eked out a living doing
manual work at the Big Houses, as he had liked to call them,
the likes of which he would never be able to afford. He had
been an uneducated Greek and had never dared to aspire
beyond his modest sphere.

Nick had had no intention of following his father's footsteps. A first at university had been the start and followed by
a rise through the financial world that had left his peers, most
of whom came from a background of Big Houses, gaping and
speechless. Now, he no longer worked for anyone. He had his
own financial empire and called his own shots. When he
opened his mouth, the world listened and paid heed.

And with vast power and wealth had come all the trap-
pings. The place in the sun, rarely visited. The country house
that he visited occasionally, whenever the ferocious demands
of work allowed him the time off. The chauffeured car, the
helicopter for those times when he needed to be somewhere
faster than a train or car could take him, the lavish apartment
in the heart of one of the most expensive areas in London.

He had long ago left behind the type of place now confront-
ing him, with its tiny handkerchief of a front garden and,
even in the forgiving cover of darkness, its signs of disrepair.
And here in the small hallway, although much effort had ob-

viously been made to brighten the interior, the cheerful primrose-coloured paint was fighting a losing battle with dodgy woodwork and carpeting that was no longer tired, but downright exhausted.

While Lily bent to unzip her boots, sighing with relief as she yanked the first one off, Nick turned to shut the front door. He was unaware of the sound of footsteps and only realised that there was someone else in the house when he heard Lily give a little yelp.

'Rosie! What are you doing up?'

'Who—' the voice was unusually husky for a woman '—is *that*?'

Nick turned around and found himself staring into a pair of narrowed blue eyes, which were glaring at him. Then he took in the rest of her—small, especially standing next to Lily, and no model's figure, although it was hard to tell because she was swamped in a fairly unflattering ensemble of dressing gown behind which peeked what appeared to be some kind of hideous novelty pyjamas.

'Honestly, Rose, I keep telling you not to wait up for me! I'm a big girl now. I can take care of myself!'

The Rose character, whoever she might be, wore the expression of someone who seriously doubted that statement.

'I have no idea how you can say that, Lily, when you've just waltzed through the door with a complete stranger in tow. At nearly one in the morning. I thought you told me that this was going to be an early one?'

'It *was* early…but…Rose, this is Nick. Nick Papaeliou. Maybe you've heard of him?'

'Of course I haven't heard of him,' Rose snapped. 'You know I don't know a thing about these models you hang around with.'

'Model?' Nick couldn't believe his ears. Nor could he quite believe the way those ferocious blue eyes were scornfully dismissing him. 'You think I'm a model?'

'What else?'

'Oh, Rosie. You have to excuse her, Nick. Rose is very, very protective of me. She thinks I'm going to be gobbled up by a big bad wolf one of these days. But that's cool. Hey, what else do big sisters do?'

'She's your sister?' Nick stared at the small, round woman who was still glaring at him, although he noticed a faint pink colour crawl into her cheeks.

'There's no need to look so stunned,' Rose said coldly.

'We're stepsisters actually,' Lily explained, smiling. 'Isn't it amazing? I mean, you hear so many stories about step-siblings not getting along but Rose and I couldn't be closer if we were proper sisters.' She gave Rose an affectionate squeeze. Even without shoes, she was at least six inches taller. 'Rosie, Nick's just popped by for a nightcap…would you mind? I've got to go to the bathroom.'

Yes, actually, she would mind, but Lily was already vanishing up the stairs, still taking them two at a time, the way she always had even as a kid. Sweet, sunny-natured Lily who thought the best of everyone, even the ones who had Health Hazard written all over their faces. Like this one staring at her, still incredulously digesting the fact that the leggy blonde with the waist-length hair, the one whom he had probably expected to escort home to a suitably empty house, was related to someone who was physically as different from her as chalk from cheese.

Rose stared right back at him. He towered over her and was dangerously good-looking, with a strong, harshly sensual face and black, black hair to match the long black lashes and brooding eyes. It took a lot of will-power not to quail before that singularly unblinking stare. She told herself that he was probably nothing more than a B-grade actor who was accustomed to playing the lead role in hammy TV dramas and didn't know when to drop the act. She didn't know why she had originally assumed he was a model. Definitely not pretty enough.

'So, stepsister Rose, do you always wait up for Lily when she goes out?'

Rose favoured him with a look of haughty disdain. She detected the sarcasm in his voice but she wasn't going to rise to it. She spun round on her heel and headed for the kitchen.

'I'm not going to apologise for being rude, Mr Papaeliou,' she said, the minute they were in the kitchen and he had taken up position on one of the chairs by the pine kitchen table, 'but Lily's been messed around by too many shallow, good-looking men and I'm not going to allow it to happen again…' She must have only just finished making a hot drink for herself because there was no need to boil the kettle. His nightcap, far from being a glass of port or a liqueur, was a mug of coffee handed to him in the manner of someone eager to see him off the premises. She stood in front of him, arms folded. 'She may not think that she needs looking after, and, sure, she's more than capable of running her own life, but when it comes to emotions my sister can be very trusting. She doesn't need to get involved with a two-bit actor on the make.'

Nick, for the first time in his life, felt himself struggling to get a handle on the situation.

'Two bit actor?'

'What else? You might play the action hero in whatever third-rate movies you've been in, but you can drop the macho act. It doesn't wash with me. All I know is that Lily is a sucker when it comes to a good-looking man with a few chat-up lines, but they never stay the course and she's had her heart broken too many times…'

Two-bit actor? Action hero? The woman had the bare-faced audacity to make him sound like a comic-book character! But he was certainly not going to allow himself to be dragged into a stand-up fight with a woman with the personality of a Rottweiler. 'Hence you're her self-appointed watchdog. That's very noble of you,' Nick said coolly. 'Does Lily appreciate your over-zealous concern? Or do you save these little speeches for when her back's turned?' He placed the mug on the table without drinking any of the coffee. 'I hate to burst your bubble, but I'm not an empty-headed male model out to sleep with the nearest attractive woman, nor am I a two bit actor with an identity problem.'

'No? Well, it doesn't matter. Model, actor…creative director with an empty casting couch…it's all much of a muchness. Lily's just emerged from a relationship that ended badly and I'm making sure that she doesn't get taken in by another man with too much looks and too few scruples for his own good. I wish there were a more polite way of warning you off, but there isn't.'

Nick was accustomed to women pandering to him, hanging onto his every word, courting him with their feminine wiles. Could his night go any more off course? From a showdown that, inevitably, would reach the gossip pages in some rag, to a confrontation with a perfect stranger who was either partially unhinged or just too plain bloody outspoken for her own good.

Before he could reply to that blazing, generalised condemnation, Lily burst into the kitchen, apologising profusely and winningly for taking so long, but she'd just had to have a quick shower because she'd felt hideously grubby and knew, just knew that she'd stunk of cigarette smoke because everybody, but everybody there had been smoking and not all of it the run-of-the-mill tobacco.

Even in the early hours of the morning and after a long day doing a tiring job, she still managed to look incredibly fresh and vital and hopelessly young. It was ludicrous that her sister could imply that he, Nick Papaeliou, who could have any woman he wanted, would be attracted to Lily.

'Have you two been getting to know one another?' Lily asked brightly and Nick, looking at Rose from under his lashes, saw her glance with muted antagonism at him. Lily helped herself to some water from the tap and then turned around and perched against the counter so that she could look at them both.

'Oh, absolutely,' Nick drawled smoothly, giving Rose a slow, meaningful smile. 'Like a house on fire…'

'Oh, great!' She turned to Rose. 'Poor Nick broke up with his girlfriend tonight and it's always nice to be in company when you're down in the dumps.'

The meaningful smile slowly disappeared as Rose raised her eyebrows and nodded her head slowly.

'I was far from down in the dumps, Lily.' He tried to smile that one off, but he was irritably conscious of her sister's eyes fastened on his face. 'In fact, our relationship was on its way out. Susanna only did what I myself would have done the following day.' How was he now having an inappropriately private conversation with two women he had never seen in his life before tonight?

'Why would you go to a party with someone you wanted to ditch?' Rose asked innocently and Nick gritted his teeth together. 'I mean, the poor woman probably thought that you really cared about her.'

'If you knew Susanna, the very last word you would use to describe her would be poor.'

'Still…' Rose allowed that one little word to drop into the silence.

Looking at her, Nick momentarily forgot Lily's presence. 'Still…what?'

'Must be awful to break up with someone you care about in front of other people. I always think that when I open the newspapers and they're full of some poor celebrity couple who end up being forced to wash all their dirty linen in public. And in a way, that's not even as bad as the dirty linen being washed in front of friends…she must have been feeling pretty desperate…'

Lily was watching this interchange with a certain amount of bewilderment.

'And on that note…' Nick stood up. Surprisingly, exchanging barbs with Rose had so completely absorbed his attention that nothing else had occupied his mind. Not Susanna, not work, and he had completely forgotten Lily's presence even though she had been standing in his direct line of vision.

'Oh, dear…leaving so soon? Well, shall I call a cab for you? You won't find one here, you know. It's not central enough. Lily…' Rose looked at her sister '…you look done in. Why don't you hit the sack and I'll wait up until Nick leaves?'

'Don't be silly, Rose.' She yawned widely. 'How can I invite Nick here for a nightcap and then disappear off to bed?'

'*I* have already given him a nightcap. It was called a cup of coffee.'

'Rose doesn't do an awful lot of drinking…' Lily smiled at Nick '…do you, Rosie?'

'I'm sure Mr Papaeliou isn't interested in my alcohol consumption.' Lord, but she sounded prim and proper.

'The name's Nick,' Nick said irritably.

Rose ignored him. 'There. You're falling asleep on your feet, Lily. Go to bed. I'll see Mr Pa…*Nick*…out.'

'Well…'

'I can lie in in the morning,' Rose insisted. 'You know you always go to the gym first thing.'

'S'pose…'

Rose guided her sister in the direction of the staircase so that the temptation of bed was just a little more irresistible. 'Well nothing. You've been on your feet for the better part of the day while I've been here, just lolling around and taking it easy.'

'If you're sure…'

Oh, boy, Rose was absolutely sure. She gave Nick a gimlet-eyed stare, but as soon as Lily had vanished up the stairs he removed his jacket and lounged against the wall, looking at her.

Rose, all at once and unbidden, became acutely conscious of her inappropriate garb. Something about the subdued lighting in the hall, the knowledge that Lily was upstairs, probably about to crawl into bed, the way he was looking at her in that perfectly still way… She tightened her dressing gown around her and clung onto her virtuous sense of authority. Revealing even a glimpse of her nightwear, namely pyjamas patterned with prancing reindeer, which had been given to her as a Christmas present by a friend who specialised in silly gifts, would undermine everything she now wanted to convey.

'Don't tell me,' he said, moving towards her, which, for some reason, she found horribly disconcerting, 'you're about to resume your attack, having frogmarched Lily to bed.'

'I did *not* frogmarch her.'

'As good as. So come on, then, let's call a taxi and get it over and done with.' He followed her into the kitchen, watched as she sat down and scrolled through the address book on her mobile phone, then made the call. While she did, she looked at Nick and tried not to let his presence overwhelm her, because even after such a brief spell in his company she knew, could just sense, that he was the sort of man who could inspire abject fear should he want to. Not exactly a people person, she thought nastily. The sort of man who picked up women and dropped them without a backward glance or a twinge of guilt. Like the poor Susanna who had been fired up enough to make a fool of herself in front of her friends.

They had fifteen minutes to talk and Rose wasn't going to waste a single one of those minutes, but before she could utter a word Nick strolled towards her, cornering her in her chair so that she could feel the full, undiluted power of his personality.

'But before you say anything, I think it's my turn, don't you?' He smiled.

Rose refused to be intimidated. Just who did he think he was anyway? She made herself breathe evenly. Up close like this, his eyes were the deepest of greens, the colour of the fathomless sea. Right now the fathomless sea was revealing some very icy depths.

'I think you should get a life,' Nick said grimly, 'and let your sister lead her own. Is it natural for you to wait up for her like a mother hen? Making sure she gets home safe and sound? You may think it natural. I, on the other hand, consider it sad, as would most people.' He couldn't believe he was having this conversation. Did he care what this woman thought of him? Did he care what anyone thought of him? True freedom, he had always thought, was the freedom from caring about other people's opinions. So why the hell was a pair of defiant blue eyes making him want to justify himself?

Rose blushed and for a few seconds was lost for words. Somewhere at the back of her mind, she knew that he was making sense, but looking out for Lily was a habit born of time and one that she couldn't seem to let go. Their parents, her mother and stepfather, had died when they were still very young and they had gone to live with their aunt and uncle who were, as they were fond of saying, travellers in search of the meaning of life. Rose had discovered that this basically meant that they moved from pillar to post at a whim, with the practical concerns of two young people being only a minor technical hitch.

Nearly seven years older than her stepsister, Rose had been the sensible one who had made sure that Lily had someone grounded to whom she could turn and so, from the age of ten, she had become accustomed to looking out for her sister. But now Lily was twenty-two. Did she really still need the sensible older sister to wait up for her?

'I don't care what you think.'

'What do you think your sister would say if she knew that you were warning me away?'

'I think she would see it for the loving gesture that it is.'

'Or maybe she might see it as an infringement of her right to lead her life the way she sees fit.'

'Who are you,' Rose spluttered, 'to tell me what I should and shouldn't do?'

'Well, not a male model nor an actor, nor, for that matter, a seedy film director with an empty casting couch.' He moved away from her chair and sat down, but pulling the kitchen chair close to hers so that there was no escaping his stifling presence. Where was he going with this particular piece of justification? he wondered.

'I don't care what job you do, Mr Papaeliou…'

'I'm in finance, as a matter of fact. And believe me, when it comes to women, I don't need to entice them with an empty casting couch.'

'Whatever you do doesn't change the fact that you're a man

who can break up traumatically with a woman, look around you, and within minutes be on the trail of another notch for your bedpost.'

Nick was enraged. Never had he been the object of such an unprecedented attack by someone who didn't know him. Without vanity or pride, he could say that people tiptoed around him, the only exceptions being women at the end of a relationship who could, like Susanna, become hysterical and accusatory, but that was something he had always easily dealt with because, and his conscience was utterly clear on this point, he never made the mistake of making promises he would later fail to keep. He never spoke of love or allowed ideas of permanence and commitment to blur the edges of a relationship. He was speechless now at her sweeping assumptions, but absolutely through with defending himself and he stood up and began walking out of the kitchen while Rose gathered herself and followed him.

She had exhausted her argument and now there was nothing left to be said. Nick obviously thought the same thing because he stuck on his coat in silence, only looking at her when he was about to leave, with his hand on the door knob, in fact.

Rose pulled her dressing gown even tighter around her. In the half light, the man was frighteningly sexy and she felt an unwelcome shiver race down her spine, like the light, trailing touch of a finger. No, he certainly wouldn't need an empty casting couch to attract women, she thought. He just had to look at them. She harnessed her thoughts back to her sister and primly congratulated herself on spotting a heartbreaker and trying to do something about it.

'Thanks for the coffee,' he said coldly, 'and the warning. Take a tip from me—get a life, spend your Saturdays doing something and then maybe you wouldn't work yourself up into a lather over your sister and what she's getting up to. I'll wait outside for the cab.'

With that he opened the door and, with perfect timing, the taxi pulled up.

Infuriated and insulted he might be, but Nick was hardly aware of the drive back to his house. There was a message on his answering machine. He played it back to discover that it was from Susanna, apologising in a trembling voice. He erased it without bothering to hear it fully out.

Damned Rose! Lurching out of nowhere like a furious little avenging angel, and now he couldn't erase her from his mind. Experienced as Nick was in compartmentalising his personal life, he was sourly aware that the abrasive woman had rubbed him the wrong way to such an extent that he spent the better part of what remained of the night brooding and not even thoughts of work were sufficiently tantalising a distraction.

The furious avenging angel, less furious now as she lay in bed some twenty minutes after she had slammed the front door behind him, stared up at the ceiling and glumly admitted to herself that the man had got under her skin. *Get a life.* The taunt rankled because it had hit its target with the unswerving accuracy of a guided missile. Twenty-nine years old, as good as, and here she was, wearing ridiculous pyjamas and still playing caretaker to a sister who no longer needed caretaking.

Where had all the party times gone? Had there been any? Tony and Flora, as her aunt and uncle had insisted they be called, had done everything to encourage a wild and carefree lifestyle. Life, she had been told so often that she knew the script off by heart, was a wonderful and exciting place to be approached with curiosity and zest. Education was fine within reason, but the greater education was the *Education of Life,* which could loosely be translated into *The Lifestyle of a Nomad*. It had suited Tony and Flora but to Rose it spelt sickening upheavals and she had fought a rearguard action through her quiet rebellions. She had developed an aversion to pulses and soya and had insisted on burgers and fries, had immersed herself in her books, studying until her aunt and uncle had finally stopped telling her to go out and have some fun, had refused to wear the gypsy skirts and patchwork coats garnered from Oxfam shops, more through a healthy sense of self-preservation than personal dislike, and had made sure that Lily was as grounded as it was possible for her to be considering their weird lifestyle.

And in between all that, the parties had never happened and by the time Tony and Flora had zoomed off in their camper van, headed for the Cornish coast, where they still now lived, the ability to abandon herself to the freedom of youth had slipped past her. She had gone to university, worked hard and set her sights on achieving everything that she felt she had lacked in her formative years. Security.

Very important. For her. And for Lily. Even if Lily gave no thought to it. With the sort of lifestyle that she led, doing jobs off and on, trying out for parts in plays or commercials, most of which she never got, she needed at least one area in her life upon which she could rely and, having seen her sister on her roller-coaster rides with unsuitable men, Rose was determined to make sure that she at least provided Lily with a core of emotional stability in her chaotic world.

Of course, rushing in with dire words of warning the day after wasn't going to work, so Rose prudently decided to leave the matter alone for a while and then, on one of the rare nights when they were both in and sharing a bowl of pasta without Lily having to rush off or Rose having to work late, she said, tentatively, 'Seen anything more of that guy…can't quite remember his name…the one who brought you back after that party a couple of weeks ago…?'

Lily, twirling some spaghetti round her fork, looked at Rose and grinned. 'You mean Nick, Nick Papaeliou…how on earth could you have forgotten his name, Rosie? I don't think anyone's ever forgotten his name before. I've seen him twice, actually.'

Rose spluttered on a mouthful of pasta and cleared her throat with some water. 'Twice! That's twice more than I thought you had, considering you never mentioned a word to me.'

'I meant to tell you, Rosie, but…'

'But what?' she asked casually, thinking of that dark, cynical face and stabbing an errant mushroom with her fork. She was reading guilt in the way her sister's eyes shifted away from her.

'I just thought you might give me a hard time. Nick got the impression that you didn't much care for him.'

'Me?' Rose laughed carelessly. 'Rubbish—the man's obviously paranoid.'

'Oh, Nick wouldn't be paranoid about anything, Rosie. I mean…he's got everything anyone could ever want or need. Apparently you thought that he was a two-bit actor.' Lily giggled. 'Wish I could have been a fly on the wall to have seen his expression when you said that. He looked outraged even when he repeated it to me.'

'I admit I may have mistaken him for someone in the acting profession,' Rose said carefully. 'I don't mean to sound the alarm bells unnecessarily, Lily, but he didn't strike me as the most reliable man in town.'

'What do you mean—"reliable"?'

'Oh, the steady-as-a-rock kind. I just think that it's so easy to be impressed by someone for all the wrong reasons.

They may be good looking or rich…and in fact they could just be bad news.'

'And I do have a history of going with the wrong guys,' Lily admitted ruefully, which was Rose's cue to breathe a sigh of relief and nod her head in vigorous agreement. 'But you're quite mistaken about Nick, Rosie. Honestly, I'm not impressed by how he looks or what he has…he's just a very nice guy.'

Nice? Nice? Were they talking about the same human being?

Then it occurred to her that he probably was a very nice man to Lily. A stunning face and a sexy body probably turned him into a very nice man indeed. On the other hand, he had had no reason to be nice to her and so had shown his true colours. He could give lessons on arrogance if her sister only but knew.

'If you got to know him a little bit better, then you would agree with me, you really would. In fact…'

'Um?'

'Well, I *was* going to actually mention this to you later…but…and this is the sort of guy he is, really cool…he's invited both of us to a bit of a bash next Saturday. Even though you called him a two bit actor…' another mini fit of giggles giving Rose a breather in which to digest this bolt from the blue '…he still stressed that he wanted us both to go along. Isn't that sweet? We'll have to go shopping. Apparently he's having something small at a very exclusive club he owns…anybody who's anybody's going to be there. And us! How exciting is that?'

'Not very,' Rose said, panicked. 'I mean…I'm not sure at all…I don't think…' Just the thought of something small at a very exclusive club owned by Nick Papaeliou was enough to bring her out in a cold sweat.

'I won't let you just write him off without a second chance,

Rosie.' Then Lily pulled out the most ancient emotional trump card in the deck. 'If you really cared about me the way you say you do, then you'll come…'

CHAPTER TWO

NICK HELPED HIMSELF to another drink. He felt restless. The party that had been arranged specifically for the benefit of Lily, though that was something she would never know, was in full swing. He had asked all the movers and shakers in the world of theatre, teased their palates by throwing in a few big names in business, the sort of men and women who were interested in promoting the Arts and were willing to put their money where their mouth was, and the supermodels were really the icing on the cake.

Not a single person had declined the invitation, even though it was very much a last-minute affair. Parties thrown by him were few and far between and had enough cachet to attract even the most sought-after celebrities.

Unfortunately, the belle of the ball, so to speak, had still not arrived. Nor had her sister.

Nick's gaze strayed once more to the door and he looked at his watch. It didn't take a genius to work out why they were late. Rose had either decided not to come or else had employed delaying tactics. It would have been a hell of a lot easier if he had not asked her along, but his memory of their last encounter had preyed on his mind and eventually he had worked out that inviting her, letting her see for herself how little he needed to pursue a woman because of her looks, would even out the score. She had dismissed him and Nick Papaeliou didn't like being dismissed. He particularly didn't like being dismissed for the wrong reasons.

He was still staring at the door when it opened. He saw Lily first, exquisite in a pale blue dress that was very simple, just a short silky shift with a very respectable round collar, saw her look round the room, searching him out, and he found himself trying to stare behind her to see whether Rose had come or not.

He finished his drink and headed towards them and as he neared them he saw her, half ducking behind the door.

'You're here.' A warm smile for Lily and then he stepped around her to where Rose was nervously hovering just out of sight of the crowd. 'And so are you. I'm surprised. I thought you might decide that this wasn't the sort of thing you were interested in attending.'

How right he was. Over four days, Rose had made several futile attempts to wriggle out of her sister's rash promise that they would both be overjoyed to attend whatever posh party Nick had arranged. She had valiantly plugged the Nothing To Wear excuse, which had been overruled before it had even had time to gain the necessary momentum, then had come a pious, self-sacrificing But I Wouldn't Want To Get In Your Way, and when that had fallen on deaf ears she had resorted to the truth, which was that she was totally uninterested in those sorts of things, big parties full of people talking at one another and peering around to see if somebody more interesting happened to be lurking on the horizon.

The truth was that she didn't want to see Nick. She disapproved of his involvement with her sister and she bitterly resented his arrogant, insulting response to her perfectly reasonable request that he take his attentions elsewhere.

Now, as she looked at him, she felt all that resentment gathering pace, like a snowball turning into an avalanche.

He looked magnificent. White shirt, black trousers, but instead of looking conventional he looked darkly, broodingly, raffishly sexy. Something about the way he had rolled the sleeves to his elbows. Or maybe it was his colouring that did it.

Rose shuffled away from the comforting wall that separated her from the rest of the crowd inside and tried not to scowl.

'It isn't,' she said shortly.

'Well, don't hide away out here, you two. Come inside and meet all the beautiful people.' Okay, he knew that that would probably send her nervous system into furious overdrive, but he couldn't help himself.

Lily, of course, responded with predictable enthusiasm, happily taking the arm he offered, while her sister looked at his other arm, also being proffered, and ignored it.

She felt awkward enough in her outfit without having to suffer the indignity of everyone looking at them, puzzling out who the short, dumpy woman in the black dress was. Lily might hang off his arm and look as though that was her rightful place. Rose, on the other hand, knew that were she to hang off his other arm the effect would be just the opposite. So she walked a little distance apart, grateful that Lily was keeping up the conversation with her bubbly chatter.

'I'll get you two a drink, shall I?'

'Ooh. A glass of champagne would be great, Nick.' Lily's eyes were everywhere, like a kid in a toy shop.

'And for you?'

Rose met his amused eyes steadily. 'I'm fine just at the moment.'

'No, you're not. I'll get you a glass of wine. It'll help you to relax.'

'I'm perfectly relaxed,' Rose lied, and he grinned broadly at her.

'In that case, you're giving an excellent imitation of someone who would rather be anywhere else in the world but here.'

He disappeared, feeling suddenly invigorated. He had never prided himself on his altruism. Sure, he gave massive donations of money to charity, but all of that he left to his financial department. In the case of Lily, he was doing a good deed for which he would get nothing in return. Except her gratitude, most probably, although gratitude was something he never requested from anyone and rarely appreciated. Yes, indeed, being Mr Good Guy was proving to be a very enjoyable novelty.

Of course, he mused, a little gratitude from her sister might be pretty satisfying.

He caught himself scanning the room, making sure that Rose was where he had left her and, sure enough, she was, although Lily was beginning to look a little edgy. By the time he made it back to Rose, it was to find her standing on her own.

'Lily's disappeared,' she greeted him.

'So I see.'

'She recognised some people from her last stint in the theatre.'

'Rude of her not to introduce you to them.'

'I…I told her to go ahead.' Rose looked at him defiantly. 'It's important that she tries to make a few connections. Apparently, that's how it works in the acting business. You can't come to a do like this and huddle on the sidelines.' She accepted her glass of wine while he deposited the unwanted champagne on one of the many handy chest-height tables that dotted the room. Tall bar stools were positioned by some of the tables, but most of these were unused. Rose supposed that sitting down wasn't conducive enough to mingling.

'No. It's all about networking,' Nick agreed.

'And I really don't want to keep you from that.'

'I have no need to network.' He shrugged. 'There's nothing I need from anyone here. They are my guests and a good time will be had by all because they offer each other opportunities. The people in the acting profession will be networking with the businessmen who make their world tick financially, the businessmen will be lusting after the models, the models will be intrigued by the celebrities—'

'And you will observe them all.'

Nick returned his gaze to her face, which was cool and assessing. He frowned.

'What's wrong with that?'

'You're like a scientist looking at the rest of the world through a microscope, examining interesting little bugs.'

'You know,' he drawled, 'maybe I shouldn't let you loose in the room, not with that knack you have of rubbing people up the wrong way.'

Rose flushed. 'I didn't realise that I was rubbing you up the wrong way. I was just making an observation.'

'The only way to succeed in life is to develop the ability to read other people.' He looked at her carefully and realised that he was intrigued by her personality, proving yet again to himself that he needed a little novelty in his life. First Lily and now her sister. Making money was predictable. Closing deals brought an adrenaline rush, yes, but it was something that was over quickly. And women…hardly any surprises there. Until now. He decided that he would spend a few more minutes with her, sparing her the trauma of mixing, in other words doing her a good deed.

'Oh, yes?' she enquired politely and he frowned at her, unimpressed with that hint of mild boredom in her voice.

'Take yourself, for example.' Oh, yes, that did the trick. He could almost see her begin to bristle. 'Here you are, hating every minute of this party, dragged along by Lily who, in her own sweet way, is as stubborn as a mule—'

'I'm not sure where you're going with this. I've already told you that this isn't my sort of thing—'

'And you would love to put yourself firmly above everyone here, but I'll just bet you feel awkward and gauche. Am I right?' Since when did a woman find his company boring? It was inconceivable.

'No. No, I don't…' She should never have worn this black, shapeless dress. Tall, skinny people could pull off shapeless because everyone would know that, underneath, they had rangy, slender bodies. And, yes, she did feel awkward and gauche, but there was no need to have the fact pointed out to her. 'Anyway, why did you ask me along if you knew that I wasn't going to enjoy myself? If you're such a brilliant reader of people, you must have known that I wouldn't fit in with this crowd.'

'It's always good to face your fears.'

'Oh, so you are doing me a favour, in other words.'

'And I notice you aren't suitably grateful.'

Rose downed the remainder of her wine and snorted in an appropriately unfeminine way. She picked up the champagne that he had left on the table and swallowed a mouthful, drawing in her breath as the bubbles went down. The little glittery black bag that she had borrowed from Lily, and which she was clutching in her left hand, seemed a ridiculous accessory. Her skin crawled at the thought that he was laughing at her, finding her awkward and gauche. The champagne seemed to be finished and she seriously contemplated another drink.

'I'm going to have to circulate now.'

'Don't let me stand in your way.'

'Oh, but you are,' Nick drawled smoothly. Two glasses on the trot had brought a pink flush to her cheeks. 'I'm running this show and it's my duty to make sure that no one is left standing next to the wall on their own, quietly drinking themselves into a stupor.'

Rose felt the colour crawl into her face as her role loomed before her in all its unmistakable hideousness. She was Lily's chaperone and her host's burden. He would fob her off on one of his guests or else deliver her back to her sister because he thought that if he didn't, she would end up making a fool of herself. Mortification replaced the light headed sensation induced by the wine and champagne and brought her crashing back down to the reality crowding around her.

'I'm not going to drink myself into a stupor,' she snapped. 'You needn't worry that I'm going to embarrass you in front of your glittering guests.'

'Embarrass me?'

'By drinking too much and falling into a heap on the floor.'

'Why would I be embarrassed if you make a spectacle of yourself?' He sighed impatiently and led her to one of the bar stools at the table closest to them. The woman was difficult and tactless and of course he shouldn't concern himself with her, but he felt an irrational need to take her under his wing. Because, he told himself, she was Lily's sister and while *he* might not be embarrassed if Rose got drunk and made a fool of herself, her sister almost certainly would. So, gentleman that he was, he would forgo his duty to circulate and spend a little time with her instead. No hardship. The crowd seemed to be doing splendidly without his input. The wonders of limitless alcohol, he thought. And of course the seduction of preening and strutting in front of people who counted. He had been keeping a watchful eye on Lily. Next to some of the more seasoned networkers, she was holding her own and drinking, he noticed, remarkably little. A wise head on young shoulders.

'I thought you were going to mingle with your guests,' Rose said, then, as if giving things a second thought, she sighed into the glass of orange juice that had mysteriously appeared in front of her. 'I'm not being a particularly nice person, am I?'

Nick shook his head, relaxing and slinging one arm over the slatted back of his bar stool.

'Well, nor are you!'

He smiled and raised his eyebrows. 'That's the worst apology I've ever heard.'

'It wasn't meant to be an apology.'

'Oh. You mean you were just making an observation about yourself.'

Rose decided to change the subject altogether. When he looked at her she felt simultaneously incredibly self-conscious, which was maddening, and resentful of him for making her feel that way.

'It's a very nice place you have here.'

'Oh, don't tell me you're going to go all polite on me now.' This happening party of his seemed to be a long way away.

'How on earth did you make so much money?'

'Ah. That's more like it. Crashing through those flimsy barriers called tact and really speaking your mind without bothering to gift-wrap anything.'

'You *did* tell me not to be polite.' Rose, who was not accustomed to flirting, was uneasily aware of a certain undercurrent between them that was thrilling and frightening at the same time. As were those amazing eyes of his, resting thoughtfully on her face. She knew that she was just being stupid but her heart was thudding inside her like a hammer and everything, all her senses, seemed heightened, stretched taut like a piece of elastic.

'So…?' she persisted.

'Worked my way up.' Nick nodded to one of the waiters who were invisibly collecting empty glasses and asked him for a whisky and soda.

'Up from where?'

'This is really a very boring story.'

'You mean you don't like other people observing you under their microscope even though you enjoy observing *them* under yours.'

Meaning that personal confidences were not part of his routine when it came to women. However, his history was no secret. Anyone could access its bare bones from the thousands of entries to be found on him on the Internet. Where was the harm in saving her the bother of looking him up, if her curiosity got the better of her?

'A simple tale of a Greek immigrant who fell in love with an English beauty,' he said casually. Did anyone know how his parents had sustained him? Had faith in him? 'They worked all the hours God made to make ends meet and to put me through private school.' Well, that was no big confidence. It was there in his profile somewhere.

'That's wonderful.'

'Is it?'

'Of course it is.' She rather thought that he would have done just fine whatever school he had attended, but, compared to her background, it must have been marvellous to have had parents who would have been willing to do whatever it took for their child to pursue a proper education.

'Where are they now?'

'No more. They both died a long time ago.' He looked away, annoyed because this was all in the past and why the hell was he talking about it anyway?

'I'm sorry.'

'And I do need to actually mingle with the people I have invited here.' He stood up and looked down at her. 'I can introduce you or I can leave you here on your own. Take your pick.'

So that brief truce between them was over. Rose was quietly relieved. Just then, she had felt something sneak up on her, something unwanted that had made her feel giddy and out of control.

'I'm fine,' she told him with a distant smile. 'You go mix. I'll have a hunt around for Lily. Sorry for having taken up too much of your valuable time.' When it came to sarcasm, she was as good as him any day.

Anyway, it was much easier now. Nearly everyone there was mellower by a fair few glasses of champagne. They barely noticed her skirting through them. In fact, Rose felt virtually invisible.

She found Lily in the middle of a small group of men, not saying much but paying a lot of attention, and very sober. That was good. For Rose, she would leave this evening behind and return to her normal life. For Lily, this was a chance to meet people, to get her face known and, for her sake, Rose hoped that the evening would turn out to be a success.

She hovered briefly on the fringe, then wandered through the crowd and, after a couple more glasses of wine, found that chatting to them wasn't the nightmare she had predicted. Somewhere Nick was lurking, although she couldn't actually see him anywhere.

Like Cinderella, she was ready to leave by the stroke of midnight. She seemed to be in a minority of one. The drink was still flowing, her sister was absorbed talking to a couple of guys, her face fresh and animated, and Rose had had enough. She had listened to people talk about other people, had eavesdropped boring conversations about scripts that had never got off the ground and arguments with directors who didn't know what they were talking about and lottery grants that should have gone to art projects but had ended up going to crazy organisations that wasted the money and went bankrupt within two years. She had eaten the most amazing finger food she had ever tasted, served by the most attentive staff she had ever seen, and refused enough glasses of wine or champagne to fill a cellar.

After fifteen minutes of trying to attract Lily's attention, Rose gave up and headed out of the room in search of a breath of fresh air.

Outside was a corridor that circled the club area and off which, like little nodules from a main stem, were rooms behind which were probably offices, although Rose couldn't tell because the doors were all shut. The floors were pale cream marble, merging into the pale cream marble of the walls, along which hung abstract paintings that looked particularly unappealing in the subdued lighting.

She drifted along, deciding to give her sister precisely half an hour more networking time before dragging her out of the place, and was about to head back when she spotted the light from under the door. It was just a narrow strip, but in the relative darkness of the corridor as bright as a beacon and she didn't hesitate. She walked right towards it and pushed open the door. She hadn't known what to expect but she certainly hadn't expected to find Nick there, installed in front of his computer and surrounded by all the paraphernalia of a home office.

'Sorry,' she mumbled, backing out, but he had already

pushed his chair away from the desk and was pinning her in her tracks just by looking at her. A further, more elaborate apology formed somewhere in her mind but didn't quite manage to connect with her vocal cords, which seemed to have seized up.

In the intervening silence, he propped his feet up on his desk and relaxed back, hands folded behind his head.

'Looking for something?' His dark eyebrows rose in amused enquiry and Rose cleared her throat.

'No. I just happened to be...'

'Escaping all the fun and laughter? Come in and close the door behind you.' He paused. 'Well? I don't bite. At least, not unless I'm invited to.'

Rose, calm, efficient, always-in-control Rose, was beginning to feel very addled. Of course, she ought to graciously thank him for inviting her to his private function, politely turn down his offer to step inside, which had the vaguely dangerous undertones of what the spider had said to the fly, and hunt down Lily pronto.

She found herself obeying him, however, and shutting the door behind her, although once she had done so her legs refused to cooperate by propelling her towards the chair that he was now indicating.

'Sit.'

'I...I'm really on my way out, actually.' Vocal cords found. Thank heavens! 'I came outside to get a breath of fresh air and saw...well, the light under the door. What on earth are you doing?' This was much better. Her brain was beginning to function. She made it to the chair and sat down.

'What does it look like I'm doing?'

'Isn't it a bit rude for the host to be working at his own party?'

'I think everyone can manage fine without me for half an

hour.' Nick shrugged and continued to look at her, his expression unreadable. She looked awkward in her dress, as if wearing dresses was not something that came naturally to her but having found herself cornered into buying one, she had opted for the least flattering. Every single woman at the party had made a very special effort to wear something that would make them stand out in the crowd. Rose, on the other hand, had worn something that shrieked *background*. Briefly, Nick wondered what she would look like underneath the shapeless black garment and drew his breath in sharply, surprised at the thought.

'Besides, there was no choice. I had an urgent phone call from Australia requesting some information to be emailed to them.'

'Do you ever stop working?'

'Occasionally.' He lowered his eyes. Something about the shape of her breasts, just discernible under the dress, was kick-starting his imagination. 'Lily seems to be enjoying herself.'

'Yes. Yes, she does.'

'But I guess you probably found the whole thing a little…boring…'

She shrugged. 'Not at all,' she told him politely.

'You looked bored every time I saw you.'

'You were watching me?'

Nick didn't like the intonation in her voice when she said that. 'It's my duty to make sure that my guests are having a good time.'

'Then I'm surprised your keen sense of duty allowed you to sneak off to this office and work.' Yet again, she had the nagging, unpleasant suspicion that she was a charity case. 'Anyway, it was very interesting. It always is, meeting people from different walks of life.'

'Now why do I get the feeling that you don't really mean that?' When she didn't answer, he added, interested against his will, 'What's *your* walk of life?'

'I beg your pardon?'

'What do you do for a living?'

'I…I work in computers.' God, that sounded dull, especially when she considered the flamboyant, beautiful people who cluttered his life. How on earth, as a businessman, was he so well connected with the media set? she wondered. Then the question was answered virtually before it was posed. He dated cover girls. Money and looks would always be attracted to money and looks.

'That's very interesting.'

'There's no need to patronise me.'

'I'm not. What exactly do you do? In computers?'

'Nothing very exciting.'

At this point, Nick knew that he should just give up. Getting anything out of this woman was about as rewarding and straightforward as pulling teeth, and if it was one thing he didn't do, it was to work at making small talk with a woman. But her awkward response was like an invitation to press harder. In front of him, the screensaver came up on the computer and he switched it off.

'What does that mean?'

'Look—' Rose looked at him steadily '—I know you probably feel sorry for me…'

'Why should I feel sorry for you?'

'Because I don't slot into your category of an interesting woman.'

'As you quite rightly pointed out, it's always an eye opener meeting people from different walks of life.'

'Well, if you really want to know, I pretty much do everything with computers. Programming, updating systems, designing websites…' She heard herself rattling off a curriculum vitae that sounded deadly dull. 'It's actually very absorbing,' she stressed.

'I'm sure it is,' Nick agreed. 'Odd that you and your sister should have ended up in such completely different worlds. Computing and acting…'

Rose shrugged and stood up. 'I've got to go and find Lily. It's late. Time to head back.'

Nick met his fair share of clever, career-oriented women in his working life. He had frequently sat opposite top female lawyers in the early hours of the morning closing deals. Several of them had even tried to flirt with him, but he had never been interested in developing a relationship with any of them outside the boardroom. Put simply, nothing could compete with the archetypal brainless bimbo when it came to relaxation. Who needed to be mentally challenged twenty four seven? He had derived enough mental challenges in his working life.

Or so he had always maintained.

Right now, he was beginning to feel inordinately curious about what the computer whiz kid did in her spare time.

'Is this a late night for you?' he asked blandly.

Rose was suitably riled by the question. 'Not particularly,' she lied. 'But there's a limit to how long I can carry on chatting to people I don't know about things I'm not particularly interested in.'

'What would you rather be doing?'

'Going to bed, as a matter of fact.'

'With anyone in particular?'

Rose's mouth dropped open at the sheer audacity of the question, which had sprung from nothing but, once voiced, seemed to fill the room with thick, electric tension.

'I really don't think that's any of your business,' she finally managed to stutter, red-faced. She turned and began walking towards the door, head held high. He might be a millionaire many times over, but that didn't give him the right to say whatever he wanted to say and ask whatever he wanted to ask, without reserve.

She was aware of him behind her before she had even reached the door and when he stood in front of her, blocking her exit, she had to clench her hands at her sides to steady her nerves.

'I like things that aren't my business,' Nick murmured lazily. 'So tell me what you do in your spare time. When you go out until the early hours of the morning.'

He towered over her and she felt as if she were suffocating. Was he laughing at her? She rather imagined that he was because he certainly wasn't interested in anything she had to say. He was bored with his own party and had decided to have a little fun at her expense. She was sure of it.

Having worked all that out, it still left her with the little problem of how to get out of the room when he was standing in front of the door like a prison warden with a taste for sadism.

The man was loathsome. Yes, he was sinfully good-looking and, yes, she could see those flashes of charm that turned women into mindless robots ready to do whatever he asked them to do, but to her he was someone who was happy to play with other people, in much the same way as a cat played with a mouse. No serious harm intended, just a spot of good fun.

'I don't have to do anything,' Rose told him coolly. 'Lily's always been the clubber.'

'And you've always been…what?' Hand it to her, he thought, she wasn't going to let herself be daunted by him, even though her mounting colour signalled her discomfort. Nor was she flattered by his interest. In fact, he would have been hard-pressed to think of any woman less flattered by his undivided attention. That in itself was an interesting concept.

'I talk when I go out with my friends,' Rose said quietly.

'And I don't need to drink to excess or have loud music blaring in the background to feel as though I'm having a good time.'

Nick could hear the implicit sarcasm in her voice and was amused by it.

'Sounds like fun.'

'Yes. Yes, it is.'

'And what do you do afterwards?'

'What do you mean?'

'When you've had fun setting the world to rights?'

'I don't set the world to rights.' Rose gritted her teeth together and reminded herself that he was just goading her and that the last thing she should do was play into his hands by reacting. 'And even if we did sit around setting the world to rights, it would still be a heck of a lot more fun than slowly getting drunk and bitching about everyone and everything.'

'Referring to anyone in particular?'

'Several in general,' she said waspishly, 'and they're all out there. I believe they're called your friends.'

If she had hoped to insult him, then she had been mistaken, because instead of being suitably offended he just burst out laughing.

When he laughed, really laughed...

Rose's skin prickled and she felt jumpy and weak at the same time, as if her bones were turning into hot liquid, no longer able to support her body.

'I'm glad you find that funny,' she said, and wondered if he, too, could detect the high-pitched panic in her voice. She wasn't quite sure why, but she badly needed to leave the room.

'Oh, I do...but you still haven't answered my question.'

'I didn't realise you'd asked one.' She gave a deep, exaggerated sigh, which she hoped would convey to him just how fed up she was with their conversation.

'About what you do after you finish discussing deep and meaningful things with your friends. In quiet rooms. Over some invigorating glasses of mineral water.' Nick grinned. In actual fact, he had headed to the office to have a break from the noise of the party, which was an event he had arranged solely for Lily's benefit. What an altruist he was turning out to be.

Work was always an absorbing diversion, but right now he couldn't care less about work because he was thoroughly enjoying himself. He was also more curious than ever to find out just a little bit more about the woman in front of him who was, right at this moment, barely managing to restrain herself from hitting him as hard as she could. He imagined that she could probably throw a pretty good punch. None of the usual female face-slapping before bursting into tears. More a sock to the jaw and then, when he was rubbing his face, another for good measure.

'I don't know what you're going on about and I think you should head back before they send out a search party.'

'Hardly likely considering most of them are far too inebriated to have even missed me, and what I'm going on about is whether, when your crazy late nights are over, you head back to your place for wild sex…do you?'

'I told you—that's none of your business.' Now she really needed to get out because something was happening and, while she didn't quite know what, she did know that it was…dangerous for her. And thankfully he stepped aside. He even opened the door for her, but before she could make a break to the safety of the crowded club he was leaning down to her; she could feel the warmth of his breath against her ear and it made her shiver.

'I take it that means *no*?'

She wanted to run but she didn't. She walked away, head held high, without bothering to dignify his smirking remark with an answer.

CHAPTER THREE

WHEN Rose looked at the screen of her computer terminal she had the strangest sensation. Instead of seeing her programme run, she saw a face. *His* face. It was infuriating. Not only had the man got under her skin at the party nearly a week ago, but he was continuing to get under her skin when she should be concentrating on her work. She couldn't figure it out because she had pointedly avoided mentioning him to Lily and out of sight should have meant out of mind.

Just as well her office wasn't the sort of cosy little place where people might notice that she had been staring at the same code for the past fifteen minutes. In fact, the big pull about Fedco, when she had joined it five years previously, had been its size. Squatting like a giant patriarch on a retail site just outside London, it had been easily accessible by car, thereby enabling Rose to avoid the vagaries of the London transport system, and, once inside, she had been able to lose herself in the enormity of the building. Her friends all joked about leaving it behind, moving on to somewhere small, chic, designer and innovative where they could really exploit their talents, but in truth the thought of being at the cutting edge of technology in some small, up-wardly mobile company terrified her. Small and cutting edge, in her head, spelt insecurity, whereas Fedco was as secure as they came, never mind that you were more a number than a face.

And where else could she sit scowling without someone telling her to get on with her work?

In between her scowls, she kept a sharp eye on the clock. She had never been one to clock-watch but she couldn't wait to leave the building and get back home, where she could put her feet up and drag her thoughts away from her sister's high-handed, arrogant boyfriend by watching a couple of hours of mindless television.

With fifteen minutes to go and just as she was finally beginning to get into her stride, an excited Maggie flew to her desk and announced, *sotto voce*, that there was a man waiting in Reception for her.

'What man?' Rose asked suspiciously, using the interruption as an excuse to switch off her computer and begin gathering her belongings.

'A dishy one.'

'I don't know any dish… Hang on, what exactly does he look like?' She could feel the colour crawling into her face.

'Oh, you know, tall and dark and drop dead gorgeous.'

'What the heck is *he* doing here?'

'*He* who?' Maggie looked as if swooning would become a real possibility within the next few minutes.

'*He* my sister's boyfriend.' Rose slammed some files into her briefcase and banged it shut. '*He* the most arrogant man on the face of the earth…*he* the person with the manners of a wild boar…*that he*…'

'Oh. Trust Lily to snap up another good one,' Maggie visibly wilted. 'Must be tough having a sister it's impossible to compete with…not that I meant…not that I mean…'

'I know what you meant, Mags, and you're right—on the looks front she's a hard act to follow…and she's nice with it…' Rose stood up, stuck on her coat and felt her stomach clench at the prospect of seeing Nick. 'Although I've got to say that this is the sort of man that no woman in her right mind would dream of competing for. One of those "love 'em and leave 'em" types of guys who see women as notches on their bedpost, the more the merrier.' The office was beginning to thin out as everybody began the exodus, off to enjoy the beginning of their weekend. 'I mean—' she leaned towards Maggie who gave a little yelp and stepped back '—the man is everything a woman should steer clear of—'

'Thanks for the endorsement.'

Nick's voice was so close to her that for a few seconds Rose didn't believe that she had actually heard him. He was standing right behind them. She turned around slowly and hoped that she was more composed than she felt. At any rate more composed than Maggie, who had launched into an awkward introduction followed by some stuttering apologies about having to dash, simultaneously backing away from Nick's unsmiling figure. Rose longed to do the same.

'What do you think you're doing here?' Attack, she decided, was the best form of defence. 'Is Lily with you?'

'No. Should she be?'

'Why are you here? Sneaking around?' He had obviously come straight from work and he looked amazing, unfairly sexy considering he had probably spent his day at a desk somewhere. Wherever it was that very rich people spent their days. At the end of a tiring working day, she always seemed to look like something the cat dragged in. Rumpled hair that had spent the day progressively rebelling against clips and elastic bands, lip gloss that had disappeared some time between her morning snack and lunch-time baguette, face that was shiny under the fluorescent lighting.

'We need to…have a chat about your sister…'

'Why?' Panic slammed into her. From experience, whenever someone had said to her that they needed to have a little chat, the little chat had never heralded good news. When she was growing up, Tony and Flora had always preceded their next, big, new adventure with a little chat. 'What's wrong?'

'Shall we take this conversation somewhere else?' He would return to those insults of hers later. For the moment, he would see to it that they leave the bustling confines of her office. He didn't have to glance around to know that he was attracting some very curious stares and, while this didn't bother him in the slightest, he suspected it would give her ample ammunition to attack him for disrupting her life.

He wondered what he was doing here. In fact, he wondered how his highly ordered existence had become so embroiled, in such a short space of time, with two sisters whom he had not known from Adam a month ago. The one, yes, he could understand. Lily was beautiful, sweet-natured and helping her had been a balm for him after the annoyance of his last relationship.

But her sister?

'No. I don't want to go with you anywhere. Whatever you have to say can be said right here.' Drugs? Debt? Pregnancy? Lord, what if Lily was pregnant with his child and too embarrassed to break the news herself? Rose tried to remember just how long Nick had been on the scene.

'Come on.'

'I'm not going anywhere with you.'

'Right. In that case, I'll just stroll out and leave you to stew in your own stubborn stupidity, shall I? You would rather make a point than listen to anything I have to say.'

'That's not true. It's just that I…can't leave yet. I still have heaps of work to do.'

'Wearing your coat? With your computer switched off?'

Rose flushed and looked away. The more she argued with the man, the more she sensed a lively interest from the dwindling number of her colleagues still around. 'Why didn't Lily come herself? Is she in trouble?'

'She…just seemed reluctant to tell you…this herself so I volunteered to do it on her behalf… Now, let's get out of here.'

It only took them five minutes to make it out of the building, but it could have been five hours. Why would Lily be reluctant to talk to her? They had always talked about everything. At least until this man had come along.

She shot him a look of pure resentment.

'You'll have to put up with my driving, I'm afraid.'

'My driver's waiting. We'll use him. I can deliver you back to your car later.'

Rose opened her mouth to protest and realised that he was waiting for the predictable objection.

'Okay.'

'*Okay?* Does that mean that you're not going to launch into a feminist rant about being able to drive yourself?'

'I never launch into feminist rants,' Rose said hotly. 'I just stand up for the things I believe in.'

'You shoot your mouth off.'

'I do not shoot my mouth off and I resent being told that I do.'

'And I don't much like the fact that you're gossiping about me behind my back. I'm obviously on your mind if you feel so strongly about me.'

'You are *not* on my mind!' They had reached his car, how she had no idea because she had been so wrapped up in defending herself.

Nick pulled open the passenger door for her and she slid primly inside, making sure, he noted, to wrap her coat very tightly around her, as if depending on it for protection.

It was out of keeping for him to ever leave work at the ridiculous hour of four forty-five, but he wasn't regretting his decision. Apart from the fact that he was doing Lily a favour, he was also enjoying himself with her sister. His palate, after years of getting precisely what and whom he wanted, was jaded. Rose, with her bristling, yapping aggression, was a novelty and who was he to resist the allure of the new?

He had also been curious to see the people she worked with, not that that had been possible given the size of the place.

'Where can we go?'

'At five-thirty?'

'Maybe we should just head back to your house. It's close enough.'

'No!' Overreacting again. And also forgetting about the little chat because she had been so wrapped up bickering. All fodder for his oversized ego. 'There's a brasserie about half an hour away. Joe's Brasserie. On Fields Road. I guess there's as good a place as any.' She turned away and stared out of the window, acutely conscious of his muscular thigh way too close to hers for comfort. Just being alone with the man in this confined space made her feel guilty. He belonged to Lily and to Lily's world. She shouldn't even recognise his physical attributes, although she gratefully accepted that she was human, after all, and, anyway, she disliked him intensely so what did it matter?

'You're tense. Why? Does it make you nervous sitting in this car with me?'

'Why should it?' Rose turned to look at him and blinked away the disconcerting impact his shadowed, angled face had on her. 'I'm tense because I don't know what you're going to tell me but I have a feeling that I won't like it.'

'In that case, take your mind off the possibilities and tell me about your job. I didn't expect you to work for such a large organisation.'

Rose shrugged. She didn't want to talk about herself or her job, but she couldn't see a way around it. 'I like it there. The size doesn't bother me. Anyway, don't tell me that your offices are sweet and small and cosy.'

Nick laughed under his breath. 'Better designed.'

'How?' Rose asked grudgingly, interested to find out how a big clump of concrete and glass could be designed into something less soulless than Fedco.

'Clever use of partitions and copious amounts of plants.'

'Right. And you did that yourself?'

'I approved it at every stage, yes. Does that jar with your picture of me striding through offices, whipping the employees and making sure that they're chained to their desks until I tell them that it's time to leave?'

'Yes, as a matter of fact it does.'

Nick laughed louder and gave her a brief, appreciative glance. When he sifted through his extensive repertoire of women, he couldn't think of a single one who had ever made him laugh.

'In that case, accept my apologies. Is this the place you were talking about?'

Rose nodded, pleased to see that it was already beginning to get busy. Brasseries in London never seemed to be quiet, and that suited her because she didn't want that weird, discomforting feeling she got when she was alone with him.

And that laugh had done something in her, made her feel oddly hot and uncomfortable.

'So,' she said without preamble as soon as they were seated at the circular chrome table and a waitress had taken their order. Orange juice for her and a lager for him. 'What is it that you wanted to tell me about Lily?'

'You're very good at cutting to the chase,' Nick commented drily. 'How much has she told you about…our relationship?'

'We don't discuss you.'

'Strange, considering you seem to discuss me freely with everyone else.'

Rose went pink but held his gaze. 'I don't think she would appreciate some of the things I might have to say and I can't put her in a position where she feels that she's having to take sides.'

'How big-minded of you.' Did the woman have no social graces? he wondered.

'I know you've been meeting up,' Rose ploughed on, 'but I don't know how serious it is. Are you telling me that it's…serious?'

'Oh, very serious indeed.' Nick sat back and took one long sip of lager, enjoying its coldness. 'I think it's now your cue to warn me off because I'm such a big, bad wolf.'

'Lily could have told me this herself.'

'Maybe she's scared of making a stand for herself because you've never allowed her to.'

'Is that what she told you?'

'I'm reading between the lines.'

'Then don't bother. You don't know anything about us.'

'I don't need case notes to see what's in front of my nose. You've always made the rules and Lily has always obeyed them.'

'If she's pregnant, then I expect you to do the honourable thing and marry her.'

For the first time in his life, Nick found himself lost for something to say and Rose watched his stunned expression without saying a word, waiting for him to be the first to break the silence. He had an annoying habit of throwing her into a tizzy and making her gabble like someone who couldn't operate the brake pedals on their mouth, but she could tell from his face that she had thrown him into a hole and she wasn't about to help fish him out.

This was the thing she feared the most—that Lily would do something stupid like fall for the man, hook, line and sinker. She hadn't seen her sister actually being even more stupid and getting herself pregnant, but if she had then Rose would be there, as she always had been, to lend the helping, guiding hand.

'You think that…' Nick shook his head incredulously. 'Shooting your mouth off again. Do you ever think before you speak?'

'What am I supposed to think?' Rose demanded, unfazed by his attack. 'You accost me at work—'

'I was doing you a favour.'

'You accost me at work, where, incidentally, you have no right to be, and insinuate that there's something you have to tell me that's so awful that my own sister just can't tell me herself.'

'And you think that pregnancy is the most awful thing that could happen to a woman.'

'No, of course I don't. When two people love each other and have a stable relationship, then pregnancy is the most beautiful thing that could happen, but in Lily's case…' She glared at him because he had started staring at her as though she had begun speaking in tongues.

'You surprise me. I never thought you would have subscribed to the Happy Ever After fairy tale.'

'What *I* subscribe to or don't subscribe to is beyond the point,' Rose snapped. 'The fact is this—if Lily is pregnant—'

'Oh, for God's sake. She's not pregnant.' Nick leaned towards her, resting both his elbows on the table, and Rose fought not to pull back because the sheer force of his personality was so overwhelming. 'Let's get one thing straight here, Rose. I'm not a complete fool. I'm no shrinking violet when it comes to the opposite sex, but I make sure to always, but always, use protection. Believe me, the very last thing I would ever want would be to find myself cornered into marriage by a scheming woman who gets herself pregnant so that she can manoeuvre her way into my bank account.'

'That is the most cynical thing I've ever heard in my life!'

Nick looked at Rose furiously. Respect was something he had commanded from other people for all of his adult life. Respect and admiration were the two things he had commanded from women. This one, white faced and disapproving, not only lacked both, but was actually sitting in judgement on him. Him! Nick Papaeliou, a man whose ability to instil fear was legendary.

He was finding it difficult to believe his ears.

'You can't be a very happy, well-adjusted human being if you think that the only reason a woman would want to go out with you would be because of your bank balance.'

'No. I am not sitting here listening to this.'

'And to imagine that a woman would be conniving enough to get herself pregnant just because she wanted your money…'

At long last his formidable self-control began once again gathering pace, solidifying into icy steel. 'Do you live in the real world at all, Rose? Or are you the archetypal computer nerd everyone reads about? The one who can do amazing things with software but hasn't got a clue when it comes to real life? Because you must be wildly naïve to think that money isn't the thing that makes the world go round. I have met more gold-diggers in my life than you have had hot dinners.'

'In which case I feel very sorry for you.'

'I think I need another drink.' He summoned across a waitress, keeping his eyes fixed on Rose. 'Lily isn't pregnant. That's all you need to know.'

'That's a relief,' Rose said sincerely, thinking it prudent not to tack on that his take on women in general left a whole lot to be desired. Yes, as she calmed down, she could see that he had a point, that women might find his wealth a pretty powerful aphrodisiac. Although, a little voice inside her acknowledged, he must know that with his looks he could be as poor as a church mouse and still have the female population lusting after him. 'And I apologise if I…went off on a bit of a tangent just then…'

'A bit of a tangent?'

'You were saying some pretty emotive things.'

Nick wondered how he had suddenly been cast as the villain of the piece when all he had done was to be perfectly truthful with her. He should have remembered that he wasn't dealing with a normal, twenty-first-century woman.

'Apology accepted,' he grated.

'So why don't you tell me why…what you wanted to discuss with me…?'

'I'm very fond of your sister,' Nick began, 'but before you jump in both feet first, let me just add that she and I are not having a relationship. At least, not in the sense in which you probably expect that we are.'

'What do you mean?'

'Do I have to spell it out for you?' He impatiently tugged off his tie and undid the top two buttons of his shirt. Was it his imagination or was this place sweltering? 'Lily and I are not having sex. We have never had sex. It has not been that kind of a relationship between us…' Since that made a first for him, he was inordinately proud of the fact that he was managing to sustain a great, platonic relationship with a beautiful woman. Not only that, but he felt no stirrings of attraction whatsoever. It had occurred to him that his relationships had become more problematic as the years had progressed. Women had invariably wanted more than he could offer and was it really worth the hassle?

'What kind of relationship is it, then?' Rose asked.

'She's a sweet kid. I know a lot of people in the industry and I've been helping her.'

'Helping her do what?'

'Helping her with her career.'

'You mean putting her in touch with…' With whom? Actors? Producers? Directors? Rose knew precious little about what went on behind the scenes in the world of acting. It was so far removed from the prosaic life she led.

'With people who could help her.'

'That's…very nice of you.' Frankly, she was slightly bewildered. 'Is that why you wanted to see me? Why couldn't Lily have just told me all that herself? Instead of being so secretive about…everything?'

'Have you ever heard of Damien Hicks?'

'Should I have?'

'Just answer the question, Rose.'

'No.'

'Well, he's an up-and-coming film producer.'

A sense of humour inserted itself in between her bemusement as to where Nick was going with this conversation. 'Not many of those roaming around in my line of work. Do they have any distinguishing features I might identify them by?'

'They're fond of cigars,' Nick answered drily. He paused. 'I met Damien when one of my companies was doing an advertising shoot in the Maldives. Not really Damien's thing now, but five years ago he was just beginning to make his mark. He did the campaign for me and I helped him finance his first film. Just a short feature, but since then his rise has been meteoric. He likes working with new talent.'

'And Lily is new talent.' Rose smiled. 'She should have been jumping at the opportunity to tell me, after all the disappointments she's been through.'

'His new film needs a lead, Rose. Don't get me wrong, he's auditioned countless young hopefuls and has come to the conclusion that Lily is the one through no doing of mine. I introduced them, got him to give her a chance and she's done the rest.'

'Why do I get the feeling that there's a *but* lurking just around the corner?'

'But,' he said quietly, 'and this is why Lily was having a hard time discussing this with you…the part will be shot exclusively in America and there's more than a fifty-per-cent chance that, once she gets over there, she'll find herself caught up in the Hollywood industry. It's bigger, there are more opportunities and with a CV that starts with a Hicks movie…'

Rose knew that the colour was draining away from her face.

'I know this is probably unexpected and not particularly pleasant…'

'And Lily wants to go to America to live?'

'She wants to give it a go, see what happens.'

'Right.'

'She also wants to go with your blessing.'

'Right.' Rose barely had any memories of a life without her

sister. They had always been there for one another and she had never given much thought to the day when they would go their different ways. That had been a bridge waiting to be crossed and she had never considered how she would cross it when it did finally loom on the horizon. 'Of course she has my blessing. I…I only want what's best for her and if there's a chance that she could make her dreams come true out there, well…who am I to stand in her way?' The words were right but the hollowness inside made her feel sick.

'Come on. Let's get out of here.'

'Yes.' She stood up and took a deep breath. 'But there's no need for you to come. You've done what you came to do and you can leave me now. I'm capable of taking care of myself.'

'Try looking in the mirror and then telling yourself that.'

Rose turned away and fumbled for her bag. She couldn't help but think that this was all his fault even though she knew that the chance he had given Lily was the greatest favour he could have granted. Was she so selfish that she would rather have Lily stay at home than take flight and find her dreams somewhere else?

But when she thought of her sister living across the Atlantic, she wanted to burst into tears.

She made a few feeble protests about wanting him to go, but she didn't put up much of a fight when she found herself back in his car being driven to her house.

'Go and sit. I'll get you something to drink.'

'I'm not thirsty.' Rose finally surfaced from her thoughts and tried to shoot him her widest smile. 'And look…' She pointed at her smile. 'Doesn't this prove that I'm just fine?'

'Lily will be back shortly. Do you want her to see you freaked out like this?'

'I am not freaked out.' She glared at him through the smile.

It was so hard to do both and in the middle of trying she felt her lower lip wobble and she knew what was coming. Not even closing her eyes could squeeze back the tears, and then she felt his arms go around her and, worse, felt herself comforted by his strength as he enveloped her.

Nick felt her melt against him and drew her as tightly to him as he could. He had never had the benefit of siblings and, yes, he had known, just as Lily had known, that Rose would be upset, but up close he was staggered by the power of her affection for her sister. He could actually feel her tears soaking into his shirt and she was sobbing, but quietly, as if ashamed at making so much noise.

He felt in his trouser pocket and located a clean handkerchief, which he pressed against her cheek, and that seemed to staunch some of her tears although when she drew back he very nearly wanted to pull her against him again.

His only experiences with weeping women had been at the end of a relationship and their tears had irritated him. What did one say to a woman at a time like this?

'I'll make sure you get the hankie back.' Rose spared him the dilemma of finding the right words. She gave him a watery smile and he did the only thing he could think of doing. He wiped a stray tear from her face with his finger, which made her remember who he was and she stepped back a little further.

'Thank you for the lift back.' Rose gathered herself sufficiently to look him in the eye. She could see the sympathy there and felt a complete and utter fool because she knew what he must be thinking: that the loser of a sister was so thrown by the thought of being on her own that she had broken down and blubbed like a baby. 'I'm glad that I've got that out of my system and, honestly, I really am happy for Lily and hope that she gets everything she deserves.'

'I'm going to pour you something strong. Or would you prefer tea?' He couldn't remember the last time he had made a cup of tea.

'I would prefer you to leave, actually.'

'No.'

'No?' Some of her old fire returned and Nick felt quietly satisfied, although he still knew that he was going to stay with her. At least until she was back to her full vitriolic self, trying to shoot him down in flames. He was fast discovering a masochistic streak in him he had never known existed.

'Go sit…' He waved in the direction of the lounge. 'I'll be five minutes.'

Less, in actual fact, as he decided to dispense with the tea-making and pour her a stiff drink instead. Much better for the nerves, he told himself.

'It was just the shock of what you said,' Rose greeted him defensively, half standing as he handed her the drink. 'What's this?'

'An old family remedy for stressed nerves.'

She sniffed the glass. 'Called?'

'Vodka and a touch of whatever juice I happened to find in the fridge.' He sat on the sofa by her and watched as she took a tentative mouthful. 'Lily is actually contemplating turning down Damien's offer if you find it too upsetting having her leave,' Nick said quietly.

'That would be mad.' Rose looked at him and sipped a little more. 'I can't believe that you've been on the scene less than a month and our lives are being turned upside down.'

'I wondered when you would get around to blaming me,' Nick said coolly.

Rose, remembering how she had felt holding onto him and sobbing, cast him a baleful look. 'I wasn't blaming you. I was just making a passing remark.' She had felt weak and helpless and protected and vulnerable, all things she had thought she had left behind when their parents had died and Tony and Flora had taken them in. For that alone, she felt resentful.

'Ever thought that sometimes life is richer when you step out of your comfort zone?'

'No,' Rose said bluntly. 'There was quite a bit of stepping out of comfort zones when I was young and I don't remember any of it making my life feel any richer.'

'Your aunt and uncle…'

'Wandering the highways and byways. You try facing changes every six months and then tell me how great it is stepping out of comfort zones.'

'But Lily may have something of the adventurer in her…'

Rose heard the affection in his voice and, yes, she could see why he felt protective towards her sister. Most people did. She had gentle, girlish, winning ways. For the first time in her life she felt a stab of pure, uncharitable jealousy, which made her draw her breath in sharply.

'Yes, you're right, she does,' Rose said coolly. 'And I don't.' Which made her a bore in his eyes because the women who peopled his life, the women he was drawn to, weren't boring worker bees like her, they were the bright, sparkly, adventurous fireflies that flitted from light to light. 'Now—' she stood up '—I really would rather you weren't here when Lily gets home. I want to have a talk with her in private and you needn't worry that I'm going to do anything that might make her change her mind. I'm happy for her.'

Nick reluctantly rose to his feet. He had glimpsed through a little window of vulnerability and, strangely for him, because vulnerability wasn't a character trait he found attractive in a woman, he wanted to see a bit more, but Rose was already walking towards the door, just the pinkness round her eyes to account for her crying jag.

'I don't expect I'll be seeing much of you again,' she told him politely as he slipped on his coat and felt in the pockets, out of habit, for the keys to his apartment.

'Why do you say that?'

'Because I imagine Lily will leave sooner rather than later. You didn't specify a time, but I guess cutting edge movie producers don't sit around tapping their feet waiting for their plots to go cold.'

'No, I guess they don't.'

'So I may not get a chance to tell you that I'd rather you don't breathe a word to Lily about my…my…'

'Crying? Breaking down?'

'My little loss of self-control.' Rose stuck her chin up and met his eyes without blinking.

She was positively shuffling him towards the front door and she pulled it wide open before he could do the sensible thing and lean against it. Because suddenly and inexplicably, he didn't want to go. Not just yet. But there was no choice.

'I won't tell her. You have my word.'

Rose nodded and, without saying a word, she quietly closed the door in his face.

CHAPTER FOUR

COMPOSING emails to Lily was becoming a combination of subtlety and creative fiction.

After Lily had been abroad for three weeks, it had become clear to Rose that life in the fast lane was suiting her sister. She waxed lyrical about the movie she was making, devoted pages to telling her all about the fabulously talented Damien Hicks and the groovy, exciting people she was working with. The flat she was sharing with four other girls, all newcomers like herself, was cheap but apparently called a condo and had a swimming pool. The adjective amazing had become a staple word in her vocabulary. Everything was amazing from the movie to the people to life in general, and Rose was relieved and pleased that it was all working out for her sister.

Which, unfortunately, didn't solve the financial problems that seemed to have been saving themselves for the minute Lily waved her fond goodbye to British soil.

The bathroom had sprung a leak, which, as the plumber had ominously told Rose, revealed all the makings of a dated system that could be patched up but would really need to be replaced at some point. Rose had opted for the patching-up job. Then the washing machine had collapsed, which had meant a new one. And now, sitting in the kitchen, she could see a damp patch on the ceiling, which didn't augur well for the dated plumbing system or, for that matter, her rapidly depleting savings account.

Rose groaned. She wondered how she could phrase the words 'need money' so that her sister didn't go into spasms of guilt and worry. Lily had already apologised for not being able to send any over, but she would just as soon as she could. At the moment, she was being paid enough to cover her rent and build a lifestyle that befitted an up-and-coming Hollywood actress, which left precious little for the crumbling house she had left behind.

Rose didn't begrudge her a minute of the enjoyment she was having. Lily deserved it. But her single income was being tested to its limits and it was getting harder to keep writing her all 'fine here' emails when the roof was falling down.

Literally.

One week later, with the damp patch still making small inroads even though the bath was out of commission, she sat at her kitchen table to the sounds of plumbers banging upstairs and the horrible prospect of going to check on them so that she could find her floorboards up and her cool magnolia walls covered with dust. They had been at it for the past two days, putting in a new, updated system. She had not dared enquire as to the cost but the sight of the shiny new copper pipes had made her blood run cold.

Lily was, according to her email yesterday, heading off for two weeks to Arizona where some of the movie was being filmed. Rose knew that she had tried to de-glamorise the whole thing, but it wasn't hard to read between the lines that she was bubbling over with excitement.

While I sit here, she thought glumly, like Chicken Little waiting for the sky to fall down. Everything else seemed to be.

The sound of the doorbell managed, just, to penetrate the sounds of the banging and Rose vaguely wondered what life had in store for her next. A kindly neighbour coming to tell her that her car had been vandalised? Maybe they had noticed a spot of terminal subsidence on an outside wall?

She pulled open the door, dressed in her very best dungarees, bedroom slippers and old jumper because dust and fine clothing just didn't go hand in hand, and there he was. The man she had avoided mentioning in all the emails she had sent her sister, the man who kept popping into her head at all the wrong times, even though she had robustly told herself that she was well rid of him.

Her response to him, lounging indolently against the door frame, finger poised as if about to summon her again, was immediate and powerful. Her stomach constricted and her eyes widened, swiftly and unconsciously taking in his lean, muscular frame and those killer sea-green eyes that seemed to burn holes through her. She had to make a mental effort to gather herself together.

'Hullo.' Pause. 'What are you doing here?'

'Still getting to the point, I see. What's going on?'

'What do you mean?' She followed his curious glance behind her and shrugged. 'Oh. The noise. Just a bit…of repair work.'

'Are you going to invite me in?'

'Has Lily told you to get in touch with me?' She had been careful not to mention a word about her financial problems, but who knew? Maybe her sister had picked up on something and, innocent that she was, might have mentioned to Nick, Nick with the heart of gold who had done so much for her, that perhaps he could just pop his head round the door and make sure that Rose was okay.

Rose instantly felt like a charity case and gripped the door knob a little harder.

'I was in the area.'

'Really? I wouldn't have thought that this would be the sort of area you would just happen to be passing through.'

'Stop arguing, Rose, and open the door.' Getting fed up with her non-argument, he pushed the door and strode in, not leaving her the option of slamming it in his face.

Nick, for the first time in years practising celibacy, was aware of the shameful truth, which was that he had been thinking on and off about her for the past few weeks. His life had been as busy and hectic as ever, his work taking him abroad, as it always did, on a regular basis, but every so often he had caught himself conjuring up her face and wondering what she was up to.

Gentle prodding had eventually elicited from Lily something he could respond to. Rose, Lily had told him in all confidence, had not sounded herself when they had last spoken on the phone. She had said all the right things, that everything was fine, but she had sounded anxious.

Nick had reacted like a man who suddenly discovered the site of an itch and realised that he could reach to scratch it. Sitting on his leather swivel chair, feet carelessly propped up on his gleaming, mahogany desk, he had immediately and piously promised to look in on her.

'You wouldn't want to have filming ruined because you're worried about what's going on over here,' he had soothed. His prospect of a weekend of solid work, interrupted only by a stuffy Saturday night do, which he had reluctantly agreed to purely for diplomatic reasons, suddenly brightened considerably.

He wasn't entirely sure why he could be bothered to hunt down a woman who rubbed him up the wrong way, but when it came to members of the opposite sex he rarely questioned his responses, safe in the knowledge that his gut feelings had rarely, if ever, let him down. Granted his gut feelings were usually wrapped up in the normal, testosterone-driven desires for a sexual relationship, but the fact that Rose was out of the ordinary in that respect didn't put him off. She had been on his mind, for whatever reason, and the fastest way to solve that problem would be to hunt her down. And Lily was a very handy go-between, giving him an excuse he might not otherwise have had.

'What the hell is that banging all about?'

'I told you. Repair work. Minor.' Rose bristled at the sight of those fabulous eyes sweeping along the banister, up to where a fine shimmer of dust obscured the small upstairs corridor. She wondered what her sister had said to him. God, what if she had begged Nick to check up on her? Lily would have thought nothing of asking such a favour because, in her eyes, Nick wasn't a shark but some innocuous little minnow, someone who would be happy to do her a small favour. In Lily's world, everyone was potentially sweet and good because she herself was.

Rose determined that as soon as her sister returned to England, she would personally teach her the ways of the world. Lily might have oodles more experience when it came to men, but her insight into human nature was sadly lacking.

'Doesn't sound minor.'

'You still haven't told me what you're doing here. If Lily put you up to this, then there's no need to be concerned.'

'Even though your house is falling down?'

'My house is not falling down!'

Nick had forgotten how easily the woman bristled. He had also forgotten how amusing he found the trait. It made a refreshing change from his normal interaction with women, which went along all the usual courses that inevitably led to bed. Bed and all its attendant complications, which he was determined to avoid, at least for a while.

'Why don't you get me a cup of coffee and tell me all about it? You look stressed.'

Rose gaped. Of course she was stressed. An army of plumbers was currently bankrupting her and now, on top of that, the last man on earth she wanted to see had waltzed through her front door, brimming over with tea and sympathy because her dear, well-intentioned and hopelessly misguided sister had asked him to. Who wouldn't be stressed?

And on top of that, she was now embarrassingly aware of her clothes, which advertised someone who was in serious danger of imminent arrest by the fashion police.

While he, she noticed sourly, fashionably dressing down in faded jeans and a rugby sweater, still managed to look fantastic.

'I'm more stressed now that you've shown up,' Rose told him and Nick immediately jumped on the slip-up.

'So you're admitting you're stressed out. Lily did say you didn't sound your normal self when she spoke to you on the phone.'

Rose mentally strangled her sister. 'Hence you were coerced into rushing over here just to make sure I wasn't about to jump off the nearest bridge.'

'That's taking it too far.' There was an almighty thump from the direction of the dust and Rose groaned, waiting for Andy's voice to summon her up, probably to confront yet another unexpected problem. Like a routine trip to the dentist, which turned out to reveal a nightmare of hidden problems, her house was beginning to revel in showing its age. A little crack there, a small spot of damp here and suddenly it was as if it had given up the fight and was now determined to fall down around her ears. And as she mounted the stairs she could already see from the grim look on Andy's face that more bad news was on the way.

'Sorry, Rose.'

Behind her she was aware that Nick had followed in her hurried wake and she could sense his attention moving up a gear.

'We've discovered something a little unfortunate…'

Rose was too afraid to ask, so she stared at him in mute silence while he shook his head and gave her a look of such profound sympathy that she feared the worst.

'Asbestos.'

Rose saw the very last of her savings flutter through the window and she balled her hand into a fist and clenched it under her chin. 'How can that be?'

'Lodged under the floorboards,' Andy said kindly. 'Nothing to look at, but I can spot it a mile away. It's not everywhere but for the moment we're going to have to put everything back in place until it's sorted. We're not trained to remove it.'

'I don't suppose you're going to tell me that you're joking.'

'Wish I could, love.'

'And I guess you don't know how much it'll cost to have it removed?'

He shrugged while behind him his guys were efficiently putting the floorboards back down. 'Best not lose sleep over that one, considering you've got no option…'

Rose saw them out and was too despondent to care whether Nick was hovering in the background with his uninvited sympathy. She didn't even care that he had been dispatched to check on her as if she were incapable of looking after herself without Lily around.

'So—' she turned to face him, slamming the front door shut

on her plumbing messengers of bad tidings '—there you go. House collapsing. Money disappearing. Stress levels high. In other words lots to report back to Lily, although I'm hoping you'll dredge up sufficient compassion to know that I would rather she enjoyed all the opportunities opening up for her in America without having to worry about what's happening to me back here.'

'How long has this place been falling down?'

Rose shrugged. 'Weeks. It's been saving itself for Lily's departure.' She sighed, too tired and depressed to argue at his presence in the house, allowing him to witness her plight. She found that he was leading the way to the kitchen, manoeuvring around the cupboards until there was a mug of sweet tea in front of her, and she gratefully swallowed a mouthful.

'And you never breathed a word to her because you didn't want her to worry.'

'There was no point. She would have rushed back over here and that would have been the end of her career, everything she has worked so hard for.'

'So you decided to shoulder the stress on your own.' He had shoved back his stool so that he could stretch out his long legs and was looking at her thoughtfully. 'Except now you're left facing bills you can't afford.'

'I'll just have to put in a bit more overtime,' Rose snapped, railing against any suggestion of pity.

'Quite a bit more,' Nick commented drily, raising his eyes to the ceiling and the source of her misfortune. Frankly he had zero firsthand experience of a woman who had to work literally to keep the roof over her head.

'Yes, well, it's not impossible.' She stared at him sourly and with inspired accuracy continued, in a tight voice, 'I guess this is a completely different world to the one you're used to, where problems get fixed with the snap of your fingers. I don't suppose you know too many women who face a struggle to pay unexpected bills and can't afford the little luxuries you would take for granted.'

'Attacking me isn't going to solve your financial crisis.'

Rose didn't care for the word crisis. It was a little too evocative for comfort. 'You have to go. I need to phone my bank manager.'

'On a Saturday?'

'I don't know why I didn't think of that before. Of course, I can call my bank manager and take out a loan.'

'Which will have to be repaid.'

'But at least I'll be able to afford the repair work,' Rose pointed out wearily. 'And if you're going to sit there and state the obvious then you can finish that cup of tea and go.'

'And in the meantime, where do you intend to live?'

'Here, of course.'

'Dust everywhere? Hidden dangers under the floorboards? And what about when you get the men in to clear the asbestos? What then? Hang around in a mask?'

Rose felt tears of frustration and anger prick the backs of her eyes. 'Oh, just leave me alone.'

'So you can wallow in self-pity?'

'I do not wallow in self-pity,' she flung back at him through gritted teeth, shaken out of her despondency by the force of rage. 'I've got my solution and as soon as the banks open on Monday, I'll be there.'

'You can't live here.'

'Oh, you're right,' she sniped with dripping sarcasm. 'I'll just get my butler to book me in at the Savoy until everything's sorted out.'

Nick stifled a grin. 'Better idea. You need money and I have it.'

'Forget it, Nick. You might do favours for my sister, but I don't need anything from you.' She gave him a mutinous look, which he chose to ignore.

Was there any woman as stubborn as this one? He felt a sudden desire to be the one who controlled the reins and melted the fortresses she had erected everywhere around herself.

'You're letting your emotions talk and emotions never solved anything. If you run to the bank for a loan, you'll spend the next few years paying it back along with the crippling interest accrued.'

'So instead I take the money from you? And in return you get what?'

A vivid image of her lying naked in his bed presented itself and he blinked it away.

'You can't hide a problem of this magnitude from your sister. You might want to protect her from everything harsh that life can throw at her, but she deserves to know the truth about what's happening over here. Give her enough credit not to be a complete fool and come hurtling back to England when she knows that it wouldn't solve anything. If she finds out that you've been keeping this from her, she'll feel betrayed.'

'Don't pretend you know my sister better than I do,' Rose retorted, but his words set up a chain of thoughts that began to gnaw away at her composure. She had always been the one looking out for Lily, but where did concern end and smothering begin?

Uncertainty shadowed her face and Nick, spotting it, jumped in. 'I'm not pretending anything, but you have to tell her. Course she'd want to fly over, make sure you were okay, but she might not if...'

'If what?'

'If she knew that I was looking out for you.' Since when had he ever looked out for any woman? The rules of his game had always been simple. No dependency, no strings attached. Rose ignited some other feeling in him. She didn't conform to his ideas of physical feminine beauty so, whatever weird stirrings he had occasionally felt in her presence, he was certain it wasn't lust. But whatever it was, it was certainly novel and to his jaded palate the thought of something new was strangely alluring.

'Oh, please.'

'I am trying to help you out here,' Nick told her irritably. 'Why can't you just accept it?'

'I don't see you as the kind of guy who helps damsels in distress,' Rose pointed out, omitting to mention the fine print, which was unless they looked like Lily or unless he wanted something from them. 'You think you ought to offer assistance because you feel guilty. By some weird coincidence, you happen to show up when all this…' she gestured vaguely around her '…is going on and you think you ought to do something because you have a relationship with Lily. You feel sorry for the plain, ungainly sister left behind trying to cope.'

'I'm not suggesting I hand over the money and walk away. You seem to forget I'm a businessman.'

'Well, what are you offering, then? Not that there's any chance I'm going to take you up on your offer.'

'Because you're a stubborn fool.'

'Because I don't like the thought of being indebted to anyone.'

'Except the bank.'

'That's different.' Rose flushed, feeling boxed in by his clever use of words.

Novelty value was fast turning into challenge and it was invigorating. 'Take a couple of months off work…'

'Take a couple of months off work?' Was the man a complete lunatic? 'Have you been listening to a word I've been saying?' She shook her head in disgust and snatched up the mugs, carrying them off to the sink. Nick swivelled round so that he was looking at her and, while he was staring, she spun around and leant against the kitchen sink, arms folded. 'You know what's happening here, the financial strain I'm suddenly under, and your breezy solution is for me to have time off work? That activity that pays the bills?'

'How much do they pay you a month?'

Rose went pink. Wasn't discussing of salary the final taboo? Not that this man would skirt round a taboo if his life depended on it.

'Well? No need to be shy.'

'What I earn is none of your concern.' She should have asked for a pay rise months ago. She was damned good at her job and worked a lot longer hours than all of her colleagues. If only she had had a crystal ball foretelling her huge household bills were on the horizon she might have been more assertive during her appraisal. She reluctantly told him, knowing that he would just carry on sitting there until she did. He didn't laugh, as she had expected him to. Instead he looked at her for a few seconds, as though weighing up something in his head.

'I'm branching out,' he told her, 'going into the leisure business. Corporate investment and the money markets pay the bills but I've conquered that challenge. Now, I'm investing some of my own reserves in building up a boutique hotel portfolio.'

Rose thought of the reserves she was investing in—making sure she didn't wake up with the ceiling on her pillow.

'What's a boutique hotel?'

'Something very small and exquisite and strictly for people

who don't want to be surrounded by hundreds of people every time they step out of their bedroom.'

'Don't tell me…strictly for the very rich because privacy costs.'

'Of course. Like I said, I'm a businessman. I'm starting with one in Borneo.'

'Borneo,' she echoed sceptically.

'Trust me…the next must-go-to destination. It'll be small, eco friendly and built to the highest standards. And here's where you come in…' Nick paused. 'You spend the next two months running the show. You set up the computer system for all the accounting et cetera, you liaise with the architects—'

'I don't know the first thing about…hotels. I can't even think when the last time I stayed in one was.'

'Which I'll make sure to put right,' Nick murmured. 'Think about it, Rose. You won't be able to live here while work's being done… I'm offering to relieve you of the stress of living out of an overnight bag on a friend's floor. I'll put you up in three separate hotels in London over the next two months so that you can have firsthand experience of what makes a good one work, and in addition I'll pay you double what you would have been earning. In return, you can try your hand at something other than sitting in front of a terminal all day long.'

Nick, who donated vast sums to charity on an annual basis, had only ever had nodding acquaintance with altruism on a personal level and he was finding that it felt good to be at the giving end of largesse. In truth, he could increase her salary multiple times and not notice the difference to his bank balance, but he was shrewd enough to know that there was a thin line between a reasonable proposition and a contemptuous act of charity for which he would probably find his hand roundly bitten off.

Because this woman snapped and snarled and yapped and bit and he was looking forward to taming her. He decided to look on it as his pet project. All work and no play…well, he knew the saying well enough and, as he wasn't playing at the moment, he would devote all of his formidable attention to digging underneath that prickly exterior to the woman inside. And doing her a good turn in the bargain by fishing her out of a pretty nasty hole.

'Don't you have people who could do the job for you?'

'Don't you have any ability to just say thank you and go away to count your blessings?'

'Why do I get the feeling that there's an ulterior motive to your offer?' Rose asked. She felt driven to find holes in his proposal even though the rational side of her was already calculating the benefits of what he was offering. She had worked long enough for the company to know that they would not have a problem in giving her unpaid leave while she sorted out her domestic situation and the thought of something different was appealing. Stepping out of her comfort zone was appealing. Appealing and frightening at the same time.

'Because you're inherently suspicious.' Nick shrugged and stood up. 'If you're not interested, then I'll leave you to get on with the messy business of sorting your house out with the help of your friendly bank manager.'

'Wait!'

She raced behind him as he headed for the front door, glancing sideways as she did so, where the shimmer of dust in the air reminded her of the generosity of his offer.

'What if I fail? I have no experience…'

'Have faith in yourself. You won't fail. I take it that that's a yes?'

'I shall have to clear it with my boss.'

'And if you do take up this opportunity…' Nick lazily appraised her, from her worn bedroom slippers to the shapeless dungarees, which, he now thought, should only ever be worn by labourers on a building site '…you'll have to do something about your wardrobe.'

Rose went bright red. It occurred to her that actually working with the man might just prove to be more stressful than sorting out her situation without his help.

'I don't go to work in these clothes,' she said coolly. 'I put them on because anything else would have been stupid.' Lily would have managed to look fabulous in faded, old clothes but she had to stop comparing herself to Lily. 'If you don't think that I'm decorative enough to work with you, then you might as well tell me now because I don't intend to buy a brand-new wardrobe for a two-month stint. And also…' she drew herself up and stared him straight in the eyes '…if I do happen to work for you, then I don't want you to think that I'm doing it because I actually like you.'

'Very tactful.'

'I'm just being honest.'

'And, believe me, I find that very refreshing, especially in a woman.' He was so accustomed to women using their bodies and their wiles to get what they wanted that the metaphorical bucket of water Rose kept tipping over him was doing him no end of good. He even contemplated the possibility of taking a little time out to show her the ropes.

'There might be some travel involved,' he continued. 'Do you have a passport?'

Rose nodded as the parameters broadened around her.

'And because you'll be working for me directly, I will set you up with an office inside my place.'

'Whoa. Stop right there. I don't think that's a good idea at all.'

'Why not?'

'Because…because it would be a lot more professional for me to…ah…work in an office environment.' She envisaged somewhere imbued with his masculine scent, with the open door to his bedroom within throwing distance. She shied away from the image with an inward yelp of dismay.

'You'll be there on your own,' Nick said, amused at her discomfiture. 'And, face it, this is my private project. I can hardly bring you into the office, sit you down and not expect you to become an object of curiosity.'

'Well, you could explain…'

'Dangerous curiosity…' Nick expanded silkily, waiting in telling silence as her eyes widened. 'People would naturally assume that because I had brought you in to work on my personal project, we were an item.'

'An item?'

'Involved with one another. Going out. Lovers. Now, I don't much give a damn what other people think of me, but I don't bring my private life to work.'

'But you…we…we don't have a private life,' Rose protested, going bright red.

'Immaterial. Tongues will wag and I can't have my power diminished. Does that answer your objection?'

'Of course, I can see your point of view, but…you have to see mine as well…'

'And that is…?' He leaned against the door and stuck his hands into his pockets.

'Well…' Rose tried to think of a coherent argument that wouldn't make her sound prissy in the process. How could she explain that just standing next to him in her own house made her feel nervous and uncomfortable, so how much more difficult was it going to be when she was working in his?

'Your virtue is perfectly safe with me.' Nick grinned. 'Like I said, I won't be there during the day, and if you're scared of being around me in my apartment, then we can always catch up on neutral territory. There's a pub just around the corner. We can avoid the cubby-holes with the subdued lighting.'

'Of course I'm not scared of you.'

'Good, because there's no reason to be, nor is there any reason to feel uncomfortable in my presence.'

Mortified, Rose interpreted his slow, amused smile as his way of telling her that he wouldn't come near her if she happened to be the last woman on the face of the earth.

'I'll let you know after I've spoken to my boss. Tomorrow some time. Is that all right?' What was she letting herself in for?

One month into her new temporary job, she was fast finding out.

A chic five-star hotel tucked away in the bowels of Covent Garden was her first project for inspection. Her brief was to examine why it worked and in detail, with a weekly report to be compiled for Nick's scrutiny. That, in addition to checking out costs for everything under the sun that might possibly be needed in the construction of a hotel. There seemed to be a hundred people, all of whom she had to liaise with, and Nick, at the end of each day, expected perfect recall and written reports on everything.

He would sweep into his apartment at six-thirty and, although he had told her that she could clear off by five and email him with her findings, she had pretty quickly sussed that, whatever he said, he expected her to work until at least six-thirty and if necessary later.

And she didn't mind. She had thought, a lifetime ago it seemed, that she would be crammed into his small personal space and, like a cat on a hot tin roof, would spend every minute there in nervous expectation of his sudden entry. She had envisaged being surrounded by his private objects, which would intrude on her, a constant nagging and stomach-churning reminder of his overwhelming personality.

But his apartment, for starters, was vast. It was also peculiarly impersonal. The abstract paintings on the white walls gave no clue to the man except to indicate his wealth. There were no photos in frames or ornaments standing on shelves. Two cleaners came promptly at eight every morning, and departed at ten, leaving the apartment spotless. Her office was no makeshift affair. It was large and kitted out for serious work and, once there, Rose had no trouble concentrating.

And then, just as she was usually packing up to leave, he would sweep in. From the office, Rose would hear the slam of the front door and the jangle of keys as he carelessly tossed them on the granite kitchen counter. Then he would appear in the doorway, tugging at his tie, leaning against the doorframe and watching her for a few seconds in silence as she logged off the computer.

It was the time of day she had been dreading. Yet now, it was the time of day Rose waited for with a sense of heady, forbidden, crawling expectation.

Tonight was no exception and she felt her stomach churn with excitement as she heard him approach. She knew it was wrong but her attraction to him was something she just couldn't seem to stuff away somewhere conveniently out of reach. It had ambushed her from behind and her only defence against it was to hang onto her veneer of professional self-control.

'I've got those costings for you.' She had trained her eyes not to stare whenever he tugged his tie off, but, like recalcitrant kids, they still always managed to sneak a look at that glimpse of hard brown chest that was revealed as he undid the top two buttons of his shirt.

'And I've got something for you…' He walked towards her, waggling a piece of paper in his hand.

'What is it?'

'Have a look.' He gave her the envelope and leant on the computer terminal, watching as she slit it open. 'We're going on a trip.' He smiled slowly as she tipped her face up to stare at him. 'A little look-see at some prime land in Borneo.' He moved round so that he was behind her chair and then he bent towards her. Rose could feel his warm breath against her neck. 'Fish out the summer glad rags, Rose. It's going to be mighty hot out there…'

CHAPTER FIVE

NICK told Rose everything there was to know about the time-table for his project and what had inspired him to pick Borneo for its location. Over a bottle of wine and some delivery Chinese food, which they ate in his ultra-modern, rarely used kitchen, he explained his connections with Malaysia, starting with an old university friend with whom the project was to be undertaken, and ending with an impassioned and persuasive belief that Borneo would soon be the rising star as Kuala Lumpur and Penang became overrun with tourists.

Rose did her utmost to play down her excitement and treat the whole thing as something that happened practically every day. She asked cool, sensible questions but her mind was running rampant with thoughts of planes and sea and lush green forests and, of course, being sequestered somewhere remote with him.

That was the most frightening aspect of the whole thing. How on earth was she going to maintain her sang-froid when she would be with him twenty-four seven? How long before her professional mask slipped and she made a complete fool of herself? Thus far, Nick had no idea that she followed him with her eyes, drinking in the powerful lines of his body, feasting on his harsh beauty, filing away throwaway remarks, the way he laughed, the slashing gestures he used when he was in a bad mood, so that she could bring them out at a later date and savour them like a guilty secret.

To him, she was the ugly duckling he had rescued out of obligation who, she hoped, was proving herself to be as efficient an employee as he could have asked for. Occasionally he teased her and very occasionally some of that teasing bordered on flirtation, but Rose, having lived her life in the shadow of her stunning sister, was a realist. Charming, good-looking men liked charming, good-looking women. A beautiful woman, for a man like Nick Papaeliou, was an essential accessory and if he occasionally flirted with his plain employee, then it was simply an overspill from his unconscious ability to charm. She shuddered to think how he would react if he ever found out about her inappropriately lustful imaginings.

She would be brought back down to earth by Nick listing her duties once they arrived at their destination.

Rose, who had been anxiously day-dreaming her way into a fictitious and awkward scenario in which he was roaring with laughter as he spotted her following him with puppy eyes as he dived into an imaginary swimming pool, surfaced to find him frowning.

'You are going to be able to accompany me, aren't you, Rose? You did say when I took you on that you had a valid passport.'

'Oh, yes,' Rose answered brightly.

'Because you seemed to be a million miles away just then.' He leaned towards her, eyes narrowed, and Rose automatically flinched back. 'Is there something you should tell me?' he demanded unsmilingly and for a few, disturbing seconds Rose thought that he had read her mind and exposed her shameful little secret.

'S-something I should tell you?' she stammered weakly.

'Fear of flying, maybe?' Nick leaned back and looked at her thoughtfully. 'It's nothing to be ashamed of. I know you haven't done much overseas travel…'

'Too busy touring the UK in search of spiritual zen,' Rose said, weak with relief.

'Right. But there's no need to be afraid of flying. Believe it or not, there's more chance of you ending up under the wheels of a car than plummeting from the sky.'

'Oh. Well, thank you very much for reassuring me that those great metal birds can stay airborne,' she said sarcastically, recovering her equilibrium.

'Then what's the problem?'

'I…don't have a problem, Nick.' She would have to take a swimsuit; she sure as hell wasn't going to take a bikini. She would take a very sensible one-piece and sneak out under cover of night to have a swim. The thought of frolicking in a pool with him made her feel sick.

'There you go again.'

'There I go again *what*?'

'Frowning and getting that distant look in your eyes.' He reached forward and before she was aware of his intention he smoothed her brow with his thumb. It was such an unexpected gesture that Rose literally jumped and gave a little yelp of shock.

'You're on edge. Why? If you're not scared of flying, then is it the unknown?'

'Yes.' She wanted to rub where he had touched and brush away the scorched sensation she was feeling. 'I'm scared of the unknown.'

'Thought so,' Nick said with satisfaction, 'although I can't understand why. You had a pretty nomadic existence growing up. If anything, I would have thought you would have found the unknown quite appealing. Don't we always long to revisit our childhood?'

Rose had done her best to discourage any personal conversation between them. She felt safer when their relationship was purely on a business footing. Yes, of course he asked about the house and the work being done on it and naturally she answered him because the house was, really and truly, the reason why she now found herself working for him. But beyond that, she was vague when he asked her what plans she had for the weekend, or how she spent her evenings or even what sort of people she met in the hotel, whether she liked them or not.

However, she was so relieved that he had misunderstood her apprehensive expression that she gratefully clung onto his fear-of-the-unknown nonsense for dear life.

'Sometimes it doesn't work that way,' Rose said distantly. She stood up and began clearing away the empty containers, which looked a little unhealthy as the leftover contents began to congeal.

'No?' Nick pulled a chair towards him and propped his feet up on the black leather. After weeks of working with her, sitting within touching range of her when they brainstormed over some niggling problem, brushing her arm with his as he leaned to consult architectural drawings, growing strangely accustomed to seeing her now when he came in through the front door, he could honestly say that he still didn't know much about her personal life. She had piqued his curiosity a long time ago but, instead of proximity doing what it should have done, and diminishing it, he was more curious about her than ever before.

Now she was throwing him a glimpse into her thoughts and, like a dog tossed a bone, he was annoyed to find himself picking it up and preparing to run with it.

'You mean you're scared of what you don't know even though you spent your formative years dealing with it?'

Rose shrugged. She had her back to him, which suited her. It helped her keep her voice steady as she spoke. 'You should be doing this, Nick. This is your house and these are your dishes.'

'But you're a woman and I'm a man. Don't women love doing things like that? Keeps them busy and happy.'

Rose spun around, but her heated accusation of sexism died on her lips when she saw the grin plastered across his face. Without thinking she flung the tea towel at him and he caught it and tut-tutted under his breath.

'I should punish you for that,' he drawled. 'Trying to cause grievous bodily harm to your employer…'

Rose felt her mouth go dry. This was the lazy, flirty voice he sometimes pulled out of the bag, with the dexterity of a magician pulling a rabbit out of a hat, and, it didn't seem to matter how many times she told herself that he was just one of those born charmers, that voice still got to her every time.

'With a tea cloth?' she said lightly. 'You must be a lot more delicate than you look if a tea cloth can inflict serious injury.' A brief, electric silence greeted this remark and Rose clenched her hands into fists behind her back. She didn't know what had possessed her to say that.

'Should I take it as a compliment that you consider me big and strong?' Nick murmured provocatively. He could tell that she would have liked the ground to open and swallow her up and for the first time since she had started working for him, he felt suddenly enraged. Enraged that he had given this woman an opportunity many would have killed for. Enraged that she continued to treat him with the studied politeness of a stranger. Enraged that every single time he had tried to get under that armour of hers, he had found himself gently but firmly repelled. Enraged now that she was back to looking at him with something like horror, as usual turning a perfectly innocent, teasing remark into something diabolical.

'Forget I said that.' Nick's voice was cool and dismissive. He even turned away.

Rose was stricken. How was he supposed to know that she shrank away from him because she was just so damn scared that if she didn't her treacherous legs would have her pelting towards him and her even more treacherous arms would wind themselves around his neck and cling?

What must he think of her? That she was ungrateful? Churlish? Buttoned up? The sort of woman who had suffered a sense-of-humour bypass somewhere along the line?

Rose wondered whether maybe she had.

'I'm sorry,' she faltered.

'What about?' Nick enquired politely.

'I'm really excited about going to Borneo…' Humourless. Buttoned up. An efficient little worker bee who actually thought that what she had to say mattered to Nick Papaeliou. He was courteous, even teasing and flirtatious sometimes, and yet here she was, lips tightly pursed, as if her maidenly honour were under threat. Clutching her precious, uninteresting private life as if one single lapse would send him into a sexual, predatory frenzy. The idea was so nonsensical that Rose inwardly cringed.

'But I guess I'm a little scared as well…'

'Oh, yes?' Nick reluctantly felt himself drawn to that simple, hesitant admission. 'Why?'

Rose sighed and went to sit at the kitchen table. She rested her chin thoughtfully in the palm of her hand and stared back down the years. She had agreed with him, initially, because he had conveniently supplied her with an excuse for her own disturbing train of thoughts, but now she thought that maybe he was right. Maybe she was scared of the unknown.

'Tony and Flora always thought that traipsing around the country would make me brave and adventurous. I think they kind of figured that some of their let's-change-the-goalposts lifestyle would rub off on me, but it never did. When you move from school to school, you end up dreading each upheaval even more than the last one. At least, that's what it did for me. It's why I like working for Fedco.'

'You can hide behind the size?' he guessed shrewdly, now fully ensnared by her dreamy, distant voice.

'I can be safe. Borneo...' Rose laughed and blinked so that he was back in her line of vision. 'Well, Borneo is just something else altogether.'

'All that heat...'

'And insects...'

Anything could happen. He nearly said it out loud and caught himself in the nick of time. 'But Tony and Flora would be pleased...'

Rose gave him a dazzling grin. 'More than pleased. They'd be overjoyed. You want to hear them on the subject of Lily. They're thrilled to bits that she's now on the other side of the world making her fortune. I think they feel that they've somehow contributed to that.'

'And what about you?'

'I would never contemplate living across the Atlantic.'

'I mean, are *you* thrilled that your sister is making her fortune on the other side of the world?'

'I've got accustomed to it,' Rose told him. 'I miss her terribly, but it helps knowing that she's happy and fulfilled.'

'And are you?'

'Am I what?'

'Happy and fulfilled.' Nick wasn't quite sure why he had asked the question. He could only think that he must be out of practice when it came to women, because experience had taught him that questions like that provoked answers he didn't like.

'Well, I'm pretty pleased with how the house is coming along.' Rose scuttled back into her shell. 'Have I told you that I'm going to have it redecorated top to bottom? The whole place is destroyed and, rather than do a patch up job, I'm going to go all the way and really have it exactly how I want it.'

'Interesting. Sounds like you're there for the long term.'

'At least for the foreseeable future,' Rose said vaguely. 'But tell me a bit more about Borneo…what else do I need to know…?'

That it took for ever to get there. That was something he hadn't told her and it was just as well as it had allowed her no opportunity to spend three days angsting over the ordeal of sitting next to him on a plane for a seemingly never-ending period of time. Rose had had enough angst on her plate just worrying about what she was going to buy to take with her.

Then there was the whole question of what exactly she was supposed to do once she got there. She might be a whizz at computers and, yes, facts, figures and financial projections were things she could handle without too much difficulty. And reporting back on her hotel, chatting to the manager, with whom she had developed a pleasant rapport, about the nuts and bolts of city chic, was within her spec…but looking at land in a country she had barely heard of and could only vaguely point to on a map?

'Okay. Spit it out.'

'What?'

'There's something on your mind. Spit it out.'

Nick snapped shut his laptop computer, sat back and gave her his full, undivided attention.

'I don't know what you mean.'

'I mean you've barely spoken since we took off four hours ago, you've been stuck on the same page of your book for the past hour and if you chew your lip any more we'll have to see if there are any paramedics on the plane. Tell me you're not worrying about what the hot weather is going to do to your hair.'

'Hardly. I stopped worrying about what my hair did years ago.'

'Relax. Enjoy the flight, as our air steward would say.' He glanced around him and then shot her a lazy, amused smile. 'Is first class all it's cracked up to be?'

Rose had had to stop herself from fidgeting with gadgets and demonstrating just how impressionable she was when it came to long-haul travel. 'And the rest,' she confessed. 'And I am very appreciative…well…for this and for…everything else…'

Nick frowned. This wasn't what he wanted to hear. Gratitude wasn't what this woman was all about. Stubborn, feisty, mutinous and often highly aggravating, yes. But grateful…no. Over the past three days, Nick had found himself looking forward to this trip. The man who had crossed the Atlantic a million times and more, who had platinum frequent-flyer cards from just about every major airline, who could afford to go anywhere in the world on a whim if he so desired, and in the company of pretty much any woman he wanted…and he had been looking forward to a business trip with a woman who made his teeth snap together in sheer frustration quite a bit of the time.

He had never been one to spend hours soul-searching, but his illogical reaction did make him conclude that his life was full of yes-men, people who would jump if he looked in their direction and silently mouthed the order.

'I don't want your thanks and gratitude,' he grated, and Rose gave him a startled glance.

'Fine,' Rose snapped back.

'So tell me what's wrong.'

'I'm not sure I'm up to what I'm supposed to do when we get to Borneo,' she admitted in a sulky voice. 'I work with computers. I don't know the first thing about building sites and conveyancing.'

'You won't have to. My Malaysian counterpart is very competent. You won't be shoved into a position where you have to make technical decisions that are beyond your scope.'

'So why am I here, in that case?'

Ah. Now, this was back to normal. Rose clambering onto her argumentative bandwagon, although her tone of voice couldn't have been more polite. He was, he had discovered, beginning to know her.

'There's more to a hotel than foundations and planning permission. Let's just say that you're here to provide the female touch.'

'Which is what exactly?'

'You argue too much.'

'Only with you.' Their eyes tangled and Rose looked away hurriedly.

'I'll take that as a compliment. It's nice to know that I can fire you up.'

Rose ground her teeth together and Nick let out a loud laugh that drew stares from the passengers sitting closest to them. 'Think about the things that impressed you most about the hotel in London, think about how they could be incorporated into a small hotel sitting in the equatorial belt. It's going to need an almighty leap of the imagination, but you know what I want…' *I want you.* The thought weaved a path in his head and he greeted it without surprise. Maybe he had known all along that she was more than just a challenge or a novelty or a refreshing break from the type of women he usually enjoyed. He wanted her. Not just her mind, but her body. Nick lowered his eyes.

Every inch of him gave the impression of a man totally absorbed by what his companion was saying. She certainly seemed to have taken on board everything he had told her in the past about his plans, even things he had mentioned in passing. Now, enthused, she was eagerly discussing them and he made sure to contribute, but the flicker of his eyes was on her mouth, soft and pink, and her breasts, shadowy outlines under her cotton pinstriped shirt as she leant towards him, her hands articulating what she was saying. Something about sunken baths and a rainforest decor that would bring the environment right into the hotel.

'I did think about buying a guidebook,' she finished, 'but I wanted to be assaulted by the place without any preconceived ideas.'

'Yes. Good idea.' Nick smiled, setting her at ease. 'Right…now let's compare some of those preliminary costings…'

How could she ever have thought that a life devoid of change and adventure was a good one?

Here she was, sitting in the first-class compartment of a plane that would deliver her first to Kuala Lumpur and then onward to Kota Kinabalu, the state capital of Sabah, places she had never heard of in her life before. And, yes, it was exciting.

She looked at Nick surreptitiously from under her lashes and felt that familiar illicit thrill. He was sleeping, his body half inclined away from her so that all she could glimpse was his profile and the gentle rise and fall of his chest.

The seats in first class could be extended to full body length and, although she was as reclined as he was and the cabin was in darkness, she was finding it difficult to sleep.

For the first time, she could sort of understand how Tony and Flora had been affected by wanderlust. The unknown wasn't scary, as she had imagined. Or rather, she amended to herself, it was scary, but it was also full of possibilities.

The strongest possibility now was that she would remain wide awake for the remainder of the trip and then be fit for nothing when they eventually landed.

But she slept.

And the next few hours so completely removed her from everything that was familiar to her that Rose, delighted and disoriented, put herself firmly in Nick's care. Connections were made, passports were checked and she just looked around her open-mouthed, until finally they were on the last stage of their travel, quickly covering the two-and-a-half hour trip towards Kota Kinabalu.

Daylight was already fading by the time they were being delivered to their hotel, but it was still very, very hot.

'It's…not what I expected…'

'You can hardly keep your eyes open, Rose. As soon as we get to the hotel, you can climb into your bed and fall asleep. Don't try and appreciate the scenery now.'

'But how is it I feel sleepy and you don't?'

'I'm an experienced traveller.' He gave her an amused, mocking glance.

The taxi swung round a corner and there, following a long drive through manicured lawns, was the hotel. As she stepped out of the taxi she was aware of a thousand tiny night sounds.

'I'm aiming for something more eco-friendly than this,' Nick murmured into her ear. 'It's big but, in terms of comfort, you'll be hard pressed to better it. Now, I shall get us checked in and then you're going to go to your room and get some sleep.'

'I wish I'd read that guidebook after all.' She yawned ruefully.

'No need. Lee Peng knows this place like the back of his hand. A living guide is a damn sight better than someone else's interpretation of a place.'

'I feel awful leaving you to go to bed…don't think that I won't be pulling my weight…perhaps if I just freshen up a bit, I could join you and we could go over plans for tomorrow…'

Nick ignored her valiant protests and checked them in while Rose loitered behind him, savouring the glassy marble flooring and the cool, colonial elegance of the foyer. Were these the perks of working for a rich man? Everything done in style, with no expense spared.

She was shown to her quarters by one of the smiling porters and only when the door closed behind her did she realise how tired she really was.

She closed her eyes on a bedroom that was all ceiling fans and bamboo blinds and soft mosquito nets and rattan furniture, and a bathroom that she would have to devote some time to in the morning as she spied the sunken bath.

And awoke abruptly, it seemed like five minutes later, to the sound of tapping from behind the blinds she had hurriedly pulled down earlier.

When Rose looked at her watch, she saw to her horror that it was already eight-thirty. She had slept for nearly ten hours. And for the first time in weeks her internal alarm system had not woken her up at three in the morning for no better reason than to fill her head with thoughts she didn't want.

The tapping on the door galvanised her into action. It was probably the cleaning service making her feel like a lazy slob instead of the working woman she was supposed to be. She wasn't sure what room Nick was in, but she would have to get through to him immediately through the operator and assure him in her crispest voice that she would be ready to start work in fifteen minutes.

No need. Rose pulled up the exquisite bamboo blinds and there he was, standing outside what was, in fact, a glass door that she could now see led to a small wooden patio, along one side of which was a hammock, next to a couple of chairs and a small table, all perfect for relaxing outside and gazing at the scenery. In this case, lush lawns liberally interspersed with coconut trees, which led down to a beach. To the left, she could glimpse the pool, just a slash of bright blue surrounded by turquoise umbrellas and yet more coconut trees in between.

But she took all this in in literally a couple of seconds.

As she had discovered, nothing could compete for her attention when Nick was in the vicinity.

'It's you.' Where was her crisp voice when she needed it? Suddenly conscious of the fact that she was still in just her nightie and the thin bathrobe she had flung on before leaping towards the door in a surge of guilt for having overslept, Rose folded her arms and tried to look composed.

'Who did you think it was going to be?'

'The cleaning service. I…I…was actually just about to phone through to you and let you know that I'll be ready to start work shortly.'

'No need to phone.' Nick gave a slight inclination of his head. 'I'm in the cabin next to yours. In fact, if you go around that flimsy wooden lattice partition, you'll be at my glass door…' He had seen her in many guises, from angry to embarrassed to primly correct, but he had never seen her like this, flushed from sleep, her skin satin-smooth, hair tousled.

Nick made no apologies to himself for wanting her. He had

recognised that kick of desire and his sole objective now was to sate it. Had she been his full-time employee, he would have done his damnedest to shut the door firmly on all thoughts of seduction, but fortunately she wasn't.

Rose tried not to look horrified at this piece of information. 'I'm sure that won't be necessary. If you want to give me fifteen minutes, Nick, I'll join you in the foyer.'

'No need to be so formal.' He leaned against the frame of the sliding patio door. 'I've ordered breakfast to be brought to my room for both of us. When you're ready, just skip across. Continental all right for you? Oh, and I thought we might as well appreciate the surroundings today. Enjoy the beach, see what the poolside facilities are…we can start in earnest tomorrow when Lee's back from KL.'

Several things he had just said converged to send her into a state of mild panic. Sharing breakfast. In his room. Enjoying the facilities.

Rose cleared her throat, wondering how she could pick her way through her objections and emerge on the other side without appearing to overreact, but he was already turning away, only glancing back to give her a nonchalant wave.

She had brought no clothes to cover breakfast with her sexy boss in his room. He had been wearing a pair of khaki Bermuda shorts and a collared tee shirt. In between the confusion of what he had been saying to her, she had managed to notice the elegant, casual ease with which he pulled off an outfit that most men would have looked frightful in.

Rose rummaged through her bags at the speed of light and tried to block out the image of his legs, bronzed and muscular, sprinkled with dark hair.

Was he hairy all over? she wondered feverishly.

Yet another thought to try and dispel as she flung on a

baggy tee shirt, all the better to hide her figure, and a pair of trousers that would probably reduce her to a puddle of perspiration by the middle of the day but which would have to do. At least until she gained a little colour and her confidence grew.

She arrived, flustered, to find him sitting on his veranda sipping a cup of coffee, legs stretched out on one of the chairs, leaving her to sit closer to him than she had bargained for.

'Gorgeous, isn't it?' was the first thing he said as she sat down and poured herself some orange juice. She could feel her heart beating madly in her chest.

'Stunning.'

He slid his eyes over to where she was staring pointedly away from him and across to the pool area. 'You really shouldn't wear trousers, Rose. Too hot.'

'I…I haven't unpacked as yet. I just grabbed these from the top of the suitcase.'

'Well, no matter. I suggest we take to the beach after this so you'll have to change into a swimsuit anyway. We can get whatever beach towels we need from Reception.' Nick relished the thought of seeing her in a swimsuit. It was hard to get any idea of her shape under the loose-fitting clothes she seemed to favour and he fancied she was more curvy than the magazines currently deemed fashionable.

'But aren't we here to…work?' Rose asked desperately. She crumbled a croissant in half as he did the same and tried to focus nonchalantly on the fact that he would have seen thousands of women in swimsuits. He wouldn't look twice at her.

'Lateral thinking.' Nick demolished one half of his croissant in a single bite and wiped his mouth with his serviette. The breeze was light and warm and very, very inviting. Yes, work was on the agenda, but he had to admit to himself that he felt very relaxed, more relaxed than he had in years.

'Lateral thinking,' Rose repeated and he nodded sagely at her.

'We have a few possible locations to have a look at and we'll do that tomorrow with Lee, but basically the rest of the time here will be…investigative work…'

'I thought we had meetings lined up. Don't we have to go over plans with your architects? What about the buildings inspector?' She had envisaged days packed with meetings and the gritty business of getting the ball rolling on foreign soil. Of course, they might share the occasional meal together, but on the hop so to speak. And he knew people in the area. Evenings, she had reckoned, he would spend with them, catching up on old times. It was what any normal human being would do.

Investigative work did not fit into her overall picture of their ten days on the island.

'There's a hell of a lot to see here. Coffee? Another croissant? Yes, as I was saying, there's a lot to see.' He relaxed back and clasped his hands together behind his head. 'Did you know, for example, that Borneo is the world's third largest island? That Sabah, the proposed site for my venture, has some of the oldest rainforests in the world? Oh, yes. There's a lot more to this place than the beach you see down there…and naturally, we have to check it all out so that we can decide where the ideal location would be. Beach or forest? Should we cater for the lazy traveller or the adventurous one? One person may be content to sit in the sun by a pool or stroll down to the beach and while away the day in a deckchair with a constant supply of cocktails on tap. Another may want to trek through the jungle in search of an orang-utan or two. Did you know that over here the orang-utan is known as the "wild man of Borneo"?'

'We're going to see orang-utans?'

'Not until we've checked out that pool and, of course, the beach.' He stood up and stretched, then stuck his hands in his pockets and stared out towards the sea. 'Fascinating place this…where else can you find rainforests and white beaches sharing the same space? You'll see for yourself, but all in good time. For now…' he nodded towards the beach '…a lazy day checking out the competition.'

And sitting in front of a lukewarm cup of coffee and a half-eaten croissant was no longer an option. It was a glorious day, the sun was hot and she had absolutely no excuse to wriggle out of a swim in the sea.

Anyway, Nick's suggestions were often thinly veiled commands. And she was being paid generously by him. Some might well say that being paid to swim in the clear South China Sea was a pretty good deal.

Rose wasn't precisely thinking along those lines as she flung clothes hurriedly into drawers while deciding which of her three black swimsuits she would wear. She was thinking that there was safety in nursing her attraction under the respectable cloak of their professional relationship. Even if that professional relationship was a little more unorthodox than most. Indeed, the fact that she worked for him in his house probably accounted for her inconvenient attraction. Made sense. After all, she had previously felt exactly the opposite sentiment before she had found herself cooped up under his roof.

She had a brief feeling of triumph, as though she had managed to solve a complex maths problem.

Then she looked at herself in the long standing mirror by the wall. As swimsuits went, this one was modest. But yet there was cleavage to be seen, far too much for her liking, and legs and shoulders and the generous proportions that always made her want to cringe…

And on a beach…with his body on display…not just snatched glimpses of bare chest where the top two buttons of his shirt were undone…where was her protection going to be?

CHAPTER SIX

THE beach was uncrowded. Too early, Rose guessed, for most of the guests. The same large canopied umbrellas that adorned the sides of the pool were in evidence along the beach, dotted here and there, and closer to the glassy, lake-like sea similar-coloured padded deckchairs were interspersed. Further along, she could see that a thin finger of land projected into the sea and from a distance might have passed for a jetty were it not for the coconut trees growing along it.

It was a breathtaking sight. Really a vision of paradise, from the white powdery sand dappled with shadows cast by the overhanging coconut trees, to the still, dazzling azure of the sea.

Rose paused and savoured the scene through the protective lenses of her very dark sunglasses. She had decided to maintain her inclination to conceal her shape by wearing a knee-length, flimsy beach dress and she could already feel the rising sun burning through it.

Along the beach, a couple of the deckchairs were occupied by early risers who were mostly reading and wearing sensible large straw hats.

Typically, Nick was nowhere to be seen and Rose was

peering into the distance when she felt a hand on her shoulder and he said, with a thread of amusement in his voice, 'Why are you wearing a sheet?'

Rose swung around and glared at him from behind her sunglasses. 'I'm trying to protect myself from the sun,' she snapped. 'It's fine for you. You can tan easily but I'm a lot fairer. In fact, coming out into the sun at this hour is not a very good idea at all for someone of my complexion.'

Which, she admitted to herself, was something of a slight overstatement given it was still quite early in the day.

He, of course, was bare-backed but for the towel swung casually over his shoulders. As promised, he had brought hers with him and he reached out to give it to her, still grinning.

'You should have brought a sombrero with you…like those practical people further along.'

Rose snatched the towel and began walking away, but slowed down at the notion that he might be sniggering as he watched her wobbly, none-too-toned rear.

She took heart from the comforting thought that this was not a holiday, this was work.

They seemed to be walking away from the scattering of people on the beach and she immediately set that particular situation right by heading towards one of the lounging chairs not far from an elderly lady who was napping with her book over her face.

'Are you going to remove that garment of yours? Because I warn you—the sun here is very hot. Much hotter than in England.'

'I've brought a notebook. I thought we might start jotting down a few things in connection with work.' She felt pleasantly secure behind the sunglasses and half watched as he spread his towel on the sand, ignoring the sun lounger, and lay flat on it. As if that weren't distracting enough, he began to rub sun cream haphazardly over his body.

'Even I burn,' he assured her. He could feel her watching him. She did that. Watched him. Nick was used to women watching him, but the concealed way she did it had become a powerful turn-on. He wanted her, but he wasn't going to get her through outrageous flirting or expensive gifts. He settled back, closed his eyes and waited for the prolonged silence to have the desired effect.

Eventually, Rose spoke, keeping her treacherous eyes away from the tempting sight of his practically naked, bronzed body. 'What made you decide to go into…well…hotels?'

'You sound like an interviewer.'

'It's only polite curiosity,' Rose said. 'Everyone has a reason for doing what they do.'

'And you went into computing because…?'

'We're not discussing me.' The sun was beginning to make her feel lazy and peaceful. She didn't want an argument. She wanted to close her eyes and let her chattering thoughts slip away. 'I bet you don't even stay in many hotels.'

'On the contrary. I'm rarely out of them.'

'I meant for pleasure as opposed to business.' She glanced down at him and realised that he was barely listening to her. His eyes were closed and she was pretty sure that his thoughts were a million miles away. She carefully inched the flimsy beach robe off and began applying a generous layer of sunblock to her exposed skin, keeping a careful eye on him because lying flat she felt a whole lot more confident about her body than when she was sitting up, where her stomach, smooth as it might be, still seemed to have the last laugh at her for having spent years guiltily avoiding the gym.

Or maybe she was simply comparing herself to Lily who

had a washboard abdomen even when she was slouching and breathing out.

Job done, Rose lay back down and shaded her face with the magazine she had brought from her room.

'Hotels for pleasure…hmm…well, maybe it's the pull of the challenge, to boldly embark on a project of which I have zero experience. There's nothing like the possibility of failure to get the adrenaline going.'

She was aware that he had half turned towards her and she kept her eyes firmly shielded behind her magazine.

'I've conquered the money markets,' Nick said casually. 'Or rather, I've made enough money to live comfortably for the rest of my life, even if I decided never to lift a finger again. Very comfortably. What does a man do when he reaches that position?'

'Retire and enjoy what life has to offer,' Rose said, surprised. 'But then, who would you enjoy it with?'

Nick sat up and lifted the magazine from her face, which immediately brought her shooting up so that they were staring at each other fully.

'Sorry,' she mumbled. 'That remark just sort of slipped out.'

'Working with computers, Rose, might not have been the best career move for you.'

'Meaning?'

'Meaning you have no tact.' Nick would have left any other woman in no doubt that overstepping the boundaries was tantamount to a still-born relationship. However there was, he reminded himself, no relationship with this woman and, anyway, she was already bristling. Of course, he wasn't about to back down and allow a woman, any woman, to invade his private space, but was he really ready for a fight? When the sun was beating down on his back and the sea glimmered invitingly?

'You mean that sometimes I don't agree with you.'

'I'm going for a swim.' Nick stood up, a profile of one-hundred-per-cent masculine beauty, and glanced back over his shoulder to her. 'Coming?'

'I think I'll just stay here, thanks, and carry on sunbathing,' Rose flounced back onto her lounger and stuck the magazine back into position.

The notebook that she had packed to remind herself that work was the reason for her lazing on a lounger on a beach remained unopened in her bag. She had a moment of brief despair as she contemplated the remainder of their stay, then she turned her thoughts to his high-handed attitude, telling her she was lacking tact. It felt a lot better to fulminate.

By the time she had worked herself up some healthy self-righteous anger, the sun was beginning its ascent and pleasantly warm was turning into baking hot.

Rose reluctantly shelved her thoughts, sat up and glanced at her watch to discover, with shock, that Nick had now been swimming for over forty minutes, and when she peered towards the horizon, there was no sign of him.

Panic slammed into her and she shot to her feet and hurried down to the water line, shielding her eyes from the glare of the sun. The beach was more crowded now, although still relatively deserted. People were in the water. A quick glance told her that Nick was not among their number.

She obeyed her instinct and forged into the sea, which was so warm that her body barely needed to adjust to the temperature.

The one continuity in her life had been her swimming lessons. Tony and Flora had nurtured a vague, hippie-like notion that swimming was akin to being at one with nature, and, with that in mind, they had insisted on swimming lessons wherever they had happened to be. The Education of Life was more important than the education of the classroom, but swimming was something they had insisted upon. And Rose had enjoyed it so much that she had continued even when classes had no longer been necessary and long after Lily had packed it in because it ruined her hair. Rose, never one to spend time agonising over the state of her hair, had found the silence and privacy of swimming a soothing balm to a tumultuous adolescence.

Feeling the water on her was like coming home.

As she struck out she wondered whether she should have run further up the beach in search of a lifeguard, but the thought of creating a scene, probably for no reason, was off-putting, never mind Nick's reaction if he returned from a simple swim to find the hotel's rescue party hot on his trail.

Anyway, it was too late to think about that.

She was pretty sure she would spot him a little further out, and then she could slink back to shore, safe in the knowledge that he was all right.

She swam confidently out but then, when the beach was beginning to look a little too distant for the sake of comfort, she felt the slow crawl of fear through her because who knew what inhabited the waters? They looked crystal-clear and perfectly innocent, but anything could be lurking in the depths. What if he had been sucked under by something? Were box jelly-fish rampant in these waters or was she mixing up her oceans?

That thought was enough to convince her that heading back to shore and summoning the search party was the best course of action.

She was hardly aware of the shape quickly gaining on her until she felt something on her waist and she spluttered in sharp, sudden panic to a stop.

'Were you worried?' Nick was laughing as he edged back from her.

Relief turned to anger and she glared at him, tempted to hit him smartly on his sexy, grinning face, but her training kicked in. Any kind of tussle in water was a bad idea.

'I was hot,' she snarled, turning away and beginning to strike out back for land.

He caught her again, this time by her ankle, and she spun around and began treading water. 'In case you don't know,' she snapped, 'it's dangerous to fight in the water.'

'Who's fighting?' He flicked his head in the direction of the promontory she had noticed earlier on. 'In case you were wondering how come you couldn't find me…I was on that strip of land. I saw you swimming out and decided to meet you.'

'Just in case I ran into problems?'

'Can't have my employee drowning on my watch, can I?'

'I happen to be a very strong swimmer.'

'I noticed.'

Rose wasn't sure that she liked the thought of him looking at her while she had been swimming.

'So…joining me? We could always swim back to shore and walk across, but better exercise this way.'

She didn't think he needed the exercise. Unlike her. But she was enjoying the water and she suddenly wanted to prove just how good a swimmer she was. She nodded and then headed strongly away towards the strip of land, invigorated as he swam up behind her, then alongside and finally in front, easily making it to land before her so that she found herself coming out of the water, dripping wet, with no protective outer layer of baggy clothing, while he sat on the sand and surveyed her at his leisure.

Self-consciousness kicked in along with all the insecurities she had always had about her body, ones which should have been put to bed a long time ago because, really, what did looks matter?

Everything about her was unfashionably big. Her breasts were not the pert, small bumps beloved by fashionistas, her hair was too uncontrollable, her frame was just too short and stocky and she was sure that her rear could have done with several thousand more trips to the local swimming pool.

And there he was. A study in casual male beauty, sitting lazily on the trunk of a fallen coconut tree.

Her modest swimsuit suddenly felt like a handkerchief tied together with a few bits of string and Rose wrapped her arms around her body in a show of feeling cold.

'I really never thought that this would be part of a working trip over here,' she said crossly, all too aware that he was sizing her up and finding her wanting in every department.

She had, he noticed, made sure to sit as far away from him as was humanly possible without it looking glaringly obvious. Coy, he thought, not for the first time, was not a word in her vocabulary. Neither were the words flirting or teasing. If she had had her notebook to hand, he was pretty certain that she would have brandished it just to make sure that he got her hands-off message.

Once upon a time, he might have been amused by that because his hands would not have wanted to be on her, but not so now.

Next to her, the women he had dated in the past were stick insects, devoid of personality and sex appeal. He wanted to tell her that instead of huddling next to him, arms wrapped around her body in an attempt to hide the glorious abundance of her body, she should revel in her womanly curves.

However he acknowledged that she would probably hit

him if he did that, so he dragged his eyes reluctantly away from her and resigned himself to the prospect of a slow seduction via harmless small talk, not a route he had ever favoured.

'What do you think of this spot?'

Rose inwardly breathed a sigh of relief. She had been half expecting something sarcastic along the lines of her resemblance to a beached whale. Scenery, she figured, she could expound upon, and she did, asking him a million questions about Borneo. Whenever there appeared to be a pause in the conversation, in she jumped to carry on the subject while the sun continued to rise in the sky. Eventually, Nick turned to her and raised his eyebrows.

'So, do you think we have exhausted the tourist angle?'

'I'm interested.'

'You're sunburnt.'

'What?' Rose automatically raised her hands to her face, allowing Nick a bird's-eye view of her luscious breasts, which her severely cut swimsuit was having a hard time concealing.

'Right there.' He ran his finger quickly along the strip of her nose and Rose pulled back with a little yelp of shock. 'We need to get you back to our towels and bags.'

'Oh, no. I've only just thought—were they safe being left on the beach?'

'As houses.' Nick stood up and held out his hand for her to take.

Flustered, Rose grasped it and he pulled her neatly to her feet, covertly watching her breasts bounce as she gathered her balance. Since when, he wondered, had he become a dirty old man, covertly watching a woman's body and getting turned on?

'You never did tell me...' Rose said as they strolled back towards their possessions, which, as he had predicted, were exactly where they had been left.

'What?' Nick enquired, staring straight ahead of him and trying to subdue his overactive imagination.

'Why you chose to branch out into the hotel business. You said that you no longer felt challenged by making money, but why hotels?'

'You mean considering I'm a sad and lonely old man still searching for the perfect woman?'

'I never said you were sad and lonely,' Rose objected, flushing.

'Just someone who had no experience of staying in a hotel for fun, an all-work-and-no-play kind of guy…'

'I'm sure you have lots of fun,' Rose stumbled, wondering how they had managed to swim out of safe waters into the perilous seas of personal conversation. It wouldn't bother him, she was certain, but it bothered her.

'Had,' Nick amended guilelessly. 'I haven't actually been out with a woman since I met your sister…'

For a few seconds Rose felt completely disoriented by that admission. He had told her that his relationship with Lily had been platonic and she had believed him. She hadn't stopped to wonder whether that had not been of his choosing and, at the thought that he might actually fancy her sister, she felt a sudden coldness in the pit of her stomach.

'Lily has been known to have that effect on men,' she said brightly, clearing her throat.

'What effect is that?'

Rose shrugged. 'Being worshipped from afar.'

'Whoever mentioned anything about worshipping her from afar?' Nick asked incredulously. 'I meant, my darling, that the night I met your sister happened to be the night I broke up with a woman and ever since then I've stayed away from the fair sex. All men need a break from complications.'

Had he just called her 'my darling'? Well, yes, not as an endearment, but for a few wild seconds her heart soared, then she registered the rest of his sentence and realised that, for whatever reason, he had decided to fill her in on a slice of his private life. He was practising celibacy.

'They do,' Rose said approvingly. 'And it's a mistake to think that sex is the answer to everything.'

Nick felt a kick of satisfaction that he had manoeuvred the conversation exactly where he wanted it. Sex. Such a small word to cover such a massive subject and, with testosterone coursing through his body, he was in the perfect mood to talk about it.

'But that's not why we're here, is it?' Rose hastened on. 'We're here to do some groundwork for your project. It doesn't matter why you wanted to go into the hotel business. That's your private matter and I know you'll agree that we shouldn't let chit-chat about our private lives intrude on the reason why we're here in the first place.' Rose felt quite proud of the adult manner in which she had grounded their wayward conversation.

One step forward, two steps backward. Nick ground his teeth together in frustration.

'Would you like me to make a list of the usual tourist sites?' Her beach dress beckoned like manna from heaven and Rose gratefully snatched it up and slipped it over her head.

'That won't be necessary, Rose.' Interesting, this feeling of having the rug pulled very swiftly out from under your feet. Interesting and not particularly agreeable. 'I suggest we use the rest of the day to do a bit of sightseeing.'

Rainforests…mountains and waterfalls…rare flora and fauna…the world-famous orang-utan sanctuary… Then a flurry of meetings and, of course, Lee Peng and his family with their abundant hospitality…supper to meet family and friends…

There was hardly time to draw breath and no time at all with Rose. Just that one morning on the beach, which, after nearly five days, seemed like a lifetime ago.

Nick had never met a woman more adroit at standing a mere five feet away from him and yet scrupulously avoiding his company. She was awash with good ideas, all faithfully detailed in her ever-present notebook and all related with an air of earnest professionalism, whenever she happened to find herself alone with him. Nightcaps at the hotel were politely but firmly rejected, with convincing yawns to back up her claims that the heat made her tired. Breakfast was always sent to her room because, and this she had told him with an apologetic smile, she liked to use the time to multitask. Eat and communicate with her friends back home via email.

With increasing frustration, Nick realised that he was gradually being reduced to the level of a schoolboy, unable to stop sneaking looks at her in her tee shirts and shorts and then fantasising about her late at night when he lay in bed staring at the ceiling and telling himself that he was behaving like a lunatic.

He could have anyone and yet when he tried to think of the many women he could have, he found his thoughts blurring and finally there she was, in his head yet again.

And here he was now. Facing another night of frustration because Rose had retired early, this time claiming the perennial headache excuse.

He looked at his watch and discovered that it was after midnight. One fifteen, to be precise, and he considered his options. Remain in bed, scowling into the darkness, or else get up and at least solve one of his problems by having a very cold shower.

He slid out from under the covers and felt the pleasantly

cool touch of tiles under his bare feet. Overhead, the fan whirred rhythmically, drowning out the little noises of night creatures outside. The prospect of a cold shower was about as appealing as the thought of switching on his computer and catching up on work, which was usually his routine when he couldn't sleep.

Nick moved quietly, without bothering to switch the lights on, and stuck on some drawstring cotton trousers, which were the closest thing to pyjama bottoms he possessed.

Making very little noise, he opened the sliding door that led onto his private veranda, from which the landscaped gardens stretched before him as a series of darkened shapes.

Borneo was proving to be a marvel of surprises. Few places, he thought, could provide such a winning combination of white sandy beaches, blue, calm sea and the spectacle that was the wonder of the rainforest.

Out of the corner of his eye, he saw something move. It was just a flicker behind the trellis separating his veranda from his neighbour's. In this instance, Rose. Normally, the leafy fronds clambering over the wooden trellis acted as a very successful screen, but in the inky blackness of the night whatever she was wearing must have been of a light colour.

Nick felt a rush of adrenaline surge through him. Without pausing to think, just acting with the unerring instincts of the predator, he circled the patch of lawn and appeared in front of her, bare backed because the night was balmy but, other than that, decently clad, if lacking shoes.

'Well, well, well,' he drawled, 'come here often?' He sprinted up the two wooden steps, not giving her time to beat a hasty retreat.

Whatever she was wearing, it was obvious she had not dressed for an accidental meeting with her boss. Her nightie was ultra thin and barely skirted her thighs. The light trick-ling from the room behind her was her cruellest enemy because it showed the full, rounded outline of her bare breasts. With a little leap of the imagination, Nick could almost see the shape of her nipples.

Rose looked at him in horror. 'What the hell do you think you're doing here?' she demanded, too shocked by his sudden appearance to even think of what she was wearing.

'Same as you. Couldn't sleep.' Ever one to take full advan-tage of the opportunities presented to him, Nick sat on the chair next to her and grinned. 'I know why I couldn't sleep, but what about you?'

Rose was literally lost for words. Never in a million years had she expected this. She could have wept with frustration because she had done so well over the past few days. She had behaved with impeccable and detached politeness and point-edly ignored him whenever she could get away with it, and when she couldn't she had fallen back on talking about work. Yes, it was an ordeal, but at least the nights were hers. And now… How dared he invade her down time? Behaving for all the world as though he had every right?

'I think you should go,' Rose said coldly, rising to her feet. She snatched up the glass of water she had brought outside with her and spun round on her heel.

'Not so fast.'

Before she knew it, he was standing in front of her, his hand biting into her arm.

'What are you doing? Let me go.'

'Tell me why you're running away from me.'

'I am not running away from you.' If only she could sound a bit more convincing, but her voice was a high whisper and, Lord, her legs were like jelly.

'You mean you've suddenly and coincidentally realised that you're very tired and need to go to bed immediately?'

'I mean…' She took a deep breath to steady herself. This situation felt so intimate. Just the two of them, eyes locked, while the rest of the world slept. His semi nudity was an affront to all her senses, filling her up until it seemed to be the only thing she could see even though she was making every effort not to. 'I mean that this is my private time and I don't want you in it. I may work for you, Nick, but when I'm in my own quarters I don't really expect you to barge in as though you own the place.'

'Hardly barging in. I saw you through the trellis and, as neither of us could sleep, I figured I might as well pop over, make sure you were okay.'

'I'm fine.'

'You don't look fine. You're shaking. Are you cold? You're wearing next to nothing.'

'I'm wearing more than you.'

Nick gave her a rueful smile. 'Apologies, but like you I didn't expect company at one thirty in the morning. It was either this or nothing.'

Rose gulped.

'I don't possess pyjamas.'

'Everyone possesses pyjamas.'

'I challenge you to rifle through my belongings.'

'I beg your pardon?'

'Let's go inside. We wouldn't want the neighbours talking, would we?' There was no chance of that. The hotel was cleverly designed to ensure that guests had almost total privacy, with only the double cabanas sharing the same veranda split by leafy trellises. Nick took advantage of her momentary lapse in concentration to walk into her rooms, which were identical to his with only variations in some of the decor to differentiate the two.

She was as neat as he had expected her to be. The little sitting area was tidy, unlike his, which always bore the signs of work in progress. She had only switched on the side light by the sofa and he preferred to leave it that way.

Looking at her, he could tell that she was on the verge of imploding and it had obviously hit home that she was in a very transparent item of clothing because her arms were once more protectively around her as she hovered by the door. Wondering, no doubt, what tactic she could employ to chuck him out.

Well, he had waited for days in a state of frustration. He wasn't going to blow this chance. He wanted her and he knew that all he needed to do was smash through her veneer of polite aloofness and she would be his because she wanted him too. The air between them had sizzled ever since they had arrived on the island. He intended to douse it.

'It's mad to be up at this hour.' Rose laughed nervously, keeping her distance. 'We'll be fit for nothing in the morning and we've another busy day ahead.'

Nick strolled lazily towards her until he was standing right in front of her. In the muted light, breathtakingly sexy and very, very dangerous. Every alarm bell in her head was clamouring, but there was still a part of her that scoffed at the notion that there might be anything to be afraid of. After all, what was he going to do? A man like that? Kiss her? Men like that, she knew, made passes at girls like her sister. They didn't look at her twice and if her heart was beating like a hammer, it was simply because she was scared of her own reaction to *him*, scared of him getting physically any closer just in case her legs gave way and she did something undignified like swoon.

'Sometimes mad can be fun,' Nick mused. 'Have you never done anything mad in your life, Rose?'

'No.' Rose laughed, this time a little hysterically. 'No—' she cleared her throat and tried to get a grip '—mad really isn't me.'

'How do you know if you've never tried?'

She had managed to somehow find herself with her back to the wall, which turned out to be not a very good idea as he now laid his hands on either side of her so that she seemed to be surrounded by him, locked in and deprived, if not literally of oxygen, then certainly of the ability to think coherently.

'Here we are, Rose…on one of the most stunningly beautiful islands in the world. Outside, the night is like black velvet and in here…well, just the two of us… Shall I tell you what my mad thought is?'

No! Her head screamed. 'What?'

'This…' Nick leant into her. She felt his hand cradle the back of her neck and she almost couldn't believe what was happening even as her skin burned where he touched her.

'No…' she protested in a pathetically weak little voice and Nick half smiled, already hearing her submission and knowing, in that instant, that his suspicions had been right: she wanted him just as much as he wanted her. His body reared up with a sudden, savage heat that shocked him, and he brought his mouth down to hers, turned on by her small whimper as she parted her lips and closed her eyes.

Rose pressed her hands against his chest and felt the hard bunch of his muscles under the flat of her hand. Yes, of course she should push him away. That was a given.

She ran her hands over his chest, contouring the outline of his flat brown nipples, and moaned softly under her breath while his mouth continued to devour hers, catapulting common sense into orbit.

When she finally surfaced sufficiently to draw breath and speak, she did manage a weak protest, but her breasts, pressed against him, were aching and sensitive. Weeks of yearning left her helpless. The feel of him was like a miracle of revelation.

What had she ever done before? Had safe relationships and not even very many of them. She had chosen boyfriends on all the right grounds: compatibility, kindness, friendship.

This man was neither compatible, kind nor her friend and, even if she weren't sharp enough to have sussed that for herself, his background spoke volumes. A life strewn with women who had stepped off the front covers of magazines, dismissive of commitment, driven but for reasons she had never valued.

Nick drew back and looked down at her. 'One last chance,' he said thickly.

'For what?' She knew exactly what he was talking about.

'For decision-making. When morning comes, I don't want to be accused of taking advantage of you.'

'I would never do that.'

'You misunderstand. We both go to your bedroom with our eyes wide open or tell me now to leave.' And what would he do? Nick thought. Have another cold shower? Go for a swim in the sea? Switch on his computer and hope that numbers, reports and figures would distract him from the thought of her separated by the thickness of a wall?

He had never been in this position before, at the mercy of a woman, and he had to restrain himself from the indignity of trying to persuade her into the decision he wanted her to make.

Rose felt his body hard against hers. What choice did she have? Common sense was a plane-flight away. For now…it was time to be mad.

CHAPTER SEVEN

THIS was as overwhelming as the first fantasies of a teenage boy, although Nick was careful not to mention that to Rose. His body didn't fail to remind him of the fact, though, as he led her into the bedroom and onto the wide, king-sized bed, still rumpled from where she had been lying, with a gap in the mosquito net through which she had slipped out, presumably on her way to the veranda.

His loose cotton trousers couldn't begin to hide the urgency of his erection, but he was going to take his time, make love to her slowly and thoroughly.

'Are you sure about this?' He parted the mosquito net and looked to where she was sitting primly on the side of the bed.

'Yes, you're right. Everyone needs a little madness in their lives now and again.'

'In which case, why do you look scared to death?'

Rose flushed and looked away quickly. 'Do I?'

Nick, on the verge of slipping off the trousers, hesitated and then joined her on the bed, pulling the mosquito net behind him so that they were now enclosed in a little cocoon of their own. He might have, in the past, made the usual traditionally romantic gestures, sent the flowers, bought the expensive meals and the expensive tokens to go with the meals, but he was not essentially a romantic man. This, however, felt romantic and she looked the part. Eyes wide, mouth parted, hands clutching at the transparent nightgown.

'You do,' he said solemnly. 'What are you afraid of? Haven't we both established that we...want the same thing?' He reached out with one hand and trailed his finger along her jaw line, then down to where her fingers were closed tightly around the shimmering, light material. 'You needn't worry. I'll be gentle.' Just talking about it was sending his normally cool, controlled nervous system through the roof.

'You don't understand...'

'You're not a virgin, are you?'

'Of course not,' Rose said indignantly, although she was guiltily aware that she really only managed to sneak into the experienced category by the skin of her teeth.

'Care to tell me about them?'

'No.'

Nick laughed. 'No need to look so shocked, Rose.'

'I suppose you do...this sort of thing all the time, don't you?'

'Sleep with women? I'm a red blooded male, Rose.'

'No, I mean... Look, what I'm trying to say is that I'm not very daring in bed, Nick.' Rose cleared her throat and looked at him defiantly. 'You can go ahead and laugh now, but that's the way it is. I haven't spent a lifetime hopping in and out of beds with men.'

'I like that,' Nick murmured. Surprisingly, he really did, although he couldn't say that he had encountered the situation before. Some of the women he had slept with were bolder than he was.

'Furthermore...'

'Furthermore?' He couldn't help himself. He leant towards her and planted a kiss on the side of her neck and he felt her shiver against him.

'I…you're not…' She wished he wouldn't look at her like that, giving her his undivided attention. 'You're…not the sort of guy…I mean, Lily normally…well, girls like Lily…'

'I'm flattered that you have such a high opinion of me.'

'I'm just talking about the way you look.'

'That's better. A bit of Rose rage.' He grinned and she smiled sheepishly back at him. 'You're beautiful, Rose.'

'Oh, please. There's no need for that, Nick.'

'Stop running yourself down,' Nick said forcefully. He gently took her fingers in his hand and unpeeled them from their stranglehold on her nightgown. Then he pushed her back onto the bed, where she fell, breathing thickly, her hair splayed out in unruly curls around her face.

What had he ever seen in those stick insects with their angular bodies and bony limbs?

He slowly pulled her nightgown over her head and there she was, in all her fulsome, voluptuous, sensual splendour. For a few seconds, Nick feasted his eyes on her and Rose looked back at him from under her lashes. Watching me, watching you, she thought, getting so turned on that she thought she might explode at any minute.

All doubts that he might have found her less attractive than the models he cavorted with were driven out of her head by the naked appreciation in his eyes.

And that did something to her. Like a dam being un-blocked, every inhibition she had ever nursed about the shape of her body flowed away in a rush of wild, abandoned passion.

Nick, watching, sensed the change of mood, something in the sinuous way she moved under his raking eyes, and with a low groan he bent his head so that he could nuzzle her generous breasts.

These weren't small tomatoes, they were heavy, ripe fruit with big, defined nipples that hardened as he lavished his attention on them, suckling and feeling her wriggle underneath him in instant response.

Her skin was as smooth as satin and felt just as he had anticipated it would. Soft and womanly.

He dragged himself reluctantly away from her glorious breasts so that he could kiss her, long, slow kisses, punctuated by her soft moans.

'Touch me again,' she whispered.

'Where?'

'Where you were before…' Never had it felt so good to have her breasts touched. Having spent a life time being self-conscious about the size of them, she felt wildly liberated at Nick's obvious delight.

'Enjoyed that, did you?' he murmured, licking the side of her neck. 'My mouth all over your breasts…your spectacular breasts… I've never seen such succulent, big nipples before.'

Rose was shocked by the sexuality of his language and turned on at the same time. His voice was dark and velvety and caressing and the way he moved against her… He was as turned on as she was, of that there was no doubt.

She reached down to touch him, but he covered her hand with his.

'Not yet, my darling. I have to take things at my pace or else I might end up letting us both down.'

'I don't understand.'

'I'm so turned on for you, I have to take things slowly.'

Rose smiled, understanding, and was filled with a sense of heady power that she could have this effect on this man.

She sighed as he massaged her breasts, lifting them to his mouth so that he could continue lathering them with his tongue, taking the nipples into his mouth and teasing the throbbing buds with his teeth. Wantonly, she arched up, thrusting herself towards him and moaning loudly as he ravaged her sensitive breasts.

She curled her fingers into his hair and half opened her eyes, following his progress down and then, as he parted her moistened labia, she fell back feverishly, hardly able to believe that she was allowing such an intimate exploration of her body.

She barely knew what to expect. Her knowledge of foreplay was limited and so her body was shameless and involuntary in its arousal.

As he flicked his tongue along the delicate pink flesh, and then deeper, sliding and rubbing her most feminine area, Rose felt herself spiralling into orbit. She writhed against his exquisite invasion and knew that she lacked the will-power and fierce control not to be tipped over the edge.

With a little tug, she pulled Nick up and he laughed softly, but obediently stopped his relentless assault that threatened to send her spinning out of control.

'That was…' Rose heard her own voice and barely recognised it. It was husky and breathless.

'Mind-blowing?'

Before she could find a suitable answer, he parted her legs with his muscular thigh. 'Now let me really blow your mind,' he murmured.

It was one deep thrust. She would never have imagined that such a powerful and impressive member could enter her with such effortless ease to fill her up. He began moving inside her, slow, hard, rhythmic and he seemed to know exactly how her body worked because every time she felt herself reaching the inevitable, shattering climax, he would ease his tempo, allowing her to come back down so that he could remorselessly take her back up again.

Somewhere along the line, she was too lost in a world of sensation to really know when, he flipped them over so that she was lying on top of him, with his hands on her buttocks and her breasts dangling down, their swollen nipples perfect targets for his eager mouth.

There was no part of her body that wasn't aroused. Bliss to feel him in her even while his mouth was avidly on her.

Bliss, even, afterwards, as she eased herself off him, wonderfully fulfilled, like the cat with a very full bowl of cream.

Yes, of course, the reality of the situation was only a thought away, but she was being mad, wasn't she? Taking chances for the first time in her life? And it felt good.

'We should get some sleep now,' Rose said regretfully, 'or else we'll be like zombies in the morning.' This was like a dream, lying here, curled into him and everything making sense because she loved him, against her will. Piercing through the dream, however, was the sure and certain knowledge that there was no way she could let him know that. Unrequited love was only bearable if it remained a secret.

But…

Rose hugged this thought to herself…what if he fell in love with her? Against all odds?

Sure, she wasn't his type of woman, at least not in the expected sense, but he was seriously attracted to her, wasn't he? And he did like her, didn't he? Put those two things together and there it was, like a root beginning to take hold in the soil, the notion that in the days remaining to them she might just discover that her love stood a chance after all.

Having fought for a life that contained no nasty shocks and

hence no surprises at all, Rose now found herself walking the perilous but exhilarating path of toying with what had seemed an impossible dream.

'I'm lying in bed with you and you talk to me about getting some sleep?' Nick ran his hand along her thigh. Sleep was the last thing on his mind, never mind the hour.

Rose smiled and closed her eyes. He made her feel wanton, something she had never felt before, and she stretched her arms above her head, tempting him with the breasts he seemed to like so much, loving the way his eyes darkened as they swept over her.

Their love-making was long and languorous. He touched her everywhere and she, emboldened by him, touched him everywhere and revelled in exploring his body.

It was five before they finally fell asleep, wrapped in each other's arms, and Rose awakened to the sun doing its utmost to get a foothold in the room.

And an empty space next to her.

The dreams she had nurtured the night before, when everything had seemed tantalisingly within reach, began to dissipate like mist in the sun, but then she heard a slight sound and there he was, standing in her doorway, with a cup of coffee in his hand.

Rose sat up, pulling the sheet up to her neck, and drew her knees up with a smile.

'For you.' Nick strolled towards her with the cup of coffee.

'How long have you been up?'

'Oh, an hour or two.'

'You should have woken me up.' She yawned and took the cup from him, hoping a healthy injection of caffeine would revive her.

'And missed the sight of you sleeping the sleep of the innocent?'

Rose marvelled that someone could look so good in a pair of baggy shorts and a fairly disreputable tee shirt.

'I don't feel innocent this morning,' she confessed, shifting to make room so that he could sit on the bed next to her. 'In fact, I feel…'

'Wicked? Decadent?' He tugged the sheet down and nodded. 'Much better. I like the view far more without the sheet covering it.'

Rose blushed and grinned and gulped down some tea. *Mrs Rose Papaeliou.* Nice ring to it, she thought.

'Something like that. I've never…just had a one-night stand. Believe it or not, I'm not that kind of girl.'

'I believe you, and whoever said that this was going to be a one-night stand?'

Hope flared but she managed to keep her expression neutral. 'Give me fifteen minutes and I'll be up,' she said, changing the subject. 'What do we have planned for today?'

'Oh, I thought we would spend the rest of our time here doing a little exploring of our own.' He stood up and shot her a wolfish grin that made her toes curl in anticipation. 'How do you feel about scuba-diving?'

Rose thought that pretty much anything in the company of Nick Papaeliou would be an inviting prospect.

And there was no Lee Peng in tow. He had flown to Indonesia for a week to oversee another building project. The various people with whom they had liaised were no longer necessary, Nick informed her.

Which just left the two of them on their own and the delights of Sabah and its surroundings.

Nick thought that boredom might set in. After all, wasn't that the way of the world? And they were in each other's company twenty-four seven.

Good old common sense told him that, without those necessary absences during which batteries could be recharged and tedium kept at bay, he was almost certain to tire of her company.

To his surprise, he didn't. She teased him mercilessly and he discovered he enjoyed it.

It was relaxing and invigorating being in her company. They scuba-dived and she proved herself pretty fearless, a side effect of having nomadic guardians, she explained, while sniggering that he seemed a little wary of the big blue sea.

They went to the local open market, which sold fruit and vegetables of every shape, size and description, many of them unrecognisable. They ate miniature figs that were sweet as sugar and drank ice-cold coconut water straight from the split coconuts that were sold in the stalls.

They dared each other to cross a bedraggled suspension bridge and then congratulated themselves afterwards by making love in a secluded part of the dense foliage and bush that fanned the river.

Without the rigid dimensions imposed by everyday life, it was easy to take that step out of sync, to explore each other without guilt and, as Rose admitted to herself, to make no attempts at holding back her headlong fall into love.

But it didn't matter because she was seeing a new side to Nick. He laughed a lot and was utterly relaxed. He had even stopped working. He took only essential calls on his mobile. Most of the time, he would glance at the number and ignore it.

Rose took that as a very good sign indeed. He wanted to spend time in her company, he enjoyed being with her to such an extent that he was willing to forgo work, and that said a great deal because, having worked alongside him, she knew that work was something Nick never, ever sidelined.

And the sex… The sex was remarkable. He was forceful, considerate, inventive and utterly irresistible.

When he looked at her, she felt the hairs on the back of her neck stand on end and one touch was enough to reduce her to instant meltdown.

After a life of carefully made choices, Rose was not equipped to defend herself against the overwhelming force of what she felt.

Anyway, she didn't want to. She wanted to be reckless.

She wanted to have his arms around her as they sat on the beach and watched the sun set. She wanted him to close that bedroom door and move towards her, every muscle in his body alert with the same hunger she felt for him. She wanted to cling to her dreams that her perfect love would be returned.

Which, on the last night of their stay, brought her to the very delicate matter of how, exactly, she might find out what his intentions towards her were.

'Tonight's meal was fantastic,' she said, which was the most roundabout route she could think to discuss the fact that their holiday was now at an end. 'In fact, the food over here has been exquisite. Such flavours. I love the multi-ethnic cuisine.' Thinking that she was beginning to sound a little like a restaurant critic, she bit back the temptation to carry the theme through.

'You're gabbling, Rose. Lie back and enjoy the stars and the sound of the sea.'

Rose obediently lay down next to him on the wide beach towel provided courtesy of the hotel, which seemed to know that sun loungers were not to everyone's taste. Especially, she thought, late at night when you wanted to be physically close to someone. Like now.

She tried to submerge herself in the ambience but her thoughts were whirring around in her head and she finally said, casually, 'Bit of a change, all this, isn't it? From London, I mean…'

'Huge change.'

'Be strange to go back tomorrow.'

'Very strange.' He sounded faintly surprised at that admission. 'But reality's never further than a stone's throw away.'

'I thought that was rats.'

'In my line of work, the two are often interlinked.'

Rose could feel him grinning in the dark but she didn't want to relax and enjoy his sense of humour, as she had done for the past few days. She wanted to pry beneath the surface and find out what happened next in their chapter, because she was sure that there would be a next.

'Will you miss…being here?' With me?

'All good things come to an end.' Nick shrugged, his hand, under her neck, hanging, almost touching her breast. 'That's just the way it is.'

'Which…' Rose decided to take the bull by the horns because they could sit around talking in metaphors all night and get nowhere '…leaves *us* where?'

Well, Nick thought with disappointment, it had to happen eventually. The bubble had to burst. He had idiotically thought that Rose, who was in a league of her own, would be the exception to the rule, the one woman who didn't start questioning the future and trying, thereby, to pin him down to promises of ever afters he had no intention of making.

'Well, I think we can safely say that your stint working for me is now over. Shy of a week or so, but we've accomplished what we set out to do, wouldn't you agree? You must be looking forward to getting back to your old routine. Are you?'

'Yes, of course I am.' In truth, she had barely missed her old job and was certainly not looking forward to returning to the grindstone having sampled the excitement of working for Nick, where every day brought new challenges. However, she wasn't a fool. She might have abandoned common sense, she might have dared to hope that her flight of fancy would bring her the result she wanted, but she could read nuances as well as the next person. Better. Over the years her ingrained sensitivity had fine-tuned her antennae and her antennae were now telling her that he was backing away from giving her a direct answer for a reason and there could only be one reason. Whatever he felt for her, it wasn't love. It wasn't even enough to give her any kind of commitment. The man who had always walked away from relationships of any depth was walking away now and Rose felt as though her lifeblood were draining out of her system.

What had she been thinking? That the way his eyes darkened when he saw her naked counted as love? Or that the easy way they talked and laughed and touched really meant something?

Inside she was hurting so much that she suddenly couldn't bear the feel of his arm around her. Outside, though, she controlled her voice and schooled her expression even though he couldn't see her face and made sure to sound as calm as she could as she started to chat about what had been happening in her old job, updates from her friends whom she had barely seen over the past few months.

'Naturally, this doesn't have to mean the end of…what we have,' Nick murmured, and Rose could feel him turn towards her. What, she wanted to ask, exactly do we have? For him, yet another pointless relationship based on satisfying sex and for her…more heartbreak, more involvement, more misery in the end.

'Oh, I think it should, really…'

'You don't mean that.' Nick turned completely towards

her and tilted her head so that he could kiss the side of her neck and Rose shrugged him off and sat up.

'I do.' She looked over her shoulder at him. Moonlight becomes him…wasn't there a song that went like that? He was just wearing an old tee shirt and a pair of faded jeans, but she knew every inch of his perfect body now, knew the lazy strength and muscular body encased in the casual clothing. She wondered how she could ever have thought that he might actually fall in love with her, the way she had fallen in love with him.

Would he return to England and be embarrassed to be seen with her? He had told her often enough that he loved her curves, found them incredibly sexy, that stick-thin, in comparison, was a turn-off. But that was here, where everything had been in a state of unreal suspension. She would bet her newly refurbished house that the minute they stepped back onto English soil stick-thin would suddenly be desirable because stick-thin represented the sort of model type he needed hanging on his arm.

He would always run true to form and she had been a fool to have thought otherwise. He was, and always had been, out of her league.

Rose stood up and dusted herself down. He, of course, was still lying on the towel, hands behind his head, probably, she thought, convinced that he could talk her round. Maybe for a few more romps in the hay back in England, where he would keep her hidden away and out of sight.

'This has been great.' She gesticulated vaguely around her. 'The scenery, the atmosphere, the romance of being out of England and in the hot sun. Now it's finishing…'

'You asked what was going to become of us.' Nick sat up. 'That implies that you consider us an item.'

'I meant in connection with work,' she lied. 'I thought it

would be awkward being stuck in each other's company, pretending that nothing had happened between us.'

'Stuck in each other's company?'

'I'm sorry. I didn't mean it that way. What I meant was…' Now he was standing up, which instantly made her feel a lot less assured. 'Look, this has been brilliant. I never thought…well, my first impressions of you weren't all that flattering but I've enjoyed every minute of being here with you. We had fun, didn't we?'

Nick couldn't quite believe his ears. Shouldn't he be the one giving the Dear John lecture? Shouldn't he be the one doing the letting down slowly and gently?

Anyway, whoever said that it had to end just yet? Sure, he didn't want a strings-attached relationship. Never had, probably never would. Which didn't mean that they couldn't continue enjoying each other until time did its thing and they both decided to move on.

'Sure, it's been fun.' He hooked his thumbs in the pockets of his jeans and stared at her. That sexy body…that light, infectious laughter… Well, this was her choice and the right one, really. 'And I'm glad you're…so calm about this…'

'What did you expect?' Rose asked lightly. 'Tears and histrionics?'

Nick shrugged and began walking back to their rooms. This was most definitely not how he had expected to spend his last night in Borneo. 'Maybe nothing so extreme,' he grated as she fell in step with him. 'You're not the tears and histrionics kind of girl, are you?'

Certainly not in public and definitely not when she'd made a complete idiot of herself.

'Not really.'

'And I'm glad about that.' He stopped and Rose continued

walking for a few steps before turning around to look at him. 'I wouldn't want to have hurt you in any way. You know me, Rose.' He laughed softly although something inside him felt slightly sick. Probably, he figured, because he had had the rug pulled very neatly from under his feet. Well, everyone needed a shake-up now and again and he was no exception. It hurt because the feeling was so damned alien to him. 'I can't give promises of commitment and settling down.'

'And I wouldn't want them,' she said quickly. 'Certainly not from you. We clicked in bed, but there's so much more to relationships than just clicking in the sack.'

Nick wasn't sure he much liked that, but he gave her a brief nod, which could have been agreement or simply acknowledgement of what she was trying to say.

'But, and I never thought that I would say this, I'm grateful to you, and not just because you bailed me out of a financial mess. I'm looking forward to going back to my old job, but you've given me the confidence to think about new pastures, not to rely on just doing the same thing day in and day out and thinking that it's fine because I know the routine.'

'Glad to be of service,' Nick told her coolly.

'Course, I'll make sure that I have all the written reports ready for you by next Monday.'

'No need.'

'What do you mean?'

'I'm no longer convinced that I'll be siting Borneo for my hotel.'

'Why not?' Rose asked, astounded at his U-turn. 'It's an amazing island. And you've put in so much time in getting to know it.'

'Yes, it's an amazing island and if tourism is to kick in, then I would rather not be the one to introduce it. It's easy for a unique place like this to lose its innocence because of rampant commercialism.' And besides, he thought angrily, Borneo would forever remind him of her. They had spent some pretty intense days together and she had imprinted too much of it with her stamp. How could he ever walk along this stretch of beach again without thinking about her? And that wouldn't do. He had let his guard down, allowed her to get under his skin, and let this, he thought, be a lesson to him.

She was delivering some heartfelt speech about tasteful and controlled tourism and the benefits to a local community and he sliced through her ramblings with dismissive ease, pleased to have her reduced to silence.

'You make some valid points, but my decision is made.' Churlish would be to make a big deal of the fact that she had, like it or not, ended their relationship. Churlish, in other words, would be to allow his ego to be involved. On the other hand, he could be as relieved as she appeared to be that the whole thing was over and, honestly, he was. Good while it lasted but all good things came to an end and it was best to part company on good terms. The ideal scenario when it came to the opposite sex, if he thought about it.

'So…' he injected some warmth into his voice as they began to stroll back to the hotel complex '…all packed?'

'Check.'

'Including those ridiculous souvenirs you insisted on buying at the market a couple of days ago?'

'They weren't ridiculous. You'll be sorry you didn't invest in a couple yourself when you get back to England and realise that they would have looked very fetching on your walls.' She kept her voice as light as she could, but now the bantering that had led her to think of what they had as something special hurt beyond endurance.

'Name two places where colourful masks would have blended in.'

'You mean against the stark white walls and expensive abstracts?'

Rose heard herself conducting this perfectly normal conversation from a distance, almost as though she were hovering over herself, watchful and detached.

When they were finally standing outside their rooms, she smiled at him, gratefully, she hoped, and stuck out her hand, which he pointedly ignored.

'That's a bit ridiculous,' he drawled. 'Yes, we've both reached the same conclusion that this was a holiday fling best left on the island, but I think shaking hands is slightly ludicrous.' He bent and kissed her on the mouth, but this was a fond, farewell kiss, devoid of the urgency and hunger she had become accustomed to, and it hurt like hell.

It did, however, set the tone for the next day, during which they were affable, polite and very, very busy. Flights, work that Nick suddenly remembered needed to be done and books that Rose decided should have been read.

She could already feel the mantle of England settling back over her long before the plane finally touched down at Heathrow.

She had feverishly wondered how they would actually part company when the moment arrived, but in all events it was an anticlimax. Nick spotted someone he knew and, before she could brace herself for the hellishness of the final goodbye, he was kissing her fondly on the cheek and excusing himself. Would she be okay to handle a taxi back herself? Just a couple of things he wanted to talk to Ed Duggins about…take care of yourself…hope the house lives up to expectations… The usual platitudes, but his mind was already somewhere else. He had moved on.

Rose went directly to her house. She had been there almost every day to supervise the work in progress and had left her painter and decorator in charge of replastering and wallpapering over the mess made by the builders.

At any rate, that was exciting. She was delivered to her door in a black cab and, once inside the house, wandered around taking in the changes, and there were a fair few of those. Terry had done an excellent job. Everywhere looked new and smelt new.

And it was all paid for. She told herself that she should be over the moon, but as it turned out the only thing she had to smile about was her phone call to her sister.

Lily was coming home. Just for a couple of weeks because the leading man had apparently done something unfortunate to his ankle. Filming would skirt around him, but her scenes were already shot.

Her voice down the other end of the phone was like a tonic and Rose couldn't help herself. For once she wasn't the one holding everything together. And for once Lily was the strong half, soothing, reassuring, safe in her own area of expertise—namely men.

'Don't worry, Rosie. I'm coming home and everything's gonna be fine. Wait and see.'

Somewhere in middle America, Lily smiled to herself as she hung up the phone—Rose needed her and that felt good, and, even better, she was going to make sure that everything really was all right for her sister.

CHAPTER EIGHT

'Now that you've been back nearly two weeks, I think it's time we went out and had a good time. I'm heading back to America next Wednesday and I can't bear the thought of leaving you alone here when you're so miserable.'

Rose looked at her sister and tried to imagine whether she was capable of ever having a good time again. Not a word from Nick since they had returned to England. Not a phone call, not a message left on the answering machine, nothing. It was as though she had never existed in his eyes.

For Lily's sake, she had played down her feelings, but her talents as an actor must have been less successful than she had thought because here was her sister now, looking at her worriedly, in fact the way she had looked at Lily many a time in the past. The shoe was very securely on the other foot.

'I'm not miserable, Lily. I'm tired. And, besides, I haven't got time to have a good time.' Rose looked at her sister over the rim of her mug.

'That doesn't make sense.'

'Sure it does. I mean, I've only been back at my old job a few days and you wouldn't believe the stack of work that was waiting for me. A lovely little collection of jobs no one else wanted to do.' Every single one of which was utterly boring, she was tempted to add, but didn't because she was determined, after her initial confession and shameful blubbing down the phone, not to make a fuss. She had lost her head and had her moment of madness and now was time to pick up the pieces and not wallow in a tide of self-pity. At least, not in public.

'But it's a Saturday, Rose.' Lily sighed dramatically.

'Don't worry about me, I want you to go out and have fun. As you said, Lily, you'll be heading back in a few days. You want to catch up with all your fans before you go.' Rose smiled at her sister. The phone had not stopped ringing since Lily had arrived back. Friends wanting to meet up and, according to Lily, who had developed a healthy streak of cynicism since working in America, not-nearly-friends who wanted to rub shoulders with someone in the movie business.

'No. You and I are going to go out tonight. Nice little jazz club in the West End. You can get your glad rags on and I'll ask a couple of people I met when I was in America who are over here as well. We'll make it a cosy evening.' Lily was not about to take no for an answer. She had promised herself that she would make sure that Rose was just fine by the time she returned to America and she wasn't about to jettison that goal. She gave her a coaxing but implacable smile.

Several hours later and Rose wasn't sure whether to be amused or alarmed by her sister's newly acquired ability to chivvy.

Chivvied from shop to shop because retail therapy was, apparently, the best form of therapy. Then from shop to beauty parlour where Rose's short nails were turned into works of art with pearly pink nail polish. Then onward from the beauty parlour to the hairdresser's, conveniently and suspiciously pre-booked, where her naturally curly hair underwent some weird metamorphosis and emerged a fabulous tumble of windblown curls rather than her usual unkempt, unmanageable mess. And brilliantly gold, thanks to some clever mixing of dyes. Lots of highlights everywhere.

Lily pronounced herself satisfied and they returned to the house energised with several carrier bags and, in Rose's case, a complete makeover.

Course, she thought, she would never be lean and glamorous like her sister, but she hadn't exactly looked fat in the dressing rooms.

'You've lost weight,' Lily announced airily, not for the first time reading her sister's mind as she dumped the bags on the kitchen table. She poured Rose a glass of wine to get her in the mood, and plonked herself down on one of the chairs. 'I kinda liked the old you,' Lily said wistfully. 'Cuddly and comfortable.'

Rose wondered whether that was how Nick had seen her. As cuddly and comfortable, like an old cushion that was just right for sleeping with when nothing better was available. She rescued herself from pointlessly worrying the thought and smiled as Lily went on to talk about the people she had met in America, and their obsession with food. They either seemed to eat too much or eat too little. Doughnut emporiums squatted alongside organic health food shops and she had seen people leaving their gyms, still perspiring from their workouts, to head directly to the nearest hot-dog stand where they would proceed to order the largest of everything.

Rose was quietly convinced that Lily would return to England. She had confided on more than one occasion, looking over her shoulder as though one of those Bigwigs she kept mentioning might pop out from behind a bush, that there was too much pressure in America to be thin, to be competitive, to suck up to the right people. Lily, having inherited

Tony and Flora's basic bohemian disregard for personal wealth, couldn't understand why everyone seemed so willing to jump through hoops for yet more money, which they obviously didn't need.

'Anyway, you're sick of me going on about this.' She grinned. 'Maybe I'll just return to London when I'm done there. My CV will be a whole lot healthier, thanks to Nick, and I can just get a nice little job in a soap opera.'

Nick. Not once had she asked her sister whether she had seen Nick. She had told herself that she wasn't interested, that the past was the past, but she knew, really, that she was just scared. Scared that she might want her sister to tell her too much. Scared that the floodgates, which she was trying hard to close, would crash open again and she would be lost.

'Right.' All assertive once again, Lily stood up, topped Rose's glass of wine with a fraction more, and ordered her to go and get changed but to do absolutely nothing with her make-up because she, Lily, would do it for her.

'You wouldn't believe the tips I've got from the girls who make me up.' She laughed. 'Believe me, it's all in the brush strokes.'

'You're chivvying again.' But Rose laughed because it was just so good not to be on her own. She had missed Lily, but only now was she realising by how much.

'And it feels good. Now I can understand why you spent your life chivvying me around as a kid.'

There was no rush and Rose took her time getting dressed. Yes, she really had lost weight and it suited her. She had also been coerced into buying a little black number that she would never have dared to have worn a few months ago. It had a plunging neckline, one of her great no-noes previously, and exposed more than a generous eyeful of cleavage. With high heels, she felt quite pleased with herself. The dress fitted snugly to the waist, then flared out to just above the knees.

By the time Lily had sorted out her costume jewellery and applied the make-up, Rose felt her spirits lift. She could almost believe her own mantra that she was well rid of Nick, that life was just about to begin, that all experience, in hindsight, was good experience, that he was little more than a dot on her learning curve brought on by temporary insanity. Of course, the two and a half glasses of white wine helped.

They took a taxi and just when Rose was beginning to warm to the idea of not staying in, Lily dropped the bombshell.

Nick was going to be there. Well, he might be there. But don't worry about it. Wouldn't it be good to prove to him how much she had managed to get her act together? There was no need to fuss. She looked fabulous. She couldn't spend her days scuttling away from the possibility of seeing him again. Sooner or later the time would come when she would meet him because she, Lily, remained good friends with him and grateful for everything he had done to help her with her career. Never run scared, that was the key thing.

Rose, despairingly, toyed with the idea of demanding that the taxi driver turn around and take her back home.

Then, if not back home, at least to the nearest pub so that she could fortify her nerves with a couple more glasses of wine.

But she was given little opportunity to object because Lily, with all her newly acquired bossiness, kept up a never-ending monologue for most of the trip, and Rose glumly took on board that her sister had a point. Why should she be scared? It wasn't as if Nick had guessed her shameful secret. He had no idea that what to him had been a fling had, for her, been the love of a lifetime. She looked good and if there was one thing he had done for her, it had been to inject a level of confidence in her appearance that she had never really had. He had made her feel sexy and the residue of that confidence was still there. The little black dress looked great and if he did turn up, big if because, as Lily had pointed out, he was mega busy and the invite had been last-minute, then she would damn well show him that she was doing fine.

The jazz club was tucked away in a side road a million miles away on the other side of London. Rose had no idea how her sister had managed to discover the place, but it was certainly popular. Despite being early, the venue was already beginning to fill up. She had no time to wonder whether she was feeling nervous about meeting Nick because over the next hour or so she was wrapped up in the business of meeting Lily's friends, a fair few of whom were American and flatteringly thrilled to be in a genuine British club and not one of those that catered for the loaded tourists.

This was new for Rose, this feeling of blending in with a crowd of people, all strangers to her. She was determined not to drink too much, but the music was sexy and, although she stuck to wine, she found her glass being replaced without her having to ask or even make her way to the bar.

The dress, she thought, was proving even more effective than she could ever have dared to hope.

Several men seemed to find her fascinating, although it was hard to tell because the atmospheric lighting bordered on downright dark. Certainly one in particular had taken her under his wing and had been responsible for at least two glasses of wine, the last of which Rose was now drinking very slowly indeed as she listened to him tell her about his latest film, a short *film noir*, which had had a very successful première at the Cannes festival.

Lily had asked a lot of her old friends, but most of the new faces belonged to the world of film and media. Rose had never met so many men who seemed to be film producers. They were very entertaining, even if she had never heard of a single one of the films they had produced. A lot of them, she noticed, sported pony-tails, which looked very trendy. Miles apart, she thought nastily, from Nick, who was as traditional as they went when it came to fashion. Long hair and jewellery on men, he had told her, were strictly for hippies, and she had laughed and accused him of being narrow-minded.

The memory made her heart constrict.

At least he wasn't around. She had kept one beady eye open so that she could take appropriate measures to avoid him, but it was now after ten and he was nowhere in sight, obviously too busy to get away.

Disappointment bit into her and she favoured her companion with a wide, reckless smile.

Which was when she spotted him, standing on the other side of the room, with a leggy red-haired woman on his arm. She looked as though she had been poured into her small silver dress.

Rose felt her heart skip a beat and, weirdly, the noise, the people, even the band playing a slow number on the little raised podium, seemed to fade away, leaving just the sight of him, as sexy as she remembered, in a pair of dark-coloured trousers and a white shirt, casually rolled to the elbows.

Well, he seemed to have managed to relegate her to the history books in no time at all, Rose thought bitterly. Less than a month and he was back to his cover-girl babes.

She gulped down what was left in her glass and concentrated on what the man by her side was saying. His name was Ted, although his friends, for reasons that escaped her, called him Splice, and he was giving her the low-down on the people he had met at the Cannes Festival, a warts-and-all account that would have been hilarious had her attention not been suddenly hijacked by her ex-lover, now excusing himself and heading for the bar while the red-haired beauty sashayed over to the nearest group of men, one of whom she clearly knew. The world of actors, models and musicians was a very small one, Lily had told her.

Rose gaily accepted another drink from Ted Splice, as she called him in her head, and was making sure not to look in the direction of the redhead just in case Nick returned to his date and noticed her staring, when she felt the tap on her shoulder.

She spun round and there he was. She'd been certain she hadn't been noticed, but he must have seen her as he was making his way back from the bar.

Rose felt her heart skip a beat, then she produced the same sparkly smile she had perfected with Ted.

'Good heavens. Fancy seeing you here. How are you?' She noticed that he failed to produce a reciprocal smile. In fact, his expression was cool and Rose was suddenly enraged that he should chuck her aside and then, as if that weren't bad enough, treat her to the cold shoulder.

'You seem to be having a good time,' Nick drawled, giving her a leisurely appraisal.

'Oh, I am.'

'Bit of a change for you, isn't it? This kind of thing?'

'Well, you know what they say about a change being as good as a rest. I hadn't expected it to be quite as large as this, but I'm having a brilliant time, meeting loads of really interesting people.'

'So I couldn't help but notice.'

His voice dripped ice and Rose wondered whether, having an ego the size of a house, he had expected her to be sitting indoors pining for him. Little could he guess that she had pretty much been doing just that until tonight.

'What about you?' she asked politely. 'Having a good time? Did you come with anyone? I guess you know quite a few of the people here anyway…' She was gratified to notice that even the subdued lighting couldn't quite hide his dark flush and she gave him her most innocent look.

'As a matter of fact, I did come with someone. She's over there somewhere.' He indicated somewhere behind her while keeping his eyes firmly fixed on her face, and Rose dutifully turned around to see the redhead looking daggers at her.

'Oh, dear. Your date doesn't look awfully happy that you've abandoned her. You'd better run along before she blows a fuse.'

Nick, whose mood seemed to be deteriorating by the second, scowled. 'My date is more than capable of taking care of herself for a few minutes.' He bared his teeth in a smile. 'Besides, I don't think she would begrudge me catching up with an old…friend…' Of course he had known that she would be there and he had brought along the arm candy to remind himself that he had done the right thing, they had both done the right thing—parted company because at the end of the day she was a settling-down kind of girl and he was a no-commitment kind of guy. That was just the way it was. He liked variety. The redhead filled that role.

'I don't think there's much to catch up on.' Rose frowned and made a show of giving his remark all the attention it deserved. 'I'm back at my old job and enjoying it and…' she could be as cool and dismissive as he was '…you were very useful in teaching me that madness isn't always a bad thing. As you can see, I've taken that advice to heart.' She laughed gaily. 'I'd have steered a million miles away from something like this in the past—as you pointed out…'

He had been useful? Nick didn't appreciate the compliment, not at all.

'There's madness and there's stupidity, Rose,' he gritted. 'Madness is breaking out of your comfort zone and coming here tonight…'

'And stupidity?' She was pretty sure she wasn't going to like his answer, but that, in a way, would surely work for her, because how on earth would she ever get closure if she carried on loving him? Let him show himself in all his arrogant glory, she willed.

'Stupidity is wearing that dress.'

Rose's mouth fell open in shock. She gave an incredulous laugh. 'You object to *my* dress?' She glanced significantly over her shoulder to where his date gave the term skimpy clothing a whole new meaning.

'That's completely different,' Nick growled.

'Oh, and why is that? Because she's tall and skinny and can carry off wearing handkerchiefs better than me?'

'Because…' Because she's as sexy as a runner bean, Nick thought savagely. He deeply resented the fact that the woman standing in front of him, flaunting herself to all and sundry, was still on his mind, despite all his efforts to wipe her out. 'Because,' he grated, 'you could land yourself in a situation you wouldn't be able to handle dressed like that. Did you look in the mirror before you left your house? Do you have any idea how much of your…you is on show?'

'It's been nice chatting to you, Nick. Now, I think I see Splice coming with my drink.'

'*Splice?*'

'That's his nickname.' Rose smiled sweetly and walked away without giving him the chance to continue the conversation. Out of the corner of her eye, she saw her sister looking in her direction and she waved cheerfully, not wanting to spoil the evening by having Lily worrying about her. Again.

The minute Lily could escape, however, Rose was dismayed to find that she was by her side and Rose just knew what her sister was going to say.

'What on earth was going on with the two of you back then?' Lily asked, jumping straight in with both feet and making Rose feel even guiltier that her sister had noticed more than she had first suspected. 'What was Nick saying to you?'

'Lily, never you mind that. I'm not going to spoil your last Saturday night in London by repeating what that man had the nerve to say.' At one in the morning, the crowd was beginning to thin out. Most of Lily's friends had headed off, with a couple of the guys insisting on giving Rose their phone numbers although she, tactfully, declined to return the favour. Still, it was flattering even if she couldn't get Nick's nasty remark about her dress out of her head.

He, as luck would have it, was still around somewhere, with the redhead clutching him possessively as if scared that he might disappear unless physically restrained. Which, of course, he would. Rose, consistently aware of his presence, made sure to live up to her statement that she was having a brilliant time. She was pretty sure that, at one point, Ted had even asked if she would consider starring in one of his productions, which had resulted in fits of laughter on her part. She had half hoped that Nick might have glanced over at that point and witnessed for himself just how much fun she was having.

Wrapped up in her mental reverie, she became aware of Lily pressing her for details, and eventually she gave in, telling her that he had criticised her dress and dared to suggest that she was somehow sending off the wrong messages and then, having done that, would be incapable of taking care of herself.

Lily was nodding, taking it all in, and finally said, 'You can't let him get away with that.'

'What do you mean?'

'You should be angry. Fuming!'

'Well…yes…I am…'

'You need to march over there and let him know that you're not just anyone. In fact, you need to let him know that you're more than capable of taking care of yourself. In fact, Splice was mightily impressed by you…' Lily glanced at her nails, painted a vibrant, deep purple. 'Nick might just want to know that he's not the only guy interested in you…'

'He isn't interested in me.'

'I'll distract Cat—'

'Cat?' What cat? What was Lily on about?

'His date for the evening. She likes to call herself that. Her real name's Nancy. I met her briefly in my modelling days.'

'I don't think—'

'Quite right. Don't think. Thinking just complicates matters.' She pushed Rose out towards where Nick was standing and holding court with several of the pony-tailed men.

There she went. Chivvying again. What was she supposed to say to Nick? She just wanted to go home, but the redhead was being suitably distracted and the pony-tail brigade was breaking up, heading off, leaving her alone with him.

'My sister wanted your girlfriend to meet a friend of hers…' was all Rose could think of saying. 'Her name's Cat, I gather.'

'She's not my girlfriend.'

'Oh. Date, in that case.' Rose shrugged as if she was bored with the business of him splitting hairs. 'It's been nice meeting you again, Nick. I'm off now.'

'Wait just a minute.' He caught hold of her arm as she

was turning away and Rose tensed. 'How much have you had to drink?'

'What I've had to drink has nothing to do with you.'

'No? How are you going to get back to your house?'

'In a taxi. With Lily.' Where was her sister, anyway? 'Or not, as the case may be.' Her skin burnt where he was holding her, bringing back memories she wanted to forget, and she looked at him with unhidden hostility.

'I'll take you home.'

'You'll do no such thing.' Alarm and panic slammed into her with such force that she took a step backwards.

'Your sister's not around and nor are any of those creeps who were drooling down your front all night.'

'They were not creeps. In fact—' she smirked '—Ted's desperate to get in touch with me. He's a movie producer, you know.' Or maybe it was advertising. She couldn't quite remember.

That clarified something in Nick's head. The woman might think that she was embarking on some crazy hedonistic life-style, but she had no idea what she was letting herself in for. He had met sufficient movie producers in his time, thanks to his history of dating women in the modelling or acting business, and he knew that kindly, thoughtful and caring were not adjectives commonly used to describe them.

'Did you bring a jacket?'

'You are *not* taking me home.' Rose looked around desperately for her sister. 'Anyway, you can't bring a date and then abandon her. How is your girlfriend going to get home?'

'Wait right here.'

Rose had no intention of doing any such thing. She tripped along behind Nick and reached her sister just as he was explaining the need to deliver Rose back to the house unless Lily was on her way out. Which she wasn't, never mind the pointed looks and contorted gestures Rose was delivering behind Nick's back.

'I've got to stay until the last person leaves,' Lily said gaily, ignoring her sister. 'Only polite. And Cat can't possibly go yet. Not when I've just introduced her to Joe Carr here. Can you, Cat?'

Rose had never seen anyone truly wriggle on the horns of a dilemma, but Cat did now. She was obviously furious at the thought of her date clearing off with another woman, even though the woman was no competition, but the prospect of networking with someone from the film industry who might prove useful later down the line was irresistible.

She did the best she could under the circumstances and all credit to her, Rose thought nastily, she did it well.

'Call me,' she purred to Nick, and then reached forward to pull him towards her. From behind, Rose watched the slender pale fingers with perfectly painted long red nails comb his dark hair and, from what she could see, he was thoroughly enjoying the kiss.

The sight made her feel sick to her stomach. What further proof could she have that he had forgotten her? Wearing a sexy black dress and flirting madly with people whose names she could barely remember suddenly struck her as very sad.

Lily, she noticed, was staring at her, and Rose composed her features into bland indifference, which was the stance she maintained as Nick ushered her out of the club, fetching her jacket *en route*, and into the sharp early morning air.

His driver was waiting outside and she climbed into the back seat of the car in silence.

'So…' Nick slammed the door behind him and turned to her '…you're suddenly very quiet.'

'I'm tired.'

'We still have a conversation to finish.'

'What conversation?' Rose looked at him with a sigh. 'We don't have anything left to finish, Nick. We've both moved on.'

Nick frowned at her. 'Which doesn't mean that I don't still have…' feelings for you. Except that there was something somehow significant about saying that. So he avoided it. 'A sense of responsibility towards you. After all, Rose, we were lovers, whether you like it or not.'

'And now you're scratching another notch on your bedpost. If it makes you feel better, I absolve you from all responsibility towards me. I don't need your misguided sense of duty, Nick. You employed me because you were Lily's friend and you felt sorry for me when I was in a financial mess. Now you feel sorry for me because—'

'I don't feel sorry for you,' he snapped sharply.

'Then what? I don't want you to involve yourself in my life.'

She slid her eyes over to him. Earlier, she had felt tipsy and mellow and just that little bit out of control. Right now, she couldn't have felt more sober. 'Do you always feel as though you've got to look out for the hapless women you've been involved with?'

'You consider yourself hapless?'

'I consider myself…changed…'

'So you said earlier.' Nick's voice was acid. 'I wasn't sure whether or not to be flattered by the adjective you used for me as useful.'

No, he wouldn't be. Useful wasn't exactly a sexy term. It was probably also a little too close to used for Nick's liking, but Rose didn't care because wasn't that what he did with all the women who littered his life?

'And people don't change overnight, Rose. You can't

suddenly turn into a woman who lives life on the edge. You've never been that kind of woman. You remember telling me how much Tony and Flora turned you off the idea of taking chances because of the lifestyle they chose? They wanted you to want adventure. Instead you found your adventure in books.'

'Yes, and now I've decided that they were right after all. I'm too young to bury myself in books when there's a whole world out there waiting to be lived.'

'And you intend to live every minute of it in revealing clothes.'

'So what if I do? What business is it of yours? You've rescued me once. There's no need to make a habit of it.'

The driver was at long last approaching the house and Rose located her glittery handbag and tucked her jacket a little tighter around her shoulders, ready to sprint from car to front door in the shortest possible time.

The frame of the redhead's fingers clawing into Nick's hair repeated itself endlessly in her head, like a snippet of film viewed in slow motion.

'I'm not trying to rescue you,' Nick grated, leaping out of the car as soon as it had stopped.

'Don't let me keep you.' Rose turned the key in the lock, pushed open the door and smiled sweetly at him.

The woman was crazy, Nick thought. Had she no idea what sort of temptation she presented to a red-blooded male? Wearing a dress like that with everything on display? Her cleavage was just a teasing reminder of her succulent breasts, which he considered outrageously hugged by the thin, stretchy fabric. If she was his, he thought, there was no way that he would let her out of the house looking like that.

'You're not getting rid of me that quickly,' he growled, pushing the door wide open with the flat of his hand and stepping inside the house before she could shut the door in his face.

Rose spun round and folded her arms. 'We have nothing to say to one another, Nick.'

'You're not to leave the house dressed the way you were tonight.' Where the hell had that come from?

'You're telling me what I can wear?'

'For your own good.' He flushed darkly and walked away from her incredulous expression, into the sitting room where he prowled restlessly before perching against the bay window so that he could look at her framed in the doorway.

'For my own good?'

'Stop parroting me,' Nick said irritably. He failed to see why she would stare at him as though he had taken leave of his senses when, as far as he was concerned, he was being perfectly reasonable and pretty decent.

'You may think you know what you're letting yourself in for, but you don't,' he informed her bluntly, and Rose's mouth fell open a fraction further. So it was fine for him to practically make love in front of an audience with a bimbo who seemed to have an allergy to fabric, but he still found it perfectly acceptable to lecture *her* about her dress code and her general code of behaviour.

She had never known anything so hypocritical in her life. She opened her mouth a few times to say something and instead succeeded in giving a goldfish impression.

'Not only is it dangerous for you to dress like that because you're giving off all the wrong signals, but you're dressing for the wrong crowd anyway. Half the men there were gay and the other half would put Casanova to shame when it comes to scruples.'

'And since you don't fall into the gay category, Nick, we both know which one you belong to.'

'We're not talking about me.'

'No, we're talking about double standards. Maybe I'm in search of an unscrupulous man. Have you considered that? Maybe my Big Change involves taking a break from the safe guy and just seeing what the grass is like on the other side.'

'You know you don't mean that.'

'Really?' Rose fumbled in her bag and whipped out the business card on which Ted Splice had written his various numbers. She waved it in the air as if proving her point, as if one small piece of cardboard were actually a key to the gates of wildness, adventure and scandal. As if she would ever, in a million years, seriously consider dating a man whose nickname was Splice.

'I didn't tell you this, but Ted and I are going out…on a date…next Saturday to…' She named the first restaurant that came into her head, which, unfortunately, was a cheap and cheerful pizza place not a hundred miles away from where she lived. 'And who knows what might happen once we've finished eating?'

CHAPTER NINE

THE advantage to the cheap and cheerful pizza place lay in its size. It was vast and, at eight thirty on a Saturday evening, brimming with families.

Nick hadn't intended to end up there. In fact, for the better part of the week he had told himself that he had more important things to do than to waste time on one highly infuriating woman. If, he piously concluded, she wanted to hurl herself into the party scene, then she could damn well live with the consequences, and consequences there most certainly would be. If she paraded her body with a type like movie producer Ted, then she might just as well have Available stamped across her forehead in large neon lettering.

Especially with this Ted character, about whom he had managed to source some information. The man had been in and out of rehab like a yo-yo, which was not exactly a notable event in the world he lived in, but Nick could not think of Rose seriously dating a guy like that. In fact, he had discovered that he couldn't think of her seriously dating any guy without feeling ferociously possessive.

Possessive over a woman.

The notion, when it first trickled into his head, was so unbelievable that it bordered on amusing. He had never been a possessive man, had never been jealous, had prided himself on his controlled approach to relationships.

Six days down the line, there was nothing amusing about it. He thought of the man's oily hands stripping Rose of her skimpy black dress, unhooking her bra, feasting his eyes on her big, beautiful breasts and felt sick.

He should never have allowed what they had to finish. That was the problem. Things that ended prematurely became unattainable objects of desire simply because basic need hadn't been sated. He had thought himself in control of what they had and only now realised that what they had had been controlling him.

But still. Going to the pizza place had not been an option. He had just somehow found himself driving over there well before she and her date were due to arrive, found himself taking the quietest and least noticeable table at the very far corner of the room where he was half shielded by an oversized plastic plant in drastic need of dusting. He found himself doing all this and it was almost as if his head had no say in the matter.

The pizza he ordered for himself as he waited was surprisingly good. The wine slightly less so, but nevertheless drinkable.

By eight-thirty, when neither Rose nor her date had yet arrived, he was smugly contemplating the very satisfying theory that Ted the movie producer had stood her up. He imagined her sitting bleakly in her sitting room, wondering whether or not to text, knowing that this was the first nail in the coffin of her new lifestyle.

She might even, he thought with a kick of real pleasure, be glumly admitting to herself that he, Nick, had been right after all to warn her off the man.

This was such a pleasing fantasy that he almost missed them. Feeling a little ridiculous because of his cloak-and-dagger tactics, Nick watched them through the fronds of the plastic plant, watched them taken through to a table uncomfortably sandwiched between two families with exuberant kids.

She had steered away from wearing anything revealing, but, instead of finding this acceptable, he darkly decided that she looked even sexier in her short grey skirt, her too-short grey skirt and neatly tailored blouse. She could almost have been going out to work except for the two top buttons of her shirt, which were undone. Nick was pretty sure that if he noticed that little detail, then so did Ted the reformed producer. He couldn't actually see the man's face because Ted had his back to him, but it was easy to imagine those beady little eyes flicking rapaciously over her body while he tried to work out the fastest way of getting her into bed.

Nick tensed and he finished his glass of wine and signalled the waitress over so that he could order something else. Coffee and dessert, because now he was condemned to remain where he was or risk being seen on the way out.

Not that he had plans to leave until they did. He sat back and folded his hands on his stomach and watched.

Rose, sitting on the opposite side of the room, was glumly regretting the impulse that had led her to this place.

She had reacted to Nick's horrible, patronising attitude towards her a week ago by fabricating a non-existent date with a man who had been flattering and pleasant enough for a couple of hours but several thousand light years away from someone she would ever have considered going out with.

In fact, there had been no need for her to telephone Ted at all, but she had been prompted into doing so for all the wrong reasons. Hurt at seeing Nick with another woman, anger that he should dare tell her how to live her life having done such a comprehensive job of ruining it, and a stubborn feeling that if he warned her against Ted, then she would damn well go out with him because the last thing she needed was Nick Papaeliou's misguided good intentions.

She had been tormented by the thought that he and his leggy redhead had probably chuckled at the silly little woman in the short black dress who was clueless to the ways of the world. That, as much as anything else, had driven her to pick the phone up and dial one of the several numbers Ted had left with her.

She had said she would be going to Angelo's Pizza Emporium with Ted Splice and she would go to Angelo's Pizza Emporium with him if only to prove a point to herself. That she was a free woman, liberated from the chains of fear that had kept her anchored all her life. Nick, she had decided as she had got dressed earlier, making sure to wear clothes that wouldn't give Ted the wrong impression, might well turn out to be just the first in a long line of many.

She had been tempted to telephone Lily on the other side of the world and inform her of this new departure, a whole brand-new set of moral codes, but Lily had failed to show the appropriate disgust at Nick's high-handed behaviour at the party and had just laughed when accused of not coming to her rescue. She had departed for America still clinging to the belief that everything was going to be fine, just wait and see.

Now, sitting in the pizza emporium, which was truly an emporium and one that seemed unnaturally full of rowdy children, Rose was in danger, not of dodging Ted's wandering hands, but of nodding off through boredom.

Ted was not only very, very fond of the sound of his own voice and enchanted with all the funny stories he had up his sleeve, but he had also confided, on the way over in the taxi, lowering his voice, as if the cab driver could care less, that his inclinations were not entirely of the straight variety.

Of course, he adored women, but…

Rose had nodded and resigned herself to an evening of listening to Ted's anecdotes and looking at her watch.

At least the place was big so that they could manage to avoid a falsely intimate setting, and once or twice, as she nibbled at her pizza and salad, she actually found herself laughing at some of the wild things he had to say.

Apparently he found her *cool* and refreshing because she was such a good listener.

'If you were a guy,' he paid the highest compliment, 'then I'd be wining and dining you and inviting you back to my place to…'

'Look at your etchings?'

Which brought them right back to square one, the main subject for the evening, Ted himself, and his trials and tribulations as an artist before he had discovered his true calling behind the lens of a camera.

It was a little after ten by the time Ted asked for the bill.

'Been a bit of a waste for you, hasn't it?' he said sheepishly. 'I should have let you know…told you where my preferences lay…'

Rose laughed and impulsively reached across the table and held both his hands in hers. 'I just don't understand why you don't come out of the closet. It's the twenty-first century, after all, and you work in a world where it's pretty much the norm, anyway.'

'Oh, it's my mum, babe. Don't think she'd be too hip to the idea and, well…she's getting on a bit… Gotta play the respect card, man, gotta play the respect card.'

'Well, if this helps at all, I was playing a part that night as well.'

'You mean…'

'Oh, no! Not that.' Rose threw back her head and laughed, then she leaned forward and whispered confidentially, 'I'm actually a closet introvert. But last Saturday, I dressed to impress and played the part.'

'Well, now we know each other's wicked secrets, I think we're going to be friends for life.'

It was turning out to be an okay evening after all, Rose considered as they stood up, and when he slipped his arm around her waist she was quite happy to nestle against him and not at all offended when they parted company on the pavement outside, after promising that they would meet up again, maybe in a couple of months time, because Ted's schedule was 'like hectic, man'.

She washed her face, kicked off the high shoes and changed into her very un-wild gear of grey track-suit jogging bottoms and a sloppy tee shirt with a faded picture of Minnie Mouse on the front.

Heartbreak had, at least, had one good side effect. Her eating habits had changed. She had lost her appetite and it had conveniently failed to return so as she sat down to finish what remained of the evening in front of a bowl of carrot sticks and some low-fat dip she rested safe in the knowledge that the pizza was not going to be accompanied by a great slab of comfort-eating chocolate.

It took her fifteen minutes of surfing the channels before she landed on one that was watchable.

It would pass the rest of the evening, she supposed. No point heading up to bed because she knew that she would be unable to sleep. It had been the same for ages. She would close her eyes, will herself to think of something mundane, like what Annie at work had done with the reports she had laboriously redone three days ago, or what would be the next stage in her programming to update the Accounts Receivables department, and then she would think of him.

He sprang into her head like sweet temptation and forbidden fruit wrapped up in one agonisingly dangerous package. And he would always be laughing at her. Mostly, he would be laughing at her while rolling around in the bed with the redhead.

She was sipping some of the green tea with lemon that she had made to drink with her carrots and dip when the doorbell rang. She consulted her watch and frowned—nearly eleven-thirty on a Saturday evening.

Much as she had ended up enjoying her evening out with Ted, she hoped it wasn't him. She was certain that she would see him again because, as she wryly acknowledged, he enjoyed talking and in the field in which he worked so did nearly everyone else, she suspected, so a good listener was a valuable find. He had also shared a major confidence with her and that, in itself, would be a strong bond between them. All very nice, but she was looking forward to an hour or so of mindless television, drifting in and out of thoughts of Nick.

She tried to wipe the disgruntled expression from her face as she went to open the front door. She was pretty much prepared to give Ted one cup of coffee, but really nothing else. His urge to confide would have to wait for a more convenient hour.

But when she pulled open the door, it wasn't Ted hovering on her doorstep. It was Nick. Rose was so startled that she remained speechless for a few heart-stopping seconds. It seemed that he made a habit of appearing on her doorstep and sending her into a state of paralysing confusion.

'What are you doing here?' she demanded coldly. 'You can't keep just turning up on my doorstep, Nick.'

'Are you going to invite me in?'

'No.'

'Why not?'

'Because I have better things to do than talk to you.'

'Aren't you dressed in the wrong clothes for the better things you have in mind?' Wrong approach. This wasn't how things were meant to develop, not that he knew quite how things were meant to develop. He had just known, when he had seen them walking out of the restaurant, wrapped around each other like a couple on the way to the altar, that he had to do something. He couldn't just turn his back and walk away because he would be haunted by her for the rest of his life and that was a consequence he had no intention of accepting. He needed to get her out of his system and he wasn't going to achieve that by antagonising her.

'I have no idea what you're talking about,' Rose informed him, her voice cooling by several degrees. 'And I don't like your attitude.'

'I apologise.'

'What?'

'I apologise. I can see your point of view. I show up here, uninvited and unannounced, without so much as a bunch of flowers or a box of chocolates…'

Rose felt the colour crawl into her skin. She didn't know what was going on but there was a lazy warmth in his eyes that made her shiver with a horrible excitement, which she tried valiantly to slap down.

'What's going on, Nick? Why would you bring me flowers or chocolate?'

'Let me in, Rose. Give me a chance to explain.' It was an effort keeping his voice smooth and even and controlled because his only thought was that Ted the reformed producer was lurking somewhere inside her house, probably in her bedroom. True, women on the threshold of a rampant affair didn't usually deck themselves out in track suit bottoms and what looked like an ancient tee shirt from when she was a kid, but who was he to tell? The woman was a law unto herself.

Poor, hapless Ted wouldn't have known what he was letting himself in for when he decided to make a play for her. He would have been expecting a sexy version of the bimbos who littered the movie world. Rose must have come as a nasty surprise. Nick was tempted to smirk at the thought, but he contained himself and did his utmost to look penitent.

Rose, conversely, was looking back at him with deep, unhidden suspicion.

'It's late.'

'I know and I'm sorry about that.'

'Stop apologising, Nick. It doesn't suit you.'

Nick shot her a winning smile. 'You're right. It doesn't. Let me come in?'

'Oh, for goodness' sake.' She swung open the door and he walked past her into the hallway and then turned around so that he could subject her to another of those sexy smiles that made her head spin.

'Go and sit in the lounge and I'll bring you some coffee,' she said, just to get rid of him while she gathered her composure in privacy somewhere.

Flowers? Chocolate? She had no idea what he was playing at, but it had sent her into a tailspin. Even as she bustled around in the small kitchen, making him his mug of coffee, she was acutely aware of him sitting in her lounge, just a matter of a few metres away. Whatever he was up to, she thought firmly, she was having none of it. She reminded herself that he had a girlfriend. A bright, sparkling, picture-perfect model with limited vocabulary. Just the kind of woman he was inevitably drawn to, never mind his brief diversion with her. And anyway, she was a free and liberated young woman now, no longer hiding behind routine and safety to protect her from the big, bad world.

She found him obediently sitting where she had told him to sit, doing nothing more offensive than flicking through one of the computer magazines she liked to read occasionally, just to make sure that she was keeping in touch with the latest technology. He closed it as soon as she entered the room and handed him the coffee.

'Interesting reading material,' he commented. Well, at least the rehabilitated producer was not on the premises. Either that or he didn't mind going into hiding for an indefinite period of time.

'Why have you come?'

'How did your date go?'

'As you can see, I'm sitting here in one piece so your fears about Ted were misplaced.' And little do you know by how much, Rose thought wryly. 'Is that why you came? Your over-developed sense of duty kicking in again? Compelled to make sure that I wasn't cruelly taken advantage of and left sobbing somewhere on my own?'

'No.'

Rose felt confused once again. 'Then why?'

'I…I'm not very good at admitting things like this, but I didn't like seeing you with other men last week at that party.'

She held onto her common sense as tightly as she could and remembered the vital truth, which was that this man was not interested in a proper relationship with her or anyone else for that matter. Which brought her neatly to the redhead.

'I'm surprised you even noticed me, Nick. Wasn't your attention on your date?'

'You know it wasn't,' Nick said huskily.

'You mean you brought a woman to Lily's party when you weren't even interested in her?'

'So it would appear.'

'Why?'

'Because I thought she might be able to make me forget that I'm still attracted to you. It didn't work.' Nick rested his mug on the table in front of him and strolled over to the sofa where Rose was curled at one end with her feet tucked under her. 'Because I am—still attracted to you. Believe me, I don't want to be, but I can't help myself.' He decided he would keep the little mortifying fact that he had spent the evening spying on her to himself. Confession might be good for the soul but total cleansing was downright stupidity.

'Have you missed me?' he asked roughly.

'I… This is mad…'

'Have you? I've been going crazy thinking about you, Rose. Ever since last weekend, I've been going even crazier thinking about you and another man.' He took her hand in his, stroked her palm with his finger and then, devastatingly, kissed the soft, tender flesh.

It was like being burnt and Rose gasped and half closed her eyes.

This was all wrong. Playing the field was one thing when it was a journey of discovery. Playing the field with this man was no journey of discovery. She had discovered way too much on this particular journey.

But when he was leaning over her like this…telling her all this stuff…opening up and whispering how much he had missed her…

She let him scoop her legs onto his lap, knowing that she should be pulling away. The redhead, he was telling her now, had barely impacted on him. In fact he hadn't contacted her since the party and hadn't slept with her. She didn't turn him on. Not as *she*, *Rose*, *did*. Music to her ears.

'I've dreamt about your body, Rose…your ripe, sexy body. I've dreamt about your breasts…'

In response to that, Rose felt her breasts harden, disobeying all the strict rules she was laying down in her head about sticking to her guns.

'Will you let me touch them?'

'No,' she said weakly.

'Things didn't end between us, Rose, and you know it as well as I do.'

'It wouldn't work, Nick.'

'Sex between us can't fail to work.'

'That's not what I'm talking about.'

She tried to wriggle her legs into a more dignified position, a position more in keeping with a woman in control of her own mind and body. However, her legs had turned to jelly. Worse, they were obeying someone else's commands, and when he ran his hand lightly along her inner thigh they fell apart, willing slaves to whatever he wanted to do.

'You tell me that you're breaking away from the shackles that kept you locked up…' His voice was low and seductive and his hands were now doing even more inappropriate things, slipping under the elasticated waistband of her jogging bottoms, easing them lower so that he could caress her stomach. 'Break away with me, Rose.'

'You should go.'

'If you said it like you meant it, then I would.' His hand left her stomach to explore upwards now, until he was cupping her breast. No bra. This was his very own wet dream. 'But you don't want me to…' He touched the tip of her nipple, which was hard, and felt her sharp release of breath. 'You want me to do this… Do you want me to do more? Do you want me to suck those big, rosy nipples?' He flicked up the baggy tee shirt and this time it was his turn to inhale as he saw the vision that had been playing in his head ever since they had last made love.

'No…yes…no…I don't know…'

He did know. He recalled how much she loved him playing with her breasts and he began to suckle one of the rosy circles, loving the taste of her and hungry for more, like a starving man suddenly sitting at a banquet. As he sucked and pulled her nipple into his mouth his tongue flicked and darted over the sensitised tip, sending her into wild throes of abandon.

Somehow their bodies moved in harmony with one another, until she was sitting up, with her head flung back and Nick positioned kneeling between her legs so that he could lavish all his attention on her breasts.

He licked his way down and pulled down the jogging bottoms along with her underwear in one smooth, swift movement.

With his fingers, he parted the delicate folds of her and inserted his tongue, wriggling it towards the honeyed sweetness of the little bud that throbbed and begged for satisfaction.

And Rose accordingly groaned and lifted her hips off the sofa, tensing every muscle in her body as his questing tongue flicked and teased and his mouth tasted every inch of her most private parts.

She reached down to try and push him away and reclaim some of her will-power, and felt her fingers curl in his dark hair, urging him to bring her to completion right here, right now.

But Nick needed more than that and he couldn't wait. He was barely aware of taking off his clothes until he was standing in front of her, big and proud. Rose opened her eyes drowsily and smiled before reaching out and taking his throbbing member in her hand, where she proceeded to give it the same attention that he had given her.

Yes, she had missed this too. Missed him and missed touching him, missed the way her hands and mouth could turn this impressive, powerful man to putty.

By the time he drove into her, they were both so close to coming that it just took a few deep, urgent thrusts to send them tipping over the edge.

Rose recovered to the dull, depressing knowledge that she had made the same mistake. She had allowed her body to do what it wanted to while her brain trailed along somewhere far behind, raising its weedy objections.

The sofa felt cramped and uncomfortable. 'I need to go and get cleaned up,' she said, and Nick, catching onto the tone of her voice and hearing the shutters begin to slide into place, turned to her and frowned.

'You're not regretting what we just did, are you?'

'We're back to square one, Nick.'

'We need one another.' She was making to stand up and he yanked her back down so that she fell onto his lap where he could easily keep her prisoner. 'You didn't hear what I said, Rose. I missed you. I missed you from the minute we parted company at the airport and I haven't stopped.'

'Which is why you felt the need to replace me.'

'I told you, I thought I needed distraction. I was wrong. I need you. I need this. And so do you. You can say whatever you want, Rose, but your sweet, sexy body tells another story.'

'It tells a different story. I want you, and, yes, I was weak, but I want more than just sex.'

'Then come live with me.' Nick uttered the words, but they failed to evoke the horror he might have expected. He had never lived with a woman in his life before, but right now it didn't seem such an outlandish proposition.

To Rose, his proposal, noble though it was, especially for a man like him, was a halfway measure driven by lust. Love would have demanded a proposal of quite a different nature. Nick wanted her, but he also wanted to keep his options open. Boredom, for him, was lurking just around the corner and he was canny enough to realise that dumping a wife was completely different from dumping a live-in lover.

And, Lord, it was tempting. Tempting to think of having this bliss, but the inevitable rider of 'for however long it lasted' was too much of a threat to her peace of mind.

'No.'

'What do you mean *no*?' Nick looked at her in stunned surprise. He wasn't even aware of her standing up and sticking on her clothes. 'What do you mean *no*? Have you any idea what sort of a leap a commitment like that takes for a man like me? To have a woman share my space?'

'And I appreciate it…'

'But you really want marriage.' He was incredulous. He had just offered her something beyond the reach of every other woman he had ever known and she wanted more.

'I really do.' Rose took a deep breath and decided that there was no point playing any more games. She sat on the side of the sofa and looked at him carefully. 'You told me that you never wanted to carry on *wanting* me. Well, Nick…' she shot him a rueful smile '…I never wanted to fall in love with you, but I did. That's why I want to marry you. You tell me that we're sexually compatible. I tell you that we're compatible in far more ways than that. I tell you that we have what it takes. So…*will you marry me*?' Rose could actually feel the hammering of her heart. If someone had asked her to do a bungee jump off the Clifton Suspension Bridge, she couldn't have felt more terrified than she did at this very moment, but what was the use trying to keep the truth to herself any longer? Pride and dignity was all well and good, but if she walked away without telling him how she really felt it would haunt her for the rest of her life. She would always wonder what if, and 'what if's were too closely related to 'if only's for her liking.

Nick looked at her, aghast.

Love? Marriage? He couldn't contemplate it. Freedom of movement was so deeply ingrained in him that the thought of relinquishing it was unthinkable.

And, anyway, since when did women do the proposing?

He felt a surge of anger that she just hadn't been able to accept his already extreme sacrifice of moving in with him.

'Don't worry answering,' Rose said neutrally. She stood up and walked towards the door. 'Your answer's written on your face.' Now, she couldn't look at him, so instead she stared out into the hallway, hearing him get dressed and then feeling him move towards her.

'I'm not the marrying type of man. You always knew that, Rose. Why couldn't you have just accepted the parameters and appreciated the fact that I asked you to live with me? It's as good as...'

Rose took a deep breath and looked at him. She had her arms folded and she could feel her fingernails pressing painfully into her forearms. If they weren't she was sure that she would be shaking like a leaf. 'Because,' she said calmly, and where that dreadful calm came from she had no idea, 'marriage is all about commitment. Real commitment. Not just the "yes, let's stay together while the going's good" variety.'

'My commitment's always been to my work,' Nick told her

baldly. 'You're the closest I have ever come to sharing myself with another human being, but marriage…'

'Just one step too far?' Rose laughed mirthlessly and walked towards the front door.

There was a flat, cold feeling inside her, but, strangely, she was still glad that she had said what she had said, given it her best shot, so to speak. She didn't think he would be back now. In his mind, he would have opened a Pandora's box and, having slammed the lid back shut, he would never make the mistake of reopening it.

'We could have had fun.' His voice was cold and accusatory.

Rose shrugged and opened the door. 'Have a good life, Nick.'

She didn't watch him leave. Instead she closed the door quietly and leaned against it. She could hear the deep revving of his car as he pulled away from the kerb and then the sound of the engine was replaced by silence and she made her way up the stairs, into the bathroom, so that she could have a shower.

When she lay in bed, she replayed in her head this last night spent together. Before, even in the aftermath of Borneo and thinking that things were finally over for good, there had been, she realised now, an element of hope and a certain restless dissatisfaction. Now, there was closure. It made her neither happy nor unhappy. She just felt dead inside.

Life would carry on and it did. On the surface, Rose functioned as she always had. Competent and reliable at work, sociable enough with her circle of friends.

Breaking out of the mould was well and truly abandoned. The only surprise was her sister's reaction. Lily was disproportionately upset at the turn of events and that touched Rose.

'You'll get over it, Lily,' she laughed wryly down the phone. 'And so will I. In a year's time, we'll both see this as just another experience in the great adventure that is life.' She couldn't stand the thought that the damage done was irreparable. Surely not. Broken hearts mended, didn't they? Every magazine assured her of that.

But six weeks down the road, and Rose still found it hard to find a way through the dense fog of misery. She felt like a robot, going through the motions while underneath everything wilted and shrivelled away and died.

She had no idea what Nick was doing and she avoided buying any tabloids just in case she was tempted to open up those scurrilous gossip pages where she might see a picture of him cavorting with another redhead, mark two. Mark one might have been a distraction, but mark two would certainly have been the truly-narrow-escape replacement.

In the midst of this never-ending battle with her torn emotions and the sheer effort needed to carry on going to work, socialising with friends and pretending that all was well in the world of Rose Taylor, the dawning realisation that something else was very wrong took a little while to filter through.

When it did, the fragile glue that was binding her daily life together dissolved like wax in a flame and the truly sickening question reared its ugly head.

What on earth was she to do now?

CHAPTER TEN

ROSE was on her way up to see him. Right now. At three in the afternoon. Right here. In his office.

Nick had no idea what she wanted. It had been nearly two months since he had set eyes on her and he had daily told himself that her disappearance from his life was the best thing that could have happened. He told himself that he had offered her the unthinkable and she had turned him down, proving his theory that women, each and every one of them, were out to change the men they purported to care about.

He had replayed countless times in his head that moment when she had told him that she was in love with him. If she were in love with him, he thought, why couldn't she have accepted what he had offered?

Because her aim had been to turn him into the domesticated animal that he was not and never would be.

It was a source of constant and relentless frustration that he still couldn't dismiss her from his head, where she had taken up residence and refused to budge.

He knew that his work was being affected. Not his ability to work, which was part and parcel of the essence of him, but his demeanour at work.

More than once he had been tempted to call her, but he

hadn't and he never would. Pride would never allow him to pick up that phone and dial her number.

But, and this was the thought that haunted him late at night when there was nothing to distract him, he longed for her. He wanted her loving him. He missed her. And he didn't know why.

Now his secretary had buzzed up that there was a certain Rose Taylor in reception, asking if she could come up and see him, and for the first time in weeks Nick felt a curious sense of peace. He immediately told his secretary that he was busy, that she might have to wait for half an hour while he wrapped up his conference call, but that he could squeeze her in after that.

Okay, it was childish of him, but she had always managed to turn him into a kid.

Then he sat back in his massive black leather chair, swivelled it to face the floor-to-ceiling plates of glass that overlooked the city of London, and turned his mind to what she wanted.

It could only be one thing. She had had ample time to think about his proposal and she had come to her senses. Nick contemplated the idea with intense satisfaction. He would even be tempted to say that he felt elated. He would have her back in his life, would have her sharp wit and clever mind and sexy body, and there would be no more talk about trying to infiltrate his life by putting a ring on his finger.

She loved him. Of course she would return. It was to be expected and Nick felt warm with the anticipation of having her back. Course, he would have to make it clear that his views hadn't changed. That a mistress was a far cry from a wife and matrimony was not on the agenda, but he didn't anticipate a problem.

After forty minutes, he buzzed through to his secretary to tell her that she could send Rose up now, and then he relaxed back, facing the heavy door to his office, and waited for her to enter.

'You've lost weight,' were his opening words as Rose cautiously entered his office and shut the door behind her.

She had prepared herself for this, but all her hours of preparation now flew out the window as she looked at him, despairingly aware that he still had as much of an effect on her now as he had the last time she had seen him. So much for time and its great healing properties.

Not wanting to leave the door because it represented her fastest route out, Rose remained hovering where she was, not quite sure how to answer his frowning observation, until he told her to have a seat. He actually stood up, pointed to the chair facing his and then proceeded to perch on the side of the desk so that she was forced to sidle forwards and sit at an awkward angle to avoid contact with his thigh.

'Well?' he demanded. 'Haven't you been eating?'

'I haven't come here to talk about my diet, Nick,' Rose answered irritably. She was aware that she was fiddling with the hem of her skirt and made herself stop. Nervous gesture. But she had a lot to be nervous about. In fact, she had spent the past two weeks in a state of near panic. Ever since she had clocked that she had missed a period. Ever since she had gone to the chemist's and bought one of those home pregnancy kits that were virtually one-hundred-per-cent accurate, leaving no doubt that she was well and truly pregnant with Nick's baby. That last time—no contraception. It had been wild and spontaneous and, unlike the very first time they had made love when they had omitted to use contraception, she hadn't been in her safe period.

And, yes, she had lost weight. She hadn't been eating properly and although, standing naked in front of the mirror, she could see that her stomach was more rounded, everywhere else was skinny in comparison to the curvy woman she had been. Who needed diets to lose weight? A healthy dose of misery worked a treat.

Not that she would look thinner for much longer.

She closed her eyes and felt suddenly dizzy. It was a good thing that she was sitting down. Collapsing on his office floor would have been a very disadvantageous way to begin proceedings.

'What's the matter?' Nick frowned because for a minute there he had actually thought that she was going to faint. Something kicked hard inside him, some inarticulate fear that she was ill. He removed himself back to his chair and tried to get himself together, because once that thought had inserted itself in his head it began to eat away at his logic, burrowing away until he was consumed with the conviction that there was something ominous that she was keeping from him.

For the first time since she had been announced, Nick entertained the possibility that she might not have come to his office because she wanted to engineer a reconciliation.

He had been on a high, anticipating her stammering admission that she couldn't keep away from him. He had even begun playing with thoughts of how the rest of his day would pan out. At his place. Uninterrupted sex. Touching her, feeling her, enjoying the things she could do to his body and all the myriad things he could do to hers.

But, now she was sitting in front of him, he could see that she was pale. This was not the demeanour of a woman looking forward to embarking on a heady and fulfilling sexual relationship with a man.

In fact, this was the demeanour of a woman who was nervous about blurting out an uncomfortable truth. Nick, astute when it came to reading other people, felt something shift inside him. He was scared, terrified in fact.

Everything seemed to slow down and he became uncomfortably aware that he had broken out in nervous perspiration. He could barely ask the question he knew he had to.

'Would you like something to drink? Tea? Coffee? I could ask my secretary to bring you some…'

Just the thought of tea or coffee made Rose feel nauseous. She went a couple of shades paler and shook her head.

'I won't be long, Nick,' she said, clearing her throat and making an effort not to be pathetic.

'No rush. Mind if I have a cup of coffee?' He buzzed through to his secretary to bring him in a cappuccino and Rose smiled wanly at him.

'Since when do you ask permission for anything, Nick?'

Since he wanted to buy some time before he heard what she had to say?

He was increasingly convinced that there was something seriously wrong with her. She looked terrible. As white as a sheet. And not because she was nervous, even though she clearly was. No, there was something underlyingly wrong, and as something close to terror continued to eat away at him Nick realised, in a moment of truth, what he had been missing all along.

He had let his own stubborn pride dictate his life. Nick Papaeliou, the man who could have any woman he desired, who had lived his life taking his pick and telling himself that his freedom was the most important thing he possessed, had clung to his vow never to commit like an idiot clinging to a lifebelt in a bath. No woman had ever been able to tempt him out of his conviction that bachelordom was the only way to go and so, when Rose had come along, he had steadfastly ignored all the glaring signs that had gradually begun to clutter his life.

He had mistaken his missing her when she wasn't around as missing her body. He had longed for her and explained it away as just a normal red-blooded-male reaction to craving a woman who turned him on. And when he had offered her the epitome of commitment as far as he was concerned, the chance to share his house with him, he had blithely assumed that the gesture signified no more than a desire to have what he wanted on tap until he became bored, until they both became bored.

Women had always eventually bored him and the fact that Rose was not included in that category had been so obvious from the start and yet so easy to ignore.

He could have kicked himself.

She had told him that she loved him and what had he done? Asked her to prove it by doing the one thing she didn't want to do: move in with him.

And now here she was and it sure as hell wasn't to set that particular little situation right.

She was here to tell him…what?

That she was ill. Thinking about that possibility made him feel instantly sick when his cappuccino was brought in and placed on the desk in front of him.

She was trying hard to be brave and meet his eyes, but she physically couldn't. He could see that and it terrified him.

'I can't have this conversation with you in my office,' he told her abruptly, and that, at least, made her raise her eyes and look at him.

'But you don't know what I'm going to say.'

'I know it's serious, whatever it is.' He pushed the coffee away from him and stood up.

Rose failed to follow suit. Instead she watched as he slung on his jacket, her fists pressed into her lap.

'I don't want to go anywhere, Nick. I want to say what I have to say here. Where it's impersonal…'

Nick shot her a brooding, sideways glance and hesitated before removing his jacket and carefully replacing it on its hanger. Then he walked towards the window and stared down at the city streets below, trying to get his thoughts in order, filled with a cold, clawing panic and the painful knowledge that he had to say what he had to say before she unleashed whatever truth it was she had come to impart to him.

He could feel her eyes on him and, sure enough, he turned around to find her watching him.

'Look,' he began, 'I'm…I don't know how to say this…' He raked his fingers through his hair and shook his head, suddenly restless and uncomfortable. 'I've never said this to anyone before…'

Rose, having screwed up every ounce of courage she possessed to tell him what she had to and as quickly as possible, breathed a silent sigh of relief that he was doing the talking. Okay, it was just a case of putting off the inevitable and it was cowardly, but she relaxed just a tiny bit.

She was also curious, even though she didn't want to be. She hadn't come to his office expecting to have a conversation, or at least not until she had told him about the pregnancy and then conversation probably wouldn't quite describe what she imagined would follow. Recriminations, accusation, bitterness—nothing that she would classify as conversation.

'Said what?' she asked, bewildered.

Even more bewildering was the expression on his face. Gone was the easy self-assurance she associated with him. In its place was uncertainty and hesitation, which was as perplexing as the dark flush that stained his cheeks.

She almost forgot what she had come to say when he walked towards her and dragged his chair round so that he could position himself right next to her, on her level.

'I…' he began. 'I…I'm glad you're here…'

He didn't look glad. In fact, he didn't look anything, at least not anything she could identify. And if he really was glad, then she was pretty sure that it wasn't a sentiment he would be harbouring for very long.

'I…the past few weeks, Rose…' He once again ran his fingers through his hair and looked away from her. 'Not good.'

In a flash, she knew where he was going. He had probably assumed that she had come to his office with a view to taking him up on his offer for her to live with him and was now, against the dictates of his pride, going to repeat the offer because he still wanted her. Want, want, want! The most distasteful and egotistical word in the universe.

She closed her mind off to her memories of him. It gave her strength to think that this man, whatever he said, hadn't wanted her enough to take their relationship that one important step further. She had declared her love and that, psychologically, must have led him to assume that she would return, grateful for the crumbs he could throw her.

'I'm not here to talk about that,' she interjected quickly.

'You don't understand, Rose. I need to talk about it. I need to talk about what a fool I've been.' He reached out and took hold of her fingers, idly playing with them, obviously, she thought, unaware of what that simple, inoffensive gesture was doing to her insides. She stared, fascinated and dry-mouthed, at his long brown fingers as they fiddled with hers, and gulped.

It was amazing that he couldn't guess the reason for her visit. Astute as he was, his mind was obviously not programmed to think the unthinkable.

'I let you go,' he said quietly, looking directly at her. 'I let the woman who loved me go.'

Rose didn't want to be reminded of that. 'I'm not here to blame you, Nick. You did what you had to do and there are no hard feelings. I haven't come to discuss the past.' She made an effort to slide her hand out of his grasp but his fingers tightened on hers, clasping them into submission.

'I've always thought that love was a complication, something of which I had no need. I enjoyed women but I didn't want them clambering into my private life and interfering with it. My goals were set and there was no place for cosy nights in and joint holidays in Italy with the eventual two point two.'

Which snapped Rose back to the present like a bucket of cold water.

'No. I gathered,' she said coolly.

'I was…mistaken…'

It took a couple of seconds for his words to sink in, then her thoughts were adrift, bobbing about in confusion as she tried to assimilate that telling, wrenched remark.

'I…beg your pardon?'

'I was mistaken,' Nick said simply. He felt a weight lift off his chest. Whatever dire news she had come to break, then she would know how he felt and it was something he should have said a long time ago. Courage, he was discovering, was something he had measured using all the wrong tools. Courage was this. Telling the only woman he had ever loved that he loved her.

Rose wasn't sure what she was hearing. She knew what she wanted to hear.

'You're playing games,' she said uncertainly. 'Please.' This time she succeeded in withdrawing her hand, which she held up because, riveting though his disclosures were, she couldn't trust herself not to start believing them, and hadn't he already made it perfectly clear that he was not in the business of love? What would he do to get her back into his bed? she wondered. Seduce her with words he knew she wanted to hear?

No. She would say what she had come to say and watch him fall back in horror. Better that than to be lulled into a false sense of security that would be snatched away the minute she broke her news.

'Just listen to me and stop…confusing me.'

Nick had the cold feeling that he had left things too late. The horse had bolted and, not only had he failed to realise what a treasure he possessed, but he had closed the stable door and returned to the house whistling a merry tune. He deserved to have her walk out on him and never look back. His punishment would be to spend the rest of his life living with his mistake.

'I…' Now it was her turn to stammer. She took a deep breath and said in one quick rush, closing her eyes to block him out, 'I'm pregnant. I'm sorry. I didn't mean for it to happen, but it has. You don't have to feel responsible. You don't have to feel anything. I came here because I felt you ought to know, not because I wanted anything from you. You're telling me now about mistakes, but I know you for who you are. I don't want money from you; I don't want time from you. I just thought…you should know…'

In a minute she would do the brave thing and open her eyes. The silence lengthened around them and into it she read an assortment of reactions. Eventually, though, she peeped at him and then opened her eyes fully when she realised that he hadn't drawn back in horror.

'You're pregnant?'

'I'm sorry,' Rose whispered.

'You're pregnant.'

'I realise this is the last thing you want…'

'I don't believe it.' Nick shook his head in wonderment. It had never occurred to him. How naïve was he? He had lurched from thinking that she had returned because she wanted him, to imagining the worst, that she was ill, perhaps fatally so. But she was carrying his child and he was overwhelmed with a sudden feeling of elation.

He looked at her and grinned.

'You're…not upset?' she asked cautiously.

'You're having my baby…' He wanted to sweep her off her feet and swing her around. 'I love you, Rose. I love you, I can't live without you and now you've given me the best news I could ever have hoped for. Lord, when you walked through that door, with that serious expression, white like a ghost, I thought…I don't know what I thought…that you were going to tell me that you were ill…that I had lost my chance to show you how much you mean to me…'

Rose's brain had registered his declaration of love and had stuck there.

'If you loved me, why didn't you say something sooner?'

'Because I didn't understand myself.' Nick smiled wryly at her. 'You crept up on me and took over my soul and, like an idiot, I still thought that I was in control. When I heard that you had come here, my world fell into place again.'

'And what if I hadn't come here?' Rose was not going to allow hope to push her headlong over the precipice. 'Would you have let me disappear?'

'I could never have done that.' Nick thought about it, thought about his pride, realised that it would have lasted so long and then he would have woken up to the fact that he couldn't live without her. And he wasn't too proud, now, to tell her that and to delight in seeing her wariness finally melt away.

'And now I'm going to be a father…' God, he felt choked

up. 'Let's get out of here. I want to celebrate and then I want us to get married.'

'What, today?' Rose laughed.

'By the end of the week,' Nick growled. 'You need looking after and the sooner I get started, the better…'

LET'S TALK
Romance

For exclusive extracts, competitions
and special offers, find us online:

f facebook.com/millsandboon

🐦 @MillsandBoon

📷 @MillsandBoonUK

Get in touch on 01413 063232

For all the latest titles coming soon, visit
millsandboon.co.uk/nextmonth